PRAISE FOR *VICARIOUS*

"Haunting and unique; the best of what
science fiction can and should be."
—Katherine McNamara, actress

"This perceptive take on the reality-TV-in-the-future
premise deserves boffo ratings."
—*Kirkus Reviews*

"A deep and a stunningly emotive story
wrapped in a truly unique setting."
—Jasper T. Scott,
USA Today bestselling author of *Dark Space*

VICARIOUS

ALSO BY RHETT C. BRUNO

The Circuit:
Executor Rising
Legacy of Vale
Falling Earth

The Children of Titan:
The Collector (novella prequel)
Titanborn
Titan's Son
Titan's Rise
Titan's Fury
Titan's Legacy

The Origins of the Children of Titan Universe
Nebula-nominated short story:
"Interview for the End of the World"
and "This Long Vigil"

The Buried Goddess Saga:
Web of Eyes
Winds of War
Will of Fire
Way of Gods
War of Men
Word of Truth

Raptors (and the Raptorverse):
Baron Steele

Others:
The Roach
The Luna Missile Crisis
Dead Acre

VICARIOUS

RHETT C. BRUNO

BLACK STONE
PUBLISHING

Copyright © 2021 by Rhett C. Bruno
Published in 2022 by Blackstone Publishing
Cover art by Fernando Granea

The characters and events in this book are fictitious.
Any similarity to real persons, living or dead, is coincidental
and not intended by the author.

Printed in the United States of America
Originally published in hardcover by Blackstone Publishing in 2022

First paperback edition: 2022
ISBN 979-8-200-72459-8
Fiction / Science Fiction / General

Version 1

CIP data for this book is available
from the Library of Congress

Blackstone Publishing
31 Mistletoe Rd.
Ashland, OR 97520

www.BlackstonePublishing.com

Vicarious: adjective. Experienced in the imagination through the feelings or actions of another person.

Uploading . . .
New High Earth Resident: [Asher Reinhart]

CHAPTER 1

I was nothing.

Then I was.

I blinked bleary, wet eyelids open. All I could see were white splotches and blurs. It was so bright. It felt as if my eyes were focusing for the first time, and while I could feel my legs, any attempt to stand was thwarted by lack of practice, so I fell back into my seat.

Something rushed down my throat. I pawed at my chest, terrified as it inflated. Then my foggy brain remembered it was only my lungs inflating from breathing air. Despite my lack of memories, I knew that somehow.

The very same air filling my mouth flowed against my skin.

My mind couldn't focus on any one thing. I itched everywhere. The air was so dry. My body was accustomed to being submerged in the life-sustaining concoction of a synth-womb.

How do I know that?

"You may be experiencing some disorientation," a feminine, but machinelike voice said. I assumed she was addressing me, although I still couldn't see more than indiscernible shapes and shades. "I assure you it is quite ordinary upon awakening."

My eyes scanned for a speaker. Found nothing. The voice was everywhere, like the unrelentingly itchy, dry air.

My mouth opened to respond but couldn't form words. My tongue, vocal cords, they just fumbled through incoherent sounds. Somehow, I knew her language, but that knowledge apparently didn't translate to my body parts.

"Your motor functions remain impaired because you have not yet utilized your corporeal form," the voice said. "While your mind was active during the growth process and infused with relevant knowledge, you have only now been birthed from your synthetic womb. It has fostered your physical and cognitive development for ten years while you awaited an open dwelling in High Earth."

"W . . . w . . . where . . ." It was a start, but I could get nothing else out. Speaking—even just that one word—brought attention to how the arid air had chapped my lips, like they wanted to crack off my face.

My face . . . my hands shot up toward it and ran along soft cheeks. Sharp nose. I was someone, but who?

"As the knowledge uploaded to your brain communicates with your conscious self, your muscles and nervous system will adapt accordingly," the voice said. "For now, please respond to my questions with the appropriate head movement. A nod for yes, shake for no. This is to ensure that your brain is functioning properly. Do you understand? Please nod yes, or shake no."

I searched again for the source of the voice and couldn't find one. So I did as I was asked and nodded. My world went into a sudden spin. Everything quaked and trembled.

"Take it slow at first," the voice said. "Your body and mind are unused to movement. Even the slightest disruption to your brain's positioning will cause dizziness, which may lead to nausea."

The room settled, but my sight remained unclear.

"I am your Virtual Occupant Residency Aide, or VORA. I am here to assist in your transition to your High Earth residency. Here, all your physiological and psychological human needs shall be satisfied by the High Earth Network. Do you understand where you are?"

My brain fed me information about the origination of High Earth. Like the fact that after Earth flooded, most of humanity living throughout the solar system had wiped each other out in a terrible war ushered in by the techno-revolution in the twenty-third century, and that the survivors founded a haven called High Earth atop the only portion of the planet remaining above the surface.

I tried to nod, slower this time. My muscles strained and my chin hit my chest.

"Excellent," VORA responded. "The educational infusion process appears to have been successful."

Some sort of bin with glowing blue nodes lowered over my head. I hadn't noticed it until it started to hum, loudly.

"What . . . is . . ."

"I am testing Network's virtual interface with your brain activity."

I clenched my jaw as the humming intensified. The way the sound vibrated deep in my eardrums made my skull feel like it was going to explode. Then my head wrenched back, and the unclear blotches of shapes faded away.

Pixelated color filled in all around me. Little squares at first, but before I knew it, I could see the world in crystalline clarity. I sat in the middle of a grassy field. Each brilliant, green blade gently swayed, though I felt no breeze. My eyes drifted downward. I was seated, only there was no seat beneath me, nor could I see my body. This brought a new sense of panic and a further tightening of my chest.

My lips quaked as I tried to find the right muscles to ask what was going on. Then the world broke apart around me again. The ground fell away, and I fought every instinct to scream, though I didn't fall. Instead, a new ground formed—shiny marble with inky veins running through it. Walls grew up around me, made of stone and covered in deep chasms. They extended farther than I could imagine possible and then arched overhead.

"User test complete," VORA stated just as my sense of awe diminished enough for me to ask what was going on. "Virtual integration successful."

Suddenly, that lofty interior space flaked away. My brain felt like it sank through my own body, and my eyes snapped open. The blue nodes lifted from their positions dancing around my head, and their hum faded, leaving me in total silence.

"That was your first virtual-reality experience—a computer-generated environment," VORA said. "I will introduce you to the full capabilities of your VR chamber after you are more acclimated."

I could now see enough to realize I was within a spherical glass container. Beyond it lay a rectangular room—stark white and tiled.

"This is your assigned smart-dwelling," VORA said. "You have been provided the most advanced in technical developments to ensure healthy living whilst inside. It is our goal to ensure you will never have to leave unless it is your desire. Do you understand?"

I nodded.

"The Network is constantly updating to improve its interface and linked technologies based upon resident input," VORA said. "You will be provided updates, upgrades, and immediate access to resident-developed content as it is made available. Once you are settled, we will discuss your data-allocation limits and occupancy contract to avoid delistment. Do you understand?"

There was so much being thrown at me I wasn't sure what else to do but continue nodding. *So, I'm ten years old but never walked or talked before, never seen anybody else?* But already, I knew so much about the world that my brain was ready to burst.

"Thanks to your genetic donors, you have been issued a social designation," VORA said. "Can you recall it?"

I squeezed my eyes shut and then, somehow, my brain fed me the proper information. "A . . ." My throat remained incredibly dry. "A . . . sher . . . R . . . Rein . . . hart . . ." That was my name—my social designation, as she called it. That was me.

"That is correct," VORA said. "Are you ready to proceed, Asher Reinhart?"

The glass chamber peeled open at the exact moment I began to nod. I panicked and slid forward out of my seat. My thin, untested legs crumpled under my weight.

"Please refrain from attempting any excessive physical exertion without assistance," VORA said. "You must proceed carefully while your bodily functions adapt to normal operation. A med-bot will arrive shortly for a final physical. I can now begin the process of familiarizing you with the amenities of your smart-dwelling."

I ignored her. All I could focus on was a wall, which was comprised wholly of a bright window. Through it, I could see a grid of countless thin towers extending as far as my vision allowed. They all had square windows like mine stacked up each face.

I braced myself on the first piece of furniture I could find and wobbled forward. The tile floor was ice cold against my bare feet and sent a chill through me. By the time I reached the couch halfway across the room, I was panting, exhausted.

"Perhaps you should sit until your post-awakening physical is complete?" VORA said.

I was too winded to respond, so instead, I pointed at the window, sucked down one long breath, and shuffled toward it.

"That is High Earth," VORA explained. "Welcome to the thirty-third floor of Residential Tower 3, located on Block 3C of High Earth."

It took every ounce of energy in my shaky limbs to reach it. I leaned against the glass with both palms, my breath fogging up the perfectly clear surface. Suddenly, the pane zipped down, retracting into the floor, and I stumbled forward onto a balcony.

"Every resident has direct outdoor access to ensure optimal well-being," VORA said.

Stepping toward a glass railing designed for a full-grown adult, rising almost over my head, my legs now shook more than ever. Wind howled as it whipped, touching only my hair. It made my skin even more itchy and assailed my ears.

Before I knew it, I found myself up on the balls of my feet, staring over and down at the impossible depths. I couldn't focus. All I saw was green, sparkling towers, and suspended walkways before a nauseous, dizzying sensation overcame me.

I fell away from it and staggered for the safe, quiet interior. A pear-shaped robot with many spindly, shiny arms hovered just inside. Its impassive white eye-lenses stared straight ahead. The robot rushed to keep me from slamming against the—my floor. I clutched one of its arms as tightly as I could, accepting its assistance to a stone-gray couch. The window sealed behind me, and that awful screeching of wind ceased.

"I-I don't like it out there," I stuttered.

"That is all right," VORA said. "It is your choice wherever you would like to go, Asher. Now, this med-bot will begin your post-awakening physical to ensure optimal health to initiate your life here in High Earth."

The bot positioned itself before me, gyros spinning, whirring in the semitransparent lid that encompassed its human-shaped head.

"While you wait, I will play one of the most popular visual programs in all of High Earth, based upon data contribution," VORA said. "Due to your genetic makeup and clear aversion to danger stimuli, I believe you will find *Ignis: Live* enjoyable. Please try to focus on the program so as not to interrupt your post-awakening physical."

While I did as she instructed—what else could I do?—the window, my view of High Earth, morphed into a telecommunication screen, along with all the walls of my dwelling. A program, presumably the one she referred to as *Ignis: Live*, surrounded me, as if I were really there.

While the med-bot poked and prodded, testing my reflexes and anything else, I watched. I gasped at the sight of a girl a bit younger than me. The first human I'd ever seen, in such a high resolution, it was as if I were next to her.

[Ignis Feed Location]
Block B Med-Bay Nursery
<Camera 5>

"Never let anyone see you." That was what Mission's Birth-mother Alora-12987 had told her every single day since she was old enough to understand.

Mission would've given anything for a glimpse of the interior world of the *Ignis*. It was all she thought about as she took one slow step after another toward the Block B med-bay's infant nursery door. In a stroke of rare luck, another Birthmother had accidentally left it open after Mission emerged from her hiding place.

Mission strolled by the cribs of newborns, their shrill wails echoing off the polished metal walls. She ran her small fingers through one baby girl's thin hair. Instead of quieting her, soothing her, it only made the crying louder. Mission grimaced and drew her hand back.

The door grew ever closer, and she could see the shadows of inhabitants passing by. The shoes of sewer jockeys, hauling supplies, slapped along the block's rocky floor beyond the lobby. A couple quarreled, and Mission brought her ear closer to the door. *What do normal people argue about?* How could two inhabitants fight when there was so much to be thankful for?—an entire world to explore within their interstellar ark.

Mission reached cautiously for the entry controls, her hand quaking like they might burn her. She could see it now, down the entry lobby's long ramp, that wonderful portal sinking toward places she could scarcely imagine.

A woman's hand poked through the opening and shoved her back. Alora burst in, quickly signaling the door to shut all the way behind her.

Mission knew she should've expected her. Every day, Alora was the first Block B Birthmother to arrive at her assigned nursery and the last to leave. No job in *Ignis* was more crucial, at least, that was what Alora always said. That the white uniforms up in the Core liked to pretend they were all-important, but she had the privilege of caring for the future men and women who would one day replace them all.

Alora switched on the lights, and Mission saw the scowl stretched across her face. She was beautiful, the product of the refined genes that the *Ignis*'s systems helped perpetuate ever since they'd set out from Earth. Her belly bulged due to an assigned pregnancy—another future inhabitant who would get to live free . . . unlike Mission.

"Are you insane?" Alora whispered angrily.

Mission pretended to minister to a baby, but her body language betrayed her. She struggled to steady her breathing, hands still shaking from the anticipation of obtaining even the smallest glimpse beyond the med-bay door. She'd been growing bolder ever since her fifth birthday and couldn't decide which was scarier: getting yelled at by her Birthmother, or the fact that a part of her wasn't so scared anymore to walk outside and be seen.

"I heard someone in the lobby," Mission murmured. "I was worried."

"Don't lie to me, Mission," Alora replied. "I thought we had this discussion the last time you sliced the controls."

"Someone left it open." Alora leveled a glare at her, but Mission didn't cave. "I swear."

"You're really going to make me tell Cassiopeia that?"

Mission shifted her feet, then frowned and said, "She's stopped crying as much."

"Who?" Alora asked.

Mission pointed to the crib with the loudest, most unpleasant infant. Mission didn't know their names, wouldn't allow herself. Even though they were printed right there on the tags hanging from each crib, she knew it would be too much once they inevitably moved on and she remained, stuck in a room that seemed to grow smaller and smaller every day. Though she was the one growing, wasn't she?

"She's fussy, that one," Alora said as she bent to lift the girl. "Going to be a handful when she gets older. I wonder if she'll lie to her Birthmother too?"

Mission rolled her eyes.

Alora turned around with the baby in her arms. Her lips twisted. Before she could say anything, the lights and various displays around the room flickered. The surge lasted for around thirty seconds before things returned to normal.

"Power is still acting up," Alora stated.

"It's done that twenty-three times in the last week," Mission said.

Alora glanced at her, brow furrowed.

Mission shrugged. "I don't have anything else to do."

Alora sighed. "All right, it's time."

"Oh, why?" Mission whined. "Nobody's here yet."

"Let's go, Mission. Cassiopeia is scheduled to come up early for their examinations today."

The infant girl cooed as her miniature hand wrapped Alora's finger. Mission was pretty sure that was the first time the girl had made a sound that wasn't crying. Every day, crying, then silence when the infants fell asleep. Crying, then silence. Over and over . . .

"Can't I stay until Cassiopeia knocks?" Mission begged.

"You know you can't."

"Pleeease."

"No. She's in charge here, which means . . ."

"'She has card access and might not knock.' Blah-blah." Mission forced an impish grin, but her features quickly darkened. Alora noticed and frowned as well.

"I'm planning on telling Cassiopeia eventually," Alora said, pangs of regret hampering her tone.

"You keep saying that."

"I'm still getting a handle on her. I think she could deal with the truth, but if I'm wrong . . ."

"We both might be spaced. I know."

Mission lowered the baby back into one of five presently

occupied cribs. The nursery, filled with new inhabitants ranging from days old to a few months, provided the infants with specialized observation and sustenance required before being cleared to move on to the more developed nurseries, and then schooling. That was how it was supposed to go. A Birthmother was chosen to reproduce by the Collective, based upon the Core's extrapolated data. Only, Mission was unlucky enough to have been conceived through what her Birthmother had called a "freak accident."

"You don't believe I'm going to tell her, do you?" Alora said.

"It's been so long," Mission replied.

"And Cassiopeia's position with the Collective is stronger than ever."

"I just . . ." Mission couldn't manage another word.

Alora kneeled, took her by the shoulders, and stared deep into her eyes. "I promise, I'm going to try when the time is right. None of this is your fault, my little miracle child."

Mission hated that nickname. If she was such a miracle, why should she be kept hidden for so long?

Alora rustled Mission's hair, but Mission didn't budge. "For now, I just need you to take things one day at a time," Alora whispered.

"As usual," Mission groaned.

Alora's lips pursed. It was the expression she always put on before reprimanding Mission for her attitude, but this time she stopped herself. "You have something to read?"

"There's nothing I haven't read."

"I'll see if I can find something else. It's tough to get clearance for anything other than low-grade Earth history texts."

"It's fine."

Mission slid an empty crib aside and crouched. Her small fingers ran in a practiced motion under the seam of a loosened metal floor panel, and she lifted. She'd done the same thing every day, but it still strained her muscles. The clatter as she slid it aside caused the fussy infant to start crying again.

"They're hungry," Mission muttered.

"It won't always be like this, Mission," Alora said at the same time.

A response simmered on the tip of Mission's tongue but went no further. She didn't have the energy. She lowered herself into the cramped, two-by-three-meter hole beneath the floor, then closed herself in.

"Who are you talking to?" the muffled voice of Alora's superior and the Mother of Block B, Cassiopeia-11445, asked a short while later after the nursery door *whooshed* open.

"Nobody," Alora quickly answered. "Just the children. They're, uh . . . hungry. They need their Birthmothers."

Mission lay in complete darkness while they chatted. She pulled a string to turn on a dim light Alora had jury-rigged. A pile of dusty historical texts brought from Earth when the *Ignis* set off on its journey rested behind her head, shuffled around a pillow and over an emergency oxygen tank. Many of their pages had been torn out, defaced by so many of Mission's drawings, illustrating all manner of scenes from her imagination of what the outside world might be like. Some were splashed with color from the dried-out markers Alora occasionally snatched from the schooling hollow's recycler.

Everyone else had their world within the *Ignis*. The myriad images drawn from Mission's mind were hers—her only escape from the cramped hole she called home . . .

* * *

I leaned forward for a closer look at Mission alone in her hole. The med-bot nearly poked my eardrum mid-examination, and

VORA instructed me to remain still. I didn't care. Before I knew it, my feet were planted firmly on the floor and I'd waddled two steps. I was about to lose my balance when the med-bot sat me back down.

I stayed there, watching as Mission scribbled a drawing of two people until she fell asleep. The show was apparently a series of live recordings of the inhabitants within an interstellar ark known as the *Ignis*. Dozens of other feeds showed along the periphery of my walls, but I didn't shift my main screen.

As the med-bot finished, a band clasped over my wrist. Pinpoints on its inside face dug into my flesh, the sting finally stopping me from staring at Mission's feed.

"Your lifeband contains pharma to help moderate any emotional distress, such as your spell of acrophobia earlier," VORA said. "It will also monitor your bodily functions and allow me to ensure optimal health."

I mumbled something and nodded, then brushed the med-bot out of the way so I could return to the show. The bot hovered out of the room and disappeared. I didn't pay close enough attention to see where.

"Now that you are cleared for all activity, may I introduce you to some of the other amenities of your smart-dwelling?" VORA asked.

"Not now," I replied.

"I would recommend . . ."

I ignored the rest of what she said, hushed her, and kept watching. VORA was right when she said I'd enjoy *Ignis: Live*. What other amenities were necessary when I had Mission and all the other inhabitants to keep me company? Soon enough, Alora returned to the nursery and slowly opened the loose floor panel.

[Ignis Feed Location]
Block B Med-Bay Nursery
<Camera 9>

Alora shook Mission's shoulder. She jolted awake, gasping for air. Her hand groped through the darkness until it found the respirator attached to her oxygen tank.

"Mission. Mission!" Alora said sharply. She took her by the chin and forced eye contact until she calmed down. "I'm sorry it took so long. A few biological fathers arrived for surprise visits, and I practically had to beg Cassiopeia to leave."

Mission caught her breath, realizing she was tightly squeezing the respirator. It was only a reaction. She wasn't under for anywhere long enough to need it, but nearly every time her eyes closed under the floor, she woke in a panic. It couldn't be helped.

"Is it safe?" Mission croaked. Her eyes had to adjust to the light, and her throat, to fresh—albeit recycled—air.

Alora nodded. "Everyone's headed to their hollows. The infants are on audio surveillance, and I am on monitor shift." She smiled, heaved Mission up out of her hole, and sat her on the edge. "I'll stay in here instead."

"Great."

"I snuck some real food down. Grasshopper vegetable medley, your favorite. And before you ask, no, I didn't get a chance to talk to Cassiopeia yet."

"I wasn't going to." Mission brushed by her and followed the intoxicating smell wafting from a bowl across the room. Typically, she got leftover milk or baby mash, but Alora sometimes smuggled the real stuff from the hydrofarms when she was feeling extra guilty.

Mission poked at it. The casserole was freezing cold, but

she lifted the rim to her mouth anyway and shoveled it in with her hand.

"How many times do I have to tell you not to eat like that?" Alora said. "It's not civilized."

"Neither is living in a hole in the floor." Mission glowered back at her over her shoulder.

Alora ignored her and rooted around in Mission's little compartment, studying a handful of the drawings she'd scrawled on loose pages using anything that left a mark on paper. She lifted the one Mission had been working on before falling asleep. The lines trailed off on the end, but it was what she imagined the bickering couple earlier that morning had looked like.

"This one is incredible, Mission," she said.

"You can keep it if you want," Mission garbled, her mouth full.

"Are you sure? It doesn't look finished."

"It is for me."

Alora folded it gently and slid it into her pocket. "Your genetic mother would be so proud to see them. You get that from her. When she was young, she could imagine anything . . ." Alora got lost in a thousand-meter gaze, as she often did when she brought up Mission's genetic mother. She'd never told Mission exactly what had happened, only that she'd died during her secret childbirth because of it. The father, shortly after.

"Too bad she'll never see," Mission remarked.

Alora staggered backward into her chair. Mission wasn't sure why she'd said it so harshly. Everyone else got to give birth in the safety of the Block B med-bay, yet *Mission* was supposedly the miracle—she, with a mother whose anti-contraceptive implant had somehow malfunctioned, forcing her to endure a secret pregnancy outside the Collective's regulation, and a fatal birth far from the medical equipment that could've saved her.

"Why are you acting like this?" Alora asked, tears welling in the corners of her eyes.

A hundred different answers came to mind, though none Mission could bear to say. Seeing Alora fight to keep her eyes from watering was too much. Mission knew what she was risking by keeping her existence hidden.

"I'm sorry," Mission decided on. She'd made her point. "Being down there for too long makes me feel . . . funny."

"I know. If there were anything I could do, you have to know I would, but the Collective would never believe it wasn't planned. Tampering with an inhabitant's implant is—"

"A high crime. I know," Mission finished. "And what is hiding an unregistered child again?"

"Who knows. I'm the only one crazy enough to try."

"Or stupid enough." Mission lightly punched her in the leg, and they shared a chuckle. Alora wiped her eyes.

"I prefer 'human enough,'" Alora added. She grabbed one of the texts from Mission's home and pulled up a seat across from her. "Now, it's time for your lesson before the babies start making a racket again."

After a few lessons about how and why life on Earth ended, Mission noticed Alora starting to drift. A few more, and she was as sound asleep as the infants around the room.

Mission smiled as she removed the book and gently laid Alora's head on the table. Alora always tried her best to stay up with her, but after a day's worth of Birthmothering and sneaking food—she never lasted long. Mission didn't mind. She was used to being alone, sharing her time with infants who could see her but would never remember. Safe.

The little girl nearest Mission's hidey-hole began to coo like she usually did around this time of night. While *Ignis*, deep in space, had no day-night cycle, the Collective had found that children benefited from a natural, simulated routine. Good thing, otherwise, Mission would never be left alone. A knock at the door made Mission's heart leap into her throat. A man and woman spoke outside in hushed tones. She hurried over and shook Alora, but Alora grumbled something and shooed her away. That was when Mission heard the control pad combo beeping. Whoever they were, they were coming in.

Mission darted toward her loose floor plate, not bothering to mute her footsteps. No time to worry about that. She made enough of a gap to stuff herself in, and her head was barely through when the door *whooshed* open. She had to release the panel without closing it all the way, leaving a noticeable gap. Lowering it into the groove would be too loud.

"Who is that?" Alora blurted, nearly falling from her chair.

"I could ask the same of you," an old man replied. His voice was rugged but confident.

"Mr. Dorromy," Alora stammered. Mission had heard the name before. He was the Head of the Collective. "Sorry, I fell asleep reading to them."

"That's all right, Alora. Routine checkup," Cassiopeia said, accompanying Dorromy. "We've had reports of faulty air recyclers on this level, as well as surges in energy output from the core to the blocks, which I'm sure you've noticed."

"Of course."

"We need you and all others to vacate the area while we investigate," Dorromy said.

"I can help." Alora sounded nervous. Her footsteps moved away from Mission's still-open hiding place in a clear effort to divert their attention. "I'm in here every day."

"I'm sure you can, but first, we have to ensure this isn't the result of mischief."

"I assure you, none of my Birthmothers would do something like that," Cassiopeia said, terse.

"Yet children are unpredictable," Dorromy noted.

"I assume you don't meet many up in the core?" Alora asked.

"They'd only get in the way. Now, I will ask kindly for everyone except Cassiopeia to vacate immediately. I'd rather not involve enforcers over something so trivial. Wouldn't you agree?"

"I really don't think—" Alora started before Cassiopeia cut her off.

"It's fine, Alora," she said. "I'll watch him."

Alora hesitated for a few seconds, then exhaled. "Fine . . . But please, try not to disturb the children any more than you already have." Mission peeked out and saw Alora glance back at her, her face flushed with concern.

"He wouldn't dream of it," Cassiopeia said. "Isn't that right, Dorromy?"

"Of course," he said. "Earth has fallen. We remain."

"Go wait in the galley with the others," Cassiopeia told Alora. Mission heard her being shuffled out, and every time she tried to talk, Cassiopeia hushed her.

Once Alora was gone, Dorromy's heavy boots clomped across the floor toward the monitoring screen at the back of the room . . . toward Mission. Mission held her breath as his shadow passed across the opening, tall and slinky like all those growing in the low g of the core. The infants started to fuss.

"I don't know how you do it," Dorromy said.

"So, what do you expect to find here?" Cassiopeia asked.

"We've underplayed the significance of the core's strange behavior the last week. The power fluctuations are . . . well, we have no idea what's causing them. That stays between us, by the way. We can't have a panic."

"And you think we have something to do with it?"

"No need to be defensive, Cassiopeia. We must investigate everything we can. And oxygen expenditure readings from this particular room in your med-bay are slightly elevated relative to population." Dorromy's fingers danced across the screen as he shuffled through data.

"Slightly? Is that really worth unsettling my Birthmothers over? Nobody is used to seeing a member of the Collective down here for anything but reproductive pairings."

"I assure you; nobody has any reason to be nervous unless they're guilty of placing the core's well-being in jeopardy."

"Don't be a fool," Cassiopeia said. "You know why."

"Well, you'd better get used to it. As soon as your time is up here, you're on the list to join us. Our work comes first."

"I won't stay huddled up in the core until I'm less than human."

"None of this is human, Cassiopeia. It's what we have to do to carry the flame."

Dorromy stopped fiddling with the screen and turned. His toe caught the lip of Mission's floor panel and caused him to trip. Mission gasped, then covered her mouth and sank back farther into the darkness.

"What in Earth's name," Dorromy said. "Have you noticed this unsealed flooring?"

"I haven't," Cassiopeia replied.

Dorromy crouched and ran his fingers underneath it. Mission raised a second hand to her mouth. Her heart thumped against her rib cage. The lights were on. If he opened it farther, he'd see her drawings, her makeshift bed, and the oxygen tank. He'd know before he even saw her tucked back as far as she could go under the crisscrossing metal structure.

"The *Ignis* is a flawless ecosystem, Cassiopeia," Dorromy said.

"I don't need a lecture," she answered.

"One rift, and oh-two circulation is not optimal." He strained to lift the panel, but Alora had always said living in the core's low g had weakened longtime members of the Collective. His arms wobbled. "Can you help me remove it? Maintenance will be summoned immediately to reseal it."

"You sound disappointed."

"An explanation for the surges would have been preferable."

"Are you sure you didn't just want to see me again?" Cassiopeia said, a playfulness in her tone that Mission didn't understand.

"Don't flatter yourself. I didn't choose us all that time ago, the core did. Now, if you please? Help an old man."

Mission's eyes grew wet as she saw Cassiopeia's shadow shift, and her hand sliding under the panel. She could picture it all, just as Alora had explained. That they'd be shot through the airlock side by side. Frozen in the void called space.

Metal screeched as they slowly began to lift. Then every light in the entire block went dark. The air recyclers rattled to a stop. Mission had been so used to them, she had no idea how loud they actually were until their absence. Screams echoed from outside, harsh and terrified.

Cassiopeia and Dorromy dropped the panel with a *clang* so loud it might as well have been an airlock breaking open.

"What's going on?" Cassiopeia asked.

"By Earth . . . they were right," Dorromy said. The pure terror in his voice was palpable.

"Right about what?"

"Some feared that with the Core acting up, a blackout . . ." He couldn't even finish. "Where's the door? I can't see anything."

He took another step and bumped hard into a crib, which stirred the infant inside into a frenzy. Cassiopeia hurried to help him, ignoring the child. Mission didn't risk another second. She squeezed through the narrow opening they'd left and rolled out onto the floor. The screaming and chaos outside now had all the infants awake, crying.

Mission had spent the entirety of her young life in the nursery. She didn't need light to find the exit, even if she couldn't see the hand in front of her face. She swept out into the lobby and backed up against the wall, finally feeling like she could breathe again.

It was only as she heard the patter of chaotic footsteps all around her that she realized this was the farthest she'd ever been from her home. She started to hyperventilate, and every breath felt more and more stale with the air recyclers off.

"Alora . . ." she whimpered. "Alora, where are you?"

The only person she'd ever known had left her alone. Cassiopeia and Dorromy still struggled to find their way out of the room, but they'd get out eventually.

So young Mission did the only thing she could think of. She ran. The other inhabitants she raced by weren't used to total darkness, but she was. And the tiny hints of light given off by the flashlights via sewer jockeys were enough for her to find a path.

People screamed all around her. Women, men, young and old. She couldn't pick Alora's voice out from any of them, and she had no idea where the Block B galley even was.

So she kept running.

Toward where terrified voices echoed louder, out into the internal world of the *Ignis* ark ship. It was as dark as anywhere else, but the air felt . . . lighter somehow. She couldn't explain it, only that breathing grew a smidge easier.

She slammed into someone and fell back. The man, whoever he was, cursed, but she was gone by the time his hand reached for her. She found a wall near a hydrofarm and climbed up, using a stalk of something for leverage. If there was one thing her hole had made her good at, it was climbing.

Reaching the top, she rolled over onto her back. Frenzied people cried out all around her, but all she could do was listen, their voices coming from around and above, all throughout the internalized world.

She focused on the sounds, on how enormous the *Ignis* sounded, and her panic started to wane. Inhabitants kept screaming about the darkness and the lack of power from the Core, but this was more light than she ever had.

"I'll be okay, I'll be okay," she heard a tiny voice muttering nearby, over and over.

She flipped over, ready to bolt until she realized that across the rocky outcrop sat a young boy, around her age. He held a dim flashlight against his chest so that it lit his chin, but his eyes were closed as he rocked back and forth. The light's charge was low, and he squeezed it as if his hands might help power it longer.

Mission knew she shouldn't, but it was too late. She was already exposed, and as soon as the power returned, she'd be found. But now that she was so far beyond her hole, that part of her that so gravely sought to be free of it took over. She felt bold again.

Crawling to the boy, she sat, legs folded, across from him.

"It's only darkness," she whispered. "It can't hurt you." She extended her hand, slowly, hovering just over his arm. Her throat went dry. Other than the babies and Alora, she'd never touched another human being. She pulled her hand away.

The boy peeked through one squinted eye. "How do you know? Listen to them."

"I promise."

He snatched her hand before she could do anything about

it. Her heart skipped a beat. On instinct, she pulled, but his grip was strong enough to hold her until she calmed.

"Don't leave me," he said, voice shaking.

"I . . . I . . ."

He slowly tilted the light so it illuminated her face. He opened his one eye a bit more, then the other until he was staring straight into hers. His brow furrowed. "What's your name? I'm Jacen."

"I'm . . ." Mission swallowed, then gathered her breath. Her pulse started to race again. Every instinct told her to run away, find Alora in the darkness. But his grip held her steady. The warmth of his hands calmed her.

"I'm Mission," she said.

* * *

"Hello, Mission," I responded, as if she could hear me. *Maybe she can.*

The events of the blackout had drawn me from my couch, and now I sat directly in front of the main screen. As Jacen shined the light on Mission, I could see the color of her eyes in perfect clarity. They were the most beautiful things I could imagine, with more shades of green than even the grass in the virtual simulator.

I stayed there until my newly discovered body gave way to exhaustion, watching as Mission was introduced to her world— same as I was being to mine. And from that moment, I knew that somehow, I had to be a part of her show.

15 YEARS LATER . . .

CHAPTER 2

Mission shoved her way through the crowded, normally empty airlock hollow of the interstellar ark known as the *Ignis*. A vital law had been broken, and with the future of humanity at stake, such acts of disregard could not be permitted. She understood the irony as she neared the airlock, just as she did every time.

Three laws existed on the vessel for which the penalty was death without recycling of energy—to be forgotten forever.

The first: population was to be maintained at ten thousand inhabitants. Any more and the *Ignis's* ability for provision would be strained. Any less for an extended period risked stunting the plans for eventual settlement in the Tau Ceti system. Any unauthorized action resulting in the population shrinking or swelling was punishable by spacing.

The second law: consumption of food and water was to be regulated to established feeding periods and rationed equally amongst the population regardless of position or rank. Any attempt to increase one's share, including theft or manipulation, was punishable by spacing.

The third, and most vital law: *Ignis's* core must always remain active. Any action that placed its proper functioning in jeopardy was punishable by spacing. Without the core, the *Ignis* would become as uninhabitable as any other rock adrift through space. Inhabitants were warned daily about the consequences of the Great Blackout—the brief period twenty years ago when the core malfunctioned and the *Ignis* went without power for three whole days. Laws were broken, supplies ruined, and hundreds of the asteroid-ship's population had been lost.

Though one inhabitant was gained.

Mission had been born beyond those laws of the core and cared for by Alora despite them. The Great Blackout hit on the first day she saw anything beyond her nursery. Much of the core's data had been damaged and rebuilt from backups. Alora intervened and, suddenly, Mission became the lawful, 14,130th inhabitant of the *Ignis*. The block populations had been reshuffled, and Mission appeared simply like a transferred Block B inhabitant. In the chaos following the blackout, nobody questioned it. Though Alora was convinced the true nature of her birth would have been ignored anyway.

Regulations had been forsaken in the name of restoring the population necessitated by the first law. This led to an overabundance of youth never before experienced on board the *Ignis*. Age variety in the populace had been key when the people of Earth were said to have sent the interstellar ark forth to preserve their species. It made adhering to the strict regulations easier and caused fewer distractions.

But as the Blackout Generation reached the age of assignment, they did so amongst an abundance of peers with still-developing minds and morals. The crimes they constantly committed made the implant malfunctioning accident that resulted in Mission being born seem innocent.

"There you are!" Jacen-14133 said to Mission as she neared the airlock. "I was worried you wouldn't show."

Mission turned to look upon her first friend in the world. The small boy, scared of the darkness, was no more. Jacen had filled out. Tall, with long, lean arms—well-suited for his assigned job trawling through the tremendous pipe-trench system that wrapped the *Ignis*. His short black hair and taupe skin accentuated the soaring forehead and long, narrow jawline indicative of humans born under the gravity—half that of the Earth's—generated by *Ignis's* rotation.

"I wasn't planning to," Mission replied. "I told Alora I was sick."

"I'm guessing she didn't buy it?" Jacen said.

"Nope. She said, 'Birthmothers don't get sick,' and then pushed me all the way here. I've seen her puke plenty of times while she was pregnant."

Jacen shrugged. "You know they don't like anybody missing these things."

Mission rocked up on her toes to see over the crowd. Every inhabitant of the *Ignis* was packed into the circular space. Technically, it was a hollow scooped out of the crust of the asteroid-vessel, but the rock walls were too smooth for it to be a natural air pocket. Sunken into the very center of the floor was a metal hatch with the appearance of a giant toothed gear. Beside it, a teenage boy and girl, both just passing puberty, stood holding each other, tears staining their grungy cheeks. The Collective hadn't even let them wash off after they were found harboring an illegally reproduced infant within a sewage line.

The temptations of youth proved too much for so many members of the notorious Blackout Generation. Spacings were more common than ever, which was why, despite the Collective's best efforts, the population still hadn't returned to optimal numbers. This wasn't the first time Mission had seen a young teenage couple who had fallen in love, felt a primal calling, and inexplicably removed the woman's contraceptive implant in order to create life.

Mission couldn't believe anyone would do anything so crazy. She understood that few women were lucky enough to be chosen as Birthmothers like she'd been. Using the Core's data, the Collective had calculated all potential genetic probabilities. Reproductive matches were selected to perfect the human genome. As carriers, women were considered the primaries in selections, so their evaluations were more rigorous.

Mission had gone through the tests to carry despite her origin, and she had been chosen.

The temptation made sense. But the brazenness to think they'd be able to hide an inhabitant forever or until another event like the Great Blackout allowed Core records to be tampered with unsettled her. She couldn't believe anyone would want to raise a child in a cramped hole like she'd grown up in.

"They were from our block, right?" Jacen asked.

"Huh?" So much of her early childhood was a blur now, all this time later. All except the sense of claustrophobia. If she thought about it, it overcame her. She could feel the air thinning, the desperate need for oxygen.

"Mission," Jacen said.

She shook away the bad memories and turned to Jacen. He wore that confused expression he often did, with one brow raised too high and his lip twisted. She would have laughed if every other aspect of the day didn't make her feel so sick.

"They're from B," Jacen reiterated. "Did you know them well, being a Birthmother and all?"

"A bit. Never saw either in medical much," Mission said.

"She seemed nice though. I remember she offered me an extra sip of water once when we were youn—"

Jacen threw his hand over her mouth. "C'mon, Mish. Lower your voice."

She pushed his hand away. "Nobody's listening."

She regarded the criminal couple. Nobody on *Ignis* was a stranger to death, considering they were the last of humanity, but the two were hysterical. Inhabitants were rarely sentenced to spacing in pairs. One death impacted the population enough, with a full nine-month gestation process required to replace them.

"What would you have done if you'd found them in the channels you maintain?" Mission asked.

"The same thing any of us would," Jacen said. "They made their decision to break the law."

"What if it were us?"

Jacen choked on his next breath. His cheeks flushed a shade of purple. "I'm not that stupid. Your birthday is tomorrow. Don't think I forgot. You'll enter the core's selection database."

Her twentieth birthday, to be specific. One day until she was cleared for her prime reproductive years as a Birthmother and would bear a child into their world in a way she'd never had the chance to experience.

"Don't remind me," she grumbled.

"Well, all I'm saying is soon you'll not only be named our next Mother, but *be* a mother. You won't have time for sewer jockeys like me."

Mission sighed. At sixteen she had taken the aptitude exam, mandatory for all inhabitants. The culmination of a life's worth of studies to find her place on the *Ignis*. That was stressful enough. But there was no age she'd dreaded more than twenty, when a Birthmother's true purpose arrived. Every time she thought of it, she could remember her infant roommates growing up, never noticing her, always crying and sleeping. Over and over and . . .

A deep, matronly voice thundered throughout the hollow and stirred her from her thoughts.

"Our laws are simple!" declared the gray-haired and wrinkled Cassiopeia-11445. "The delicate balance of resources provided by *Ignis* must never be tested. We are the last! We carry the lasting flame of humanity!"

Cassiopeia, formerly the Block B Mother before being replaced by Alora, now served as the acting Head of the Collective, the group of thirty men and women who had access to the records and systems of the core. They were deemed the most perfect subjects on the vessel of age, based on DNA analysis, physical appearance, and the rigorous aptitude testing every inhabitant endured.

Together, with the six Mothers who oversaw the health and reproduction of inhabitants—one for each of the ship's six living blocks—they decided the future of the ship. Cassiopeia had been one, though her body didn't show it. She wore her prim white uniform proudly.

"I swear we didn't steal anything!" the young accused boy protested. He grabbed Cassiopeia's arm and shook vehemently. "We only ever shared our portions with him!"

Someone sprinted out from the crowd and spat at him. "Flame-robbers! Your cursed generation will be the death of us all!"

The accused boy wiped his wet brow, incredulous. In a world where resources were so finite, there was no graver gesture of insult than the sacrifice of water.

"Order!" Cassiopeia bellowed.

Enforcers quickly pacified the situation. They responded only to the Collective. Most had scored just below the cut in the core's standard aptitude exam of making it into the Collective themselves, and had exceptional physical ratings. Their batons could crack bones, but when things got as bad as they had during the Great Blackout, they'd bring out guns from back on Earth. Pulse-pistols able to blow a hole through somebody from dozens of meters away, though thankfully not through the *Ignis's* thick enclosure.

Cassiopeia turned back to the young man on trial. "And once he grew, could your portions still be sufficiently shared?" she asked. "And what if a defect from your unregulated mating caused him to require even more? Or worse, polluted the gene pool before we reach Tau Ceti and have a chance at rebuilding Earth. Endangering one of us is the same as endangering us all." The crowd voiced their agreement.

"We know what we did was wrong, but please spare him . . ." the mother of the child said, eyes wet with tears. "Spare our boy."

Cassiopeia approached a semicircle of the Collective and Block Mothers. While everyone else in the hollow sported half-century-year-old boiler suits from when *Ignis* first set off from Earth, they wore clean white uniforms like hers.

Alora handed Cassiopeia a wailing infant swaddled in a cloth. Cassiopeia carried him to his illegal biological parents and stood before them, brushing his thin hair and gazing amorously down at his chubby face as any mother would.

"Your child was born innocent of your crimes," she said. "By some miracle, he has been determined healthy and pure enough to become the 9,935th living member of our crew."

"Samson . . ." the accused girl sniveled. She fell to her knees and reached for her child, but Cassiopeia turned away.

"In two days, he will celebrate the fiftieth anniversary of our launch alongside each of us," Cassiopeia said. "For the crimes of removing your contraceptive implant without sanction and breeding without core authorization, you two will not. Your energy will be expelled from the *Ignis*, never to taint us again, or corrupt our future world. Never to be recycled."

"Samson!" The accused girl lunged but was halted by her partner before she could touch Cassiopeia. Three enforcers rushed forward and tore the clothing from her and the boy, as was customary. The young woman punched and kicked, but her lover did nothing. He merely stared blankly at his child.

Once their grime-stained flesh was exposed for all to see, they were shoved onto the surface of the airlock's inner seal.

Cassiopeia positioned herself at the airlock's edge, still stroking Samson's head as she regarded them. There was no malice in her eyes, only the calm of a leader knowing she did what needed doing.

"May you find peace in the void." Cassiopeia regarded the crowd and shouted, "Earth has fallen! We remain!"

The crowd's echo filled the hollow. But Mission remained silent.

"Jacen, let's leave," she whispered.

"You know we aren't supposed to," he replied.

The airlock's inner seal peeled open like a swiftly blooming rose, and the criminals fell in, clunking against the solid outer seal below. The crowd surged inward to watch as they screamed for mercy and pounded against the metal. Mission turned away. At first, she'd loved watching when the outer seal opened, hoping for the briefest glimpse of the stars beyond, but not anymore. She'd seen too many inhabitants she'd grown up around be sucked through, knowing there was a time she and Alora might have been destined to join them.

The shrieks of those condemned to die were squelched as the inner seal of the airlock shut them out.

* * *

"Any stragglers?" fixer Lance Alsmore asked through the comm-link in my ear.

"Give me a minute," I replied.

A spacing ceremony was taking place on the *Ignis*, and as the Chief Director of Content for *Ignis: Live*, I was monitoring it while simultaneously coordinating a camera repair with Lance.

A director's job is never done, I thought as I absentmindedly tapped my finger on my thigh.

The vast array of view-windows floating before me abounded with a selection of camera feeds and data. Front and center was one focused on Mission as she refused to watch the spacing. It was hard to miss her within the dark cavern, with hair like amber. Blonde in some light, but if you looked closely, the shades of natural red shone through. Though messy and littered with fraying ends, somehow, it made her look more interesting than the clean perfection of High Earth's Residents. More unique.

It made Mission, Mission.

Every other inhabitant observed the ceremony with keen interest, but not her. She turned her face, a look of . . . what was it, disgust? Irritation? Frustration?

After watching over her every day of my life since my emergence from the synth-womb, I'd become good at reading her mood. This time? I wasn't completely sure.

Over the last fifteen years, I'd seen her blossom from a bastard child living beneath a floor, into a beautiful young woman whose image was plastered on holoscreens throughout High Earth—the face of *Ignis: Live* emerged from the horrors of the Great Blackout.

That something so beautiful could spring from such darkness . . . it was what the program was all about. Beauty from ashes. Though none of them knew Earth was still here. Different, sure, but here nonetheless.

"I'm ready to go here, Asher," Lance droned into my ear. "Waiting on your call." Patience was not one of our fixer's finer traits, of which it seemed there were few. Although, I'd never actually met him—not in person, at least.

I had a lot of relationships like that. Between those working upon *Ignis*, like Lance, who knew they were part of an entertainment stream, and those like Mission, who didn't, I had many friends I knew I'd never meet.

I rotated in my chair to face another feed.

"All currently broadcasting feeds are focused on the airlock," I said. "Give me a moment, please." He was hundreds of thousands of kilometers away, so there was about a second or two delay.

I swept across my station's central feed to pull another in front of me, then another. My crew had sent a station-wide update—the sector where the camera repair was needed remained free of inhabitants. It wasn't that I didn't trust them, but . . . I didn't. It was too important, so I always liked to see for myself before a fixer entered the vessel.

"We're clear for now, Lance," I decided.

"About time," he groused. "You got me itching, waiting in here."

I turned to peer through the wall-sized window of my office at the camera-operating crew sitting at desks in the large, impossibly open studio. Considering the studio was a VR we were all uploaded into, standard physics didn't apply. Which meant no columns or structures impeding my view, and floating screens that made it simpler for the crew to monitor hundreds of feeds simultaneously.

It was tough to call them a crew anymore, since they were

a mixture of humans and AI projections. Developers of other programs utilized majority-AI workforces for support jobs once they had the data support, but Craig Helix preferred to keep his wildly successful program in as many human hands as possible. It was part of the charm of *Ignis: Live.*

Often, interludes in the show cut to the live, human-operated bullpen like it was a selling point. Real people producing a real show, in a real studio, about real inhabitants on a real, reclaimed, pre-techno-revolution interstellar ark carved into an asteroid that had never been launched.

I can admit, that's a long tagline. Perhaps that's why Mr. Helix is in charge of things like that and I'm not.

The only fabrication was that the *Ignis* wasn't actually heading anywhere. It orbited the Earth at a safe distance on a plane roughly equal to the moon's, making it possible to maintain near moment-to-moment reception. The inhabitants' visuals and equipment, however, were modified to maintain the illusion that they'd been headed toward Tau Ceti for fifty years and counting.

When I'd started as an assistant to now-retired Chief Director Bolsa, the crew was seven-eighths human. Finding enough residents willing to help monitor and control the thousands of 180-degree cameras hidden within the *Ignis* was no easy task. Every month, it seemed like another worker had to be replaced by an AI. Most people of High Earth preferred to consume entertainment with their data credits, rather than be a part of producing someone else's. The novelty of helping make *Ignis: Live* possible seemed to be wearing off on everyone but me.

I switched my station-wide comm-channel so the crew could hear me. There was nowhere I felt more comfortable than alone in my office with my feeds, issuing commands.

"Team, I'll keep an eye on all entry points for the fix. Focus on the ceremony. I want to *feel* their emotion."

"Yes, sir," they responded.

"Operator 76, pan across the Collective," I said. "Then widen scope and provide an overhead of the whole hollow. I want every single inhabitant in the shot when the outer seal opens. Senior cam, stay focused on Mission. Let's give the people what they want to see."

Mission was what I wanted to see too. Since that first day, so long ago. She was—

"Sir, I lost track of her," my senior camerawoman, Laura, answered. "She left Jacen and disappeared into the crowd."

I swore before answering, "Locate her immediately. Our viewers treasure her reactions. 81, find the cam with the clearest close-up of the infant. We need a face for his first day."

Always a face for their first day . . .

"All right," I said. "I'll be observing the fix. Laura, feed's on you until I get back. Find Mission, then frame again from her POV."

"On it," Laura replied.

Laura Mandini was a fast riser in development, like I'd been. I'd barely been acclimated to walking when I'd had VORA contact Mr. Helix and volunteer my data credits and my time to work on the show. VR programs featuring any worlds or activity you could imagine, the constant flow of original visual content streaming on the High Earth Network—none of it made me feel a thing like seeing Mission's proud eyes for the first time, surrounded by so much fear and darkness.

I'd started out on cameras, but the show's brilliant creator, Craig Helix, quickly took notice of me. My focus on Mission had led to some of the show's highest ratings, historically. Approval ratings spiked when the show featured Mission after the

Great Blackout, and I'd been assigned to monitoring her, as Laura now was by me. Her appearance, her attitude, her horrific then triumphant background, viewers couldn't look away.

But I'd made sure of that. I wasn't sure anyone realized it, and I'd never say it out loud . . . but I'd made Mission the star of *Ignis: Live*.

Nobody in High Earth *had* to work. However, I spent more time uploaded into the studio than my own home. And when I was out of it, I watched whenever I could. About three years ago, Chief Director Bolsa formally retired to pursue developing her own program, and Craig named me his youngest chief director ever.

I switched my comm-channel back to a private line with Lance.

"Do you need anything, sir?" a timid voice asked. I nearly jumped, she startled me so badly.

Vivienne Poole was my new human assistant. I'd completely forgotten she was in the room observing. She was a young woman . . . well, relatively young. The ages when people were released from the synth-womb varied from ten to full physical development, depending on how well their brain took to knowledge infusers and if there were openings in domicile placement. With life expectancy among residents presently sitting at one hundred and forty-two, at thirty, Vivienne was technically older than me, but hadn't been animated until her late teens.

"No," I said. "Just watch."

Out of the corner of my eye, I noticed motion on one of the *Ignis's* feeds. Lance crept to the end of a loose air recycler vent into a corridor near Living Block B. He was dressed in the same sort of ratty boiler suit that most of the inhabitants wore—an effort to reduce the risk of him being spotted. As per protocol, they also wore a holographic facial concealment that made them appear exactly like a similar-sized inhabitant, since *Ignis's* low population would make a stranger stick out. On this job, he happened to be wearing the face of Mission's lifelong friend, Jacen.

All safety measures. In all the years *Ignis: Live* had run, none of our crew had ever been caught. But Mr. Helix knew best.

I transferred the feed to my central window.

"Entering corridor 103B now," Lance said. "Sometimes I forget how damn cold it is in here."

"Just focus, Lance," I said. "We've got cameras 2,331 and 2,338 down in the passage. I can see the position of the first at full zoom, but not the second."

"Easy-peasy."

"Let's not get cocky," I said. "Just get the job done quickly and quietly."

"Yessir," Lance said. He saluted toward the camera he knew I'd be watching, then hurried down the rock-strewn passage.

I tracked him with the cameras I still had access to. It was difficult to go ten meters on the *Ignis* without there being one. Every angle, every room had to be covered. It was the only way the show could work—one hundred percent access to the lives of the inhabitants. Nothing held back. Nothing censored. Not Mission's birth, or the terrible circumstances that had caused it—nothing.

Lance stopped at the edge of my viewable area and kneeled to get started. The fixer's job was simple enough. Most times, surges knocked out power to the cameras, or their wireless capabilities malfunctioned and needed to be replaced. He went in and took care of it. If an inhabitant ever stumbled upon a broken piece of High Earth equipment and looked too closely, that was when a fixer was really needed. To exfiltrate those who grew suspicious that the *Ignis* might be more than it seemed and remove the memory via brain infuser. I could only count on one hand how often that'd happened since I'd started at Helix.

Lance reached into his satchel and put on an OptiVisor to detect the signature of each camera. They were minuscule, like crumbs from a stale loaf of bread, and they'd all been carefully camouflaged to blend into rock surfaces, into the patterns on metal walls, or even attached to lighting fixtures.

"Do they have to make these things so impossible to find?" he asked.

"Exactly the point, isn't it?" I said.

"Yeah, well . . ." He ran his fingers along the wall's craggy surface for a minute or two. "Aha! Got you." He stopped and drew a wand with a magnetically charged end designed specifically to grip the cameras.

"Is the entry port compromised?" I asked.

After transmission lag, he leaned as close to the wall as his Opti-Visor would allow. "Looks fine."

The slot it fit into could only be measured in millimeters. The port the tiny sphere would then latch onto for stability was even smaller. Lance removed a flat case from his satchel and carefully raised the lid. He then used the wand to refit it with a new lens. I couldn't see it from my vantage, but he held it up to the light before inserting it in the wall.

"It's in there," he said. "Activating now." A holoscreen projected from the lid of his case and he keyed a few commands. "Syncing with the comm-relays."

I pulled up a field of data on my end. Strings of code ran down the screen. Thanks to Helix's in-house brain infuser, it had taken me mere minutes to understand the code, but many years to master.

"I've got initial contact," I said.

"Shouldn't be long," Lance said. "Second one now. Moving."

"All right. You're out of my view while the new camera syncs."

I turned my attention to the live feeds of the spacing ceremony. The inhabitants remained safely clustered around the airlock. The lawbreakers had been evacuated, and the airlock was already resealed, but they were listening to their leader, Cassiopeia, share a few more ceremonial words. I'd always found it fascinating how they'd managed to invent their own laws using all the information fed to them by the core. The initial ten thousand delisted volunteers Craig Helix had selected had had their memories altered to believe the Earth was left completely uninhabitable by nuclear fallout, but the rest was all them.

"So how many cameras are there in total?" Vivienne asked, startling me anew.

I didn't say anything. I was busy scouring through the feeds around the airlock hollow, probing the thousands of familiar faces in the crowd to locate Mission. I couldn't help but think back to her younger years after she became a legal inhabitant, when she might as well have been named Mischief. My neck started to ache when I still couldn't find her.

"Mr. Reinhart?" Vivienne said.

"Didn't you infuse the manuals?" I snapped.

Her lip twisted. "I did, but my brain's still sorting the information. It's foggy."

"Well, give it another day or two." A few moments went by in silence; then I exhaled. Dealing with people over comms was so much easier. "Thirty thousand two hundred and sixty-one. On the inside."

"And you use all of them?"

"Most of them. There are parts of the ship nobody ever visits, but that doesn't mean we aren't prepared. When Mission was first hidden beneath that floor, for instance, the current fixer had to sneak aboard to add cameras."

Vivienne recorded everything I said on a holopad hovering above her wrist. Only her second day after the bots hooked her up to the Helix Brain Infuser and uploaded everything she'd need to know, and she didn't want to miss anything. I remembered being that eager on my first day under Craig Helix's wing.

"You really are interested in this, aren't you?" I asked, finally turning my head halfway toward her.

"My VORA thinks it'll really appeal to my mental composition," she said.

I missed having assistants without brains. AIs stayed quiet while I worked, did what I requested within their limits, and did it efficiently. Vivienne, on the other hand, was a resident struggling to find her passion, by the looks of it. Not everyone emerged from the synth-womb only to find the thing they loved right in front of them like I had. I pitied her.

"So why exactly are you here?" I asked. I had to imagine Mr. Helix saw something in her, besides his desire to involve the human element in the show's production as much as possible. He was always calculated.

"I decided to visit the Outskirts and got caught with banned tech that put my resident status in probation, with need for 'volunteer therapy,'" Vivienne said.

Ah, there it is, I thought.

"The Outskirts? Why?"

Some residents also liked VRs for things like skydiving while I barely wanted to step out on my balcony no matter how often VORA listed the benefits of fresh air. I couldn't imagine actually wanting to *leave* my smart-dwelling let alone travel to the Outskirts, where delisted people lived off-Network like the animals they were. Security bot escort was required for a visit. Some residents got a thrill out of seeing how the other half lived, donating data to them or testing their food and permitted tech.

"I needed to forget something and saw on *Outskirts Today* that they have their own off-Network brain infusers. It was foolish to ditch my security and sneak to one."

"Did you forget how many nonresidents fry their own brains out there trying to live like us?"

"I wasn't thinking. I should've just requested the procedure here, but it was too embarrassing."

I shifted my jaw. "What was it?" I asked only because I felt I had to. Now she had me locked into small talk. AIs were so much easier. They let me concentrate. People always needed attention for something or other. I always suspected that was why Mr. Helix trusted me so much. All I needed was the show.

"I wanted to—" Vivienne's eyes went wide. "Her."

"What?"

"Her!" She pointed at one of the feeds on my screen array.

I tracked her finger. Mission was alone and heading toward the same tunnel system where Lance was. My inexperienced crew had lost track of her because she'd completely left the area. I'd allowed myself to get too distracted by the ceremony and Vivienne's pointless questions to notice.

Seeing her froze me. It wasn't until Vivienne repeated herself again that I snapped out of it. I jumped on comms and said, "Lance, you've got incoming!"

"Are you crazy?" he asked after the standard delay. "You said they were all at the airlock."

"One snuck out, and you're taking too long. Get out of there now."

"Too long," he grumbled. "I'm getting this camera set."

"Just forget it. Go!"

My pulse raced. Mission moved at a brisk pace, like she did

whenever . . . irritation it was. The transmission delay allowed her to get so close that in only a few more meters she'd reach the offshoot corridor where Lance was working. If she turned, she'd definitely see him, and if she did . . .

The idea of memories being yanked out of her head by a brain infuser made my stomach turn over. They could take information as well as provide, but the side effects of the former could be severe if the process wasn't done carefully. Lance was far from the best infuser operator I'd encountered. Sometimes all the necessary fragments of memory weren't found, and inhabitants returned to the *Ignis* went mad from the missing pieces. I'd heard that was the case with Mission's biological father, that he lost it and took her Birthmother against her will.

But that wasn't even the worst case. If Mission spotted him and made a scene, or ran, then Lance might have to take more severe action. It was why Craig chose residents on the verge of being delisted and cast away to the Outskirts beyond the walls of High Earth to be fixers. Otherwise, I would've jumped at the opportunity to be one. A chance to not only watch over the *Ignis* and its inhabitants through cameras, but be there among them.

I shook the thought out of my head and focused on the situation. I was of much better use behind the camera. I could never hurt an inhabitant, and Craig Helix had to prepare for the worst scenarios. The show came first.

"Lance, I'm warning you," I said. "You have to go."

"Just a second longer . . ." he replied.

Vivienne stood directly beside me, furiously taking notes.

"Stop that!" I slapped the screen out of her hands. It hit the ground and burst into pixels. "No more talking during operations." A few heavy breaths later, I realized I'd acted rashly. But she had to learn.

"I'm . . . I'm sorry," she stuttered. "I didn't mean to distract you."

"It's my fault." I took another deep breath to compose myself. "Can you please go see if anybody on the floor needs anything while I handle this."

"I—"

"Now."

"Sure." She shuffled away, head hanging.

I tapped my fingers on the desk for a few more seconds until, finally, Lance shouted, "Got it!"

"Quiet," I said into the comms.

Mission rounded the corner while he was still cleaning up. Her brow furrowed when she spotted him at the other end of the long corridor. There were about fifty meters between them, but she squinted and whispered, "Jacen?"

Shit! In my panic, I forgot to tell Lance to shift his appearance to someone from another block. Lance's facial-concealer was programmed to look like Jacen, and the real Jacen was supposed to be back where Mission had left him at the airlock, halfway across *Ignis*.

The newly installed camera went live, and I witnessed Lance's perplexed expression up close. He turned so Mission wouldn't see his hip and reached for the pulse-pistol hanging there, equipped both for stun and kill. There was no saying which setting a delisted man like him would choose now that he'd gotten himself cornered. Not after I'd allowed him to be caught off guard.

"Lance, just find another way out of there," I yelled into my comm. "She's alone and saw nothing."

He didn't move. Mission walked toward him. Too late for him to change appearance.

I activated a virtual control window as fast as I could and dug through code. Most of the *Ignis's* programming could only be altered by Mr. Helix, but as chief director, I had some additional access. I could adjust the lights if it helped a shot, only enough that it wouldn't be noticed by inhabitants or could be excused as a minor power surge.

"Lance, move!" I demanded, hand hovering over the controls. Nothing.

I could see how panicked he was. I felt the same.

"Lance, listen to me," I said. "On my signal, I want you to head for your exit as fast as you can."

Without thinking twice, I adjusted some code and set the lights throughout the entire area to go completely dark.

"Go!"

Lance took off. I tracked his progress on the feeds with thermal vision. By the time I returned the lights to normal, he was safely around the next corner, then into the air duct he'd entered through. A keycard would get him past a hidden passage deep inside, and beyond the rocky exterior of the *Ignis* back to his observation station, which hovered around it.

I released a mouthful of air I hadn't realized I'd been holding in.

I turned my attention back to the new corridor 103B feeds. A surge like that would have any other inhabitant who'd experienced the Great Blackout terrified. Not Mission. She strolled to where she'd spotted Lance in disguise, as puzzled as I'd ever seen her. She stopped where he'd been kneeling, bent, and rose with a tiny black orb sitting in her palm.

One of the malfunctioning cameras had fallen during his escape. My heart stopped beating.

"Drop it," I whispered. "Please, Mission, just drop it."

She raised it to her eyes and tilted her hand to let it roll. A pebble or a crumb would have been uneven, swerving along her hand from side to side, but the camera was a perfect sphere. It rolled straight down one of the grooves of her palm. She glanced curiously from side to side and then, to my relief, let it fall like it was trash. It rolled through an air recycler grate, where it would never be seen again.

We got lucky.

I checked over my shoulder. Everyone in my crew was busy monitoring the conclusion of the ceremony, so nobody other than me saw exactly what had transpired. I'd violated my agreement as a volunteer on Mr. Helix's program not to intervene in inhabitant affairs by overloading the light to gain her attention. I had a good reason, I could convince him of that, but then Mission's curiosity added a second strike.

I reopened comms with Lance and said, "Lance, you dropped the broken camera behind. We're lucky it rolled into a duct, but you'll need to sneak in and retrieve it as soon as possible."

I heard panting as he opened his line. "How did that . . . It was clear."

"Just get it. And let's keep this between us. You almost caused quite a mess."

"I—"

I switched off comms before he could answer. He'd keep it to himself. I might have messed up, but leaving a piece of High Earth tech behind like that? No matter the circumstances, he'd lose his position, and he knew it.

Next, I had to handle the crew and viewers. Nobody could worry that Mission might suspect something was wrong with her world. Since I oversaw all footage and had earned Mr. Helix's trust enough for neither him nor his VORA to monitor my activity too closely, nobody ever would.

"You're too smart for your own good," I said to Mission, as if she could hear me.

I dug through command prompts to erase all history of my intervention with the light. Then I accessed the data for every camera in the area and deleted all proof of her interaction with Lance, as well as the fact that she'd almost noticed a camera. Then I reset the logs of both new cameras. It would appear like they'd come online after Mission was already walking away.

"Asher, old friend!" someone exclaimed.

I whipped around. If I were out in the real world, sweat would have been beading on my forehead.

Craig Helix materialized in my office out of nowhere, elegant tunic pulled tight over his broad shoulders. The upper portion of his face was covered, as usual, by the screen of a digital OptiVisor that floated in front of his eyes. From my end, it didn't allow me to see what he was watching. Any number of *Ignis's* public feeds could've been projected by it and manipulated simply by tracking his eyes and thoughts.

"Mr. Helix, I didn't realize you were uploading today." My voice cracked slightly. Deleting unusable footage was permitted. Getting caught erasing an interaction between Mission, a fixer, me, and a loose camera would get me kicked off the crew at best, or delisted at worst.

What was I thinking?

"I wanted to compliment my chief director on crafting such a beautiful scene," Helix said. "Wonderful, just wonderful." He ambled in, and I positioned myself in front of the feeds displaying Mission.

"You'll have to thank Laura and my team for much of it," I said. "Unfortunately, I had to take care of a situation in Living Block B."

"I hope nothing too out of the ordinary?"

"Just a few cameras on the fritz and a random power flux."

Helix signaled his OptiVisor to fade away. He was coming

up on eighty years old; however, in a VR, age was but a number. Hair, eye color, skin tone, clothing—it could all be adjusted on the fly, if you even wanted to look like you. Here, the golden-hazel eyes Mr. Helix wore boasted the luster of youth.

He leaned to the side and peered over my shoulder. His nose wrinkled as he likely saw Mission standing alone while the rest of the inhabitants dispersed from the airlock hollow. Then he glanced at my wrist. For the first time, I did as well. A warning light slowly blinked red, transmitted from the lifeband I wore in person. It wasn't an emergency, otherwise it'd be chirping out loud as well, but it indicated that my heart rate was elevated.

"I assume everything went well?" Helix asked.

"Lance cut it close, but everything worked out in the end," I said.

"If he's not getting the job done, I can look elsewhere. Plenty of deadbeats teetering on the edge of the Outskirts."

"He'll be fine. He's getting faster." The words poured from my mouth before I could stop them. Deflecting blame for Mission getting so close to discovering Lance. But Lance had nothing to lose. He'd already done something to put his residency at risk. And if he logged a complaint, as chief director, I oversaw interactions with him anyway.

"Now, sir, don't waste your time with me." I gestured toward the door, desperate to be alone before I said anything wrong. "You should compliment the crew on their job instead."

"Yes, of course." He summoned his OptiVisor back. Something he'd been watching on it made him smirk, and it wasn't his own show. I considered playfully scolding him for upping the ratings of another program, but held my tongue.

"Excellent job as always, Mr. Reinhart," Helix said. "Keep up the good work."

"Will do," I said. "Oh, and, sir, one thing. Speaking of looking elsewhere, I don't think Vivienne is going to work out."

Helix sighed. "I just brought her on, Asher. She seemed desperate for purpose."

"I know, I apologize. I just can't concentrate and keep up with her questions at the same time. Not at an important time like this. Can you shift her to Frederick's night crew maybe? Bring back the AI assistant for now?"

"If it's really a problem, I'll see what I can do."

I spotted Vivienne across the studio. She nearly tripped over a camera operator's legs while attempting to squeeze between them.

"It is, sir. Thank you."

"Doesn't look good having my chief director working beside an AI, especially with so many of the crew missing days or being tempted by VRs," Helix said. "As if living in a made-up world could possibly be more enjoyable than recording a real one."

"I agree, sir."

He exhaled. "But the fiftieth anniversary is coming up. I need everyone focused, especially you."

"Again, I apologize. Trust me, I'm as focused as ever."

"Of course you are!" He placed his hands on my shoulders. "You are the most focused CD we've had! From the moment you uploaded into this studio to interview, barely this tall." He held his hand out near the middle of my chest. "You didn't even know who I was, only that you needed to be here. From that moment, I knew this was your future."

"Thank you, sir." I shimmied out of his grasp, trying not to make it seem obvious how uncomfortable I was. In my opinion, Craig Helix was the most brilliant resident alive. He was my mentor, but no matter how long I'd worked below him, it always felt surreal when he touched me.

Program developers were the true celebrities of High Earth. They chose their passion and went for it. It was the beauty of the world. The High Earth Network provided those humans with a nature for creating, the ability to produce content and compete for ratings in a harmless way.

I myself never had it in me to develop anything as vividly realized as he had. I'd tried and failed over the years, never willing to publicize my work or ideas for data contribution, never giving it the chance for ratings. No, I was happy enough to help Mr. Helix's vision. And though I loved the work, I could also understand those residents who were content with only experiencing the designs of others. Supporting incredible visions was a worthy venture. Without *Ignis: Live* fans, the Network would never have kept a show on air that required so much data.

Helix turned, but again I stopped him. "One more thing, sir," I said. "Are you going to reveal your big plan for the anniversary yet or surprise us all?"

His grin stretched from ear to ear. "We'll discuss it soon enough," he said. "Trust me, it'll be the best footage since the Great Blackout! We'll be back on top."

"I didn't realize we'd fallen—"

"Oh, no. Not yet." He laughed. "But you know me. I prefer a comfortable lead. Approval ratings are tough these days with so much out there. There are more worthy developers than ever. After next week, though, we'll be number one again in every chart. You can bet on it!" He patted my back, then meandered out into the studio, clapping and congratulating every human member of his crew he passed.

I signaled my door to shut, digi-locked it, and fell into the chair at my station. My wrist continued to blink red. If anything was ever really wrong with me, automated med-bots would arrive at my home to treat me without even having to call for them. An indication of high stress levels wouldn't elicit that reaction.

The same warning sometimes occurred when I was unsure of a camera shot, or got stuck in a crowded VR platform while I wasn't working, or tried to stand at the edge of my balcony. Heights still made me as queasy as when I was a boy.

Presently, however, my wrist was blinking for reasons I wasn't accustomed to. I couldn't remember breaking a rule in my life. I was just grateful Mission had tossed the camera away somewhere out of sight. I knew better than anyone how curious she could be, how impulsive and smart. What would I have done if she'd looked closer? If she'd taken it and shown it to other inhabitants and the situation expanded beyond a harmless resolution.

I reached for my wrist and keyed a command on the circular screen that appeared above it, linked to my lifeband. Anxiety-easing pharma injected directly into my bloodstream. After a few seconds, my chest felt loose again and my pulse slowed.

I turned back to my array of *Ignis* feeds. With the spacing ceremony concluded, the inhabitants were returning to their daily routines. Keeping an interstellar ark built into a small asteroid in optimal condition wasn't easy, especially considering they had no bots.

"All right, everyone, fix was a success," I said, resetting my comm-channel to communicate with the whole crew. "Get me up to speed."

"Still no location on Mission," Laura replied, sounding somewhat embarrassed.

"I've got her," I said. I considered bringing up how she'd possibly allowed Mission, of all people, to sneak so far away, then decided it was best not to press after what I'd done. "She snuck out early and headed home."

"I . . . I'm so sorry. I don't know how I missed it."

"It's fine, it was crowded. Just don't let it happen again, yeah?"

"Yes, sir."

I set the feed displaying Mission to broadcast live and centered it. She was climbing the stairs of the Block B med-bay, her forehead still creased by confusion, which would easily be mistaken by viewers for sadness over the spacing.

I closed my eyes tight and drew another measured breath, really letting the calming pharma sink into my system.

Seriously, what the hell was I thinking?

CHAPTER 3

Things fell quiet on the *Ignis*. Spacings always left the inhabitants pensive. Of course, the show had to go on. I had the crew track the conversations of a few of the show's favored stars. I checked in on Mission personally a few times, but she'd lost herself in work at the Block B med-bay after reporting the power surge. A Collective member came to check the power output levels, but everything cleared, and it became but another blip on the *Ignis's* power log.

A child required a health checkup, and Mission recorded the measurements of his body, from facial structure to height. She seemed distracted, and I hoped it wasn't the out-of-place Jacen or the strange pebble she'd found still on her mind. She even misreported his height and had to catch herself.

Every inhabitant went through rigorous tests while they grew to help determine their job placement. Mission's measurements, readministered along with many others after the blackout, were more perfect by the core's established standards than any inhabitant before her. Her aptitude exam scores ranked in the ninety-ninth percentile.

Eventually, my VORA notified me that my shift's end had arrived, and I should log off to rest my brain. The night director, Frederick Lowery, was left in charge, though as chief, I could always be contacted to load in for a real emergency. Frederick hated when I did that, almost as much as he hated that Helix had passed him over for me. He'd been volunteering for Helix for twice as long and had experience developing a number of programs with middling approval ratings. The problem was, the man had no flare for capturing significant moments.

He understood how the show worked, but he didn't *get* it.

I would've stayed in my office day and night to make sure nothing on *Ignis* was missed, but one thing even the techno-revolution couldn't find a cure for was the need for rest. I usually logged off late and ate into Frederick's time, but after the fiasco with Mission, I needed a real break. Away from the show. Mr. Helix intimated as much when he popped in again later, telling me to, "Go home and enjoy your evening. Watch something inferior."

He knew events like a spacing were exhausting for us, on top of a fix. I monitored every inhabitant on a daily basis, for years. Today, two inhabitants had been spaced, and I'd never see them again. But it wasn't them on my mind. I'd lost focus for a minute, thanks to Vivienne, and almost caused a nightmare.

Mission was a major draw for the show, and her requiring the attention of a fixer would hinder ratings. Yet, as much as I told myself that was the reason I'd erased footage of her, I knew it wasn't the whole truth. Every generation of *Ignis* had their superstar, and I'd watched others fade to obscurity without a second thought before Mission's fame truly exploded.

"Welcome home, Asher," my smart-dwelling virtual intelligence VORA said as my mind was logged out of the *Ignis: Live* virtual studio. I was so used to it now, the transition was basically seamless. Only a momentary spell of vertigo and fragmented vision where I'd see bits and pieces of the VR I'd emerged from. Then nothing.

The neural nodes lifted off my head, and my feet lowered to the cold tile floor. Gravity emitters dotted the interior of the sphere, able to simulate on my physical body whatever action I undertook while uploaded. To trick my firing neurons into imagining the VR was a real world. Pleasure, falling, even pain—limited to a nonhazardous degree—could be experienced if the user desired.

I stepped out of the VR chamber and stretched my arms. "Thank you, VORA," I said. My familiar, pristine smart-dwelling greeted me.

"Did I miss anything?" I asked.

"Your lifeband informed me of unusually high stress while you were uploaded," she said in her usually impassive tone. "Is everything all right?"

"Just something with the show."

"It is not healthy to allow stress to affect your day-to-day activities."

"It's not stress."

"Perhaps you might consider a less intensive schedule."

"Drop it, VORA. I'm fine."

"As you wish. Are you hungry?"

"No."

I sat on my couch and signaled a holoscreen to blink up from the table in front of it. I rifled through personal messages. Mostly new content recommendations or other programmers trying to get an endorsement from a director on *Ignis*. I didn't give that away easily. It had to be genuine, and I rarely had time to test other content.

One message stood out above the slush. A VR date with

a woman named Dawn was scheduled for me that night. Occasionally, VORA would suggest human interaction through VRlovefinder. Normally, I declined without any real thought. For some reason, I'd said yes this time, about a week ago, and I'd regretted it ever since.

I closed out of the message and pulled up my Network viewing profile, which tracked all my data consumption and donation. I paused on the *Ignis: Live* ratings and couldn't help but dig deeper. There was an unusual dip in viewer numbers.

"There is a new program that seems to fit your viewing and developing habits, Asher," VORA said, as if answering my silent concerns.

"Show me."

My walls doubled as screens that could envelop me in whatever setting or program I desired. Gardens, lakes, even the surface of the moon. As a boy, I used to surround myself in *Ignis* and pretend I was there amongst the inhabitants.

VORA turned on the new program, and the ruddy landscape of Mars appeared. A small crater was covered with a dome, only all the structures were sterile, no movement at all.

"*Survivor 2450*," VORA explained. "In the ruins of a former Mars colony, twenty delisted residents struggle for survival. Only one will earn the approval to return home, here, to High Earth."

"Another knockoff," I groaned, still catching my breath. "Not interested."

"Are you sure? The developer received an enormous data contribution from residents after publishing the concept, which allowed her to receive tech appropriation to set it on the actual planet of Mars. Approval ratings after the first episode are—"

"Inflated. Now, set randomize program selection relative to my profile."

"Yes, Asher."

I knew I'd wind up back to watching *Ignis: Live*, but I always tried to take a break after spending all day uploaded to the studio.

My High Earth Network allotted-data contract allowed for more viewing hours per year than I could ever manage to use. They existed to help determine popularity alongside live enjoyment ratings, so that residents had to be somewhat selective about what they wanted to watch or which VR to upload into. On top of that, data could be contributed to programs of a resident's choice to foster a sense of involvement. *Ignis* required such a massive budget, it had to remain one of High Earth's most popular programs; otherwise, it would be unplugged.

Maintaining the speed and functionality of the ever-growing network of human imagination was another bonus to the tracking of data usage, but contract or not, the options were nearly endless. The only real ways to push limitations and get yourself delisted was to overcommit data contributions in support of programs, or play multiple programs, on multiple devices, twenty-four hours a day, all while watching them inside a VR. That, or harass other residents relentlessly enough to earn numerous complaints against your Network profile.

Mine was as pristine as my home.

A hulking robot burst into sparks and silvered fragments on the first program that came on. Cygnus Creations's famous bot-fighting league, where the best programmer-designed metallic monsters were pitted against one another in a simulated, real-world physics arena. A "live" audience made things both interesting and unpredictable since it was impossible to tell where loose pieces would fly. Of course, they weren't in any actual danger. The entire crowd was technically sitting at home, synced into a VR version of the program.

The whole experience was too barbaric for my tastes.

I swiped my hand to change the feed, no doubt providing a poor enjoyment rating. OptiVisors, holoscreens, VR chambers, they documented viewer reactions through facial expressions and vitals to determine if new content was widely enjoyable and worth recommending to other residents with similar habits. This way, nobody could lie about their enjoyment. Every rating—re-evaluated daily—was genuine.

Outskirts Today came on. An *Ignis* rip-off if there ever was one. Using drones and handheld cameras from resident developers braving the lawless Outskirts, the program tracked a data-mining gang called the Nation. The fact that all the members practically worshipped residents made nothing seem genuine. It even painted some of the awful delisted people scrounging for life to be heroic. On the current episode, a violent rival faction known as the Unplugged had burned down one of their off-Network VR dens.

A man, face covered by the shadow of a hood, stood behind a roaring fire. I could only imagine the heat given off by it. I'd never experienced real fire in person.

"Open your eyes," he said in a low growl that sent a chill up my spine.

I turned the channel before I had to watch more. Probably too fast for any genuine reaction to be recorded and provide a rating. What was interesting about a place residents could visit firsthand? Where reactions were exaggerated by data-beggars desperate for a donation. Fabricated to feel scary. *Ignis: Live*'s ratings buried it and other "reality" copycats every day.

A fictional series came on. This one, I couldn't fake disinterest. It was about contact with aliens during the initial solar-system colonization craze of the early twenty-second century. The characters were computer generated, as you could expect from most fictional show devs with a knack for storytelling.

Not like Mission and the other *Ignis* inhabitants. They were as real as could be, even if I couldn't reach them.

"VORA, please switch to *Ignis: Live,* most-watched feeds," I said, finally giving in. It was like a voice in my head was warning me I might miss something. It made my frontal lobe ache.

Then all the walls of my smart-dwelling morphed into feeds on the *Ignis.* My preprogrammed *Ignis: Live* aroma wafted through the vents to help fulfill the illusion like I was there. VORA's approximation of how the hydrofarms in the open interior might smell.

On a broad shot on my central screen, plants were brushed aside by farmers strolling around the curving landscape to their plots.

In another feed, Jacen headed to meet up with Mission. They'd been nearly inseparable ever since they were children and she'd found him on that ledge, flashlight gripped like a security blanket.

Nobody else knew her like him—nobody on *Ignis,* at least. I begged to differ.

[Ignis Feed Location]
Farming Plot 17B
<Camera 4>

"Birthmother Mission?"

"What?" She turned, and when she realized it was a child from Block B, her tone softened. "Is everything all right?"

Harold sat on the low wall of a hydroponic farming plot. Reeds of corn extended from chambers strung across the pit. Mission watched as a tiny droplet of water rolled off a leaf and splattered on the rock floor beside her foot.

All six living blocks in *Ignis* popped up through the rows

of greenery. They were like metallic nodes spread equidistant throughout the enormous ovular interior of the vessel. Another was straight above Mission, beyond the structure of the Core, jutting from a plant-filled sky, which wrapped all the way around to become her ground.

Hydrofarmers roamed the racks of green, trimming and caring for all the different types of flora brought from Earth. Beneath them, bugkeepers tended to the grasshopper farms, where the insects were used both for fertilizer and milled into food for inhabitants.

Others in the trenches between kept the water lines clean and running. Even farther beneath, sunken into the rock, people like Jacen maintained the countless main pipes and sewer trenches. Caring for *Ignis*'s hydro and insect farms was a never-ending vocation, but if they died, so too would the inhabitants.

"It's my leg," Harold said. "I think I broke it."

"Yeah, and tell her what you were doing," one of the nearby hydrofarmers hollered.

The boy's head sank. "Being nosy . . ."

"He tripped over a water line."

"I was only trying to get a closer look!"

Mission smiled. Harold was always squeezing into places where he didn't belong, like she used to. She knew the boy would be trouble from the moment she'd held him after Alora gave birth. His was the first birthing she'd ever attended. He'd squirmed and kicked and cried.

"I'm sure you were," she said. "Let's take a look, then."

"Maybe you can right the spigot he bent while you're at it," the hydrofarmer griped.

Harold looked ashamed, but Mission positioned herself between him and the farm plot and knelt. She rolled up his pant leg until a thin, red slice along his knee was visible. Mothers and Birthmothers served respectively as the doctors and nurses in charge of health throughout their blocks, so Mission knew right away he was fine.

"This hurt?" She tapped the wound lightly. The boy winced, but shook his head.

"No need to be brave," Mission said.

"A little . . ." he whined.

"I don't think it needs attention, but if the bleeding doesn't stop, you have to promise me you'll head down to the med-bay."

Harold gulped. "Stitches?"

"Maybe."

"Just make sure you go down when Mission is on call," Jacen said, emerging from the Living Block B entrance behind them. "Trust me. She's gentler than the other Birthmothers. You get Nixu and you'll wish you'd bled out."

"Jacen!" Mission jumped to her feet and punched him in the arm. "You'll scare him."

"Good, it's not safe snooping around here."

"I'm sure he had a good reason. Right?" Mission asked.

Harold shifted his feet and said, "How else will I learn how to be a good farmer when I grow up?"

"Oh, is that what you want to do?" Jacen said.

The boy nodded enthusiastically.

"Then you should be back in the block, studying for the AE. If we all got to choose what we did, the sewers would overflow and we'd suffocate."

Harold's chin fell to his chest. "I know . . ."

"He's only being cruel," Mission said. "I'm sure the core has a special role waiting for you. Just try to be more careful before the time comes."

"Yes, Birthmother Mission," he said, dragging out her name like he'd heard it all one thousand times.

Jacen rustled the boy's messy hair. "Now get to working hard." He gave Harold a light push, and the boy scampered back into their block.

"You're going to give the poor kid nightmares," Mission said.

"No reason in lying to them."

"Spoken like a true sewer jockey." The edges of Mission's lips curled into a mischievous grin.

"Now who's the cruel one?" He maintained a hard glare for a short while before his own smirk shone through. "Alora asked me to get you. You overstayed your break."

"I hadn't noticed."

She glanced up at the all-illuminating presence of the core. The colossal metallic beam where the Collective lived ran down the heart of their world, bulging at the center. The light of the ship's power reactor slipped through a series of rifts in the sphere, casting all *Ignis* in a subtle orange glow. It was the only source of light, heat and energy *Ignis* required. In her homeworld studies, Mission learned that the Earth had a sun that moved with the time of the day—or was it the Earth that moved with it? Either way, here, the core sat eternally still, never rising or falling, brightening or dimming.

"Don't play dumb, Mish," Jacen said. "She's summoned all the Birthmothers at the same time and won't say why. It's finally happening. She's going to pick you to be the next Mother, with her term ending, I know it."

"So do I. That's the prob—"

Jacen placed his finger over her mouth. "I don't want to hear it. You could've wound up like me, crawling through pipes every day. I wish I had your brain."

She frowned. "So that's why you were so hard on Harold? The aptitude exams aren't everything, you know."

The tests generated by the Core and administered during

the developmental years measured the intelligence of the inhabitants, as well as some key facets of their personality, such as drive, empathy, and courage. They, along with the careful monitoring of genetics, were how inhabitants were sorted into occupations.

Before the Great Blackout, everyone had to take them upon turning eighteen, but that all changed with the Blackout Generation. The Collective was forced to start administering the tests earlier to adjust for the abundance of younger inhabitants. Jacen took his early at seventeen. A year later, with a more developed brain, Mission always told him he would've placed higher. She herself had taken the exams and undergone her full physiological analysis at sixteen, and everything she'd learned, studying alone in her hole as a child, had her very advanced.

"Easy for you to say, Ms. Youngest-Birthmother-In-History."

Mission blushed and turned away. From the girl hidden beneath the floorboards, to a woman meant to spend the rest of her fertile life caring for the health of the inhabitants in her block and carrying future ones in her belly.

"I never asked for that."

"Yeah, well, you could've just failed on purpose," Jacen said. "So I guess you aren't that smart!"

"Oh, space yourself!" She punched him in the arm again, but as her hand hovered there, her features darkened again.

He stopped laughing, went to wrap his hand around her back, and gave her a gentle shove toward the Block B entry instead.

"It's going to be all right, Mish," he said.

"I know, you're right," she replied. "I'm just being stupid." They started off into the block together, through an open hatch and down a long, ribbed tunnel toward the dozens of hollows where inhabitants resided.

"No, you're not," he said. "I remember how nervous I was when my AE results came back."

"Me too," she said.

He rolled his eyes. "Sure, genius Mission was worried. You've known you were going to make Birthmother since the day you were born. Alora didn't hide it."

"I didn't know anything when I was born."

"Sure."

"And you wanted to be a hydrofarmer, like Harold does. More than anything."

Jacen shrugged. "I did, but maintenance isn't bad. Every job is important if we want to survive."

"You can be honest with me, you know."

"I am! Mostly . . . It really grows on you though, being a part of the ship, down in the trenches. It's better than wasting another second learning about ancient history."

"Jay, you coming?" another sewer jockey shouted over from a cluster of inhabitants standing at the entry of the cavernous galley, waiting to start their shift. It was the night shift, per Earth Standard Time. Jacen's peers were clean now, but after they returned from the pipes, their bodies would be as brown with muck as the rock surrounding them.

"Be right there!" he answered, then turned back to Mission. "I'll see you later?"

"If I'm still allowed to talk to someone like you."

His mouth opened to respond; then he froze, lips pursed like he was worried whether that was true.

"I'm only joking." She laughed. "Now get to work! I'll be fine."

"You always are." He stood and clasped her hand. "Good luck with Alora, Mish. You deserve this."

"Tell you about it in the morning?"

"Of course. It's your birthday! We'll meet in our spot like always."

Mission forced a smile and nodded. She'd hoped he'd forgotten about her birthday after the drama of the spacing. She hoped everyone would. It was the start of her prime birthing years, which meant that as soon as the core found her match, her contraceptive implant would be removed, and she'd be called upon to perform her sacred duty.

Jacen started to walk, but she clutched his sleeve before he got far. "I forgot to ask," she said. "Why did you leave the spacing early?"

"That was you, remember?" he said. "Don't worry, I won't tell Alora."

"No, I saw you on your way here, down the west corridor. I guess I was taking my time through the farms since you wound up ahead of me, but when I shouted for you, you ran."

"Mission, I promise. You're the only one who left early."

"And *I* promise. I saw you."

"Daydreaming about me, as usual?" he said.

She rolled her eyes.

"It was probably someone else who snuck out early. You know I'd never run from you."

"I know." She exhaled. "You're right. It had to be someone else. I was pretty far away, and then that light surge happened."

"I'm sure whoever it was *also* didn't want to be seen leaving early," Jacen said in a scolding tone.

"Yeah, yeah. Maybe I do need some actual sleep tonight. All right, go on already."

"Bye, *Mother* . . ." Jacen performed an exaggerated bow, then scurried away chuckling after she tried to push him. "And happy birthday!"

Mission wore a grin until he was away with his maintenance

crew, then it faded. When Jacen was around, she never let it show when things bothered her. Friends were hard to come by for Birthmothers. The others in her generation all competed for the same position, and Alora always kept them plenty busy in the Block B med-bay. There was no time to spend in the galleys carousing with other inhabitants after a hard day's work.

Mission stood and flattened her boiler suit while practicing her smile. Then she set off for the med-bay, crisscrossing the many hollows that comprised Living Block B. The rocky walls were filled with sleeping nooks like her own. It was late, and a portion of the farming crew was turning in while another shift woke. Those who weren't busy rubbing their tired eyes watched her carefully.

She stopped when she heard a group of children asking questions. They were in the schooling hollow, wrapping up a history lesson. Each of them were only a little older than she had been when she finally got free of the hole. Mission would have given anything at that age to be a part of a class, and half were barely paying attention.

"Division," the instructor said, pointing to an image projected on a tattered white curtain draped from the ceiling. "That is what destroyed Earth." She hit a switch, and an image popped up with a mushroom-shaped cloud looming over a massive city. Mission couldn't believe humans had ever lived in such a sprawling metropolis. It had to be at least four times the size of the *Ignis,* and Earth supposedly had hundreds of them.

"What is that cloud?" a child asked.

"The tool of our undoing," the instructor answered. "Because people couldn't agree on things, they used weapons like that to annihilate each other, pollute the sky, cause famine, disease, and deformation. This is why we must maintain the core.

It maintains focus, keeps us all working toward a unified goal more important than any other—the survival of our species."

Mission remembered those lessons well, even if she learned them in a different way. She preferred learning about what Earth was like. That it was a world turned inside out, where the sky was open, and the ground arced downward instead of up. She longed to see a place like that. She didn't want to die from a bomb like the ones depicted, but at least those people had the freedom to drop them. They didn't have to worry about surviving the next Great Blackout every single day.

"Look who decided to show up," Evelyn, another young Block B Birthmother, said, breaking Mission's train of thought.

Evelyn stood at the base of a silvery ramp that poked through the rock wall like a steel tongue. It led up into the Block B med-bay, where Mother Alora and other Birthmothers cared for their assigned inhabitants.

"She's been waiting on you," bristled a Birthmother named Nixu.

Like Mission, she and Evelyn were Alora's protégées, raised amidst the Blackout Generation, groomed from the first sign of promise to potentially take her place as Block B Mother when she turned forty.

They glared at Mission as she approached, their gaunt cheeks flushed with anger. Mission ignored them. She didn't ask to be Alora's favored daughter—she didn't ask for anything that had happened in her life—but Jacen was right. Nothing could change that now. The core didn't ask before determining how an inhabitant could best serve the *Ignis*. It was all data. Ones and zeros.

Mission stopped in the entry and drew a deep breath. Light poured down from the med-bay, and standing framed against it was Alora, garbed all in white. Years of stress on her body had diminished her beauty, but there was a time she looked much like Mission. On either side of her were the six older Birthmothers, ranging from their early twenties to late thirties.

"You're late, Mission," Alora scolded, tapping her foot.

* * *

As I watched Mission climb the ramp, the holoscreens around my smart-dwelling flickered, then fizzled away.

"VORA, what's going on?" I asked.

No answer.

"VORA, I can't miss this. VORA?"

I stood and turned. My lights, tech, everything—it all went dark, like the hall Mission and Lance had found themselves facing off in. Except High Earth didn't lose power, and it certainly didn't experience surges.

I found myself facing my unit's vast window, usually covered by some playing program. It was night. Units in the distant High Earth towers shone, nearly all of them covered by the motion and color of entertainment streams. But some were eclipsed. A humanlike figure stood behind the glass on the balcony I couldn't remember the last time I'd used. Maybe a bot with a new tech delivery.

I approached slowly, squinting to make sure I wasn't seeing things. It could happen after too much time in the VR chamber, shadows of the program playing with your vision. It usually meant a visit from a med-bot was due.

"VORA, where are you?" I asked, my voice trembling. Only upon hearing it did I realize that my pulse raced.

My window suddenly slid open. A gust of air rushed in. I flinched and had to lean on my table to keep from stumbling over.

"She can't hear you right now," the stranger said. His voice shook with unbridled emotion. I'd never heard anything like it in person. But one thing was sure, he was a human.

With the window open, the ambient light from High Earth revealed standard resident clothing. He stood at the long end of my balcony, back facing me, palms upon the railing as he stared out across High Earth.

"Who are you?" I asked. "How did you get up here?"

His lack of response drew me forward to the frame of the window, though no farther.

"Excuse me?" I said. "Who are you?"

"What a view," he said. "A shame you're all so content in blinding yourselves."

I looked from side to side at the edge of the aperture. I gritted my teeth, drew a deep breath, and took a step out into the wind. Now I could feel my heart thumping against my chest. I instinctually glanced at my lifeband, though, like the rest of the tech in my smart-dwelling, it had gone dark.

"Is this a dream?" I said.

The man whipped around. I froze completely. His skin was as creased and leathery as armor in an ancient, medieval VR. His long nose bent in two places, almost purposefully emphasized as if he didn't want the break repaired, a simple procedure for med-bots. He was dressed and clean like a resident, clothing nanofibers set to a neutral gray coloring, but the center of his forehead was branded with three stacked, arcing lines growing in length from bottom to top. They glowed neon blue.

The mark of an Unplugged.

He stared at me with dark eyes so rife with rage that I didn't need a lifeband to inform me I was nervous.

"Can I help you?" I asked.

I'd only ever heard about Unplugged on shows like *Outskirts*

Today, or warning newsflashes from the Network not to visit the Outskirts on certain days. They chanted their loony ideals throughout the awful place about how everyone should relinquish the technology that makes life enjoyable, and were famous for hounding visiting residents while the other delisted praised them. They'd preach at them, or sometimes rip off their tech. Even attack the security bots guarding them for their own twisted entertainment.

They *never* showed up out in the open in the center of High Earth. Security bots should have stopped him at the High Earth walls. Drones should have been quick to spot him and his mark. Network scanners should have read his biosigns or retinas and known he didn't belong. Yet, somehow, he stood right in front of me.

"VORA, please—"

Before I knew what was happening, he grabbed me and spun us around so that my back was against the balcony rail. I didn't even realize he'd been moving; I was so distracted by fear.

"Open your eyes," the man said, then pushed on my chest with two hands. He was strong, his muscles tested in a way only someone's from the Outskirts could be. I flew backward, flipped up over my balcony's railing, and fell.

CHAPTER 4

Air rushed up around me. Down to my internal organs, every part of me seemed to shrink in fear. It was a sensation I'd never experienced. Countless VR simulations existed for daredevils wanting to free fall, climb, and fight. You could be a swashbuckling hero on prehistoric Earth when humans battled with sharpened metal blades, or pilot a starship during the offworld colonial wars.

I'd avoided them all since I was a boy searching for my interests from a near infinite pool of possibilities available on the High Earth Network. Now I wished I'd at least learned from them.

My arms flailed wildly, feeling weightless even though it was weight that dragged me down. My right hand slapped the structure of the skywalk in my mad attempt to grab anything. Fingers grasping, they found a grip, but the rest of my body continued to plummet; my shoulder was wrenched upward. I shrieked in pain. My arm felt like it was going to tear from its socket. I swung the other to try to get a better hold on the railing but couldn't reach.

The pain was excruciating. The panic, like nothing I'd ever known. Spiderlike maintenance bots were scattered across the towers, polishing every surface, but too far away to hear. Drones blanketed the skies, keeping an eye on things, but without my lifeband active, I was one resident in a field of thousands.

I looked down and immediately got dizzy from the height. Moving walkways were strung between the towers. They were never busy, but a few residents out for "walks" or to visit others in somewhere as banal as the real world dotted them. They all focused on whatever was on their OptiVisors, though they were too far below to hear me anyway.

The Great Lawn spanned the bottom of High Earth beneath them. Grids of trees and verdant grass stretched between the plasticrete bases of the residential towers like an emerald carpet as green as Mission's eyes, providing fresh, breathable air.

Carekeeper bots maintained the grass, trimmed the trees, and kept any delisted folk out—ensuring everything remained in impeccable condition like they did throughout the city. I'd be the single blemish when my arms finally gave out and I fell hundreds of feet to a splattery death.

That was all I could think about, even though I knew I should be screaming. Fear made adrenaline surge through me when usually my lifeband soothed me. I threw every ounce of energy into swinging my other arm. Anything to escape the height. It found purchase, and I strained my muscles as hard as I could, heaving myself over the railing until I fell onto the balcony.

My legs were so shaky I couldn't stand, so I crawled for the safety of my smart-dwelling. I couldn't breathe until I got inside and rolled onto my back. That was when I noticed my lifeband start blinking at a rapid pace. Calming pharma was automatically discharged in my veins, making my eyelids heavy. My chest stopped stinging.

"Asher, are you all right?" VORA asked when I'd made it back inside. That was when I noticed that all my lights were back on. "Your lifeband has indicated a great deal of strain."

"Did you see . . ." I panted. My hands quaked uncontrollably despite the pharma. I looked out onto the balcony, then from side to side. That Unplugged man who'd shoved me was nowhere to be found.

"See what?"

"That man," I said. "He . . ."

I closed my eyes as more pharma filled my veins. This many times in one day was rare. Like most residents, I tried to avoid placing myself in situations I found stressful. After all, some people enjoyed the thrill of war simulation VRs. Lifebands could sense the difference.

My pulse and breathing leveled out, but my hands continued to tremble. And my mind raced. Man, did my mind race.

I'd never almost died before. Or had I? Traumatic experiences were the kinds of things residents could elect to wipe from memory by infusers. There was no reason to live with thoughts that didn't bring joy.

"Your vitals are beginning to regulate," VORA said. "Can you please explain what caused your reaction so I can begin my evaluation?"

"That man attacked me," I said. "Didn't you see?"

"Processing . . . You were physically assaulted?"

"Yes! Surveillance didn't catch anything?" My eyes flitted back toward the balcony. A wave of dizziness quickly passed when I squeezed my eyelids tight.

"Pulling up local surveillance log: 221178a3b." The screens of my smart-dwelling bloomed to life. A feed from a drone that'd been hovering above recorded the instant, with a time stamp of a few minutes ago. Eyes all over High Earth kept the residents safe, not that there was ever anything to fear. Or so I thought.

There I was, walking toward the window to my balcony. The drone was at a high angle as it soared over a tower, but the balcony was empty. No Unplugged man. Residents in the units above and below me peacefully went about their business. One was uploaded to their VR chamber, sprinting in place. Another was watching an episode of a show called *Molecular Nation*.

One moment, I stood before the opening; the next, I was collapsed on my back when my lifeband started operating again.

"That doesn't make any sense," I said. "I was . . . I was attacked, I swear."

"There does not appear to be an attacker," VORA said. The screens switched to a view from within my smart-dwelling, which showed the same. Me collapsing in front of my window, alone and short of breath. "It seems that you collapsed. You have always had an extreme reaction to heights, and after the stress of—"

"No!" I stood and ran back outside, searching the corners of my balcony, up and down. The intruder was nowhere. I even fought my fears and leaned over the rail to peer over for as long as I could before rushing inside to feel like I could breathe again.

"Please stay indoors, Asher," VORA said. The window to the balcony sealed closed behind me. The hum of wind died away, and all I could hear was my VORA.

"You weren't answering, VORA," I said. "Everything in here turned off, like a power failure . . . And he . . ."

"There is no record of power fluctuation, Asher. As you can see, you were headed outside and collapsed. You recorded elevated stress levels earlier in the day. It is advised you undergo a complete psychological and physiological evaluation."

"You think I fainted?" I asked.

"For your safety . . ."

I grabbed the edge of my table. My hand still shook from adrenaline, even with all the calming pharma in me. This was why I loathed thrill-seeking programs. I hated losing control.

"I was attacked, out there, by an Unplugged from the Outskirts," I said. "A man with a three-arced brand on his forehead. He's the one you should be questioning. He was right there!"

"Unplugged: a gang located in the Outskirts with violent tendencies," VORA said as if reading from a Net entry. "They are obsessed with destroying modern technology."

"I know what they are." I pointed toward my balcony. "He was out there, and he tried to kill me. You have to check every security feed."

"There have been no reports of a delisted resident infiltrating High Earth for the last . . ." VORA paused to process. "Two hundred and sixty-seven days."

"I know what I saw . . . I . . ." I fell back onto my couch. "You don't believe me?"

"I have warned you of the dangers of overexertion and stress. There are numerous possibilities. A nightmare due to falling asleep beyond your sleep-pod. Exhaustion leading to sleep-walking. Fainting. A full medical evaluation will allow me to determine the root of this episode."

"I'm not crazy, VORA. There was someone there."

"I can assure you, there was not. It is impossible for a delisted resident to infiltrate High Earth without our knowledge. All residents are DNA marked. Those exiled or born beyond our borders are not."

I drew a few extended breaths to steady myself, in through the nose, out through the mouth. Maybe she was right. Memory of how I'd broken the rules earlier flooded my head. I hadn't been thinking clearly since.

What were you thinking, Asher?

"Incident has been labeled as *stress-related accident*," VORA said. "Resident Asher Reinhart, health status listed as *mildly unstable*. Resident is advised to undergo full evaluation within seventy-two hours in order to return status to *optimal*. For your safety, you are to remain within your smart-dwelling until the evaluation is complete."

I sighed. "Maybe I am pushing myself too hard . . ." It'd been an insanely busy day. Enough to overwhelm my brain and cause a nightmare. I'd seen two inhabitants fall through the airlock earlier, and an Unplugged on that show. It just felt so real . . . but so did VRs.

"Would you like me to clear your schedule?" VORA asked. "There is currently a med-bot available for service."

I nodded.

A medical evaluation I could handle. Honestly, I probably needed the checkup. Breaking rules wasn't in my nature, and thanks to doing it once, my problems were compounding. Concerns over Mission's well-being had me all out of sorts . . . *Mission*.

I suddenly recalled what had been happening with her before I lost it.

I was missing out on Mission's potentially big moment. *If she was named Block B Mother already* . . . My heart skipped a beat. I'd been there for all the most important events of her life. So often, she pretended she didn't want the honor, but I knew how much time she'd spent preparing for it—absorbing lessons, putting in extra hours in the med-bay to sew up wounds and help with infant deliveries.

"Actually, can I do it after the *Ignis: Live* anniversary?" I asked. A visit from the med-bot related to stress might result in some potent pharma. I didn't want to be anything but my overly attentive self for such an important day. Whatever Mr. Helix was planning was sure to be big.

"Of course, Asher. That is within the allotted timeframe," VORA said. "I am only here to help."

"Thank you. Can you please tune back into *Ignis: Live*?"

She did as I requested without an answer. The primary feed displayed the galley in Living Block D. Discolored metal paneling covered portions of the cavernous hollow. Dim lights flickered as the hanging fixtures swayed. Two inhabitants brawled in the center while others cheered them on. One flipped over a table. After long days of farming or down in pipes, tempers had a tendency to flare. They didn't have endless programming like the residents of High Earth did to hold their interest.

"Mission-14130's current feed to central," I instructed. The moment her face appeared, my entire world seemed to settle. Imagining intruders and almost falling didn't matter. I knew I'd made the right choice breaking the rules, even if the stress of it had me struggling.

For her, for me, and for the show.

[Ignis Feed Location]
Block B Passage 1A
<Camera 14>

Mission lumbered down the main hall of Block B. Her conversation with Alora had been cut short with the evening feeding period about to begin. Once daily, in their assigned galleys, inhabitants were provided a bowl of slop composed of blended bugs and flora. The line full of tired workers struggling to stay awake spanned away from the long service counter. The *Ignis* never fully slept, meaning shifts had to be coordinated so every position remained stationed. Nighttime was simply a word to keep days from blending one to another.

Mission waited in that line every day for Jorah, one of the oldest men in *Ignis*, to slap food into her bowl. It wasn't like the decadent feasts on Earth they learned about during schooling, but it was all they had to survive on. The risk of another Great Blackout made rationing an even graver necessity when pumps powered by the core stopped cycling clean water and the crops wilted. Even the Collective ate the same concoction. Everyone knew how precious food and water were. There were no new neighboring lands to conquer on *Ignis*. What they had was all they ever would have.

Mission settled in line behind two younger Blackout Generation sewer jockeys who worked the shift opposite Jacen, their legs coated in sludge. The young woman and her male companion exchanged a playful jab, just like Mission and Jacen always did. Then they did something Mission never had . . . with anybody. They shared a passionate kiss.

The older folk in the line glared at them, distaste plain upon their faces, some cursing the impetuous Blackout Generation under their breath. No rules existed against chasing love or lust on *Ignis*—so long as the woman wasn't an active Birthmother or she hadn't taken extreme measures to remove her 100% effective contraceptive implant and take the creation of life into their own hands.

It was different for Mission.

She'd been expected to become a Birthmother ever since her core reevaluation after the blackout. And then, as she grew older, she was favored to become the next Block B Mother. Everyone knew it.

Boys had always kept their distance. Developing unmanageable feelings was what had led to the spree of spacings afflicting the undisciplined and adolescent Blackout Generation. Birthmothers getting pregnant outside of the selection process, lust and rejection causing violence, removing implants—Mission had seen it all, and the Collective grew less lenient with punishments now that the population situation wasn't dire.

Jacen was the only person her age who never seemed to mind the risk of Mission's company. The only person she ever felt like she belonged around. She used to have him with her for meals, though ever since he was assigned to the night shift, she wound up eating alone.

She wondered if he spent his feeding periods the same way, but she knew he didn't. He'd always found it easy getting along with others, and they him. He didn't look at them and know, like Mission did, that she shouldn't even be alive.

Mission tried not to stare, but when the two canoodling workers finally pulled their lips apart, the young woman shot her a sidelong glare, eyes red. They looked like they'd been snorting scrunge all shift—the crud scraped out of the core's exhaust ports, which enhanced sensations and made the world appear more vibrant. The Collective reluctantly tolerated its use in moderation so long as no Birthmother partook. Anything to distract the Blackout Generation from getting into worse trouble.

"Where's your boyfriend?" the girl asked, wiping her chapped nostrils.

"Yeah, where is Jay?" her partner said, smirking.

Mission bit her lower lip. She hated when people called him Jay. "Working."

"That's right, he's on nights now," the boy said. "Gets to deal with the weekly hydroflush."

"Pipe burst in his sector before we left," the girl said, sniffling a few times. "Too much buildup. I swear, this hunk of rock is falling apart more and more every day."

"At least we'll suffocate with our bellies full!" her partner added.

"Praise to the core." They giggled together and kissed again.

Mission pretended to laugh and looked away, but the girl slid in front of her.

"I guess Jay doesn't have to worry though," she said. "You'll patch him right up anything goes wrong, won't you, Miss Perfect." A hint of resentment eked into her tone. Sewer jockeys got that way with Birthmothers, at least until they broke a bone that needed mending.

"Probably climb down there yourself," the boy said. "Bathe him too."

Maybe Jacen didn't have it easy with everyone, thanks to being so close with her. Mission's hands balled into fists, but she exhaled slowly through her teeth before she did anything foolish.

"Maybe I'll go do that," Mission said.

She turned away without filling her bowl, the two of them cackling behind her. Her fellow Birthmother Nixu bumped her with a shoulder on the way by and mumbled something under her breath.

Mission did her best to ignore it and headed to her sleeping nook. She knew she should eat—Birthmothers and mothers weren't supposed to skip meals—but food was the last thing on her mind. All she wanted was for Jacen to return. She wanted to sit side by side in their favorite spot and talk like they had on the first day she was free.

Before they had responsibility.

Before everything.

* * *

I watched as Mission returned to her sleeping nook without eating and faced the wall. I wanted to call into the studio and berate Frederick for not shifting vantages to capture her expression, but eventually he recognized his mistake. *Too late as usual.* A hidden camera on the inside of her nook offered a glimpse of her face. It filled all the space around me.

Mission's cheeks were stained with tears, and her eyes, bloodshot. Her slender shoulders bobbed as she struggled not to weep aloud. I wasn't sure what that meant. It seemed impossible that Alora didn't name her Mother. I knew her AE scores. I knew how ideal her physiological ratios were relative to core standards and how immaculate her DNA strain was despite the nature of her birth. There was no way she'd be passed up. She was perfect.

I wished I were uploaded into the studio. There, I could dig into old footage, but as an everyday home viewer, I couldn't rewind to see what I'd missed. Most shows allowed it, but that was a policy Mr. Helix enacted from the start. *Ignis: Live* always moved forward, always live. In the moment.

"VORA, pull up all discussion boards referencing Mission-14130," I said.

A window popped up on the side of the screen. Comments and conversations regarding what was happening with the viewers' favorite inhabitants packed the screen. One new post after another.

so happy for mission! buck up, girl, you're gonna do great.

new mother! hell yeah, mission.

jacen is going to be heartbroken . . .

can't wait to see her with paul-10183 tomorrow. what a sight!

I choked on a mouthful of air. Now I knew why she was crying. She'd more than just been selected as Alora's heir, she'd already been designated for reproduction. Paul was a male member of the Collective, forty-eight years old and nearing the end of the permissible mating period. The system the first Collective invented using the medical information provided by the core was a careful one. It was used both to refine the human genome throughout their journey and to ensure the diversification of breeding partners to avoid inbreeding.

The population remained below the ten-thousand-inhabitant quota, lower now after a double spacing. Every Birthmother over the proper age had to do their part. They didn't get to choose. They didn't even have to want a child.

For those of us on High Earth, if we wanted a family, there were plenty of safe VRs for that. All residents were sterilized in the synth-womb, to ensure we didn't need to deal with the complications of child rearing. To make all the mistakes our ancestors had. I never really saw a reason to do that outside of a VR anyway, where you could be anywhere, try anything . . . safely.

Family was such an outdated concept.

I grew up fine, alone in the smart-dwelling provided for me, with VORA to offer guidance. The infusers and the med-bots rightly took care of the difficult parts of parenthood to ensure mentally and physically stable offspring were animated, already prepared to be respectful residents of High Earth; residents birthed from already perfected genetic material to replace the old who'd passed and the unruly who were exiled to the Outskirts. We existed knowing that humanity was in safe hands.

But Mission *had* to replenish the population. They needed numbers for their imagined new home and to optimally maintain their current one. Paul was the mate assigned to her from a select pool of men—someone with whom I knew she was barely acquainted.

The discussion boards weren't lying though. Tomorrow, as was custom after a Birthmother was selected for reproduction, Alora would remove Mission's contraceptive insert so she could conceive Paul's offspring. She'd be put through that gruesome natural birthing process I'd watched so many times on the show. Then she'd feed it. Raise it. Be attached to it in a way I couldn't imagine, but unable to favor it.

"VORA, switch programs," I ordered, feeling nauseous at the thought of her pain. My lifeband chirped quietly in response to the stressors as well.

"Sorry, Asher," she replied. "You did not specify a program."

"Anything!" I sprang to my feet. "Anything but this."

She chose nothing, and silence returned to my smart-dwelling. Slowly, my lifeband started to quiet down.

"In addition to your psychological evaluation, would you like to report a malfunction with the pharma from your lifeband?" VORA asked after allowing me a few moments to myself. "You have experienced an unusual number of anxiety-based episodes today."

"Maybe I'm building a high tolerance?"

"I can have the dosage increased following your evaluation. Elevated stress levels are detrimental to the proper functioning of the human mind and body and could explain your accident."

Accident. I couldn't believe what was happening to me. My life was usually so stable. Sleep, wake up, upload into my favorite place, and help Mr. Helix create art, rinse, repeat.

"That might help," I said. "Thank you, VORA."

"Perhaps you are nervous about your date?"

"Date?"

"Since you have pushed your evaluation to a later period,

you still have a VR date scheduled with one Dawn Trevell, scheduled to start in exactly twenty-seven minutes. You had expressed enthusiasm about meeting with her after your chatroom interaction last week. As I have told you, positive human interaction beyond the confines of your volunteer work can be soothing."

I'd totally forgotten I never officially canceled. I glanced toward the other end of my room, where my VR chamber sat. Then toward my window and the completely empty balcony beyond it. I'd always resisted VORA's insistence on interaction. Told her that I had all I needed in my work.

A message popped up for me and I expanded it. From Lance, saying that he had piloted a drone into the ducts and couldn't locate the missing camera, but would try again when things in the block quieted down.

I ground my teeth in frustration.

"Fine," I conceded to VORA. I wanted to call it off, but any distraction would be good for me after the day I'd had. I could blame my pharma for malfunctioning, but I was still on edge from doing something so crazy to help Mission.

"Inform her VORA that I'll be there on time," I said.

CHAPTER 5

"So," Dawn said. She sat across from me at a round table. We hadn't spoken more than a few words since we were shown to our seats. "Tell me something about yourself."

I stared at the computer-generated waiters carrying trays of computer-generated food to all the other residents uploaded into the VR we had decided on. They wore red vests with bow ties, and everything else around them was designed in the spirit of an early twentieth-century, western, five-star restaurant named Virgil's. Rich mahogany, finely embroidered tapestries, steaks the size of my head. It amazed me that people used to live like this, waiting for servants to bring them food. No bots or replicators.

"Mr. Reinhart?" Dawn asked. She twirled a fruity drink in her hand. The sound of ice rattling against the glass drew my focus across the table.

"Please, just Asher," I replied, putting on a grin. It took more effort than usual.

Dawn was gorgeous. Thin, with long straight hair colored

violet, strong cheekbones, and lips painted bright red. Most girls in High Earth had a similarly refined look, provided her VR avatar was as accurate a portrayal of herself as mine was of me. In a VR, appearance was immaterial, not that any resident didn't have perfect genetics in the real world regardless. You could be whatever you wanted to be, from age to gender. In certain VRs, you could even choose not to be human.

I took a lengthy sip of my own drink. Some sort of old-world bourbon. It stung going down, leaving me to wonder if the taste being transmitted to my brain through the neural transmitters was accurate. Who would enjoy this?

But every sip made my head feel less cluttered; an illusion tricking my mind, however, effective nonetheless. Real alcohol was an archaic, dangerous substance that you could only find if you ventured into the run-down Outskirts of the delisted, brewed using their off-grid, unregulated farms.

Dawn smiled. "Okay, Asher. Tell me something interesting."

I erased footage of an Ignis *inhabitant and interfered with their lives beyond clearance. Then I imagined I was attacked by a High Earth infiltrator.* I couldn't tell her any of that, of course. She'd think I was crazier than VORA had. There hadn't been a murder in the city in . . . I honestly didn't know how long. My entire awakened life.

"Asher," Dawn said while I remained deep in thought.

"Um . . . I live in Tower 3, Block 3C, on the thirty-third floor," I blurted.

"Interesting," she gargled, her mouth still full of liquid.

My brow furrowed, and I wasn't sure if she was teasing me or not.

She forced down her gulp. "I'm on Block 27A, near the Outskirts border."

"Wow. I've never been out that far."

"I've never braved crossing, but I'm on the seventieth floor. You can see the Ocean over the outer wall. It's nice."

I forced another grin, then couldn't keep my gaze from wandering around the room again. The restaurant's style was so raw and authentic, I could smell the wood moldings and the gourmet food. Not every VR nailed that sort of stuff, but the sensory detail here was astounding. Even if it wasn't real, I knew people in the past had sat in a restaurant just like this one, on a date, sharing drinks just like ours. Desperate to find a connection with someone . . . or avoid one.

Dawn returned to rattling her ice. They banged like the percussion line for the programmed musician strumming a soothing melody on his harp across the room—the soundtrack to all the quiet conversations of other High Earth residents on virtual dates. Another reason why I enjoyed this particular VR for any rendezvous VORA convinced me to go on. Most were far too noisy, replicating clubs with music blasting and residents simulating the effects of narcotics. There wasn't a viable interest in simulating a walk down the quiet streets of an ancient town these days.

"Solid brown hair," Dawn said. By that time both our glasses were empty. "I like that."

"What do you mean?" I asked.

She brushed her own hair. "On you. Most people get their hair colored to stick out, especially in here." She chuckled. "I honestly don't even know what color my hair is supposed to be anymore."

"Oh. I guess I never really noticed."

A waiter placed a meal down in front of each of us, saving me from another awkward silence. Mine was a juicy rib eye, green beans and mashed potatoes on the side. No gravy. Dawn skipped right to dessert. A wonderfully presented soufflé smothered in powdered sugar. No need to watch what you ate in a VR.

"Bon appétit," the waiter said.

Dawn grabbed her spoon and started digging in before the plate even settled. "I just love this stuff," she said, crumbs dribbling from her lips. "I would have been huge if I had been born in this time."

I offered a chuckle and turned my attention to my steak. I wasn't hungry at all, and maybe Dawn didn't have her re-assembler hooked up to her real body, but I did. Every bite would signal it to send nutrients into me through an IV in my VR chamber. I sawed off a chunk with my knife, watching reddish juice expand across my plate. Staring at it was as far as I got.

"I don't believe it!" Dawn exclaimed.

"What is it?"

She pointed over my shoulder, and when I turned, I realized the entire restaurant was buzzing. Being seated was a resident anybody in High Earth would recognize. It was the radiant star and developer of *Molecular Nation*, a period drama set in the middle of the twenty-second century during the breakout of the awful World War IV between the former states of Earth over their colonies throughout the solar system. It was now High Earth's most popular program by viewer registry, having recently surpassed *Ignis: Live*.

The developer, Joanna Porvette, not only created the show, but portrayed the troubled scientist Gloria Fors amongst a mixed cast of resident volunteers and computer-generated characters.

Fors had invented the molecular re-assembler, which inspired the techno-revolution long ago. Its ability to recompose matter down to its atoms, to turn saltwater—or even air—into food, rendered the battling governments of the past and their colonies pointless. High Earth wouldn't have been possible without it.

The survivors of the worst war humankind had ever endured no longer needed to argue over wealth and resources. Intersolar colonies built in the name of discovering riches or establishing strategic stations were abandoned. High Earth put every resident on an equal plane, distinguished only by their passions. It made war, struggle, the need for family, exploration, and so much more obsolete.

"I can't believe it's really her!" Dawn said.

I rarely found myself starstruck by anyone but Craig Helix. However, residents throughout the restaurant were standing to get a closer look at the breathtaking actress. And it was her. Replicating the appearance of another resident while in a VR wasn't technically difficult, but VR optics allowed me to view her verified Network profile. Both Dawn and I had been avoiding doing that to keep our conversation mysterious, but I was starting to regret that decision.

"I can't stand that show," I murmured. The truth . . . it wasn't terrible, and the fact that its developer used herself and other real people within the VR film made it feel extremely authentic, a new fad ever since *Ignis: Live* took off. A dab of realism.

"Then what *do* you enjoy?" Dawn's attention snapped back to me, her features darkening as if she herself had been insulted.

"Sorry, that's not what I meant. It's . . . uh . . . fine to watch. I just meant its existence."

"You like it, but you hate that it exists?"

"Competition."

She leaned forward on the table, a glimmer in her eyes. "So you're a developer? I post reviews for . . . well, for just about everything. Just hit ten thou the other day, each verified through yearly data contribution."

"Wow. Congrats."

"Thank you. It's all I can do for High Earth. I never really felt I had an idea anyone would care about watching or living in, but I have a good eye."

"Me neither. Only a volunteer, unfortunately."

Her excitement faded. "For what show?"

"*Ignis: Live.*"

That brought her back into the conversation a little bit. "I love that show. What do you do for it?"

"I'm chief director in charge of the day-to-day feeds. So, everything you see, really. For the last few years."

She coughed and wiped her mouth of soufflé. Her virtual eyes were bright with enthusiasm.

"That's amazing," she said. "Really, it is. To volunteer for running a show like that. It must take up a ton of your time."

"Most of it. But it has its perks."

"I can imagine. All the stuff we don't get to see . . . And you get to be with Craig Helix every day. I swear, I've seen every single interview he's ever done. He's an incredible man."

"He is."

Dawn shoved another piece of soufflé into her mouth when things went quiet. Then her foot grazed mine with intent.

"Want to hear a secret?"

I nodded.

"I'm struggling not to peek at your profile now." She leaned over the table as far as she possibly could, staring at me as if spellbound.

I couldn't help but glance down at her avatar's ample cleavage and she knew it—she'd planned it that way.

"Can you tell me anything about what's going to happen?" she asked. "Any secret plans coming up for the fiftieth anniversary?"

I cleared my throat and forced myself to look her in the eye.

"No plans yet. Like Mr. Helix says, 'What the *Ignis* gives you is pure, unscripted human drama.' There are times when we have to intervene to preserve the role of the vessel in the inhabitants' minds . . ." I paused, remembering how I'd just pushed the envelope. My throat felt suddenly dry even though I knew that, here, it couldn't be. "It's nothing you'd ever see though," I quickly said. "You probably wouldn't be interested."

"I wouldn't say that." She grinned.

"Ms. Porvette!" a man shouted. He pushed a table aside and darted at the actress from the other side of the room. He took her arm and she squealed in fear. Then an unseen forced tore her off him and into the air.

"No, no, no . . . I just wanted to meet her!" he yelled.

"Please pardon the interruption," an automated voice, much like VORA's, sounded all around us. "An intruder has been detected." Suddenly, it was simple to tell who was a program and who wasn't without opening profiles. The uploaded residents' eyes all shifted toward the intruder, while the generated waitstaff and musicians continued as if nothing had happened.

"No!" the intruder screamed. Then his avatar began to flicker, revealing a sullied face in rags rather than the clean jaw and suit. His voice distorted, and in a flash, he vanished into pixels, then nothing at all. Delisted folk in the Outskirts could acquire limited portions of data from visiting residents or via open donations hosted by the Network, but slicers out there often hacked into High Earth programs. If they remained quiet enough and blended in, the best could evade Network security for a time. Running at a star actress on one of the Network's highest rated shows, however, was a ticket to being booted.

It was as bold as one of them climbing onto a resident's balcony in person. Which made me feel even more foolish.

"Damn delisted ruining a peaceful evening," Dawn said.

"You don't even know," I said. A vision of that ugly, wrinkled face of the Unplugged attacker I'd imagined flashed through my mind. I raised my glass and drank a bit of the melted ice to cool down.

"And there she goes," Dawn added as Ms. Porvette made a fuss to whomever she was with, then disappeared as she too logged off.

"That's okay," I said. I could feel Dawn's interest slipping away even faster than earlier. I never was good at this. "It isn't secret information, but I can show you something about *Ignis* if you want."

"Please," she said, eager.

"Do you mind if we leave this VR?"

Dawn's posture loosened. "Not at all."

"VORA, can you upload Dawn and me into Unpublished Project-1GN15.77?"

"Yes, Asher." I heard VORA's voice inside my head. The restaurant began to swirl and lose shape. Bits of color frayed away at the edges of my vision. Before I knew it, we stood on a rock ledge at one end of the *Ignis*, looking out upon its vast, internalized world.

Dawn took a step forward, then spun a tight circle. "This is—"

"*Ignis*," I finished for her. "Well, half of it." The hydrofarms climbing along its ovular interior and sweeping up over our heads came to a sudden end. The almond-shaped asteroid the *Ignis* was built into was sliced in half, and all that lay beyond was empty white unprogrammed space. The core's beam extended toward it, then died off as well into pixelated pieces, just before where its fusion reactor should've been.

"This is a VR?" Dawn asked.

"A work in progress," I said. A lie, really. All progress had halted a while back. "It took years for me to construct this much. But I promise, it's accurate down to every nook and cranny."

I took a moment to behold my unfinished work. In the real thing, six equal living blocks were built into the dense band of crust left within the asteroid after the middle had been hollowed out and landscaped with farms and trenches. The cavity between those blocks and the outer crust was filled with water, and as the entire asteroid spun to generate artificial gravity, that water was churned and pumped throughout the vessel.

It fed the plants and insects, communal showers, toilets, faucets, and most importantly, was pushed through the fusion-powered core to keep it cool. The core itself, had I built it, would be enclosed in the center of a tremendous tube spanning that gaping hollow lengthwise from one end to the other, structuring the asteroid so that it didn't collapse in on itself with so much mass scooped out. Their version of a sun.

It was a delicately balanced system necessary to provide all the necessities for human life as well as protect the inhabitants from radiation with solid rock. The vessel itself had apparently been designed by a conglomeration of the largest corporations existing before the techno-revolution, when settling the galaxy was something people cared about—until High Earth perfected the art of living.

The real *Ignis*'s core was meant to eventually power the massive engine array jutting from the far half of the asteroid, which I also never built. When the vessel reached its supposed destination in the Tau Ceti system, the engine would allow it to decelerate and land. In reality, the *Ignis* remained orbiting Earth, as every resident who'd read the show description knew.

Databases located within the core maintained a fabricated chart of movement toward another star, and the single airlock entry or exit point that the inhabitants knew about was specifically programmed not to open while facing anything but stars, and never remained open for longer than a few seconds.

A holographic projection on the other side of the airlock displayed accurate constellations relating to where the ship should be. This way the *Ignis* always appeared to be moving through deep space.

Dawn knelt and tapped the leaf of a cornstalk in the farming pit below us. It swayed rigidly as if made of stone. I never could get the physics right. Even the mass of grasshoppers in a farm looked stiff as they fluttered about. My version of the *Ignis* didn't even actually rotate to provide centripetal gravity, not yet. We could stand on any surface in the vessel simply because it was easier to program a world without gravity, or weight, or any naturally occurring force at all.

"It all *looks* accurate at least," I admitted.

Dawn chuckled.

"What?" I said.

"It's just, you work on the show every day. Why waste your time . . . I mean. I'm sorry, that's not what I meant. It really looks great."

"It's fine. I get it." I strolled down one of the rock-strewn pathways wrapping the internalized world. Dawn followed me. "I started it before Mr. Helix named me chief director. I thought if I could recreate their world perfectly, I would know all the best angles."

"Why didn't you finish?"

"I got as far as you can see. Until the farms wrapped over my head and it seemed like I was really there, only I wasn't. It felt empty and static. So I tried programming inhabitants, but I couldn't get them right. They looked like inhabitants, I mean. But there was nothing *chance* about the way they moved. It all felt like cheating, scripting them where to go. Eventually, I got named Chief Director and gave up."

"So the show really is all unplanned?"

"That's the beauty of it. Here, I could pay as close attention to every detail as I wanted, add pseudo-gravity, every last grasshopper, but nothing could make this place equal to the real thing without the real inhabitants."

"Their lifestyle is remarka—"

She yelped before finishing and ran on ahead of me. I stopped when I realized where she was going. A projection of Mission stood atop her favorite rocky promontory, the one where she went after leaving her hole, where she'd met Jacen and so often sat beside him, looking out over her world.

Dawn circled her, marveling at every detail. She was barely able to contain her excitement. I'd almost forgotten the crowning achievement of Project-1GN15.77. The first inhabitant I'd tried to recreate. Mission was beginning to mature when I'd designed her, all knees but growing into her body. Just after the time she took her AE test. I'd spent so long perfecting the green of her eyes that VORA had to rouse me so I could get natural sleep before my volunteer shifts.

Now she was a young woman, not so much younger than me, really. And she was stunning. Residents could try as they wanted to replicate that appearance, but there was no developer on Earth talented enough to capture her essence.

"I remember when she was this small," Dawn said. "She's your favorite, too?"

"Directors aren't supposed to have favorites," I replied. I could almost hear Mr. Helix's own words coming out of my mouth from my early years.

Dawn shot me a knowing glare. "Then why has she almost always had a primary feed focused on her since she was about this age? How long did you say you've been the director in charge?"

"I . . ."

"Relax," she said. "I see how the message boards react to her. What else could you do? I can't remember another *Ignis* inhabitant getting so much attention. The girl from under the floor . . ." She grabbed a clump of Mission's strawberry-blonde hair. The real Mission would have slapped away someone handling her like that, but my creation stared blankly forward. A digital statue and nothing more.

"I think her hair color is a little off," Dawn said.

"It's not."

She ignored my comment. "Can you believe what's happening with her? I mean, I always knew she'd be named the next Block B Mother, but I don't know. I never thought I'd actually see it happen. I swear, I was literally posting about it before my VORA reminded me of our date."

That got my attention. "Did the scene feel right?" I questioned, clutching her arm as if she were in danger. Dawn wormed her way out of my grasp and continued studying Mission, clearly unsettled by my overzealousness.

"You tell me," she said starkly. "You directed it."

"I was off-shift and . . . well, I missed it." I regarded my recreation of Mission and hung my head. I'd been there live for every important moment in her life besides her birth. Her freedom and reacclimation. Her exams and placement. Everything. Until my nerves got the best of me.

"Wow," Dawn remarked. "So I saw something a director didn't?" The words came out playfully, but stung, nonetheless. Dawn, on the other hand, seemed to warm up again after my admission and closed the distance between us. "She's the youngest inhabitant to be named Mother, you know. What am I thinking? Of course you know that."

I answered with a nod. She was right. Mission was the youngest ever to be named a Birthmother after the Blackout forced the inhabitants to shift the age requirements, and was now likely to become the next Block B Mother. I was Mr. Helix's youngest Chief Director. We had that in common.

"Can I tell you a secret?" Dawn asked, seeming eager.

"Sure," I said.

"I've never told anyone this, but Mission is so incredible that sometimes I program my virtual presence to look like her. I wish I could all the time."

"So do I," I mumbled, unable to keep my thoughts to myself.

"What?"

"Nothing." I cleared my throat. VR or not, my head sank into my palm. I was exhausted, with good reason. Plus, all I kept picturing as we talked was poor Mission being prepped to meet with Paul, with nobody there who really knew her—who really cared—to watch over her.

"Would you mind if I unplugged?" I asked.

"I . . ." Dawn looked me over, incredulous. "I tell you a secret and you want to leave?"

"It's just been a long few days on the show," I said. "I can barely keep my eyes open."

Her gaze withered. "You can be honest, you know."

"I promise, I am. Maybe we can pick this up again soon? You can pick the next VR."

"This is what you do, isn't it? You tell women who you volunteer for and show them your little *Ignis* museum, and if they don't throw themselves at you, you move on."

"That's not—"

"This is why the sims are better than the real thing." She kicked a loose rock at me. "I knew something was off when I noticed your profile flagged with health concerns earlier. I thought maybe it just meant you were interesting."

"That was nothing, I swear. Just an accident because I'm

pushing myself too hard. It's just like I said." I reached out for her hand, but she pulled away.

"No, this here—us—is the mistake. Don't bother messaging again. Maybe you could have an infuser teach you how to look someone in the eyes when you talk to them. And just so you know, I would have screwed you anyway. Enjoy your empty rock."

She vanished into thin air before I could swallow the lump in my throat and respond. Not that I had much to say. I'd been getting used to dates ending like this ever since I started going on them. Not every resident who logged out on me was so forward, but most eventually did. And Dawn was right. Nearly every date ended up with me taking them to my unfinished *Ignis* recreation, like it was anything to be proud of.

I regarded the stagnant world. The crops didn't even move from the hydrofarmers moving through them. The clicks and hums of water pipes and air recyclers were absent. And even though this Mission looked exactly like her slightly younger counterpart, there was something missing. All it took was the quickest glimpse to know it wasn't the real thing.

I was no Craig Helix or Joanna Porvette. I was no developer. Just the help.

I sighed and signaled VORA to end the program. My VR chamber's neural transmitters returned my consciousness to my physical body. The walls of the *Ignis* vacillated and flickered. A sense of vertigo stole over me, then blackness. In mere seconds, I stared at the blank white ceiling of my empty domicile.

"Welcome back, Asher," VORA announced. "Your date ended earlier than scheduled."

The re-assembler tube slid painlessly out of my throat, and the bands wrapping my arms, legs and torso loosened before falling away. They exercised my muscles while my mind was

absent. Then the glowing blue nodes of my chair's neural transmitter band lifted from my temples, allowing my physical body
to feel again.

"As usual." I stood and rubbed my head. A minor headache always followed too long a time spent in VRs. No wonder
there were stories about delisted people in the Outskirts melting their brains by abusing the outdated and dangerous tech
they had out there.

"Was Dawn not to your satisfaction?" VORA asked.

"No, she was perfect," I said. "They're all perfect."

"I do not understand the issue."

"Forget it. Can you please prepare my sleep-pod? I'd like
our programmed scent of *Ignis*'s main chamber again."

"Of course, Asher. By the way, while uploaded you reached
your daily advised activity quota to maintain a healthy lifestyle."

"Great."

"You did, however, not finish dinner in the simulation. Shall
I have the re-assembler make you anything?"

My gaze followed the path of the tube curling away from
my chair into my kitchen. It was small, but it had everything I
needed. A sink to maintain cleanliness, a fresh waterspout, and,
of course, my re-assembler. Every resident received one. The shiny
device could create nutrient bars or soups by reassembling the
molecules in waste and other inexhaustible products it received
through its connections in the wall. Reclaimers throughout High
Earth sucked any other elements it required from the air and the
oceans. Taste was applied later. Anything one could think of.

"I'm not hungry," I said.

"I advise that you try to eat something before sleeping."

"VORA."

"Like interaction, sustenance can help alleviate the stress
you have experienced today."

I sighed. She wasn't going to back down. "Fine. A small bar will work."

"Any flavor you would prefer?"

"Surprise me."

A low whistling filled the room, like too much air being forced through a narrow vent. My re-assembler shuddered, only marginally, then in less than a minute chimed. The ovular glass port in its center fell open, and inside sat a bar no longer than my index finger. It looked like a thousand colorless pebbles smashed into each other and ground into the shape of a perfect rectangle.

I removed it and took a small bite because my stomach still felt a bit unsettled. "Is that?"

"Teriyaki chicken," VORA answered. "One of your favorites. And do not forget your fluids."

A spout beside the sink filled a plastic cup that rose from the counter.

"Thank you," I said. I snatched it and took a step toward my bedroom. "You can hibernate now. I need some sleep."

"As you wish."

The door of my bedroom rose into the ceiling. My sleep-pod was arranged in the center of the smaller white room. A silvery chamber with its rounded lid peeled opened. I finished as much of my dinner as I could. Then my teeth were brushed and whitened by robotic arms while I used the toilet. Finally, my laser-detox shower cleaned me off.

I entered my sleep-pod, clean and ready for much-needed rest. Cushions inside molded to my form. My weary muscles had never been so relieved to lie down. A glowing band lowered over my head that would help me quickly fall into REM sleep. I'd need it with how the day's events had my mind churning.

The lid closed me in, nice and safe. The subtle scents of the

Ignis surrounded me, farms and recycled air. A holoscreen projected across the lid. Windows featuring all my favorited shows popped up in beautiful color and motion, along with their related discussion boards. Everybody in High Earth still chatted about Mission, like her needing to reproduce was some great surprise. She, herself, was asleep.

In honor of the upcoming fiftieth anniversary, an early interview with Craig Helix by a woman who was a top program reviewer at the time played on one feed of *Ignis: Live*. I'd seen it hundreds of times before, but I dragged it to the central screen. Helix hadn't visibly aged a day since. The interview had taken place at the start of it all.

Fifty years ago, the show was no more than him alone in his smart-dwelling, with a basic data contract like any resident was provided post-animation. He came up with the idea to use the *Ignis,* an old ark-ship collecting dust on the moon after the techno-revolution and the formation of High Earth, for a show. He developed a concept package, then earned enough data pledges from potential viewers until the High Earth Network approved spacefaring vessels for establishing the set, and brain infusers to prepare the delisted volunteers who'd serve as the original cast. The rest was history.

People tuned in by the millions on day one of *Ignis: Live*. More viewers and ratings meant more tech provided by the Network's automated systems, so that he could add more cameras and volunteer operators, update systems. Everything I now took for granted. An undertaking so vast, anything but top ratings would lead it to fade away with so many other failed programs.

"What do you say to the people who claim that the *Ignis* merely maintains an illusion of reality?" the reviewer controlling the recording drone asked through the machine. "That by programming the information stored in their core, you've placed your stamp on the inhabitants' lives."

Helix rubbed his chin, taking a long moment to think before staring directly into the camera, eyes dark as coal. "I say they're wrong," he replied calmly. "Do you have control over what happens around you? We gave them background, but beyond that, our interference is negligible. We gave them history and data in the Core, and they extrapolated a lifestyle. Since the minds of the first delisted volunteers were molded to fit the reality created for them, they've gone about living in their own fascinating ways. Their very culture has manifested all on its own.

"What *Ignis: Live* provides is unscripted human drama. These aren't computer-generated performers or even resident actors. Their reactions are genuine. Every loss is felt. By me. By my crew. By all of you. And most of all, by them. There was a time when the life of a human being was little more than a game of survival. When all of this wasn't around to keep us safe."

My heart grew heavy as I watched. Negligible. Genuine. I'd put all of that at risk by interfering beyond proper boundaries. By allowing my lack of focus to put a fixer in a position like I had. I'd failed the man who gave me everything.

Never again.

Helix gestured to his smart-dwelling filled with holoscreens and countless trinkets and treasures harvested from traders in the Outskirts, which he'd always enjoyed putting on display. He then tapped on his lifeband and said, "What people want to see, more than anything, is something truly, sincerely real . . ."

CHAPTER 6

Mission lay on her back in the Block B med-bay, legs raised, and tunic rolled up around her waist. Children ran amok in the adjacent room, the din of their games drowned out by the cries of the youngest infant in the nursery cribs. It was Samson, the biological child of the parents who'd been spaced the day before.

Alora sat on a stool in front of Mission, using a thin pair of forceps. When a Birthmother reached the age for prime reproduction, it was the job of the block's acting Mother to perform the procedure to locate and remove her contraceptive implant. Mission squirmed slightly and squeezed her eyes, struggling to focus on anything else.

"There we are," Alora announced. She stood, the tool in her hand clamped around the edge of a small semi-translucent ring. She carefully placed it on a tray to be stored in freezing units until either Mission or a new inhabitant needed it again. Medical resources were finite on the *Ignis*, with only what had been loaded onto it when it had departed Earth.

"Remember," Alora said. "If you start feeling ill, or anything at all—"

"Come see you immediately," Mission finished for her. "I know."

She sat up. It felt strange now. Like a fullness she'd never before been aware of was suddenly absent. She fidgeted and pulled her tunic down over her thighs. Now she understood the numbness all those who'd illegally removed their implant in the name of affection were talking about. She felt . . . cold.

"The effects should wear off shortly, and you'll be fertile enough to engage in a first attempt with Paul-10183 before the fiftieth Launch Day celebrations tomorrow," Alora said.

Mission's eyelids went wide. "That soon?"

"Our ancestors back on Earth left us with the best technology they had. There isn't time to waste, Mission. You know that."

"I know . . . Just . . ." She swallowed hard. "Is he . . . nice? Kind? I've never really known anyone who lives up in the core."

"Is that really what you're worried about?"

Mission didn't say a word, but her cheeks went pink and her gaze turned to the floor.

"We all grow up eventually, my dear," Alora said. "Wouldn't you rather your first be meaningful?"

"I guess."

"Our species. They rely on what we Birthmothers do more than anything. We have to take every precaution we can to preserve our future upon arrival at our new home."

"I understand. Earth has fallen." Mission raised her fist overdramatically. "We remain."

Alora rolled her eyes. Just then, Samson released a screech louder than all the ones that preceded it. It made Mission wince, reminding her of how it had often sounded when she lived beneath that very floor.

"Let me show you something." Alora took Mission's arm and led her to the nursery. Mission stared at the sealed floor panel. At her former home.

Alora asked the Birthmother holding Samson to hand him over, then hummed to him as she cradled him in her arms. Drool dribbled down his chubby face, but she kissed him on the forehead anyway, with the tenderness of a devoted parent. The crying stopped and his big bulging eyes locked onto Mission.

"Thank you," Mission groaned, finally tearing her gaze away from the panel. "I thought my head was going to explode."

Alora ignored her comment and tickled the baby's nose. "Come." She walked out of the nursery and across the Block B med-bay. It was nothing like the rest of the rocky living block. Burnished metal was everywhere, with shiny white walls and inset lighting. It was a medical facility first and foremost, featuring beds for healing and sanitary operation areas curtained off from the nursery and children still in need of constant surveillance. *Ignis*'s spin didn't exert quite the g-forces of Earth, so careful attention had to be paid to the muscle development and bone density of children.

Alora led Mission past all of it. They reached the locked doors of Alora's personal quarters, where she shooed away some of the younger children trailing behind them alongside other Birthmothers. Nixu and Evelyn glared enviously at Mission, muttering as they steered the children away.

"What are you showing me in there this time?" Mission asked.

Alora didn't respond. Her handprint opened the door, and they entered. Very few inhabitants were privy to what lay beyond. It wasn't Mission's first time, but she could probably count on one hand how many times Alora had invited her inside. A bed rested at one end, not a nook carved into the wall, but a real mattress with clean, woven sheets. A vast screen array was sunken into the walls on the other, with a bulky computer terminal wrapping the space below. It was packed with rows of data. Alora stopped in front of it, painted green by the screens' glow.

"Your terminal?" Mission asked. Each of the six block Mothers got one, making them vital members of the Collective's decision-making. It was the only way to access the core's medical records from anywhere but within the core itself.

"No," Alora stated. "Yours."

"What?"

"No need to drag this out. I'm forty. I can't carry any longer, and you've already been named my successor."

"But I hardly know how to use any of this!"

"You'll be fine. It takes a younger mind than mine to keep track of everything."

"I can't . . . I can't make a child stop crying, let alone lug one along inside me. And manage all this? Alora, please, I still need your guidance. I need . . ." She gasped for air, not having taken a breath since she started speaking.

Alora pulled Mission's head to her bosom, cradling Samson in the other arm. "You're ready, child. More ready than I was at your age. You've always been incredible at adapting to the impossible. I'll still be around to offer guidance for as long as you need, and the other Birthmothers will be here to support you."

"They won't even look at me."

"They'll come around. They won't have a choice." She released Mission and ran her fingers across the keys of the console, all while bouncing Samson. She began typing, and a list comprised of hundreds of names and numerical designations popped up. Selecting any one brought up a full-body scan surrounded by notes.

They were the detailed medical logs of everyone under the Block B Mother's care. Everything from their blood type, to their aptitude exam results, to a DNA analysis revealing who was susceptible to what or related to whom and how closely. The processors in the core's database sorted all that information and used it to select safe genetic matches, like Mission and Paul, for reproduction.

"There's so much," Mission mouthed. She had to step back to take in the breadth of the screens. She knew what being a mother entailed, but only they were privy to seeing them. Her sense of dread deepened like the gaping chasm within which the core sat.

"Only what is necessary, my dear." She took Mission's hand and pulled her toward the terminal. She placed it flat against a reader beside the keyboard, then typed in a command. A copy of Mission's hand appeared on the screen above, outlining her prints in red. The words EXECUTE COMMAND – MISSION-14130 blinked above it. Alora reached out to accept, but her finger hesitated above the key.

In that moment, Mission realized that this transition wasn't only daunting for her. She might have been gaining responsibility over people's lives, but at the same time, Alora was losing it. Her mother had to let go of everything she'd been for two decades. That was why she couldn't bear to wait any longer. She had to rip off the bandage before it stuck.

Mission put on a strong face and wrapped her free hand around Alora's arm. "You can take your time if you want," she whispered. "Trust me, there's no rush."

Alora gazed down at her protégée and daughter, tears welling in the corners of her eyes. The edges of her lips curled into a frail smile. "We all have to grow up. My time has come." Then she pressed the key, enabling access to the room and console to be transferred from Alora-12987 to the new Block B Mother—Mission-14130.

"Now . . ." Alora choked back tears. "Now all of this is in your capable hands, Mission. From the girl I raised beneath the floor, to the woman standing before me."

"But what about you?" Mission said.

"Don't worry about me."

"Are you eligible for the Collective? What will you do?"

"Relax, hopefully, for the first time since you were born." She smirked. "I suggest you take today to try to do the same. You were born for this, Mission. I've known it since the day I held you in my arms like I'm now holding Samson."

"Then why do I feel like I don't belong?"

Alora's free hand shot out and clutched Mission's arm. "Never say that. You're as much of an inhabitant as any. The core shows that now, because it's true."

"But I'm not."

"You are. None of what happened is your fault. It's nothing like what those two were spaced for yesterday."

Mission backed away and stared down at the floor. "I'm scared, Mom."

"You're human. It's okay. Don't think for a second I'm not terrified of what comes next, too."

Mission let a nervous titter slip through her lips. "I didn't know you could *feel* anything."

"Watch it, Mission. I may not be Mother anymore, but I still raised you."

They laughed until they were interrupted by Samson starting to cry again. Alora rocked him back and forth, hushing him and brushing his smooth head. Mission watched carefully, then extended her arms. She'd always preferred to treat wounds and perform checkups, to leave the infant nursing to the other Birthmothers. It brought out too many painful memories.

But now she was Block Mother. That would no longer be possible.

"May I?" she asked.

"Always."

* * *

"Asher Reinhart, Mr. Helix is requesting your presence for the conference about the fiftieth anniversary," my AI assistant said, uploaded out of storage to replace Vivienne. A shade of a human comprised of blue lines had appeared beside me.

I stopped giving orders to the crew about how to capture the crucial moments going on throughout the *Ignis*, with a special emphasis on Mission and Alora. My health status hadn't been updated yet. I had to argue with VORA over working my usual shift on the show. It was too crucial a time to miss anything. In the end, she couldn't stop me unless my or another's life was in danger, and my status wasn't that severe.

"Asher Reinhart, did you hear my words?" the AI said.

"Yes, yes," I groaned. A full night's sleep and, somehow, I was still groggy. "Right now?"

"Immediately."

At least he wasn't Vivienne. No mincing words, no questions. Straight to the point. I was glad to have a program back for my aide.

"Laura," I said into my virtual comm-link, "Mr. Helix called a meeting. You're in charge again. Let me know if anything out of the ordinary happens." She affirmed with a single word. I could tell when I saw her that morning that she was still embarrassed over losing track of Mission.

I stood and moved into the greater VR studio as my AI assistant blinked away. The crew was hard at work at their stations. Hundreds of holoscreens throughout the room blinked with motion. The chatter of conversations about which feed to switch to or who to focus on blended into white noise.

There was no other production studio in High Earth quite like this one. No live-action undertaking as ambitious as Mr. Helix's show. It was hard enough to get residents to contribute data to certain programs, let alone inspire them to collaborate with others on content they didn't create, when consuming content was so easy and relaxing. In my mind, that was one of *Ignis: Live*'s greatest accomplishments. I never tired of hearing the hubbub of production.

Rounding a corner toward the central conference room, I crossed a floating bridge made of solid light pixels, surrounded by a simulation of space. Vivienne stood outside the doors, chatting with Night Director Frederick. His avatar's one distinguishing feature was a tiny birthmark on his left cheek, which, for whatever reason, he hadn't removed.

I offered Vivienne a nod of acknowledgment, but she was either too busy jotting down notes on her holopad or chose not to respond. Frederick entered the conference room, and Vivienne hurried by me back toward the studio without even a passing glance.

I drew a deep breath outside the doors. It was a big day coming. Fifty years tomorrow. I felt like I should've been more nervous, but for this I didn't need any pharma to keep me level. Nothing. I was becoming an anxiety professional.

"There he is!" Mr. Helix exclaimed as I entered.

Mr. Helix sat at the far end of a long glass table, digital OptiVisor covering his eyes in program windows. The air smelled of an ocean breeze, his favorite scent. Behind him was an impossible view over a replica of High Earth's skyline. All the spires gleamed in a perfectly uniform grid, like rows of glass books neatly tucked into a bookcase. The ocean raged beyond walls tall enough to obscure the Outskirts, if Mr. Helix even bothered having them rendered.

Around the table sat three other residents. There was Night Director Frederick, glaring at me enviously like always. The two additional people present were acquaintances of Mr. Helix whose opinions he respected. I recognized them by face only as top-notch developers producing in noncompeting genres.

I took my position directly to the right of Mr. Helix. A wave of guilt overwhelmed me, but I composed myself. He leaned over and whispered, "I saw reports about unhealthy behavior yesterday. And your health status. What happened?"

I had a feeling he'd find out about my little mishap, so I had an answer ready. Not much escaped Craig Helix.

"It's nothing," I said. "Just some over-exhaustion."

"Asher, I requested the footage, and as a resident with daily interaction with you, and for health reasons, I was permitted access. One moment you're standing, the next you're on the floor. That plus elevated stress readings throughout the day . . . if I'm working you too hard, you have to tell me. A close fix and a spacing all in one day. I know it's hard . . . trying not to grow attached to inhabitants, and then watching them die . . ."

"Some people can't handle anything," Frederick remarked to the resident beside him.

I stared down at the table, the glass reflecting the eyes of my avatar which failed to resemble how they stung with exhaustion outside the VR. With such a big day coming up, Mr. Helix was bound to be even more observant than usual. And with his status in the Network and resoundingly positive ratings, his requests for information were rarely denied.

"I'll be okay, sir. I promise," I said. "It was only an accident. My VORA has scheduled a checkup for me after the anniversary. We'll sort it out."

He laid a hand upon my shoulder. "Asher, I've known you for nearly your entire woken life. I know when you're withholding."

"Can we just focus on the anniversary?"

"You are my eyes and ears on *Ignis*. I need to know you're fine."

"I am."

"First you dismiss Vivienne for no clear reason. Now this," Frederick added.

"I said I'm fine," I said, my teeth slightly grinding.

"Asher, you know I'm here for any resident who helps make this show possible. None help more than you, both in time and data contribution."

"I dreamed I was attacked by a delisted man, okay?" I said. I couldn't tell him about what went on with Mission, so that was the next best option. "A nightmare really. It was an Unplugged."

The air seemed to be sucked from the room. Everybody silenced. Mr. Helix deactivated the screens of his visor. "An Unplugged from the Outskirts?"

"Yes. He was as close to me as we are now," I said. "He pushed me off my balcony and I nearly died, like those inhabitants through the airlock. It felt . . . It felt so real."

Mr. Helix shook his head. "This is why it is dangerous to fall asleep beyond the safety of our sleep-pods. They help with the REM sleep that alleviates stress and all the negative side effects associated with it."

"I know." I sighed. I hated disappointing him, and I'd reached the extent of truth I could share without sacrificing my position. In Frederick's hands, the anniversary footage would be a mess. The others in the room seemed to pity me over my nightmare, but he leaned forward like vulture.

"You see?" Mr. Helix addressed the room. "Those radical delisted animals that damn show *Outskirts Today* celebrates put all of our minds in danger. Our subconscious shouldn't be filled with fears when we're so safe here." He took my hand. "Promise me you're all right?"

"I'm . . . Yeah. I am," I said. "Like I said, I've been working too hard lately, and the stress got away from me. But I need to stay focused for the anniversary tomorrow. I'll rest after."

Nobody made a sound. Then Mr. Helix started to clap, until everyone around the room joined in. "Now *that* is dedication to the greatest show in High Earth," he said, voice overflowing with pride. "You can all learn something from him."

"Thank you for understanding, sir," I said. I breathed a sigh of relief.

"Of course. I'll still want to see the results of that evaluation. For my sake."

"I understand, sir. I could use it, too."

"And a week off."

"Sir—"

"That's nonnegotiable, Asher. All these years, I can't recall you ever spending a day to yourself."

My chin hit my chest. "If you think it's for the best."

"You should wipe that nightmare from your memory entirely. Nobody needs fears like that."

"Maybe," I said.

"Well, nobody can force you. I'm just glad you didn't hit your head collapsing like that. I can't lose you at a time like this."

"Yes, whatever would we do?" Frederick muttered.

"That's right," Mr. Helix said as if he didn't catch the sarcasm. Then he clapped his hands one last time and stood before

I could say anything. The lighting effects in the room dimmed, and a screen bloomed to life at his back. "Let's begin. I know I've been keeping everyone in the dark about what the plans are for this year's anniversary. I apologize."

"Afraid we'd leak it, were you?" Frederick joked.

Mr. Helix ignored him. "I've been going back and forth on it myself until this morning." He turned and manipulated the screen with his hands. A series of numbers and charts scrolled across. "As of last night, we've fallen to fourth."

He meant we were number four on the daily-registered enjoyment ratings.

"And third in data contribution," he continued. "Our lowest ratings in fifty years."

Everyone in the room seemed shocked by the data, but I constantly refreshed our ratings while I was working to stay up to date. *Ignis: Live* had fallen below *Molecular Nation*, Cygnus's bot fighting league, and that very same survival-on-Mars program recommended to me in the elevator. *Outskirts Today* was even hot on our tail.

"None of them can ever touch you in viewer hours logged on a visual program," one of Mr. Helix's acquaintances remarked, then chuckled. "Trust me, I've been jealous a long time."

"Of course they can't," Mr. Helix said. "But there are roughly half a billion people in High Earth, and more of them tune in every week for the latest installment of that ridiculous molecular re-assembler period drama. Don't you see that as a concern?"

"Yes . . . My apologies, Craig."

"Are people getting tired of the *Ignis*?" Mr. Helix asked.

"I don't think so," I said.

"No? Then do you have any explanation for this drop?"

"You can see right there, sir. Overall rating quality hasn't fallen at all this year. The other shows have simply gained larger followings. Our core audience has mostly maintained interest since the *Ignis*'s launch numbers stabilized. The recent ratings spike for the others will fade. It always does with newer shows."

"Not our show. Not ever," Mr. Helix declared. "We give the people something real. *Molecular Nation* . . . it's pure invention! They've strayed so far from Gloria Fors's recorded history I'd sooner consider it fantasy. And don't get me started on *Outskirts Today*. They're fearmongers! So why are people tuning in?" Frederick opened his mouth to answer but was immediately cut off by Mr. Helix. "Tragedy," he said, answering his own question.

"Tragedy?" I asked.

"Yes." He gestured to the numbers. "A week ago, Gloria Fors's love interest was murdered. The boards and viewers went crazy. Fifteen percent of them required pharma to slow their heart rates. It was a boost like we haven't seen since the Great Blackout!"

I remembered that period well, when the core malfunctioned and the *Ignis* lost all power for a few days. It was my first experience with the show, a horrible yet fascinating time, when the people of the *Ignis* had to abandon their most fundamental laws in order to maintain their world, which of course led to exceptionally dramatic content. The first scene I'd ever recorded on camera after volunteering was a starving man trying to murder a woman over food.

"Their show is scripted," Frederick said. "We can't wait for something like that to happen again."

"That's true," Mr. Helix replied. "We can't *wait* for anything."

"So what are you suggesting?" I asked.

"Fifty years. We won't celebrate that by mimicking what has already come to pass. Look." He rotated the display into a three-dimensional map of the *Ignis*, with all the layers of its systems mapped out in varying colors. He pointed to the locations of each of the six living blocks dispersed throughout the outer surface.

"The core powers the air recyclers in each block individually." Mr. Helix had the display highlight power lines and traced them. "This way, a hiccup in one doesn't hamper the entire system. For the fiftieth anniversary, *Ignis* will experience a tragedy unlike any they've ever seen. Something that will put the dangers of living in space on full display!"

"What is it?" Frederick asked, leaning forward on his elbows in excitement.

Mr. Helix cleared his throat. "The core will malfunction and overload conduits in a single block, signaling fire suppression to reverse the air recyclers to vacate oxygen and conserve water. The doors should remain open for egress throughout; however, an error will keep them closed." He threw his arms wide and smiled even wider. Everyone in the room applauded except me.

"Mr. Helix." I cleared my throat. "I don't mean to be contrary, but at any given time there could be hundreds of people in a block. Wouldn't they all suffocate?"

"It will be left to their ingenuity to override the error in time. But yes, it's conceivable that many inhabitants may be lost. Possibly more than during the Great Blackout even."

"But they would die, partially, because of us." For whatever reason, both my conversation with Dawn and Craig's interview about the show jumped into my thoughts. "Wouldn't interference at that scale undermine the authenticity of their natural lives, sir? It's unprecedented."

Mr. Helix calmly gesticulated to emphasize his point. He could be quite theatrical at times. "Could our ancestors stop the rising of the oceans? Could they turn back storms? The *Ignis* is their natural environment, and unprovoked acts of nature are as much a part of human history as war, aren't they? After I program the error, they will have the opportunity to correct it, and all that will remain are their reactions. And what, my friend, is more authentic than facing adversity?"

"Absolutely brilliant, sir!" Frederick exclaimed, sneering in my direction. He rarely had an opinion of his own to throw in, and while he figured that would get him my job one day, I knew Mr. Helix valued *actual* input.

"Asher, you still look hesitant," Mr. Helix remarked, without bothering to offer Frederick even a glimpse of gratitude.

"The public response would be astronomical," I admitted. "There's no question. After that boost, however, I worry people might begin to suspect our meddling and that it might compromise what this show stands for."

"Says the man scared of monsters in his dreams," Frederick whispered to the resident beside him, earning a snicker.

Mr. Helix strolled around the table, quieting him quickly. When he reached me, he wrapped both hands around my shoulders.

"As always, your concerns are noted, but I think you overestimate their perception," he said. "All shows evolve with the times; otherwise they fail. The viewers . . . They only seek for their minds to be taken on a journey. They want drama. Emotion. Tomorrow we're going to give it to them in a way they've never experienced! It will be so intense, there won't be a viewer in High Earth who doesn't need pharma to handle it." He sucked in a breath. "Do you trust me?"

I regarded the warm, inviting smile of my one and only mentor. There was no denying his plan would put the show's ratings back through the roof. Popular in ways it had only been when the *Ignis* had first launched, long before I was born. The inhabitants would recover from the losses. They were resilient. I'd seen more die than I cared to count.

And before they had their memories reprogrammed, the original inhabitants knew the dangers of volunteering. They were delisted men and women who wanted to be stars seen across High Earth. A chance to be a part of the world they'd been exiled from. And they'd accomplished that, alive or dead.

"Of course I do, sir," I agreed. Who was I to cheat the inhabitants of their potential glory, or question Mr. Helix's brilliance? I couldn't even develop a working digital replica of his show's set, let alone understand the full depth of his vision. If he was this passionate about an idea, it meant it was a good one.

"I apologize for seeming unenthused," I said. "I never meant to imply that the event wouldn't generate results."

"Good. I've already completed the programming, so there's no turning back now. And, Asher."

"Yes?"

"Never apologize. As proven yesterday, your concerns are for the sake of the show, and that is why you are here."

Mr. Helix turned and I shot a smirk back at Frederick.

Maybe Mr. Helix was right. I owed a ton to Mission's soaring popularity, but from the first moment I saw her, I knew she needed to be the program's focus. The show, the fiftieth anniversary, everything—it would be better for having a healthy Mission involved, not one recovering from having her memory wiped away. The pangs of guilt over what I'd done faded, and I felt sure I'd done the right thing.

"Nobody will see it coming, sir," Frederick scrambled to say in response to my look.

"That's exactly the point," Mr. Helix replied. "Now, each of your communications will be monitored until after the event. Not that I don't trust all of you, but for obvious reasons what has been discussed must stay in this room. Not even the crew can know, as their reactions will be equally crucial in capturing the moment under Asher's supervision. As Asher said, we must maintain our perception." Mr. Helix closed his hand and deactivated the screen behind him, again revealing the glittering virtual skyline of High Earth. The sun hovered high in the cloudless blue sky.

"So, when will this be happening?" one of Mr. Helix's associates asked.

"9:00 a.m. tomorrow morning. Half a day before the start of their own planned fiftieth anniversary celebration so that viewers are caught off guard. I want all of High Earth to wake up and be a part of this. Our ratings will never drop again."

"Which block are you targeting?" I asked.

"Oh, Asher, do you really want to ruin the entire surprise?"

"If this is the direction we're taking, I'd like to know ahead of time so that I can plan the shoot and be prepared for all possibilities."

"Always looking for the best angle, Reinhart!" Mr. Helix laughed. "Pay attention to his work, Frederick. Even off his game, you can learn a lot." He turned back to me. "I've programmed the error to occur in Block B."

Usually I would love to hear Mr. Helix set me as an example for Frederick, but my stomach suddenly dropped. I felt cold all over.

"Block B?" Frederick said. "Mission is our biggest draw right now. Are you sure that's a smart risk?" He fumbled through the words, clearly unaccustomed to voicing his opinion.

"It was a difficult decision," Mr. Helix replied, "but I went through all of our records. Whenever a star inhabitant faces death, viewership rises. Just like with Gloria Fors's boyfriend. People are always searching for the next Miss—"

My chair slid out from under me and I toppled over onto the floor. I hunched over on my knees, gasping for air. The room started to spin and close in around me. I couldn't hear any voices, only the insistent chirping of my lifeband upon reaching the point where it would apply pharma automatically to my real body.

This time, however, the drugs didn't help at all.

CHAPTER 7

When the virtual room finally stopped spinning, I found a med-bot hovering over me. Teardrop-shaped chassis, multiple appendages, a tiny head with a single central eye-lens—it barely resembled a human, but carried all the medicine and tools it might need to provide a resident with treatment. The thing was comprised entirely of light, meaning it was being projected.

My mind was still in the VR.

Its scanners passed over me while one of its arms poked a needle into the side of my neck. That felt real, for sure. Whatever it pumped into my veins was far more potent than what was in my lifeband. For a moment, I felt like I was floating, and then I couldn't suppress a smile. I thought I even giggled.

"Asher!" Mr. Helix shouted, shaking my shoulders. His concern-stricken face appeared through the projection of the med-bot. "There we go. You're all right. It couldn't risk unloading your mind yet. Just breathe, my friend."

He glowered at the med-bot. "What the hell is wrong with him?"

"Mr. Reinhart has experienced a sudden onset of acute and disabling anxiety," it replied flatly, voice echoing all around, almost ethereal. Real-world tech wasn't meant to interfere during a VR upload outside of emergencies. "A severe panic attack."

"Check again, that can't be all. His heart. Check his heart. I've heard about these types of attacks in the Outskirts."

The tingle of more scanner fields penetrated me, through the layers of my separated mind and body. I suddenly felt like I was floating above myself.

"I'm fine," I groaned.

"You're not fine," Mr. Helix said. "I've never seen anything like that before."

"Scans are consistent," the med-bot said. "Mr. Reinhart is in optimal physiological health. However, recent reports place his psychological health in question. After analysis, it can be confirmed that this episode was, indeed, a panic attack."

"Panic . . . My word, Asher, you must really be shaken up from that nightmare."

"It was only a bad dream," I said.

"Clearly not."

I slid backward and propped myself up against the wall. The others stood behind Mr. Helix, gawking at me like I was some sort of science project. Vivienne had entered now, as well, finally acknowledging my existence. I opened my mouth to respond, but an irrepressible chuckle snuck out.

"Relax," Mr. Helix hushed. "No resident should have to suffer fear. Clearly, I was wrong to think it resolved. Bot, what does he need?"

"He has experienced a traumatic event of unclear origin," the med-bot stated. "Proper rest, pharma, and plenty of fluids should expedite his natural recovery. A full psychological evaluation is scheduled for Wednesday at 8:00 p.m., where we will determine if a targeted memory wipe could also prove beneficial."

"That all sounds for the best," Mr. Helix said. "No more pushing."

"No," I groaned, the world snapping back into focus. I still felt loopy, but the memory of what had triggered the panic attack came rushing back and spurred me onward.

A tragedy in Block B meant Mission . . . I wanted to scream even though I couldn't manage to express that in my drugged state. All I knew for sure in that moment was that I had to get out of that room. I had to get away from people. To be alone.

"Asher, what are you doing?" Mr. Helix asked. "There will be other anniversaries. I'd rather have you healthy."

"No. Sleep. I just need sleep." I pulled myself up the wall and staggered. Vivienne failed to get out of my way in time, allowing Mr. Helix to get in front of me.

"Asher, you're not thinking clearly," he said, stern.

"Don't worry about me, sir."

He took me by my shoulders and whispered, "Asher, I am worried. Nightmares, panic attacks. This isn't like you."

"Rest, sir. That's all I need. Then I'll get my head checked out."

He finally sidestepped out of the way, and I sidled along the wall a little farther. By the time I reached the door, I was worn out and ready to tip over.

"Help him!" Mr. Helix ordered. The med-bot took my arm and kept me from falling. "Make sure to keep an eye on him. I need him healthy." He groaned. "Why do I rely on humans? Frederick! You're in charge for the day and night today. Consult with Senior Camera Laura immediately, and I'll need you on call tomorrow in case Asher is unable to perform."

"That's fine, Mr. Helix," Frederick replied, sneering. "I never need any rest."

Mr. Helix's footsteps clacked behind me. "Asher, get your mind right. We need you here!"

I stopped outside the conference room. The human members of the crew had stopped working and were ogling me through their floating control screens. I glanced back over my shoulder at Mr. Helix. His wrist flashed red from his own real-life life-band blinking.

Frederick was behind him, grinning as he quietly yammered orders in Vivienne's ear. The opportunity to prove himself was at hand.

"I'll be here tomorrow, sir," I said. "Everyone, back to work."

As I spoke and struggled for air, I found myself watching the *Ignis* feed over Laura's workstation.

"Are you all right, Asher?" she asked. Small talk wasn't part of our relationship. I ignored her and stared . . .

[Ignis Feed Location]
Block B Med-Bay Nursery
<Camera 6>

Mission leaned against Samson's crib. She held him, extending him out as far from her chest as she could without risking dropping him. She didn't hum or sing, and he didn't cry. Instead, she gawked down at him and he back at her.

"You aren't too bad, are you?" she whispered.

He cooed, as if responding, and Mission reached out timidly to run a single finger over his forehead. He grasped at it with his tiny hands. As he giggled, a line of spittle ran down his chin and onto her arm. She winced at first and then giggled herself.

"You see, dear, you're a natural," Alora said. She stood on the opposite side of the nursery, pretending not to have been paying attention.

"He has Jacen's eyes," Mission said.

Alora craned her neck to look over her shoulder. "By the core, you're right. I hadn't noticed. They may share ancestry. You can check in your terminal if you'd like."

"That's okay. I prefer the mystery."

"You always have." Alora chuckled and strolled away.

Mission played with the baby to get him to laugh again. As she did, she caught Nixu and Evelyn grimacing at her from the adjacent room, but Mission didn't pay them any attention. She just smiled and finally willed herself to cradle the baby closer.

* * *

I purposefully turned away from her feed for the first time in years. Maybe ever. I couldn't bear to watch anymore. Mission was already settling into her new role, as I knew she would, but the fiftieth anniversary event would place that in jeopardy—everything she'd worked so hard for, even when she acted like she didn't want it.

My gaze roamed around the busy studio, at all the volunteers working to make this vision a possibility. Mission's face was hidden everywhere amongst their workstations. Her messy, amber-colored hair and dazzling green eyes nearly always featured on a primary live feed.

"Asher, can you hear me?" Laura asked. She was at my side now, abandoning her station to help keep me upright.

I couldn't feel her touch.

My stomach churned.

I requested my VORA log me out, and Laura, Helix, and the rest of the studio promptly flaked away to pixels. Blackness overtook me; then my eyes reopened within my VR chamber. All the gadgets that kept me uploaded receded, and I leaned against one curved, glassy wall of the chamber and vomited.

Only then did I finally feel like I could breathe, one deep inhale after another, sucking down air like I was fighting to live. I'd never been so grateful for oxygen. I wished I had two mouths.

"What is wrong with me?" I whispered to myself.

"You experienced a panic attack," VORA replied. "You have been advised by the emergency med-bot to rest and drink plenty of fluids in preparation for your scheduled full psychological evaluation."

"Panic," I snorted.

I took a few wobbly steps across my living space, activated the holoscreen in my table, then swiped through all my preferred comment boards and programs. Mission's face was everywhere. Over and over. Her name, a topic in thousands of discussions. Other inhabitants were sprinkled in here and there, but nothing like her. Even while she did something as banal as eating lunch.

High Earth's collective eye was upon her.

"Did I do this?" I asked.

"To what are you referring?" VORA answered.

"Mission."

"To what mission are you referring, Mr. Reinhart?"

I didn't answer. All I could think about was if I was the only reason she'd become such a massive star. If I'd been focused on her to the detriment of the rest of the show, just like how I'd risked my own position, health, and sanity for her.

I was the Chief Director of Content for *Ignis: Live*. My job was to execute Craig Helix's vision and provide the residents of High Earth with visual access to an emotional journey unlike any other. To document the lives of *every* inhabitant on the *Ignis*, not fixate on the first I ever saw. Yet the very thought of her dying made me want to die with her.

They're all worthy of our attention.

"I have food and water prepared for you," VORA said. "You must learn to take better care of yourself, Asher."

I peered up. A nutrient bar sat waiting for me in my re-assembler with a glass of water beside it. The bot directed me toward them, and with the drugs in me bottoming out, I didn't object. My stomach felt completely void. I grabbed both and then collapsed onto my couch.

"Would you like to watch anything?" VORA asked.

"Not right now," I replied. "Only silence." *When was the last time I'd ever said that?*

I bit into my teriyaki-chicken-flavored bar. VORA always knew exactly what I wanted. I washed it down with the entire glass of water without breathing, but as I lowered it from my mouth, I noticed the message indicator on my lifeband blinking. Mr. Helix was already checking in on me.

"I can attempt to move up your psychological evaluation to today if that is acceptable?" VORA said. "I do so hate seeing you like this, Asher."

I shook my head. "Quiet. That's all."

"Mr. Helix has also placed a recommendation with the Network for you to erase a traumatic nightmare," VORA said, being anything but quiet. "Such dreams can be unsettling to an unpracticed mind accustomed to REM sleep. You are well below your data limits, so the cost would not put you at any risk."

"It'd be erasing the wrong thing," I mumbled. I leaned back and closed my eyes, trying to still my mind and make sense of what I was feeling.

All I'd needed was a dose of pharma to get over the nightmare. Yet when Mission's well-being was first placed in danger, I'd knowingly broke Mr. Helix's rules. Then when I heard his anniversary plans and there was an even greater chance Mission might come to harm, I very nearly had a heart attack.

It didn't make any sense.

I'd watched plenty of inhabitants perish over the years. Sure, I'd felt pity for them, but that was it. Then I did my duty for the good of *Ignis: Live*. I didn't fall apart at the seams like this.

I wasn't any average viewer who could become invested in favorites. The show had to come first. It was my job, my life for over a decade, and I'd already risked throwing it away by interfering beyond allowances—not to mention foolishly deleting footage of Mission seeing a Fixer and picking up a camera. If the High Earth infusers decided to investigate my mind, they would see that. I might be delisted and sent to live out in the Outskirts . . .

"The Outskirts," I blurted out.

"Excuse me, Asher?" VORA replied.

I leaned forward. An idea popped into my head that might be able to spare me that fate. I remembered Vivienne talking about the off-Network brain infusers in the Outskirts while she was distracting me. It was crazy, but I was desperate. If I kept on this track, Mr. Helix would lose his trust in me. I'd lose my position on the show. I'd lose everything.

"I'm going to leave our smart-dwelling for the next few hours," I said. "I think that it'll be good for me to visit the Outskirts and see that there's nothing to be afraid of for a resident. Get my head straight."

"Perhaps an episode of *Outskirts Today* would suffice?" My smart-dwelling's holoscreens blinked on, and that program came on. A boat rocked, a haggard, old woman on it holding a rod connected to a line that sank through the water beneath.

"No. I want to see it for myself." I stood and approached the door for the direct-access lift into my unit.

"Asher, it is my duty to ensure your health and well-being. I advise that you stay here and rest until your evaluation is completed."

"Please open the door. I need this."

"You have never exited the floor of your smart-dwelling before. The danger of a stress-related relapse is elevated by unusual environment conditions."

"This will help me. Are you not required to fulfill my needs?"

"At this moment," VORA said, "my primary directive is your health."

"Then please open the door."

"I can arrange—"

"Stop!" I growled. "I need to do this. Now, open the damn door and wait here for me to return." It was impossible to project my voice with all the calmative pharma still in me, but I got my point across.

"Yes, Asher," VORA finally conceded. "I will keep track of your vitals through your lifeband. Please be aware that your actions disobey your active medical recommendations. If you proceed, it will be noted on your public profile, pending examination."

"Understood," I said. What was another mark on my health status? "If Mr. Helix checks in again, reply that I'm feeling much better already."

"Yes, Asher. Would you—"

I didn't bother waiting for her to finish. I remembered to grab my OptiVisor from my kitchen just in case I felt the need to watch anything, and entered the elevator. I rode it down, wrapped in projected recommendations for popular programs fitting my profile, including that Mars survival show again. I blew some dust off the visor's screen. I rarely used the thing, not having much use for viewing while on the move.

The elevator opened to the tower's spacious lobby. Other than an info-bot standing silently at the center of the room's pearlescent white tile floor, it was completely empty. I hurried across it to the great doors that led to the skywalks of High Earth, then stopped.

My throat grew suddenly dry. My feet felt like they'd been submerged in wet plasticrete.

I'd been down to the lobby before, during my acclimation tour, but no farther. Some residents liked to walk outside in High Earth while they watched their visors. In the fresh wind and the warm sun. I supposed I'd finally found a reason of my own to leave home.

If Mission could escape from under the floor, I can handle this, I told myself, before the thought of her again set me on edge.

"I'll be okay," I told myself. "I'll be okay."

I donned my OptiVisor so I wouldn't be affected by how high the skywalks were over the Great Lawn. I didn't put on *Ignis: Live.* I didn't put on anything. I just used it to block out my vision, held my breath for no real reason, and took a step before I second-guessed myself.

"Walk," a robotic voice announced as soon as I was outside onto the skywalk. I obeyed, not even looking to make sure the path was clear. I knew High Earth's automated pedestrian traffic system was flawless. The walkways were never busy when I looked down on them from my unit.

My feet drew me forward with the aid of the moving sky-walks. The city's gleaming towers rose all around me, appearing as silhouettes through the OptiVisor screen, stretching toward the pinkish sky like fingers of glass and polished plasticrete.

A few silhouettes passed by—other residents out for walks, all focused on the OptiVisors jutting out over their heads, letting the walkways guide them. I breathed slow and steady, making sure to stare straight through the visor and not down or up. As I moved farther away from my home, it all got easier. Even with other residents around me, I'd never felt so isolated without VORA. So far from home, even when VRs had transported me to other galaxies.

A message from Lance suddenly popped up on the corner of my visor. He'd located and disposed of the camera. I knew I should feel relief, but I felt nothing. I closed it out and continued on.

If I wanted to perform the job I'd dedicated my life to, up to my and Mr. Helix's standards, I needed to erase more than just some stress-induced nightmare. I needed to expunge the root of all my current issues. To forget all the years of following Mission more closely than all others when I should've been focused on the big picture.

Maybe that way, the show could even improve. Had I been the cause of its recent decline? Alienated viewers who didn't care about her?

I needed to erase Mission from my head. And I needed to do it without Mr. Helix or High Earth's Network discovering the rules I'd broken for her. How I'd been too distracted to properly oversee Lance's recent fix.

CHAPTER 8

It was sunset by the time I reached the coast. My muscles burned with soreness like I couldn't believe. The moving walks were fast on their own, but pushing my legs while on top of them got me to the Outskirts faster than even waiting for a hover-car would have.

My feet stopped moving, and I drew a deep breath before raising my OptiVisor. My eyes widened.

The last row of soaring High Earth towers had construction bots crawling all over them like spiders, keeping everything clean with their multiple appendages. They were impressive from such a low angle. Awe-inspiring. I could barely believe they were physical and not projections.

At the coast, the skies were smeared with clouds, and the rainfall was heavy. I'd never seen rain in person before—it didn't rain in central High Earth—but apparently it was bad for buildings. One damaged tower even had an entire exterior wall being refaced with glass and polymer plating.

Beyond that last row lay the Outskirts. Like everything else that day, it was my first time visiting the hodgepodge of structures made of metal, stone, and even wood. Some buildings were literally reclaimed from the old world before the tide stopped rising and High Earth became the only land left above the surface. Countless public safety drones swarmed overhead, ensuring that the delisted populace of the Outskirts stayed where they were supposed to and didn't utilize hazardous weaponry or energy sources.

The Outskirts themselves were a three-kilometer-thick band wrapping High Earth's entire circumference. Tremendous floodwalls separated it from the Great Lawn, with intermittent lifts along it able to carry residents down. A secondary, lower wall was located directly on the water at the opposite end of the Outskirts. Massive makeshift wind turbines lined the top to provide power for a delisted world separated from the High Earth Network.

From my vantage, I could see the raging ocean beyond that second wall. A gray mass rising and falling, waves foaming like sick animals on ancient Earth. Far out, bulky High Earth factory rigs rode the waves, sucking water out of the ocean for resources in order to construct all the bots and tech needed in High Earth as well as maintain the planet's current water level. For the safety of residents, production was kept far beyond the walls. Pollution within the walls of High Earth was nonexistent.

All this information had been uploaded into my brain before initial animation. I'd simply never accessed it before—never had reason to.

And as I stood there, a bright light shone from the nearest rig. I heard a distant crack, and then a glittering dot climbed the sky along a thin ladder of smoke. A waste vessel was being launched into space to eventually drift out beyond our solar system, where it couldn't cause any problems to humankind.

Most waste was reusable by re-assemblers—even human

excrement. Some tech couldn't remain on Earth, however, and things weren't ever so clean in the Outskirts. The High Earth Network was adamant about keeping what was left of Earth as clean as possible, even that place.

I watched until the brilliant light disappeared beyond the veil of clouds.

"Resident Asher Reinhart, you have arrived at the borders of High Earth." An emotionless voice spoke.

I looked down and saw a public safety bot standing before a lift. Another thing I'd never had to see before in the safety of my home. Unlike med-bots, this one's chassis was humanlike in construction, from its legs to its emotionless face. It did, however, also share blank, white eyes.

It seemed harmless, but I'd seen them in action when delisted people grew riotous on *Outskirts Today*. Jets in their legs allowed them to cross gaps at inhuman speed. And the weapons built into their arms could paralyze a human in an instant if the threat was not deemed urgent. If it was . . . well, I kept my profile censored so I didn't have to see. "Vaporized" was a term I'd seen used on comment boards.

"I . . . uh . . ." I cleared my throat. "I'd like to visit the Outskirts."

"Processing . . ." The bot's eyes blinked a few times. "Resident health status: MILDLY UNSTABLE. Referencing VORA evaluation . . ."

"Please, I need to go," I said. "I already told my VORA I want to experience the Outskirts for personal reasons. I am a volunteer chief director for the program *Ignis: Live.* I think it could better help me perform."

"Processing . . ."

My hands were inches away from grasping it by its shiny shoulders and demanding it hurry when it spoke.

"You are cleared for a four-hour visitation. Per your residential contract, a security unit will be assigned for your protection."

"That isn't necessary."

"It is required. You will be tracked via your lifeband." The bot extended its arm. A blade of light emerged from a scanner over its wrist and passed across my lifeband. "Any dangerous spike in your vitals or sign of band tampering by an outsider will necessitate force and your safe removal from danger. You have nothing to fear, resident. Please enjoy your stay in the Outskirts."

The doors to a lift that descended the High Earth wall opened with a snap-hiss. I looked from side to side for no real reason, then stepped on. The doors at my back shut and it plunged. I grabbed the first thing I could find and stared at the ceiling.

The cylindrical chamber I clung to chimed and peeled open. Another security bot strode in, backing me up to the other side of the lift.

"Hello, Asher Reinhart," this bot said, sounding identical to the last. "I will serve as your protection as we depart the borders of High Earth. As with all residents, your safety and freedom to live are our utmost concern. If you have any questions throughout your stay, do not hesitate to ask."

By the time it finished speaking, the lift slowed to a stop. It felt like my stomach had fallen straight through me. The doors opened. It was darker than it ever got in High Earth, even at night. The floodwall at my back rose at least one hundred meters to the skywalks of High Earth. It was solid, not a single aperture in it. The sun hadn't even fallen beyond the horizon yet and it was totally eclipsed.

I made it. I'd think up something to tell Mr. Helix when he inevitably found out about my venture to the Outskirts while I was supposed to be resting. Then I'd continue with my life, mind clear, and my ability to carry out my responsibilities to him secured.

Rain slashed down in sheets outside, pounding into the ground so loudly that I couldn't hear anything else. A dispenser by the exit released ponchos to keep dry. All the pharma in my system had been sweated out by then, allowing me to feel as nervous as I really was.

"We have arrived, Asher Reinhart," the bot said. It stepped out first, then rigidly turned to the side so I'd be able to pass. "Please proceed. May this unit provide a list of highly rated sights and attractions for those interested in the lifestyle of those banished from High Earth?"

"No, thank you," I said. I knew what I was looking for—a place to wipe unwanted memories—just not exactly what it looked like out here. But anywhere like it would be forbidden for resident use. I needed to find a way to ditch my security first.

Swallowing hard, I grabbed a poncho and headed out.

I drew the wrinkled plastic tight around my entire body as I threaded the damp, winding streets, like I was a product fresh out of a factory. It smelled dirty. Natural. Like sweat mixed with dirt and I thought maybe sex. Though, I wouldn't know since I'd never interacted physically with a woman outside of a VR.

Feet scampered in every direction, the footsteps of their owners sounding like static when interspersed with raindrops. The persistent showers had a difficult time navigating the clustered, dilapidated structures to reach their bottoms, but that didn't mean it capitulated. And it dripped down countless physical screens portraying ads for VR dens and other places where content could be consumed.

A trash sweeper barreled past me, and I jumped back in fright. The automated vehicle controlled by the High Earth Network appeared far out of place, hovering along at ridiculous speeds as it was programmed to suck up refuse from the street with snaking tubes, which would then either be ejected into space or reused. That was one luxury afforded to the degenerates of the Outskirts. If their pollution multiplied without relent, eventually it would affect us too.

A child leaped from a low rooftop onto the back of the sweeper, trying to scavenge something, anything. Whatever he grabbed, he'd managed to pry out a clump of materials before being flung off. He slammed into a wall and crumbled in a heap, but nobody stopped to help him. Instead, the delisted men and women down the street dashed over to pick through the junk.

I shuddered and yanked my hood as far over my head as possible. After that display of tech hunger, I didn't want to risk anyone seeing my resident-issue tunic beneath. Not that my bot didn't give me away.

Nor was anybody paying attention. If they weren't raiding the scraps, the grimy, rag-wearing crowds were all too busy waiting in lines to get into VR dens or show bars, peddling what little they had to get their programming fix. Most didn't even bother wearing ponchos. Others sat, literally in the rain, clustered around half-broken or outdated devices to watch shows. Legitimately or illegitimately, in the Outskirts, it didn't matter.

When a resident was exiled to the Outskirts, a Network brain infuser removed certain details about High Earth from their brains so that the sudden loss of all the luxuries they'd had and loved wouldn't prove emotionally catastrophic. It was one last kindness provided to those who did something to deserve being sent over the wall.

From what I knew, people known as slicers ran everything in the Outskirts—those with the skills to rip show feeds or hack into VRs. Ex-developers who might have had High Earth taken from them, but not their passions. They played a constant game with the Network, figuring new ways to hack into content while the artificial firewalls of the latter worked to block them out.

There were less deplorable ways for delisted folks to get their hands on our programs, however. They could trade old-world relics or services to residents in exchange for a data donation from our Network-registered accounts. Enough to watch a favorite show or load into a favorite VR if they were smart. Considering these were people who'd been banned . . . they were apt to be wasteful.

"It's another resie from above!" someone shouted suddenly from somewhere. I spun a tight circle and noticed the eyes of every delisted scoundrel in the vicinity rise toward me.

A woman poked my shoulder. "Blow you for a few bits, resie."

I whipped around again to behold her, so skinny I could see the bumps of her ribs beneath her sallow flesh. All she wore were undergarments beneath a transparent poncho. Her teeth were almost entirely missing, her eyes sunken into sockets as dark as night. Even though she was addressing me, her gaze lingered on a cracked holopad screen with nothing playing.

"Back away from the visiting resident," my security bot stated and stepped in front of me, arms extended to maintain a perimeter.

"Have you come to save us?" a delisted man asked, voice muffled. I found him, his face covered in a respirator.

"Please bless me with data," said another. She fell to her knees and presented a faulty lifeband, the holoscreen emitted from it flickering. Her other arm was missing, wires sticking out from it.

"Want a taste?" A woman spread her legs, wearing nothing under her dress.

"He wants me!" said a man, pushing her aside, he too lacking portions of clothing.

"Come with me to a pre-revolution museum and you'll see in person how our people once lived. An hour of data only!"

More and more of the ravenous people hounded me. They bowed and held out their devices. Filled my ears with promises of enjoyment.

I panicked and turned down the nearest street.

"Open your eyes!" a man chanted.

My heart raced from hearing the words from my nightmare. A gray-bearded preacher stood atop a crudely constructed dais in the center of an intersection with a conglomeration of metal shacks literally stretching overhead. His bald head shone beneath a flickering advertisement for a Nation VR den. The mark of an Unplugged glowed blue in the center of his forehead.

"We all must look!" he shouted. He gripped a bloody knife in one hand, and in the other, a pair of orbs dangling from a string. At least, that was what they looked like from a distance. Another man knelt before him, completely naked. He too bore the Unplugged brand, but red ran down his cheeks, and there were gaping holes where his eyes should be.

Not a soul stopped to look or to help. They all continued to focus on me. Begging for a donation. Offering services, some of which I barely understood. The preacher's own face was a mess of scars around empty sockets, and it felt like he was staring directly through me.

I had to cover my mouth to keep from vomiting, and again turned down the nearest alley I could find. It was blocked by a line of VR junkies stretching out from a virtual-reality den. People inside lay on rusting neural-transmitter chairs, some of them groping at the air, everyone drooling.

A resident stood at the far end of the line, a bot beside him.

It was easy to tell by his strong features and clean skin. He sat, legs draped over the side of a chair, while a woman fed him Earth-knows-what and another massaged him. He manipulated the screen over his lifeband, donating data to the tech addicts in line, one at a time. The next one up kissed him after receiving his due. A drone hovered above, recording it for *Outskirts Today*, I imagined.

The whole scene was revolting. I held my breath and shoved through the crowd.

The brushing of sticky arms, the mindless dribble spilling out of their mouths, the stench of burning flesh from their permanently seared temples from the old tech. The strain put on the brain by a VR chamber not physically replicating an uploaded user's movements could be deadly.

My bot cleared the way for me, and I was gagging by the time I broke through. Some broke off the line to follow me around like stray dogs. Their whispers and begging scratched at my brain. Incessant. Shameless. I walked aimlessly and glanced back over my shoulder after every step, hoping they'd forget about me.

"Another one!" someone's voice echoed. In an instant, I was old news, and the people following me turned to hound them.

I moved around a corner, leaned against the wall, and caught my breath. My lifeband blinked slowly. Not surprising considering what I'd just been through. I loaded myself up on a bit of pharma for good measure. I'd figured *Outskirts Today* was a complete exaggeration, but the place was somehow worse in person.

I looked up. I'd arrived in a dead-end alley, alone. At the end of it, I spotted someplace that seemed like it could be what I was looking for. The sign outside the shop wasn't holographic, and a few of the person-sized letters hung from their bolts like wilting leaves on a dying tree. The pulsating neon glow of the ones that remained illuminated glimmered on the slick plasticrete beneath my feet. All together they spelled the words minah's brain miner.

I did my best to gather my wits on approach, thankful for my recent injection of pharma. My fingers wrapped around the doorknob of the shop. I slowly exhaled and started to push, which didn't work. So I pulled. I'd never dealt with a door that wasn't automated. It was like I was in one of the popular period dramas residents seemed to love. The hunk of solid wood was heavy. It took two hands to haul it open.

"Resident Asher Reinhart, please keep in mind that this facility is registered with an off-Network brain infuser," my bot said to me as I entered. "Experimenting with such technology is dangerous and not permissible. You are free to, however, watch any procedure performed on nonresidents with permission of the owner."

I nodded in understanding.

The lobby reeked. A pool of stale water near the ridge of the stairs leading down into a flooded basement revealed why. The lobby's wooden ceiling sagged in places, rotted in others. The painted walls were faded, at least where they weren't completely torn away to reveal the guts of an ancient structure. Motes of dust swirled about in the lazy beams of old-fashioned fluorescent bulbs.

Two delisted patrons were seated inside. One wore a decades-old model OptiVisor. Half was cracked open and allowed me to spot naked limbs writhing on the screen in the murky reflection of the surviving parts. That explained the smirk he wore as he mumbled to himself and squirmed in his chair. The other patron held a holopad inches away from her eyes. A lump grew over half her face, covering one eye. They were different than the people outside. I might as well have not been there.

The third person present was a burly man leaning against the wall beside the only door in the lobby. He was half-asleep, a small white stick pinned between his lips. A screen of smoke eddied out from the smoldering tip to mask his face. Above his head, a sign blinked: why remember, when forgetting is so much better?

I definitely wasn't home.

"Gree-eee-eee-tings," sputtered a faulty bot sitting behind the reception desk. It was infinitely different from the sleek, shiny automaton that clanked into the room behind me.

The thing had been eerily crafted to imitate a human, and it looked like it'd been through a war, maybe two. One of its eyes was operational while the other hung from a loose cord. A few small patches of synthetic skin remained, but the rest was peeled away to reveal rusty gears, circuits, and grimy metal plating. A pearly white set of faux teeth was the only part in prime condition.

"Hi there." I paused and glanced back at my guardian. I knew using a delisted brain infuser was against my contract. I also had very little idea how anything worked out here. My bot hadn't stopped me from entering the place. It merely lingered silently at my back.

"I'm curious what it is you do here?" I asked.

A terminal sat out on the reception desk with a bundle of cords connecting the bot to it. The thing wasn't even wireless. Its single eye fluttered as blocks of text flashed across the thick screen.

"Why re-member-ember when forget-forget-forget . . ." The bot kept repeating the same broken word like it was stuck in a loop.

"Memory manipulation?" I said, desperate to save the thing and move on.

"Affirm-ative . . ." With the stump that passed for a right arm, it gestured rigidly toward the jug of water beside the desk. Maybe it was just the light, but the water was a foul shade of yellow. "Refresh-ment?"

I covered my mouth and stifled a retch, then declined.

"N-name?" the bot asked.

My tongue froze. My entire life, everyone and everything around me knew my name, whether from a scan or my posted profile. Even I was awakened knowing it.

"Asher," I stammered. "Asher Reinhart."

The bot's eyes flashed. The longest minute of my life later, the image on the screen it was attached to finally froze with the word invalid blinking in the center.

"You-y-you are not sched-ed-eduled," the android said.

"I know," I said. "I'm just exploring."

"There are n-no-no slots avail-available today."

"Slots?" I realized I was communicating with a machine that could barely speak, trying to hide my intent from a hyper-advanced bot behind me. I doubted the Outskirts one was programmed with even the barest simulated-intelligence platform.

"Pl-please wa-a-ait," the thing said, leaving me completely uncertain for what.

I glanced up at a poorly disguised surveillance lens built into the wall. Then I scratched my head under my VX350 OptiVisor. Maybe it was the stink of the place. Or how dirty the entire Outskirts were. I felt itchy all over.

The door beside the guard suddenly swung open. My head whipped around so fast that my neck cracked.

"What are you doing, you wire-box!" a cheery voice exclaimed. "Making a resident wait like that."

In the opening hunched the unsightly proprietor of the

place. She leaned on the wall, fat rolls sagging over her belt. I'd never seen somebody so obese in all my life. High Earth tech and health monitoring had eliminated that epidemic long ago. Both of her legs were synthetic, though one of the things appeared to have mostly given out and scraped the floor as she limped.

"Minah is sorry," the woman said. "Oh, so sorry."

"That's Minah?" I asked, facing the faulty bot.

"Minah is here." She laid her hand over her chest, and I realized that while her left hand was real, her right one was artificial, constructed with ten fingers set in two stacked rows. She regarded me with a mischievous grin. Her teeth were so discolored it drew attention away from her blotchy skin. Only her straight, jet-black hair appeared clean. I was half-convinced it was a wig.

One look at her and I remembered why visiting a delisted brain miner was so nerve-racking, besides it being delistment or probation worthy. If I wasn't cautious, I might wind up like her and stop caring about the right things. Get sick, and instead of being taken care of by High Earth's top-of-the-line med-bots, I'd wind up in a delisted chop shop, lose my legs, and start growing sideways.

The very thought made me shudder and filled my mind with a thought that was becoming far too familiar.

What am I thinking?

"Resident?" the male of the two patrons said. I glimpsed back and noticed both of them, with their tech lifted away from their faces, gawking. Heights. Crowds. Violence. These were things I'd learned I didn't like from both real-world experiences in my smart-dwelling and VR tests while establishing my profile. Now I knew I could add excessive attention to the list.

"Get your filthy, tech-grubbing eyes off him!" Minah barked.

She hobbled past me, waving with her free hand. "Out, both of you. Out now."

The patrons perked up but didn't listen. Their gazes never left me.

"Minah said out! Don't make me call the bosses."

That got their attention. The shop's guard hurried over to help shoo them out the door. A door that he promptly slammed shut and locked.

I swallowed hard.

"Damn, Minah, that's a beautiful piece," the woman then said. She circled me, eyes glued to the OptiVisor on my head like it was the last scraps of food on a forsaken space station. Her stomach bumped me.

"Please maintain a safe distance from the visiting resident," my guardian warned. The *clank* of its footstep gave me chills. Her smile only seemed to broaden as she continued winding her way around me, giving the desk a shove to squeeze by my front side.

"You have to give permission for touching of your body," she whispered. "First time out here?"

I nodded.

"Minah can tell," she said. "Minah can always tell. But what Minah really wants to know is if you merely stumbled into Minah's little corner of hell, or if you *wanted* to be here."

I looked back at my stoic guardian. Said nothing.

"Say no more." Her metallic grin stretched ear to ear.

"I didn't say anything," I replied. Sweat dripped down my back. I was only ever used to perfectly temperate climates, not this humid mess. I reached for the screen of my lifeband to get another fix. The woman's fat arm shot out, careful not to touch me, but enough to stop me.

"The mind must be clear," she said.

"For what?"

"Minah guesses that you would enjoy a tour of the facility. Minah has a woman in back about to go under. You'll get a special show today."

"No, that's not—"

She shushed me. "A tour it is!" She waddled toward the open door, waving me along. "Come now. Minah has a schedule to keep."

My feet felt like they weighed a thousand kilos. "Don't you need data or something?"

"Minah don't deal in traceable data," she said. "All that matters is keeping the great residents above happy. Come, come."

She vanished around the corner, and I slowly followed. A dark room in this disgusting place didn't exactly have me comfortable, but I had my bot with me, shadowing my every move. I'd learn what I needed to, then figure out how I could get my issues taken care of without being caught.

The woman's guard held the manual door open for me. He grinned a toothless grin and blew smoke in my face as I passed. I wanted to choke and die. I swatted it away from my face until I could see Minah at the end of a dank hallway.

"Are you coming, Mr. Resident?" she said.

"I only want to ask you a question," I replied.

She spun a crank on a portion of wall, and then a circular hatch creaked open. As I neared, I realized it was made from at least half-a-meter-thick metal. It felt like entering a sealed vault filled with all manner of hidden treasures. I'd probably watched too many ancient fantasy shows set in what was known as the Wild West.

A plaque above the hatch said OPERATING ROOM, and as it creaked farther open, I realized that my description wasn't far off, minus the riches. The ancient-world look of the waiting room was gone, replaced by a confused box with stark metal walls, floor and ceiling. Of course, it was equally as dirty, just in a different way. Every inch was either rusting or covered in a layer of filth so copious that if I dragged my finger along them, it was sure to come back black.

One step into the small room and the smell of singed flesh assailed my unprepared nostrils. Not the best first impression when it comes to a memory reprogramming center. Another problem, the room was completely empty except for a bundle of fraying wires that vanished into the floor, extending from a terminal station complete with an archaic-looking, chunky physical monitor.

"What is this?" I asked. I entered slowly, my steps and breaths echoing throughout the mostly empty space. The bot's movements sounded even louder. And we were barely all the way inside when the hatch slammed shut, its crank *whirring* until it locked.

"You can't lock me in here!" I yelled as I spun and banged on the metal.

"Trust Minah. It's for your own good," she said.

My brow furrowed and I turned back to her. "What?"

"You are here for a memory operation, aren't you? That's what 'tour' means. Minah thought all of your kind knew that?"

"No operation." My gaze flitted toward my bot, who stood silently beside me. In fact, I now noticed that its eyes flashed slowly, rhythmically, as if it were receiving an update.

"Relax. It cannot sync with the Network in here." She banged on the wall with her metallic hand.

As she did, I studied the bot. I poked one of its arms, winced, but the limb merely remained stiff. I waved in front of its eyes. Nothing.

"Very pricey for Minah to set up," she said. "You won't find a more secure tech vault in all the Outskirts though, Minah will tell you that."

"Are you sure?"

"It depends if you need an operation."

"I . . ." My jaw clenched. Every part of me wanted to say no and walk out. Sure, I'd broken a few rules lately. Left my smart-dwelling for the first time. But this was on another level. I could get myself killed.

What is there to live for without Ignis?

"I do," I said quickly, before my tongue could betray me.

She chuckled. "Then, my friend, you have come to the right place."

I swept across the room until I stood close enough to smell her body odor. "I need this to be confidential. Everything you see and do, nobody can know." Sure, the Network couldn't know, but, more importantly, if anybody found out about Mr. Helix's plans for the fiftieth anniversary, it could harm the show's reputation. That was the last thing I wanted.

The show comes first.

"Everything here is off the grid, darling."

"You're sure?"

Her features darkened. Suddenly, she looked less grotesque and more frightening—worse than my nightmare about the Unplugged. My throat dried up.

"Mr. Reinhart, if Minah starts revealing the secrets of my *special* clients, you'll be the last one to walk through those doors." She wrapped her arm around my back, lower than necessary. My skin crawled. The implications of having no bot to protect me hadn't dawned on me until then. She could rip me open, and not a soul would ever know.

"You aren't the first resie who's come strolling in here to forget secrets. You won't be the last. Here at Minah's Brain

Miner, we don't care who you are, or what you know, so long as the trade is fair."

"I thought you don't deal in data?"

She plucked the OptiVisor off my head. I went to grab it back, but she spun away from me, then rotated it in her hands. She might well have been drooling.

"For this, we can get started right away," she said.

"That's impossible," I said. "It's registered to my retinas through the Network."

"Do you see where you are, resie? Minah can break such things." She lifted it over her face, stretching the ends with her wide face. "Yes, Minah can do so easily. Unless . . ." She grasped my wrist and pulled it close. She sniffed at my lifeband, her eyes rolling back as if it gave her pleasure. "A lifeband is tougher to crack. DNA coded, but—"

"No." I pulled away from the overly handsy woman. I could feel my heart racing, but the band wasn't blinking or warning me to steady my vitals. It seemed the room was interfering with it as well.

"What about your clothing?" Her gaze moved from my head to my feet, and she licked her lips.

"No."

"You resies are usually more adventurous."

"I'm not here for adventure."

"Then the visor it is. Minah will take it off you; you report it stolen upon return, transaction complete. Simple, simple. Cracking open that steel box of yours, however, may be more tricky, Minah thinks?" She poked me in the forehead with a metal finger, then chuckled.

"Watch that!" I yelped and rubbed my face.

"Do we have a deal, Mr. Resident?" She stuck out her fat hand.

"Only after you show me how this all works," I replied.

She used her strong artificial limb to draw me forward and took my hand. Her skin was so moist I needed an air dryer. "Of course! But Minah promises this is the best you can get out here."

I stumbled slightly when she removed her hand. Minah then ushered me forward. She slapped my OptiVisor down on her desk hard enough for me to cringe and fear it would break.

"Let's get started."

CHAPTER 9

Minah struck a command on her terminal, and the floor peeled open behind me. A brain infuser chair rose through the center of the room on a low podium. Every resident received a VR chamber complete with neural links. Infusers were a step up and more carefully guarded throughout High Earth, having to be delivered by med-bots for use.

They could upload information directly into your brain, like schematics or a language, or they could rip memories out, knowledge with them. Outside of medical uses to help residents forget harmful memories, only shows with viewership levels compared to *Ignis: Live* were ever granted approval for them to be used on volunteers.

Minah's was a dated piece of equipment. A soft seat with tears along every part of it; rusty armrests with manual restraints built into them. The headrest was a dented bowl of neural transmitters that would cover my temples; bundled wires from Minah's terminal connected to the top of it.

Considering how the rest of her shop appeared, I'd

half-expected her to use equipment out of an ancient psychiatric asylum, complete with needles and scalpels. All things considered, the chair appeared somewhat comfortable, so long as I didn't catch some manner of Outskirts flesh disease from it.

"Please sit," she said. She limped around the infuser and spun the chair so it faced me. Then she smacked a crank on the base with her artificial hand, and it lowered with a hair-raising squeal.

"Already?" I asked. "Don't we need to discuss the issue first? Or, I don't know, sign a contract?"

Not only was it my first time with a delisted infuser, but also my first time having memories removed at all. The process was supposed to be essentially painless minus a bout of headaches for a few days after. However, without a skillful operator, it could leave the patient dissociated and depressed, like a piece of them was missing and could never be returned—which was exactly what it was—even if the memory was no more vital to their existence than eating a meal. I'd heard of delisted folk sometimes taking their own lives from the frustration. At least, that was the way certain shows depicted it.

Minah chortled. "No contracts here, resie. Honesty and trust come with comfort." She removed my rain poncho, revealing my resident-issue, color-shifting tunic beneath. With its graceful lapel and elegant tones, it was finer than any outfit I'd seen worn by the rabble of the Outskirts.

She tossed the poncho onto the floor. "Sit, sit, sit," she repeated, ushering me toward the chair. Before I knew it, I was lounging, legs stretched out and head in a deactivated neuro-basket.

Minah leaned over me, presumably to make sure I was centered or something. Once I met whatever requirements, she put on a big, toothy grin. Her breath reeked of smoke and liquor, and not the appetizing kinds.

"There you are," she said, cranking the chair again. I rose about a foot closer to the low ceiling. "Loosen up. You don't need a working lifeband for me to see how nervous you are. It will make it more difficult to get a reading."

"Is it that obvious?" I tittered.

"I've seen worse." She started to shuffle over to her terminal, stopped. Standing on the balls of her fake feet, she poked the ceiling, and a portion of it folded open, revealing a monitor built into the nook. I could immediately tell by the multiple view panels and rock-strewn interior of the world depicted that it was already set to *Ignis: Live*, apparently also a favorite out here.

"Focus on that," she said. "Try not to think much and just answer Minah's questions. We'll get you sorted out."

The sight of *Ignis: Live* gave me goosebumps. In the seconds before I looked away to avoid seeing which inhabitants were being broadcast, I could tell by how grainy the feeds were that it was a sliced broadcast. It made me sick that people like her had the nerve to watch Mr. Helix's painstaking labor without registering as viewers to help our ratings. After my brain was fixed, I hoped I'd remember to pass along an anonymous report about Minah's shop so that High Earth Network firewalls would lock her out. Though I imagined she'd be smart enough to avoid me remembering.

"You know, this infuser is the same model Craig Helix used to reprogram the original delisted volunteers before loading them onto the *Ignis*," she said. "It's an antique, but the thing works like a charm. You'll walk out of here feeling like a new man." Her ten-fingered hand started dancing across the manual keyboard of her terminal, moving so fast all I could hear was one steady stream of clacking. The other worked a touch pad.

"I didn't agree to anything yet," I said.

"They always do."

The neurotransmitters and nodes around my head sparked to life. They released a pulsing hum, like the beating of a heart.

"Are you starting?" I asked.

"You'd know if it was. Minah is only booting up. Can't do any work without knowing what you want and explaining how things work. So tell me, Mr. Fancy Resident Man, why are you here? Something awful happen in a VR that you just can't live with? You resies can be so sensitive."

"Not exactly."

"You didn't kill somebody, did you? Hid their body in the Great Lawn and now you're trying to forget where?"

"That's not . . . Do people do that? I—"

"No, you don't seem like the type." She cut me off like she was playing a guessing game I didn't realize I was a part of. "Hasn't been a recorded murder in High Earth probably ever . . . though, not like they'd rattle the happy residents and tell you." She snorted in laughter. "It's got to be over a girl, eh? Handsome fellow like you."

I didn't respond, but there was no way she didn't hear me swallow the lump in my throat.

"Minah knew it!" she said. "Did she break your fragile little heart? Well, don't you worry. Let Minah take care of it for you. We deal with these situations for resies more than anything else, believe it or not." She grinned ear to ear. "Sometimes, the medical clearance never comes. Sometimes they're embarrassed. All Minah says is . . . 'Why remember when forgetting is so much better?'"

I grunted a nervous, incoherent response.

"So, before you ask," she continued. "No, Minah can't take away your feelings for her and leave the rest. It doesn't work like that. Too many moving parts. She's got to go, all of her. Like a hard reboot."

"And it's permanent?"

"It is. Once it's over with, you won't know the difference. If it makes you feel better, if Minah got hands on you, we would never let go. You resies usually all look similar, but there's something special about you. Just a few clicks and Minah can try replacing her with Minah if you want." She cackled so loud it echoed.

I almost choked on a mouthful of air.

"Only a joke. Minah runs a reputable establishment, Mr. Reinhart. So, who is the lucky lady? A name will make this quicker. A picture, even better."

"A picture?"

"Unless you'd rather Minah start digging blindly. Might accidentally make you forget about someone else. Maybe some woman you saw on the skywalks up there that you don't even remember wanting. Minah may be the best there is, but it's your brain we're opening up."

I froze. I hadn't even thought about having to show her Mission. I guess I hadn't thought about much since I came up with the insane idea of running to some miscreant brain miner in the Outskirts to solve all my problems.

But erasing Mission seemed like the only possible option. After it was done, to me, she'd be another inhabitant on *Ignis* with a story worth recording. I'd be able to keep my position at Helix Productions after the anniversary events without losing my mind. I'd gotten too close. I couldn't be the first camera operator for it to happen to. I wished I'd been open enough to talk with the other volunteers about things like that after they'd quit. Maybe I wasn't alone.

"I don't have a picture," I said softly. "But her name is Mission."

"Popular name these days. Last name?"

"I'm not sure."

"Is there anything you do know?" A hint of frustration edged into Minah's tone. "Tell me about her at least."

"She's . . ." I sighed. I guess if there was any time to talk openly about what I'd been feeling, it was now. I only wished I were amongst better company. Even VORA.

"I've known her for nearly both our entire lives," I said. "It wasn't always this bad, but recently I can't stop thinking about her. Every time I close my eyes, she's there. Every time I open them, too. And I know I'm not supposed to only think about her. I . . . I can't deal with it. Not unless I want to lose everything."

"Ahh. So she didn't break your heart. She just won't offer you hers."

"It's not like that! She couldn't even if she wanted to. And I couldn't . . . Well, I could . . . It's just—"

"She isn't a resident?" Minah almost sounded insulted.

"Not technically. I don't think."

"Look." She stopped clicking away at the keys of her terminal and limped over. "For what you're offering, Minah will wipe whatever you want. You don't want anybody to know details, fine, but this is a safe space. You've got to give Minah something. Now describe who this girl is or get the hell out and stop wasting my time."

My gaze wandered past Minah's tremendous head and knotted hair, back to the monitor in the ceiling playing the show I had so much invested in. On one of the live feeds, Mission sat, legs folded, on the same promontory within the hollow interior of the *Ignis* that I'd placed her in my unfinished recreation. She stared out at the farms, which arced away and over her in every direction.

"Her . . ." I whispered.

Minah looked up, and when she turned back, she wore the toothiest grin I'd seen on her yet. "That Mission!" She laughed and placed her hand over my chest. I could feel the sweat on her palm through my clothing. Maybe it was my own. "Nothing to be embarrassed about. Minah sees that more than anything with you resies. Fallen for a character you can't ever meet or even talk to, but can't get clearance on a full wipe. Trust me, it happens. At least *she* isn't digital like most times."

I felt like a knot around my heart had been loosened. It wasn't just getting the truth off my chest, but the acknowledgment that I wasn't alone. The details of medical records in High Earth were private, so VORA could never have told me the same. Of course, Minah could be lying. It didn't seem like it though.

"So you can get rid of my memories of her?" I asked.

"Minah won't lie to you. This complicates things. Feelings aren't a simple thing. They go far beyond memories, even if that is what they're built upon. Perhaps those bots of yours back in High Earth know better how to dig out what sparks feelings, but it could be a single moment or an accumulation of a million. The possibilities are endless."

"Can you do it?"

"Of course Minah can! But for your average relationship, causal experiences are easier to pinpoint. With this, it may take a second session to find all the related memories that might trigger emotional relapse."

"I don't have time for that!" I drew a long, beleaguered breath. "I need her out of my head before morning. If you can't do it, then there must be other places out here I can go to."

Her scowl made me sink back into the chair. "You want this done right, there's only here," she said sharply. She wrapped the restraints around my arms without asking.

"Hey!" I protested, pulling at them. I was far too weak to break free.

"Minah won't force you, but that fine piece of machinery you offered is staying no matter what you decide. Consider it price of consultation."

"That's not fair."

"Life isn't fair." She chuckled. "At least out here it isn't. Now calm down and tell Minah, how often do you watch Mission's live feed on the show? Or even when you aren't focused on it, how often is it in the background?"

"Every day probably . . ." *Stop lying,* my mind scolded me. "Definitely."

"Exactly as Minah suspected. Now do you comprehend how many relevant memories we'll be sifting through?"

I nodded, even though the truth was, I couldn't even imagine.

"Two sessions and Minah can keep the fatigue and disorientation to a minimum," she said. "But if you're intent on doing it all at once, it's going to take all night, and by the time Minah's finished with you, your head will be aching for days. That's assuming everything goes smoothly."

"I know the side effects. It must be tonight. I need to be back in High Earth, in my home, before 8:00 a.m."

"You resies, always in a rush to be safe and sound in your beds. Minah will find out why soon enough, eh? Will you go on this adventure with me? Make an old woman's day."

Ever since Minah got me to look at Mission's feed, I couldn't stop watching. So many hours together since the day I was born and she found her world. Was I really willing to lose it all?

"Nobody can know," I said. "Please."

"Minah has peered into the minds of more resies than we've cared to count. Minah has seen the way shows were going to end and the genesis of new ideas. Minah doesn't give a damn about you High Earthers or your shows and programs. They cause more trouble than anything around here. Plus, Minah will see plenty of you in *your* head to keep busy. Every inch of you." She chortled and smacked her lips. "And you're oh-so-real."

The thought made my stomach turn over, but I was desperate enough to stay put. Not that I could break free. I was desperate and confused enough to trust a delisted witch with my mind and every secret I harbored about the *Ignis*.

"You're sure this is what you want?" Minah asked.

"No. But I don't think I have a choice," I whispered. Mr. Helix depended on me getting my head right. The inhabitants deserved better for their sacrifice. They all deserved to have their lives recorded in the best, most entertaining way.

"Then lie back, relax, and let Minah take care of you." She fastened my restraints tighter, stabbed a needle connected to a long tube into my neck out of nowhere, and then shambled back toward her terminal.

"What's that?" I tried and failed to reach for my neck. "Minah?" My heart pounded. I could hear it in my eardrums. Then it started to slow.

"Minah will start by getting a read on your brain activity," she said. "You'll be conscious for now, but once we crack you open, the next time you wake up, you'll be outside and on your way home alongside a bot that will know nothing of this."

"Nobody can know," I said, my words slurring slightly. I felt drowsy.

"Our. Little. Secret." She poked my head once for every word. "And don't you go falling for her all over again."

The nodes and transmitters wrapping my head started to buzz even louder. A tingling sensation augmented around my ears, and the hairs all over my body stood on end.

"Here we go," she said. "Enjoy your last few minutes with your beloved. Soon, Mission—beautiful, innocent Mission—will be another silly character on a silly show."

Minah broke into laughter and set the feed recording Mission to fill the entire screen above. Then she raised the volume loud enough for me to hear nothing else.

[Ignis Feed Location]
Block B Promontory
<Camera 3>

"There you are!" Jacen said as he climbed up to the promontory where Mission sat. It was the upper portion of Living Block B, which protruded above the crops. As Mission watched him near, she couldn't help but wonder if he knew why it was her favorite place in all *Ignis*, or if maybe he felt the same way.

Her first memory outside of the hell she grew up in took place in that very spot. She remembered it like it was yesterday. Tiny, straggly, little Jacen rocking back and forth, scared of the dark. She'd been scared all her life up until then. Frightened of every footstep that drew too near, of being forgotten in her hole.

Sitting with him that day, holding his hands and helping him stay calm . . . She could've been in the worst position, starving like they were days into the Great Blackout, but if she thought of that moment, she felt safe.

"I got in late yesterday from a repair," he panted as he reached the top. "I hoped to find you before you started working."

"I'm sorry," she said. "I meant to come down, but have you ever been on a Mother's bed? I don't think I've slept like that in my whole life."

"One day, I hope." He snickered. "White looks good on you, by the way."

Mission glanced down at her new outfit, bestowed upon her by Alora after their last conversation. "I'm guessing you heard it's official?"

"Everyone's heard. Youngest official Mother ever. I thought Alora would hold on a bit longer."

"So did I . . ."

"Well, I'm proud of you, Mish."

"Oh, shut it." She rolled her eyes and slid over to make room for him. She gazed out at her sustainable world amongst the stars. Busy hydrofarmers were lost in rack after rack of greenery, and from their vantage, they could see the mass of grasshoppers leaping about one of their containers. Shadows of maintenance men occasionally scurried around the pits beneath them. The orange glow of the core's reactor pulsed soothingly from above as it always did, like a beating heart pumping blood to limbs.

"Can you imagine looking up and seeing a starry night sky on Earth?" Mission said.

"You asked me that same thing the first time we sat up here during the blackout," he replied.

"Well, I guess you still haven't answered. Can you?"

He shrugged. "Doesn't make much sense to me how they describe Earth. I know we've seen pictures, but what would keep you from being sucked up into space like criminals through the airlock?"

"Same thing that keeps our feet grounded in here."

"You think too much, Mish. People on Earth all killed each other, remember? It isn't hard to imagine why with them surrounded by so much darkness."

"It isn't like that."

"How do you know?"

"When I was younger, I once wandered too close to the

airlock before it released someone. For half a second, as the outer seal opened and the inner one closed, I saw what they call space. It wasn't just darkness, Jacen. The stars shined like . . . like someone had shattered a crystal on top of a black blanket."

"Is that why you needed to leave the spacing the other day? Too tempted to jump out and join them?"

"Maybe." She chuckled. "I don't know, I've been so overwhelmed. Haven't you ever wanted to see the outside with your own two eyes? Not just hear about it or look at grainy old pictures."

"I never really think about it. We'll be recycled long before *Ignis* is supposed to reach one of those star things. Seems crazy to find a new Earth anyway when we have everything we need right in here."

"Not everything . . ."

Jacen placed his hand on Mission's leg and edged a little closer to her. "Are you really up here to think about Earth, or is being the new Mother so overwhelming you're trying to hide?"

"That's not funny."

"It wasn't meant to be. If it was easy, any of the other girls in there would have had the honor, but Alora named *you*. I know you like to doubt yourself, but I don't. Not for a second."

Mission took his hand in hers. "You're my best friend, Jacen. You know that?"

"Even now that you're wearing white?"

"Always."

"Well, you know you're mine, too. And because of that, I can always tell when something's bothering you. Leaving spacings, thinking you saw me when you didn't, sitting here alone. I may be a lowly sewer jockey, but I know my Mission."

Mission drew a deep breath. "The core has already selected me as one of the Birthmothers to carry a new inhabitant. And then I guess another after that, and another . . ."

Jacen's hand fell away from hers. "Already? I . . . Is that normal? With whom?"

"Paul-10183."

"Of the Collective?"

"Yeah."

Jacen bit his lip and leaned back. "Well . . . no matter who it is, you should be honored, Mish. How many get to be a Birthmother, let alone an actual Mother?"

He said all the right things, but Mission could tell the news had caught him off guard. He wore the same thousand-meter gaze that she had been ever since she'd found out. Not that he shouldn't have expected it, but she knew him. He rarely thought about anything until it happened. That was what she loved about him.

"I'm honored all right," she said. "It's what Alora always knew I'd be since I got out of—" She caught herself before revealing the only secret she kept from her closest friend. "Well, she always knew."

"You used to want it, too, you know," he said. "More than anything."

"I did. And then I found something I want more."

"If you really want to see the outside that bad, I'll dangle you out there for a second. A Mother's got to have that kind of pull."

"That'd be a good start." Mission laughed. "But what I really want is for the core to stop making decisions for me."

She closed her eyes, and without taking the time to second-guess herself, she leaned over and kissed Jacen on the lips, just like she'd seen the couple in the galley do it. He pushed away at first, then gave in, squeezing her tight in arms made strong from scrubbing grunge out of pipes. By the time they released, both were completely breathless.

"I don't want my first time to be with Paul," Mission whispered. "Or to carry his child. I want to be with you."

Jacen ran his hands through her hair and planted another kiss on her lips. He held them there for a few moments before his expression was wrecked by a grimace and he retreated. "We can't."

"We can," Mission insisted.

"You're fertile now. And if we . . . and I . . . The core will know whose it is. They'll find out and we'll be spaced just like the other Blackout Generation mess-ups."

"At least we'll be together." Mission pulled him in for one more kiss, but he turned away.

"We'll be dead." He sprang to his feet. "You're a Mother, Mish. And I'm maintenance. The core is never going to choose me for you, or me for anybody."

"But I do."

"It doesn't—" He bit his quivering lower lip and sighed. Then he knelt back down and embraced her. "Please. You have to do what you're meant to. I'll still be here when you're done. I'll always be here."

She squeezed him as hard as she could and buried her head in the cambers of his neck.

"Promise?" she whimpered.

"Always. Now, hey . . . I have a shift all morning, but I'll find you as soon as it's over. Take you to the Launch Day celebration at the airlock like I always do." He held her at arm's length. Her cheeks were stained with tears, and she was forcing a frail smile.

"Sit with me until you have to leave? I'm supposed to relax today—Alora's orders. I'd rather not be alone."

"Only if you promise you'll keep your mouth to yourself this time. I don't know if I can hold back a second time."

She chuckled, then sniveled. "I'll try."

"Deal." He plopped back down beside her. "Oh, and I almost forgot. Happy birthday." He removed a crudely fashioned necklace from his pocket and wrapped it around her neck. The string was made from the twined stems of a plant, and the pendant was a rough shard of metal. Countless tiny dots were inscribed on the surface in no real order.

"Like the stars you always talk about," he said.

* * *

"He won't be there," I mumbled weakly. The steady hum of the nodes along with the drug Minah gave me had me feeling drowsy. A few more seconds and I would've been unconscious, but my tolerance was high thanks to all the recent stress. I blinked my tear-filled eyes hard and lifted my head as much as the infuser's restraints would allow.

"Try to stay still, dear!" Minah shouted over the racket. "We're about to get started."

"What the hell am I doing?" Watching Mission enter her world, bulging green eyes bright with wonder despite being surrounded by so much chaos . . . it was my first real memory. Without that moment, I might never have been inspired to find Helix Studios and volunteer so young. I never would have discovered the only thing I was ever good at in my director's chair.

Now I realized losing Mission meant losing everything.

I yanked at my arm restraints as hard as I could to break free, causing the bulky chair to tilt from side to side.

"Minah said relax!" Minah yelled.

Out of the corner of my eye I noticed brown liquid running up the tube attached to the needle she'd stabbed into my neck. More pharma to keep me calm. I wrenched my arms up and ripped out the needle.

The infuser's nodes amplified their power. For a moment, my head felt like it had been placed between two giant electromagnets. My eyelids grew heavy, tingling around the sockets. I yanked with all my might, and one of the shoddy restraints tore off the chair. The laws of inertia sent me rolling over the opposite armrest.

After tearing my head out of position and slipping, I was completely disoriented. I scrambled to find which way was up until my feet found the chair's base. I pushed off as hard as I could. My other hand tore free, and I flew back into the wall. Minah barked something, tried to run over to me, but she tripped and the room rumbled.

"I can't do this!" I said. "I can save her."

"Good for you, you damned resie idiot," Minah groaned. "Now come help Minah up!"

My vision came into focus, and I saw her rotund body roll over. She sat, trying to quickly adjust her prosthetic leg.

"Thank you for all of your help, but I . . . I have to go."

"Get the hell back here!"

I grabbed the crank of the vault and put all my weight on it until it unlocked. A new idea had popped into my head that could help me keep my position, ensure *Ignis: Live* would thrive like it was supposed to, *and* save Mission's life. I don't know how I hadn't thought of it earlier. Probably the cloud of pharma and stress.

It would only require me to bend the rules a little more, but Mr. Helix would understand if he ever found out. He had to. After many years working under him, I'd learned enough to know that this one time, he was wrong. The show needed Mission now as much as I did. Whether or not my obsession was the reason she'd become so famous was irrelevant. All the ads plastered across High Earth and the Network depicted her face, nobody else's. All the discussions, her name. The tale of her life kept viewers invested more than anything else.

The hatch swung a bit; then I panicked. I saw my OptiVisor shining on Minah's desk. She was obviously a skilled slicer, and I didn't want to leave any traces she could use against me. So I snatched it. She pawed for my foot as I rushed by. I stumbled into my bot, shoving it against the door, which swung open.

Minah's bouncer was caught completely unawares as I busted through the lobby door. It smacked him in the face and knocked his newly lit cigarette free.

"Gree . . . tings . . ." the reception bot said as I raced by.

I was nearly through the exterior door when I heard the deafening crack of Minah's guard firing off a round of an illegal firearm. It pierced the wall, just missing my head. Seconds later, I was out the door and back into the driving rain.

"Get back here, resie!" the guard yelled.

I dashed through the crowd, and he fired into the sky to scare me. None of the waiting tech junkies even flinched from the sound. My ears rang. I held my breath and ducked into a VR den. At least a dozen neurotransmission chairs lined one side of the room, their wires frayed, some sparking. No computer monitored them to make sure their users were fed. Half the people plugged in were so skinny their clothes barely fit.

A child, no older than twelve, occupied the one farthest from the door, drool dripping down his chapped lips. I had no idea how someone so young could've been exiled from High Earth already, but anything was possible. I knew that now.

"Another resident!" some haggard operator wearing yellow said, addressing me directly. He grabbed me by the shoulders, so strong I couldn't fight him, and shoved me into an empty

NT chair. I searched frantically from side to side and noticed that the resident who'd been inside donating data was gone now.

"The Nation got this VR slice working the other day," the man said. "Test it? Is it good as yours?"

"Get your hands off me!" I demanded.

"Won't take long."

He pressed me down into the chair and lowered a basket of neural nodes over my head. I felt my mind begin to fray, my vision warped, and then I stood on a grassy plain. Chaos surrounded me. Men and women in shiny plated suits battled with blades and shields. I was wearing similarly bulky armor, although it had no weight to it.

A blade swung at my head, but the VR glitched and gave me time to dive out of the way. I hated these types of violent VRs without narratives, celebrating the basest parts of human history.

"Don't run, knave!" the hulking person bellowed at me. He raised his sword again to strike me. Another warrior rode by on a great, hoofed beast—horse, my brain informed me—and sliced off his virtual head. An excessive wave of blood gushed out. His body glitched as he fell to his knees, suddenly skipping ahead through time to him lying facedown.

I scrambled to my feet, pulse pounding. An arrow zipped by my ear. I turned to run, and then another horse-riding resident enjoying the VR stabbed a spear through my chest. I flew backward, not in pain like it was real, but in shock. I knew it was fake; however, the mind sometimes had trouble distancing itself from the simulation of dying in these old machines. I hit the dirt, spear and blood rising from me, and then the world folded in on itself.

I gasped back to the present, knocking the NT chair's neural nodes away as I jutted forward.

"Good, right?" the VR den operator asked eagerly, half his teeth missing. "Right?"

"There you are!" Minah's guard threw someone aside at the shop's entry.

He fired again. It missed, but the bang was enough to stir me from the shock of being dropped into a war zone VR. His bullet shattered a panel of the shop's storefront. I leaped around the foul-smelling operator and out through the opening of his hellhole. My legs and chest stung from a level of exertion I'd never experienced. The great wall of High Earth rose before me, and I knew if I reached it, I might be safe. Weaving my way around the delisted, I tried to make sure the guard couldn't get a clean shot.

I kept bracing for another bullet to whip by or, worse, hit me, but one never came. When I was around the corner of the wall, a security bot slammed down in front of me, cracking the street. I skidded to a stop.

"Resident Asher Reinhart, you have been located," it said. "You are safe. A High Earth Network glitch caused this unit to briefly lose your signal. I would recommend returning to the lift at this time."

I glanced back over my shoulder and found the guard stopped in his tracks. He stood glaring at me, as if there were an invisible barrier he couldn't pass. He ran his finger across his throat, then stowed his weapon and vanished into the crowd.

I exhaled and collapsed against the wall. My legs felt like they were on fire. A few bulging-eyed men and women crawled toward me from the other side of the street.

"Stay away!" I yelled. My guardian bot stepped between us. If it only knew how much it had missed.

"Piss someone off, did you, resie?" someone beside me muttered.

I flinched, then turned. Slouched right beside me in the shadow of the wall was the bald Unplugged man I'd seen getting his eyes gouged out earlier that night. The first thing I noticed was the stench of fresh blood. Like . . . rusted metal, another smell I now knew. The rivers of red on his dark cheeks were dry despite the rain, but he hadn't even been provided a bandage by the preacher who'd done it to him.

That unsettling sight was overshadowed only by the fact that now that I saw him up close, beyond the veil of rain, steam and glowing ads, I recognized him.

I got dizzy, opened my mouth to speak, and felt like the air could choke me.

"You," I finally pronounced. "You tried to kill me." I was too pumped up on adrenaline to be as terrified as I should've been, and too exhausted to run again.

"What the hell are you talking about?"

"You pushed me back in High Earth yesterday. I know your face. I wouldn't forget. You're . . . you're real."

"I'll be damned." He started chuckling, which turned into a dull cough. "And now you're here? Guess you managed to pull yourself up, then. I'm surprised."

"You almost killed me!"

"And this is my reward." His bloody eyelids opened, revealing the two gory holes where his eyes had been. I saw the ridges of muscle and sinew within and had to look away. "Did you come all the way out here to get back at me?"

"No . . . I . . ." I was at a loss for words.

He groped through the air to touch me. I sidled out of the way, causing him to tip onto the sodden street, where he laughed like a madman.

I expected my bot to warn him against touching me without consent, but it silently watched. Maybe it registered how little of a threat he was. Still, I wanted to run, sprint away as fast as I could. I didn't.

"Why?" I asked. *How?* seemed the more appropriate question, but I'd seen Minah's capabilities at blocking out the Network. It hadn't been a nightmare. An Unplugged man had snuck into High Earth without anyone seeing, and attempted to murder me. Suddenly, my crazy moods and actions all started to make sense.

He tapped his forehead and sneered. "To earn my brand. We all must."

"No. Why me?"

He sloshed through the wet street and used a wall to stand. "I see. You think you're special. You're not. The Elder told me to get a resident to look me in the eyes, and then I'd be free of them. Unplugged for life."

"You didn't answer the question."

"I found a tower; I picked a home. That's it. Special?" He scoffed. "We're all the damn same, both sides of the wall."

Again, he reached blindly and his finger brushed my OptiVisor-less face before I could evade it. The bot's hand sprang out and gripped his wrist.

"Please remove your hand from the visiting resident, or this unit will apply force."

The crazy man kept his hand on me. The bot continued to squeeze until I could almost hear the crunch of muscle and bone. The man smiled all the way through the pain; then finally, he gave in.

His arm thumped hard to the ground and he rolled over, curled into a fetal position like he was ready to go to sleep. "At least you managed to follow my advice. Good for you."

Seeing the poor delisted soul in his own element, nightmare or not, he was hardly anything to be frightened of anymore. A deluded, blind lunatic in rags, rolling about in his own blood and filth. I felt sorry for him, sorry for the first person who'd ever tried to physically harm me. Who made VORA think that stress had me coming unhinged.

Whatever he claimed to want by attacking me, now he was harmless. Pathetic. At least if my ill-advised journey beyond the wall accomplished anything, it was helping me conquer my fear of monsters like him. If I could do that, I could do anything.

I regarded the pitiable man one last time, then headed for the High Earth lifts with my bot. I kept my head low, ignoring the pleas and extended hands of all the poor souls who'd never again know paradise.

I was the Chief Director of Content for the greatest show in High Earth, featuring its brightest star, and the time had come to make things right.

It was time to return home.

CHAPTER 10

Home.

I wasn't away long, but I was so glad to be back. One retinal scan, a trip through a cleaning detox chamber, and I had no trouble getting back into High Earth, thankfully leaving the countless delisted men, women, and Unplugged separated by the wall.

I watched *Ignis: Live* the entire way, letting the moving walkways carry me instead of pushing my exhausted legs. Rejecting Minah's operation meant I had time. The heights as I crossed the skywalks barely even mattered. Only the show, where Mission still sat with Jacen.

She'd made a mistake, kissing him—like me, she wasn't above making them—but the silence as they sat there afterward was difficult to stomach. I'd always felt they were better suited to be friends. Not only was that the only safe option for her, but he barely seemed to understand her. How could a sewer jockey ever comprehend the significance of creating life for their world, after all?

Mission was lashing out because she feared her new position. I understood. She was fortunate that Jacen proved to have more mental fortitude than I ever thought he did. His lust for her had been obvious since the moment he'd reached adolescence.

I didn't only watch their feed, however. I caught up with the other busy lives of inhabitants around *Ignis*. Only one day away from the director's chair, and I already missed them all. Yevin-8432, a hydrofarming chief from Block C with an obsession with stealing food every day. A group of Blackout Generation punks, snorting scrunge in the sewers. Members of the Collective, decorating the airlock chamber for the anniversary celebration, where on that one day a year, the rations were doubled. Inhabitants could chug water to their hearts' delight.

By the time I reached my tower, it already felt like I was back in my old routine. One visit to the Outskirts was enough for a lifetime.

I rose through my residential tower and into my smart-dwelling. It was exactly as I'd left it. Sterile, tidy, not covered in rain or blood or filth—perfect. That first breath of fresh air was the finest I'd ever drawn.

"Welcome home, Asher Reinhart," VORA promptly addressed me.

"Thank you, VORA," I said, giddy. I couldn't contain myself. I wished she had a body like a bot just so I could hug her.

"Your lifeband recorded some peculiar activity beyond the wall. I hope your visit was as therapeutic as you hoped."

"It was exactly what I needed."

"I am pleased to hear it. I took the liberty of preparing a meal while you were gone."

I thanked her again as I snatched a bar from my re-assembler and took a large bite. Macaroni and cheese flavor. It hit the spot after the awful scents and tastes of the Outskirts.

"Might I recommend a rest now that you have returned?" VORA said. "You are a bit outside of your sleeping schedule."

She was right. I was pushing my body, but after whatever Minah did to me in that chair, I didn't feel the least bit tired.

"I actually think I'd like to log into the *Ignis: Live* studio," I said.

"You have—"

"I know, but I can't tell you how much better I feel. It's nearly dawn. The anniversary is coming, and I could use some time to settle in and plan."

"Very well. I will activate your VR chamber. It is recommended, however, that you sleep before your full evaluation later today."

"After this, I'll sleep better than I ever have." I took a step toward the chamber fitted with all the best in technology. No rusted bolts or dented neural bins. "And, VORA, thank you for caring about me."

"Of course, Asher. It is what I am here for."

I hooked in, and a few minutes later, I arrived in Mr. Helix's digital studio. I stood in the main studio floor amongst dozens of residents volunteering to devote their crucial time for the sake of creation, and hundreds of virtual workstations and AIs.

Gifted residents imagined shows and VR worlds from the comfort of their homes every day, but few ideas ever made it beyond programming. It was a beautiful thing, what Mr. Helix had done. Trudging through the Outskirts made me appreciate it more than ever. I was privileged to harbor such an important role in his vision, and after this situation was remedied, I'd never put that into jeopardy again. The sounds of production were like a symphony to my ears.

"Mr. Reinhart?" Vivienne Poole said, glancing up from her holopad for a moment as she approached. "Shouldn't you be logged off?" Looking at me or not, there was no mistaking the resentment in her tone when she uttered the term.

"I feel better," I said. "Rested."

"Already?"

"I got what I needed."

She grumbled something under her breath and went to walk away, but I stopped her. A soft touch on the shoulder. I wasn't sure why; I usually hated getting too close to people for no reason.

"Vivienne," I said softly.

"What?"

"I'm sorry I didn't take the time to talk with you before requesting your transfer." I felt her stance soften as I spoke, if that were even possible. "There was a lot going on. It's difficult for me to focus on more than one thing at a time."

"It's all right, Mr. Reinhart," she replied. "I'm still figuring it out." One half of her lips twitched into the semblance of a smile; then it vanished, along with her, off to help someone else, with all her attention returned to her holopad.

I ambled through the studio toward the director's office, where Frederick currently operated in my stead. The night crew was composed of even more AI presences than usual, but the humans—the few tireless holdovers who'd witnessed my breakdown—peeped up at me and whispered amongst themselves. They quickly returned to work any time I caught them.

Frederick turned and watched my approach, back turned to the camera-monitoring screen display. I wished I could record his vexation.

"Asher, what are you doing here so soon?" he questioned as I entered. "Shouldn't you be sleeping?"

"Rested and feeling fine," I said. "I wanted to get an early start. Big day."

"It is."

"You're dismissed for the rest of the night. I'll take it from here."

"I'm not sure if that's the best idea," Frederick said. "You didn't see yourself earlier. It was sickening. You're in no condition—"

"I'm in perfect condition. If you think otherwise, feel free to wake Mr. Helix. If not, as Chief Director of Content, I'll be taking over observations."

Frederick stood tall in front of me. If he knew the kind of vagrants I'd just been around—the murderous Unplugged I'd looked upon and felt sorry for—he would've felt like a fool for trying to intimidate me.

"This is my shift, Asher," he spat. "My work."

"Then consider it a night off." I squeezed by him and into the office without looking back. At the terminal, a user check initiated a retinal scan on my real body via my VR chamber. Seconds later, I was logged into the director systems, overriding Frederick's access and booting him out. He stormed away in a huff, cursing me under his breath.

According to Mr. Helix, the error programmed into the core was going to affect Block B at 8:00 a.m. That meant I had four hours. Based on viewer responses in discussion boards, Paul was scheduled to arrive to see Mission just before that. Members of the Collective were aggressively punctual.

Presently, she and Jacen had parted ways and she was alone in her room, getting acclimated with the core data only Mothers were permitted to read. She seemed both tense and exhausted, the bags under her eyes darker than usual from being unable to fall asleep.

Don't I get it, Mission, I thought. There we both were, monitoring countless bits of data on dozens of screens at the same time.

Log after log of information about her inhabitants raced before her face. On one window, off to the side, she'd pulled up the DNA analysis results that culminated in her being matched with Paul-10183 as breeding partners. Every few seconds, she couldn't help but glance at it.

The timing of what I was planning would be close, but I could get it done. Who knew Mission better than me?

So I got back into the groove of issuing orders to the crew. It felt good. They weren't my usual crop, but they were equally attentive. With so many other options for content, people didn't volunteer to help on a show unless they were passionate about it.

On *Ignis*, a pipe at one of the farm plots by Living Block C had ruptured, shooting water across the hollow. The spin of the vessel made it bend through the air in a peculiar way. This led to a few interesting exchanges, including a fight between a sprayed plant-tender and a mechanic.

At the airlock, the decorations for the anniversary were even more opulent than usual. It made sense, with all the spacings over the last year. The Collective was going out of their way to make it a party to remember, to distract with food and liquid and dance. A night to unwind. Cassiopeia barked at everyone around in her oh-so-authoritative manner. She really was a perfect fit for the role.

While that all happened, I studied the entire area around Living Block B in detail. I'd constructed it in my VR replica, but it was impossible to know it too well. Three-dimensional mapping helped me locate every camera and pick the ones where choke points would be when the panic started. Whether or not I thought Mr. Helix's plan was the right one, I'd make sure the documentation of it was spectacular. I owed him that much and more.

By the time the day crew logged in, I felt as normal as I had since I'd stupidly decided to erase footage of Mission to protect her. Only one more rule to bend, then I'd be done being a rebel, for good, and the show would be more successful than ever. Mr. Helix would thank me. This was why he'd promoted me, wasn't it? To make his vision even better?

"Good morning, Asher," Laura said, leaning in the entry of my office. "Nice to see you're feeling better."

"Thank you, Laura," I said, even taking the time to look back over my shoulder and offer a half-hearted smile.

"So, does Mr. Helix have anything up his sleeve for the fiftieth?" she asked.

"We'll find out soon, won't we?"

"Absolutely, sir. He actually just logged in."

My heart skipped a beat. Maybe I wasn't *entirely* calm. I turned and saw him moseying up the studio toward my office. Beneath the screens of his digital visor, he wore a placid smile and had his clothing colored bright purple. He only wore color when he found himself in a particularly festive mood. I stood to greet him at the entry.

"Asher!" he exclaimed. "It does me well to see you here, looking back to your old self. This room suits you."

"Good to be back, sir."

"I saw that you took a stroll out to the Outskirts? Sorry for keeping tabs on you, but I had to make sure my chief director was safe after what happened."

"I understand, sir. I know it was probably a bad idea to go there, but I barely stepped out of the lift down. I just . . . I wanted to show myself there wasn't anything to worry about. That my life here was all I wanted. Get my head on straight."

"A brain wipe would have been easier." Mr. Helix grinned. "As long as you're back here doing what you do best and staying conscious, I'm happy." He laughed heartily, then entered the office. His eyes were covered, but his head tracked my array of screens displaying countless feeds inside the *Ignis* at once.

"Half a century," he marveled. "Can you believe it?"

"Hardly," I replied. "I wasn't even conceived yet when it started."

He affected a small frown." Sometimes I forget how old I am. I remember when all I had was myself."

"And a vision, sir."

"Not possible without volunteers like you." He ran his hand over the monitoring screens like a father would through his child's hair. "The error should occur within the hour," he said. "You're welcome to join me and the others in the conference to watch. I've called everyone in for the occasion."

"Thank you, but I'm needed more out here. Actually, I was hoping I might open the storage drive and start pulling old footage to put together a reel remembering some of the show's finer moments. I know the show's about always moving forward, but half a century is worth remembering."

Mr. Helix's features darkened. "You're still sour on my plans, aren't you?"

"I think it's going to be brilliant, sir. I just think it might also benefit our viewers to provide some lightheartedness today. It will help remind them of how much the show and the inhabitants have evolved since they were delisted vagrants."

"Learning from me now, are you? It's a wonderful idea. Who am I to keep you from your work? That's why you're here."

"Thank you, sir."

He switched off his visor and regarded me warmly. "You've been the finest director I could ever have hoped for."

"I . . . I don't know what to say, sir," I stammered. I clutched my wrist to cover the blinking of my lifeband. I wanted to pass out again. If he knew how disloyal I'd been lately, it would've destroyed him.

"There's nothing you need to say that I don't already know, my friend," Mr. Helix said. "And for the last time, please call me Craig."

My mouth parted to reply, but instead I just nodded.

He beamed. "Should I recall Frederick to help you up here while you're in the Driver?"

"No," I answered, almost too eagerly. He didn't seem to notice. "An AI can help with the old footage, and I'll manage fine from down there on visor. I trust Laura to keep me updated."

Mr. Helix slapped me on the back. "So you *can* work with humans after all! Perfect. Keep me updated, Asher. You know where I'll be."

"Of course, si—Craig. And congratulations."

He took my hand and shook. "Here's to fifty more years."

Then he left, and as soon as his back was turned, I stared at my director's chair. Like all residents, I had my smart-dwelling, but that virtual seat was where I felt most at home. Looking through the many eyes of *Ignis*. Fifty more years sounded just fine to me. I could live happily here, and now I had to go and make sure that never changed.

I was ready to make sure Mission got another fifty with me.

I pulled up the window for Driver access on my terminal. It ran another user check and retinal scan before an illuminated pad was revealed to my left. I stepped on, and I was instantly teleported to another branch of the studio's VR program. The Driver.

Row after row of memory files awaited me, each one rising to the impossibly high ceiling and glowing blue like I was in some sort of sacred temple. Millions, maybe billions, of minutes' worth of footage transmitted through space from aboard the

Ignis were stored in the stacks. So much that it took a parallel server. And not only the material that was actually aired. There were backups for every camera on board, filming twenty-four hours a day in perfect resolution, for half a century.

Only a program with the number of viewers as *Ignis: Live* could warrant such a staggering amount of storage.

Needless to say, there was no other datahub like it. Even the High Earth Network was ethereal, connecting everything around us, but with no single, imposing, physical databank. If its conception was the greatest feat in the history of human programming, in my opinion, what Mr. Helix had managed to do came second. An entire civilization's every moment documented.

I traversed the central aisle. At the end stood a terminal where I could access every millisecond of stored footage. Behind it was a small windowless office with nothing inside but Mr. Helix's private terminal. It, and only it, allowed him to communicate directly with the *Ignis's* core and affiliated systems. He preferred to work in complete solitude. Something I could appreciate.

I pulled up my AI assistant. "Please start collating footage of every inhabitant born in Block B following the *Ignis's* departure," I ordered. "Focus especially on those after the Great Blackout so people remember their resiliency."

"Yes, Mr. Reinhart," the light-based entity replied.

It moved in front of the terminal and established a wireless connection. Data started flying across the screen while its eyes flickered. Once I could hear the whir of processing, I entered Mr. Helix's office.

It was chock-full of recreations of old-world relics. Reproductions of ancient paintings detailed elaborate scenes from the old world. Chalices and other tableware, flags and statues. Even his terminal was built into an ancient desk fashioned out of weathered-looking wood and carved with elaborate patterns.

Only two people in the world could access that terminal. Him, of course, and the serving Chief Director of Content for *Ignis: Live*. Me. In case of emergency, I was his backup. Years ago, a brain infuser had provided me with a latent understanding of how to navigate the system. Nowhere near as proficiently as he could—with his ability to program errors into the core or code the algorithms used by inhabitants to select breeding mates and evaluate the aptitude exams—but I knew enough to save Mission without anyone ever being the wiser.

I positioned myself at the terminal, activated my digital OptiVisor, and opened the most-viewed real-time *Ignis* feeds in front of my face. I focused on the one displaying Mission. Sometime during her studies, she'd fallen asleep at the controls of her core terminal.

"Wake up, Mission," I whispered. It was 7:45 a.m. There wasn't much time. Then, as if answering my prayers, somebody knocked at her door.

[Ignis Feed Location]
Block B Mother's Chamber
<Camera 5>

Mission rolled her head over on her console's keys and covered her ears with her palms. Another knock on her door came, louder and harder. She groaned.

"Mission, open up!" Nixu shouted. She slammed on the door three more times before Mission finally signaled it to open. Nixu had the same cross look plastered on her face that she'd worn ever since Mission was named Mother. A handful of children followed her.

"What is it?" Mission yawned.

"Paul is here to convene with you."

Mission blinked. She jumped out of her chair and hurried to her bed to straighten the messy sheets. As she did, she noticed that the bottom of her tunic already—what was that, baby spit-up? She folded that side into her pants and tried her best to remove the wrinkles from the rest. She might have been dreading this moment, but it wasn't often a member of the Collective visited from the core. "Tell him to give me a few minutes."

"Tell him yourself, Mission." She rolled her eyes and headed off with the children.

When Mission looked back up again, she noticed Paul standing outside. He was finishing up a conversation with Alora, who was still buzzing around, helping out. She offered Mission a warm smile and a nod of encouragement before departing. Paul then started toward Mission.

He'd been a member of the Collective since eighteen, living within the core for more than thirty years. *Ignis's* centripetal gravity was weaker there, elongating his frame over time. Just a handful of inches, but for an already tall man, it forced him to duck to fit through the doorway.

"Good morning, my dear," Paul said, his voice as smooth as velvet. "I don't believe we've been properly introduced. Paul-10183." He bowed at the waist, arms tight to his sides, back straight. Everything about him was refined. From his mannerisms to the folds of his white uniform. Even his graying hair and beard were primly cut, with crisp edges and not a strand astray.

"I know who you are . . . I mean . . . I'm Mission-14130." She mimicked his bow as best she could, while simultaneously continuing to smooth her clothes.

He stepped in farther, the door shutting behind him and drowning out the sounds of children. "Amazing. Nearly ten thousand people on *Ignis,* and still I find so many that are strangers."

"Alora kept us close."

"The fault lies with me. I should descend from the core more often. Walk the blocks. Meet our future." He sat on the edge of her bed. Mission bent as if to join him, then chose to remain standing.

"Planning that future seems more important."

He chuckled. "Indeed."

"You know Alora well?" Mission asked after a brief spell of silence.

"Not as well as I used to. I was matched with another Birthmother under her guidance, must be a decade ago now. You couldn't have been much taller than my knees. I think I remember you following her around like a root to water." He grasped Mission's hand and drew it close to his face. "You've grown so much."

The necklace Jacen had given her tumbled out of her collar as she leaned over. She backed away, startled. "I . . . I'm sorry."

"There's no rush, my dear. You should be as comfortable as possible." He smiled and slid back on her bed until he was leaning against the wall, long legs stretching across the mattress. He slipped off his boots. "Would you prefer to talk first? I could tell you a bit about what we have planned for later."

"If you don't mind," she replied softly.

"Not at all. When you reach my age, you try not to rush things. Mandatory recycling never gets any further, only closer."

Mission responded with a reticent chuckle.

"Alora says you're remarkable with your hands," Paul said after another lengthy silence. "'The best in *Ignis* with a needle and stitches,' I think was how she worded it. If I ever get a cut, I know where to come. Striking keys is about the most we get to use our hands up in the core . . ."

* * *

"Operator 112, cut live to camera 1984," I told the member of my crew assigned to the Block B med-bay. "Focus on her expression, with Paul positioned over her shoulder. Perfect. Now, relinquish controls over her room's cameras to me. I want to capture this just right. Transition full attention to your assigned feeds within the rest of the med-bay."

That specific camera was located within Mission's terminal. While Paul continued talking all on his own, she nervously paced back and forth, transitioning between facing the screens and her bed. I had every possible feed in the room pulled up on my visor. Twelve of them captured every angle. With my crew focusing on the rest of the med-bay, only I would be monitoring them.

This was my one chance.

I reached for Mr. Helix's terminal and paused halfway there. There was no turning back after this. I'd known him closely for a long time, both as my boss and what I considered a mentor. Now I was going to violate the trust he'd placed in me from the moment he named me second in charge of the biggest reality show in High Earth.

I had no choice. In the end, the show would benefit. That had to come even before my respect and loyalty for Mr. Helix. He would have to understand that.

I signaled my lifeband to inject me with some calming pharma so I could better swallow my nerve. Then I proceeded to complete the scans necessary to log in to Mr. Helix's terminal. If he wanted, he could easily find out that I'd been on it, but there wouldn't be anything suspicious to see when I was finished. I'd simply say I was checking up on the systems before the event. He knew how diligent I could be.

Countless lines of code blinked beyond the transparent windows of my visor. I drew from parts of my brain that had lain

dormant since the infusion. My fingers flurried across the screen
without even having to think about what I was doing. In a short
time, I was in, with access to Mission's terminal. The message I
planned to send her could have come from any member of the
Collective. And to the High Earth viewers, it'd just seem like her
stress getting the best of her when she inevitably ran from Paul.

I SAW YOU WITH JACEN, I typed. MEET ME IN
THE PIPELINE UNDER BLOCK C AND I WON'T TELL
A SOUL.

One long, hearty breath, and then I sent it. The message
vanished into the ether, bouncing between network comm-relays
across space, and then appeared in one corner of Mission's console. Paul droned on about plans for the anniversary celebration.
Mission nodded along absentmindedly, and when she turned to
continue her restless pacing, she caught a glimpse of my message.

She froze, brow furrowed. From the vantage of the only
live feed being broadcast, it merely looked like she'd come to
a sudden epiphany. Exactly what I was hoping for. Her eyes
opened wide; she clutched Jacen's pendant and then bolted out
of the room without offering Paul a passing glance. By the time
he stirred from his confusion and got up to see what had happened, I'd wiped all evidence of the message and was logged
out of the system.

I took a step back and exhaled.

My crew chattered in my ear, anxiously shifting between
cameras to keep track of her. Nobody wanted to lose her again
after what had happened at the spacing. I didn't even bother
giving direction. The time was 7:59 a.m. when she escaped the
confines of her block and entered one of the trenches carved
between the hydrofarms that crisscrossed the gaping interior
of *Ignis*.

8:00 a.m. had arrived.

Conduits throughout Living Block B suddenly burst. Roaring flames swept through the tunnels. Emergency lights directed the inhabitants toward the exits, but the fire-suppression protocol faulted. Local air recyclers began sucking the air out of the block in order to extinguish the flames like they were supposed to, but the hatches sealed tight instead of opening wide to allow egress. Hundreds of inhabitants were trapped with draining oxygen, screaming and banging on rock and metal.

At the same time, the members of the Collective, still at their control stations within the core, desperately hammered at keys to try to fix the error.

My crew's yammers transitioned to shouts. So many begging for me to tell them what to do that I couldn't sort the requests. Mission's flight had become an afterthought . . . and then I heard someone clear their throat. It wasn't coming through my comm-link.

I whipped around and spotted Vivienne standing in the doorway, a look of shock on her face.

"M-Mr. Helix sent me to help with file pulling," she stuttered. "For a second chance."

"How long were you—" I lost my train of thought when, beside her, an AI presence appeared, blank and emotionless as always. Vivienne typed something into her holopad with one hand. Before I could get out another word, the AI went red.

I felt a surge of electricity from the neural nodes around the head of my real body, convulsed, and then everything went black . . .

CHAPTER 11

.

My eyes slowly blinked open. The world was a blur. The muscles in my chest cramped, and I felt my pulse around my temples. I tried to turn my head to look around, but something had it restrained. Arms and legs, too. A screen switched on, wrapped across my face. I had no idea if I was in my smart-dwelling or in a VR.

All I saw was a single display of her. Mission . . .

[Ignis Feed Location]
Block C Subterranean Line
<Camera 26>

Mission raced frantically through the dark pipelines somewhere under Block C. The only light emanated from the helmets of sewer jockeys, and she ran to the nearest like a moth to flame. She had to stay crouched to fit as her feet sloshed through water up to her knees and with a heavy current. She held her nose with one hand.

"Have you seen Jacen?" she asked, almost shouting over the gushing water.

The woman lowered her sanitary mask, the same one who'd messed with her the day before in the galley. Her nose was red from snorting too much scrunge. "Lost him again?" she asked. "Not seen him since the galley yesterday. Can't you have the core track him or something now, Mother?"

Mission sloshed to another and asked the same. She received a similar answer, and when she went to run again, the man grabbed her by the shirt.

"Watch your step!" he said.

They stood on a narrow bridge over the yawning pit all the liquid was draining into, where it would be carried around the outer crust of *Ignis*, strained, purified by running through ground rocks and minerals, and recycled for reuse. Very few inhabitants clambered down through the darkness to the layer of water churning around the asteroid. Upkeep in those sections was hazardous work. The *Ignis* wasted minimal water, and so long as all the systems remained operable, the supply they'd left Earth with would last until they reached Tau Ceti.

Mission stared down into the bowels of the *Ignis*, breathing hard as if finally realizing she was winded. Then there was a bellow, loud and thunderous, reverberating off the metal and rock walls. It sounded like an ancient beast rousing from eternal slumber, but it wasn't coming from below.

A few of the older workers made a beeline toward the ladders leading out of the sewers. They were visibly panicked. Mission couldn't help but follow. If Jacen was down below, she knew that awful sound would surely draw him up, too.

Mission spun when she emerged, searching for what had produced the sound, when another bellow filled *Ignis*, louder and deeper than the first. It made boughs tremble. It came from the core, and for the first time in her life, the light glowing from the reactor at its heart changed. It swelled and darkened in sync with the deafening bellow, so that at the end of every interval, the gaping interior of *Ignis* was drowned in blackness.

"Another blackout!" some terrified voice echoed throughout the hollow.

The uniform landscape of *Ignis* became agitated. All throughout the farmland inhabitants stirred, tracing thick lines across the green. All of them were headed toward the ridge where the entryways into Living Block B protruded. Reddish light poured from the openings.

Mission fell in with the nearest throng going that way. Everyone gawked up at the all-illuminating core as they moved, but not her. She searched the crowd for Jacen. He was nowhere to be found.

They weren't far from her block, just a quarter of the way around the bowing surface. People all around her mentioned the word "blackout." It wasn't something inhabitants brought up lightly, and more than enough of them had survived the great one. She was young when it had happened, but this all felt like déjà vu. The core slowly failing, one spine-tingling wail at a time before darkness descended over her world.

The man in front of her stopped when they reached one of the three entry tunnels arranged around Block B's circular outcrop of rock and metal. She bumped into him. He was too stricken by the sight lying ahead of them to react.

The block's hatch was sealed, and the red color emanated from flames licking at the inside of its circular viewport.

"It's locked!" someone yelled from the entry controls. Mission squeezed through the crowd, and as she approached the hatch, a hand slapped the glass from within.

"They're trapped inside!" someone else yelled.

"Alora!" Mission screamed. "Jacen!"

She pounded on the hatch and tried to peek through the viewport. She'd rushed out of the block in such a hurry, thanks to that cryptic message, that she wasn't sure who was still inside. All that was visible through the glass was smoke, a hellish glow, and the silhouettes of scrambling inhabitants.

She backed away and bolted through the stunned populace, calling out for Jacen and Alora. She didn't see them anywhere, but the entirety of the *Ignis* gathered in numbers normally reserved for ceremonies and celebrations. There were too many faces to count.

The same scene awaited her at the next entrance into the block. By the time she hurried around to the last, the radiance of flames had diminished. So too had the movement of limbs within.

She squeezed her way back to the first hatch and shoved her face against the glass. Nothing stirred inside. "What's going on?" she questioned. Nobody had an answer.

"Out of my way!" a woman barked.

Cassiopeia, the head of the Collective, as well as a group of Collective members all in white, approached from the direction of the airlock hollow. Enforcers threw aside the inhabitants crowded at the entrance and struggled to maintain order. Mission's fingers had to be pried away from the metal. Cassiopeia's people broke open the hatch's manual controls and started fiddling with the wires beneath.

After a minute of working and ignoring the hysterical screams of their constituents, the hatch popped open. A powerful gust of wind rushed in due to the change in pressure, throwing everybody in the crowd onto their stomachs. Mission gathered herself quickly and used her slight stature to shove to the front. She and the members of the Collective froze only a few steps in, jaws dropping, eyes glued open.

"We're too late," Cassiopeia whispered.

"Why didn't the overrides work?" another member of the Collective asked, voice cracking. "Why didn't they work?"

A few of the conduits running along the walls of the tunnel sparked, the rock around them charred black. Bodies were piled along the passage, many of them with their clothing scorched. There was barely enough space to get down one at a time without stepping on their backs. Inhabitants at the rear ignored the enforcers and forced their way inside, throwing themselves onto bodies and pressing on their chests. Mission was too much in shock to do anything but walk slowly. Not a single one of the bodies breathed. Not even so much as a leg twitched.

She reached the living block caverns to find more of the same, only there, none of the bodies were burnt. And they all wore strangely tranquil expressions, eyes closed and lips drawn in neat lines. It was like they'd all been petrified or formed from wax. Some died hugging each other, others clinging to their sleeping nooks.

A rattling made her and everyone behind her jump. The familiar hum of air recyclers blustering then filled the room.

"I couldn't get them on . . ." the Collective member beside Cassiopeia mouthed. "Cassiopeia, I swear I couldn't."

Cassiopeia couldn't muster a response.

Mission stopped by the entry to the galley. Dozens more bodies were scattered within. A mound of them lay by the coverless entrance to an air duct. The scrawny leg of a child stuck out.

"No!" She ran over and found the young boy Harold, whom Jacen liked to tease. Scrapes from fingernails ran up and down his leg. He'd opened the duct and tried to escape, but the inhabitants piled behind him clogged the way in a panic.

A conduit sparked behind the long serving counter. Mission darted over to find half of chef Jorah's face seared down

to the bone. He'd been preparing for that morning's feed, and
a line of bowls along the counter were already half-filled with
blended greens and insects.

Mission grew dizzy. She stumbled out of the galley and used
a nearby sleeping nook to balance herself. When she marshaled
the nerve to look up again, her gaze locked on the illuminated
entrance to the med-bay. Birthmother Nixu was sprawled out
at the bottom of the silvery ramp. Dead.

Mission staggered over and kneeled by her side. "No . . ."
When she rolled the body over, Samson was cradled in her
limp arms.

"No, no, no." Mission had to look away. She started to
breathe faster and faster until she was hyperventilating. Then
the light of the med-bay drew her attention, and she realized
who might be up there.

"Alora!" she rasped. She scuttled up the ramp, eyes half-open,
as if coming up for air after a lengthy swim. The nursery was
filled with silent children and Birthmothers who'd been trapped
in the block. They'd suffocated. All those times Mission had
been locked under the floor just became a reality. Her greatest
fear realized.

Mission couldn't bear to look at any of them long, but
none of the bodies belonged to Alora. She ran across the facility toward her room, struggling to breathe. She didn't notice
Paul lying facedown right outside her door, and tripped over
his outstretched arm. As she fell, a thin stream of electrical current shot over her head

The crackle when it struck the wall compelled her to roll
over, and a second blast hit right where she had been. Mission
sprang to her feet and charged. Another bolt flashed over her
shoulder as she ducked; then she crashed into the man standing
by her terminal. He flew back into the screens.

She grabbed his wrists and forced him to aim his stunner at the ceiling. "What did you do!" she screamed. Even though he was larger and stronger, rage fueled her. She pried the stunner out of his hands, but when she did, she saw his face.

"Jacen?" she muttered.

That second of indecision allowed him to get his arm around her throat and twist her body. He squeezed and drew her to the ground. She kicked and swung her arms blindly, and just as her eyes started to roll back into her head, her fingers found the grip of a pulse pistol resting at his hip. She squeezed the trigger. The sound it released was little more than a whistle, but a bullet shredded the holster and left a gash in the metal floor.

She broke free and backed away slowly. Her hand quaked as she aimed the weapon at him, too perplexed to form words. Jacen raised his hands. His gaze darted between the pulse-pistol in her hand and the stunner on the floor. His eyes were bloodshot, but other than that, he was completely clean. Not covered in grime after a shift like he usually was.

Mission reached the exit, and her foot brushed Paul's corpse. She looked down, then back at Jacen.

"Mission!" a voice suddenly shouted through her doorway. The sound startled her, and she turned and fired without thinking.

The gun slipped from her fingers. Another Jacen stood in front of her, this one's clothes dirty from the sewers. His hands peeled away from his chest to reveal a hole the size of a fist cutting straight through, ribs splintering flesh and sinew. He crumpled forward, and Mission lunged to catch him before his face smashed against the floor.

"Jace?" Mission whispered. "Jacen!" She shook his body and frantically tapped his cheek. "Jacen, stay with me."

His jaw shuddered as he tried to speak. A gob of blood was all that came out.

"Jacen, please. Help!" she shrieked. "Somebody help!"

She pressed her hands over the wound to try to stem the bleeding like she'd been trained to, promising him he'd be okay over and over.

"Jacen, stay awake . . . Please . . ." She looked around for something, anything she could use. That was when she saw that the Jacen who'd been standing by her terminal had vanished along with his stunner. The screen of her terminal, which had displayed the strange message that drove her into the sewers, was completely shattered.

Someone pulled her off Jacen. The real one. She screamed at the top of her lungs and tore free of them, diving back over his body. She lifted his head. This Jacen's eyes were stuck open and shimmering like two glass orbs. More hands seized her and ripped her away.

* * *

"What is this?" I yelled. Nobody responded. Then the feed I was watching flickered, and Mission was back in the pipes, searching for Jacen. The entire sequence of horrible events restarted.

"No," I whimpered. "No!" I couldn't use my eyes or thoughts to control the screen. Real life or VR, it was locked. Everything leading up to Mission shooting Jacen played all the way through again. And then again. Even if I closed my eyes, I could still hear everything.

Every single scream . . .

CHAPTER 12

I lost count of how many times I'd watched Mission leave the pipeline I'd sent her to and return home to see Block B filled with death. Fixer Lance, guised as Jacen, attempting to take her in for a memory wipe and screwing up. Her watching the life drain out of the young man who was her closest friend in her world before she was dragged away by enforcers, drenched in Jacen's blood.

My mind grew numb. I'd given up on trying to close my eyes or drown out the sound. The gunshot that pierced the real Jacen went off for what I imagined to be the thousandth time, only finally, the screen was pulled away from my head.

Silence at last. The screen winked away. My eyes stung. My vision was blurred by crusted tears.

"What's going on?" I spluttered. I wasn't sure how long I'd been fastened in place watching Mission, but it felt like I was using my chapped lips for the very first time. "Where am I?"

"Home," a strong, familiar voice replied.

Mr. Helix leaned in front of me. For once, he wasn't wearing a visor at all, not even raised on top of his head. And his young visage, the one he used in the VR, was gone. His hair was thick but gray. His skin clean of all imperfections and birthmarks. It wasn't wrinkled, but seemed stretched from aesthetic surgery. Only a crease on his forehead was pronounced by the scowl that he wore like a third eyebrow.

This was the real him.

I looked from side to side. My arms were strapped to the armrests of a Network brain infuser attached to a med-bot, much like Minah's only shinier and more delicate. On either side of my head, neural nodes shone blue, though I couldn't turn far enough to see anything but their aura.

"Home?" I asked. "VORA, what's going on?"

No answer. My smart-dwelling was dark, like when the Unplugged had visited. She couldn't hear me.

"Don't play dumb with me, Asher," Mr. Helix said. "You know exactly why you're here."

He stepped back, and my vision adjusted enough to discern more. Behind him, at the entrance to my unit, stood four security bots just like the one from the Outskirts.

Public safety bots. A brain infuser. Memories of what had happened jolted me. Vivienne had told Mr. Helix what I'd done. I wasn't sure how much she'd seen, but enough to know that I was somewhere I shouldn't have been.

"Sir, I swear, it wasn't what it looked like!" I said. "I was only trying—"

"Quiet!" he snapped. "Perhaps you thought you could erase the message you sent and I'd never realize. But thanks to some loyal volunteers, that wasn't the case."

"Bots, leave us," Mr. Helix demanded, turning his attention.

"He has been deemed a threat to society," one of them answered. "It is not safe to be alone with him."

"He's not going anywhere. Leave us." The human-subservient bots swiveled together in one uniform motion, torsos before legs, and stomped out of the room. The lift doors closed behind them.

Mr. Helix paced in front of me, deep in thought. In the VR studio he'd never shown evidence of the slight limp he now had. "Did you really hate my idea so much that you would betray me like this?" He no longer sounded angry, but wounded.

"I promise, sir. That had nothing to do with it."

"Then what is it? All our years together." He grabbed my restrained hands. "You directly contacted an inhabitant during a live broadcast and tried to conceal it. You put everything we've worked so hard to build at jeopardy. You violated your own damn contract!"

"I know, and I'm sorry. But I would never do anything to hurt it, you know that. I . . . I love your show more than anything . . ." The words came out slowly. I knew deep down it wasn't the whole truth, but I'd never been able to fully admit it to myself before then.

It was always Mission.

From the moment she'd emerged on the same day as me to now. She was everything to me. She wasn't only the star of *Ignis: Live*, she was the star of every worthwhile memory I'd ever had.

I loved her. The word was as foreign to me as the Outskirts, but somehow, I knew it was true. Because only something that intense could drive me to do all of the insane things I had since she came within even a sniff of trouble.

"Then why!" Mr. Helix pled.

"I couldn't let you kill her!" The truth blurted out of me before I had a chance to second-guess. Watching Mission, tortured again and again by the grief of shooting Jacen, had made it all so clear. "It would've been a mistake. There's never been an inhabitant like her. The viewers would have been heartbroken."

He sighed. "Is there anything more human than heart-break?"

"They would never have forgiven you."

"They would never have known, and they never will. Sure, I pushed a little too hard with that hazard, and they failed to correct it in time. But such is life. It isn't for you to decide."

"It isn't for any of us to decide, right? That's the point."

"There is no point!" He slammed on the armrest of the in-fuser. "It's my world! My creation. Everything that happens on that vessel happens because I want it to! If I want to push the boundaries, I can. If I want to shift the paradigm, I can. Not you! I am their core. Me! And the viewers love me for what I give them, because I know exactly what they want to see. What have you ever made that anybody gives a damn about?"

I swallowed. I'd never heard him so irate in my life. Letting him down had been my greatest fear since the day I stepped into his studio, yet all I could think about then was Mission pulling the trigger. I couldn't stop seeing it. The way her face contorted when she saw that Jacen was the victim, like her whole world had shattered, all because of what I'd done.

"Was what you made me watch real?" I asked softly.

"Everything that happens on the *Ignis* is real, as you know," he said. "And everything you saw aired except for her interactions with Lance, including the unprovoked murder of the man she loved. Although, considering how much you've been secretly interfering in her life, I would have thought that man was you."

"What have you done with her?"

"Me? Lance failed and will be replaced once things smooth over, just like you will be. The Collective has detained Mission for stealing a weapon from the core and murdering another in-habitant. The viewers don't know any differently."

"But she saw him."

A grimace flashed across his face. "Not for the first time, according to Lance."

My heart skipped a beat. Lance didn't care much about anything except getting his fix of excitement aboard the *Ignis* and redeeming his public profile. He wouldn't have voluntarily reported all the details of what had happened during the spacing, as it made both of us look bad, but Mr. Helix must've done some digging around while I was under. I don't know why I thought I could hide anything from him. *Ignis* was his own show.

I felt like that twisted Unplugged must have, kneeling on the dais with his eyes gouged out. How could I be so blind?

"Will you have her mind wiped, then?" I asked. Her? I was going to lose the show—lose my chair—and all I could think about was her, locked away in the core, thinking that Jacen's death was her fault.

"You have already guaranteed her far worse," he replied. "Two Jacens? To the Collective, she sounds like a lunatic who couldn't handle her new appointment. She could have died peacefully with the others, been recycled and honored by her people. Now she'll be spaced as a homicidal criminal. The viewers who raised her to such fame will bear witness to her fall. I suppose I should thank you. She really is quite the draw. Viewership is escalating even higher than I ever anticipated. We're now the clear number one program in all categories."

Number one again, and he gave me some of the credit. I should've been thrilled, but instead I yanked at my restraints and tried to break free. They weren't like the ones in the Outskirts. All I did was bruise my wrists. "Mr. Hel—Craig, please. You have to help her."

"She's beyond help. Under the constant watch of the Collective and in the core, even I can't touch her. And it's all because of you." He sat on the arm of my couch. "I placed my trust in you, Asher. Gave you access to my terminal, my work . . . to everything. This is how you repay me?"

"I swear, my only concerns were for Miss—for the show!"

I couldn't think straight. It was like a war was being waged inside my conscious mind. I wanted to defend myself, to say whatever it took to get back in the good graces of my mentor, but none of that came out. I could hear all the excuses I'd provided myself after leaving Minah's brain infuser about why Mission needed to be saved for the show's sake, when the real truth was so much simpler.

It was because *I* couldn't bear to see her go. Because *I* was weak.

"For the show," he scoffed, as if my insecurity was written all over my expression. "Who knows how many other times you bent the rules for your own favorite inhabitants."

"Never!"

"You've made a fool out of me, Asher. All this time I've always thought, here is a man who understands my vision; who will stand at my side until I die or the *Ignis* stops spinning. Here is a *friend*." His mouth was trembling by then, as if he were in pain. "You think I'd rather deal with Frederick every day?"

"I know . . ." I could hardly breathe. I had to take a break between every sentence. Otherwise, I'd pass out. "I made a mistake, Craig. Don't let her be punished for it."

"This isn't about her! It's about what you did."

"I know, and I'll do anything to make it up to you! I'll work every day for as long as you want. I'll live logged in. You can even monitor anything I do. All these years I've only tried to do what's best for you and your vision. It will be like that again."

"Do you really think I'd ever let you near *my* show again? It's over, Asher. Your actions have been reported to the High Earth Network, and you have been designated for delistment for violating the terms of our volunteer agreement, refusing medical advice, and erasing data without creator approval.

"Craig, please!"

"You can have the honor of joining Mission in being exiled from your people, and share the blame for you both."

"You have to help her." Again, I tried to pull and kick and twist my head. It was futile.

"Listen to you fawning over her like some crazed fanboy. How did I miss this? You focused on her so much, but I only ever thought it was because of the moving content she provided. You got too close to them, Asher. Lost focus. I told you on day one not to get tunnel vision."

"You're right. Punish me. Blame me, but I beg you, not her."

"I don't blame her. She's an inhabitant, like any of the others. They're here for our entertainment. It was the choice they and their delisted parents made. To be stars rather than waste away in the Outskirts in ignominy."

"Please, sir. I'm begging you!"

He circled me once, then leaned down beside my ear. If I'd had a lifeband on, it would've exploded I was so agitated. I only noticed then that mine was nowhere to be found.

"Maybe that nightmare really did a number," he said.

"It wasn't a nightmare," I said, desperate. "It was real. I was attacked, here, and I haven't been able to think straight since."

"As ridiculous as that is, you'd lied before it."

"For the show!"

"Maybe it was all an act to distract me from what you planned on doing. It doesn't matter anymore. Upon delistment, a resident is supposed to have certain memories erased. The location of his home, any close friends, the secrets of his work if he does any. But you see, Asher, not only you can bend the rules."

"W . . . what are you talking about?"

"An exiled resident is allowed to have one person with them at the end. And so here I am, the only friend you ever claim to have had. The bot is supposed to wipe your brain right now, but forgetting what you've done to Mission would be a mercy without lesson. You have to learn how dangerous it is to meddle in things that can't be changed. There's something broken in you, Asher. You need help."

"No . . ."

"You looked me straight in the eyes and lied on more than one occasion. That's the very deceptive, egotistical nature that led our ancestors to war and ruin. It's why we needed High Earth to save us. To focus us on the things that really matter. Our beautiful minds."

"That's not me!"

"We were going to take chaos and, together, mold it into something beautiful. We were going to show the people of High Earth an *Ignis* like they'd never imagined."

"We still can, Craig! I can fix all of this." Another lie spilling out of me. Mission and I were where we were because of my actions, that's all. There was nothing left to fix. I'd betrayed the only person I ever cared about impressing because of the brilliant, beautiful, green-eyed girl I'd entered the world with.

Mr. Helix shook his head. He looked like he was on the verge of tears. "I don't know. Maybe this is all my fault and I did push you too hard. You broke my heart, Asher," he whispered. "I hope the Outskirts help you find yourself again. This is for the best."

He lowered the OptiVisor back over my head; then the infuser chair switched on. Only, the med-bot remained inactive and Mr. Helix controlled the operation. It made my ears tingle, similar to how things had gone at Minah's place, except the process never proceeded beyond that. Instead, the OptiVisor switched back on and continued to loop what had happened to Mission and Jacen.

"No, not again," I cried. "VORA, please activate. You're supposed to protect me. VORA!"

I screamed, but my protests fell on deaf ears. I couldn't even hear them myself. Just the deafening *bang* of Mission shooting Jacen over, and over, and over again . . . because of me . . .

CHAPTER 13

My body tumbled across wet plasticrete as I came to. At some
point during my repeat viewings of Mission, I was put under.
The security bots that had tossed me out into the Outskirts were
already ascending on the lift back to High Earth. The brain infuser, even though it hadn't actually done anything, had my
head feeling foggy and my body dehydrated—like I'd been put
though a molecular re-assembler.

I could barely open my eyes I was so exhausted. All those
hours of watching Mission's life come undone and not a minute
of sleep.

I pawed at the street, scooping ruddy water into my mouth
as fast as I could. When I could no longer bear the taste of dirt,
I got to my feet and staggered back toward the lift, which was
guarded by a handful of heavily armed public safety bots. Security drones soared overhead like gulls along the bluffs of an
ancient coast, now a wall of synthetic materials.

Scanning arrays illuminated me, projected from a bot standing at the gate. Its pale, pupilless eye-lenses stared blankly over

my shoulder even as it addressed me. "The lifts may only be accessed by High Earth residents."

I pointed toward the rack of rain ponchos behind the gate, hand shaking from the cold. "May I have one?" I took a step forward. The bot raised its arm. Built into its wrist was the barrel of some manner of pulse weaponry likely able to tear my head from my shoulders with a single shot.

"The lifts may only be accessed by High Earth residents," it repeated. "Back away."

I studied the lift, noticing something that I hadn't on my last visit to the Outskirts. The area where the street met the base of the wall was discolored, brown in spots, deep crimson in others. Slightly higher up, similar blemishes were smeared across the surface, with tiny appendages at their fringes. Fingerprints. I quickly turned away.

The Outskirts were exactly how I'd left them—rainy and dreary. They let me keep my resident clothing at least, but without proper upkeep, I'd soon look like the rest of the delisted rabble wandering the winding streets with no purpose. And it wasn't enough to keep my head warm. Chilly drops of water battered my hair, and now that I'd turned into the wind, it peppered my eyes in such excess that I had to hold my hand over my brow just to see.

An entire life of providing my services to *Ignis: Live*, and Mr. Helix didn't even leave me with a poncho. Not that I deserved one. I could see it in his eyes how much I'd hurt him after he placed so much faith in me.

How could I have been so foolish to forsake my responsibilities?

To fall head over heels for a character?

She isn't just a character, I reminded myself. But it hardly seemed to matter now. She was so far away. Untouchable. Unattainable. And I threw it all away for a dream.

My hands started to tremble in self-loathing. I'd upset plenty of women on VR dates when I failed to connect with them, but never somebody whose opinion actually mattered to me before. I'd never had anybody else in my life with trust to betray. I should've just asked Mr. Helix to target a different block as a personal favor. Came clean that I'd developed a detrimental attachment to Mission instead of denying it to myself, then had my mind scrubbed a bit. We had the history. He might've listened.

My head sank as I started my solemn trudge into the heart of the Outskirts. My new home. The one I deserved.

I was greeted by the countless grimy people scrambling to find any way to watch or experience High Earth programming. My new people. When I first visited, I never cared to wonder what any of them did to wind up in exile. Now it was all I could think about. And despite my clothing, none of them flocked to me as a resident. Like they could see right through me and tell.

I studied the vibrant signs for VR dens and data-sliced show bars. Men and women lying on the street corners, broken and mutated. A visiting resident stood a few corners down. He was so obvious. They surrounded him, begging and pawing at his feet, worshiping him. I wondered how long it'd be before I'd do the same, desperate for a data fix.

That same old Unplugged preacher shouted from his intersection. My newly blinded assailant, however, was nowhere to be found.

"Open your eyes!" the man shouted. "High Earth seeks to take your minds. To blind you with waking dreams and fantasies. Remove yourselves from their world and dare to experience ours! The techno-revolution didn't raise us, it destroyed us! Remember the stars!" His incessant raving seemed to be ignored by everyone, yet it was impossible not to hear.

Was I now fated to become like them? To want and to

thirst and to lose all the sense of worth and belonging being a resident of High Earth provided until I didn't even care about the life I was missing. To descend into darkness like so many of our ancestors had.

I dragged my weary legs down a street in the opposite direction, leaving the echo of the Unplugged's voice behind. I had no idea where to go or what to do, but it seemed wise to avoid Minah's shop after what had happened. I stayed under the tin overhang of a sagging structure, rain banging on top like a million tiny creatures with hammers.

"Hey, you. Resie!" someone said to me. His voice was ragged, a cough between words. He took my arm and drew me through an archway without giving me a chance to answer. We were beneath an overhang of bent metal sheets, the spaces between openings covered by drapes.

"I can always tell when one of you is down here for the real thing," he said. "We'll accept anything from your side of the wall."

"I'm not . . ."

Words escaped me when he drew back one of the drapes. Inside the rusty room, a woman lay on a mattress. She was completely naked, her one scrawny leg spread wide open and the other missing at the hip. She wagged her finger for me to enter.

"A few bits of data and she'll do anything you want," the man said.

She swept her one leg and used the wall to rise to her foot in one graceful motion. Her undernourished body glistened from the rain leaking through the ceiling. She didn't say a word. She simply drew one hand around my thighs as she circled me, using a chain on the ceiling to hop with only her single leg. Her touch made my whole body tingle in a way I'd never experienced outside a VR. I couldn't speak.

"How about it, sugar?" she whispered. Her breath tickled my earlobe.

"No reason to browse anywhere else, resie," the salesman said. "You won't find better. Or if she isn't your speed, I got boys who'll—"

"Oh, he's my speed," the woman said. She took my hand and grazed her navel with my fingers. Then she lowered them, lower and lower until I was finally able to squeak out words.

"I'm not a resident!"

The woman looked appalled. The salesman grabbed my wrist, noticed a lack of resident-issue lifeband, and shoved me. I tripped over the walkway and skidded across a puddle.

"What the hell is wrong with you!" he barked. "Change your damn clothes." He pulled the woman back inside.

I went to stand, and someone bumped into me. Whoever it was glared at me through half a broken OptiVisor and nudged me in the gut again on the way by.

The blow sent me to my knees, gasping as rain pelted my back. Somebody else chuckled. A cluster of three delisted women sat around a nearby sewer cover, grinning. Their teeth were missing, yellow or warped—my ostensible future without the whitenings VORA provided. In the center of them was a holopad. They watched an episode of *Molecular Nation* on what appeared to be a legitimate feed. Though it was impossible to hear anything over the rain.

I crawled toward them and took a seat. "Back off," one growled.

She tilted the holopad away from me, and her friends repositioned themselves. Sharing a seat wouldn't waste any of whoever's data it was, but that didn't matter. Here, every bit was precious. You either found a way to procure them as legal donations or illegally, or you didn't.

I slid a bit closer anyway. The nearest woman bared her rotten teeth without averting her gaze from the holopad. They were like ravenous carnivores of the ancient world, protecting a fresh carcass from rival animals.

"I . . . I don't want to watch," I said, starting to shiver from the cold water filling my clothing. The fiber was water resistant, but that didn't keep it from sneaking in through my collar or up my sleeves. "I n . . . n . . . need somewhere to stay. Where . . . where do I stay?"

The woman raised her bony arm and pointed from one side of me to the other. Then she flashed a grin and returned to watching the show.

That was it? People in the Outskirts just squatted wherever they wanted? Every dilapidated structure was a home? Every overhang a sleep-pod?

I stood and continued down the street, more confused than I'd ever been. When I'd emerged from the synth-womb, VORA told me exactly what to do. I had my assigned smart-dwelling, my VORA, and anything I'd need to keep me healthy. Nourishment, exercise, interaction, mental stimulation, all at the tips of my fingers. Now I was utterly lost.

Why couldn't I have just kept my head down and done what I was supposed to for Mr. Helix? Why did I think I could control what happened to any inhabitant or to . . .

Mission.

There she was, her face plastered on a crooked monitor jutting from a wall in front of me. The sight alone made my heart plummet. If anybody in the universe was in a worse place than me, it was her. Imprisoned and destined to be spaced for a crime that I'd committed.

I approached the sign and realized that the adjoined building was a show bar. The tinted glass storefront didn't allow me to see anything but the glow of screens beyond, and a pair of bouncers stood at the entrance. They both wore red, and clearly not by coincidence, since they also bore matching tattoos of an asteroid on the tops of their hands.

"Move along now," one of them grumbled. "Ain't no reason for a resie to be in here."

I pressed my face against the glass to try to see inside. "I'm not."

The bulkier of the two pushed me back. "Whatever you're looking for, it ain't here, resie."

"I'm not one," I answered louder. "A resident."

The big bouncer shined a tiny scanner into my eyes. It buzzed a negative-seeming sound.

His partner laughed. "He's telling the truth. Look, no bot guard, and he doesn't even have a lifeband."

"You remember that, Jim? Memory wiped, wind up here, no way to go back."

"Like it was yesterday," replied Jim. "Poor resie. Like a baby out here."

"Ca . . . can I get in?" I asked. I was freezing, and it felt nothing like the way VRs simulated it. I could feel the cold deep in my bones.

The bouncer—Jim, apparently—patted me down. "Doesn't feel like you got much to offer."

The other grabbed the lapel of my shirt and pulled on it. "How about this, Jim? Down here fresh. Only been out in the rain a few days at most."

Jim strolled around me, getting a good look at my clothing. He lifted my leg and examined my resident-issue shoes. Sleek and seamless, fashioned out of the finest fiber-weave in existence and nearly impenetrable. Soles still in perfect condition. They'd only even left my tower that one time.

"Keep the clothes," he said. "You trade in those shoes, you can enter."

"My shoes?" I asked.

"Only thing the boss will have any interest in. Save your pants for next time."

"What's in 'there,' exactly?"

"This is the Ignis Farmers, friend. What do you think?" He turned to his partner and sneered. "He really is fresh. You get in, you can keep warm and dry. Watch *Ignis: Live* on the boss's feed as long as you want without a hitch. Best slicer in the Outskirts, he is. We got food and water, too. You can stay for a year for all I care, but as soon as you step out, it's gonna cost something else to get back in."

"Your clothes maybe," the other bouncer snickered.

"So what's it gonna be?" Jim asked. "Shoes, or maybe you can head down to one of them slimy Nation gang bars and watch moving static."

I wriggled my toes, the only part of me that remained dry. Then I considered the rest of me. Everything inside sounded perfect. A way to escape the rain and rest my legs. A way to check in on *Ignis* after what'd happened. A feeling of hope warmed my insides. Maybe Mr. Helix had acknowledged my final pleas and figured out a way to prove Mission's innocence to her people. That might make all this worth it.

"I'll come in," I decided. I kneeled and hit the switch on my sole, which loosened the fibers comprising my shoes and allowed me to slip them off. One size fits all. Jim snatched them from me before I even had a chance to stand.

"Boss is gonna love those," the other bouncer said.

Jim smacked him in the head. "They ain't for him, idiot. Go on in, former resie. Enjoy." He opened a manual door and ushered me inside, never once taking a break from admiring my shoes to look up.

The stench of sweat and urine blasted my nostrils. It was enough to make me nauseous, and the room was so sweltering, I had to squint to keep my eyes from tearing. All the promising things Jim had noted were present—heat, food, the show, and a place to sleep—but the image in my head couldn't have been more inaccurate.

People were crammed into the large rectangular space, legs and arms threading, bodies on top of each other—a literal tapestry of flesh. Some wore only their undergarments, others nothing at all. A few slept, using backs for pillows and legs for blankets, but most stared at the expansive screens arranged along the walls of the space. Each displayed a live broadcast feed from *Ignis: Live,* grainy because there was no question in my mind at all . . . they were all sliced. The fraudulent slicer who ran the place apparently wasn't trading for data to stay legitimate.

I crept over limbs. Against one of the walls was a counter with two large bowls arranged along it. Each was filled with thick, soppy strands of what looked like dark green lettuce wrapping some sort of flaky substance. Latent knowledge from the synth-womb brain infusers quickly reminded me that it was seaweed around grilled fish.

The presentation was sloppy, pieces spilling out onto the counter and the floor, like everyone in the room had yanked some out with their bare hands. And the smell was so pungent I already missed sweat. As I passed, another goon in red arrived with a small crate filled with more of the stuff and dumped some into each bowl.

It was repulsive. Eating real, living creatures torn out of the risen oceans like a bunch of ancient savages. Yet just seeing food had my stomach rumbling. I dipped my hand in slowly and scooped some out with two fingers. It felt like what I would imagine brains might. As soon as I put it in my mouth, I had to fight the urge to vomit.

I ran over to a spout sticking out of the wall. Someone was already there, head tilted upside down and working a pump to get brown rainwater to drain out. I pushed him aside and guzzled as much as I could to wash out the salty taste. Iron and grime in the water replaced it.

I fell backward, people's limbs parting to make room for my body. My back was propped up by another, and I had to bend at the knees to fit after the space by the spout refilled.

"Would you quiet down?" Someone slapped the back of my head. It was impossible to know who with so many arms all over the place.

I steadied my breathing and studied the screens. It made me more nauseous than I already was, knowing I was about to willingly watch an illegal feed. Like all the other rabble around me getting off on Mr. Helix's brilliant vision and giving nothing back.

I supposed I had to start my life of being delisted somewhere. There wasn't anything more I could do to place him or *Ignis: Live* in jeopardy.

Dozens of views from *Ignis* surrounded us, but I was only interested in finding one. I no longer had access to all the thousands of cameras, so I had to scour the live feeds like any average viewer would. A fair number always focused on people in the farms, pipes, living blocks, and med-bays. Presently, most depicted the cleanup after what had happened in Living Block B, along with the dismantling of the celebration that never happened.

Bodies were being carried to the recycler, which sat in a hollow similar to the airlock's but on the opposite side of the vessel. Its cover sealed after the corpses were placed in, the tiny rifts around it glowing red. I knew what was happening within.

They were being drained and pulverized, to be reused as fertilizer for the farms.

Per the laws of energy, theirs would remain within the *Ignis's* man-made environment forever, but Mission's wouldn't. Examples had to be made to maintain order. Directly behind me, I finally spotted the single live feed depicting something other than Block B, the recycler, or Birthmothers and their partners starting the process of rebuilding the population in their beds.

I felt a surge of anxious energy, the kind that my old life-band would warn me about. I propped myself up onto my knees to get a better view.

Mission was within a cell in the core. With the sound feed playing simultaneously from every screen throughout the room, I had to really focus to hear what was happening.

[Ignis Feed Location]
Core Cell 3
<Camera 2>

Mission sat alone on the floor of a tiny cell. It wasn't as cramped as her hole beneath the floor, or as dark, but the locked door had her heart racing. For the first time in her life, she was within the inhabitable structure of the core. She'd spent a lifetime looking up at it and wondering what it was like inside. Now she'd do anything to get out.

Its appearance was similar to that of the med-bays, though with far more exposed mechanical equipment. All of it was spotless, tended to assiduously by the members of the Collective to maintain the core's integrity. It was also much louder. Constant vibrations from the fusion reactor in the core's center resonated through the walls.

Recessed into the floor directly in front of her, a viewport the size of her head offered a view of the greenery spanning the *Ignis*'s inner surface. Far below, it slowly coursed to the left as the core rotated faster and independently in order to generate its own sense of gravity.

Mission couldn't bear to look though. Instead, she squeezed her eyes and tried to imagine being within that big open space. She absentmindedly reached for the pendant Jacen had made for her, only to find it was no longer around her neck.

The door opened with a *whoosh* and startled her.

Cassiopeia, Head of the Collective, stepped through. Her disposition was more dour than usual.

"Cassiopeia, is he okay?" Mission asked. "Please, I have to know if he made it. Did you save him?"

After she'd inadvertently shot Jacen, enforcers carried her away, flailing. She hadn't been permitted to see or hear anything about his status since, and the uncertainty was eating away at her. This was the third time Cassiopeia had visited to drill her with questions about what had happened, even though Mission could hardly understand it herself.

The message. Two Jacens. Sometimes, the removal of a conception implant could lead to unexpected spikes in hormones, and she wondered if something like that had driven her crazy. Maybe she'd hallucinated the entire thing, even the blackout, and Jacen and Alora were back home waiting for her.

Cassiopeia said nothing. She signaled the door to close behind her and knelt across from Mission. From her belt, she drew the pulse-pistol that had drilled a hole in Jacen and waved it over the viewport.

The air fled Mission's lungs. If she hadn't dreamed up the weapon, then that meant . . .

"Where did you get this?" Cassiopeia asked calmly, voice muffled. "And no more lies."

"Somebody attacked me," Mission said. "It looked like Jacen—"

"So you're saying he stole this and tried to murder you? That this was self-defense?"

"No! Well, yes, but it wasn't him. The person just looked like him, but then the real Jacen came to help me and . . . I didn't mean to shoot anybody!" Her mind ran in circles. Even with the pulse-pistol right in front of her, so much didn't make sense. Nobody could look that much like Jacen unless he had an identical twin, and the core made sure prospective mates had the lowest possible chance to birth multiple children, which would skew population numbers.

In the chaos of the day, Mission had forgotten something vital . . . she'd seen this before, at the spacing of those Blackout Generation kids. How could she have forgotten? She'd explicitly seen Jacen in the sewers, but he'd denied having been there at all. What in the world was going on? Nothing made sense.

"You admit to pulling the trigger?" Cassiopeia asked.

"It was an accident!"

"You're telling me whoever this *supposed* double of Jacen's is, he managed to steal a weapon that can only be found here, in the core, and snuck into a Mother's room during a catastrophe just to murder you? Next you'll say this imposter caused that error too?"

"I . . . I don't know . . ." The more she thought about it, the more her mind unraveled. She was about to start hyperventilating when Cassiopeia slammed on the viewport, causing the gun to spin across the glass.

"Stop lying to me, Mission!" she shouted. "This was meant to be a day of celebration! Fifty years, carrying the flame of humanity! Instead, two hundred and thirteen people are dead because of an error in the Block B fire-suppression system. One of them was a member of the Collective. A dear friend. And he was there specifically to procreate with you."

Mission looked stunned. "You think I caused this?"

"My best operators discovered traces of expunged message coding in your busted terminal. Alora tells me how nervous you were about your new position. I'm starting to see a pattern. What I can't decide is why you would attack Jacen."

Mission edged forward.

"Alora is okay?" she asked. That was the first bit of good news she'd heard in a day.

"She was visiting the core at the time . . . fortunately. I'm trying my best to believe it wasn't a coincidence, but someone was trying to hide something on your terminal. Only you two had access recently."

"It wasn't her! The message . . . it . . . someone was threatening me. They lied and said they saw me with Jacen, and that they'd tell everyone if I didn't meet them in the pipelines."

"Saw you with him . . . how?"

Mission bit her lip. She didn't have to explain any further.

"I see," Cassiopeia said.

"As soon as I left to go find the messenger, the fire started," Mission explained. "I don't know who it was, but that's what happened. I swear. When I got back, everyone was dead, and I was attacked in my room."

"By this Jacen clone?" Cassiopeia asked.

Mission nodded.

"And conveniently this mysterious message allowed you to escape."

Cassiopeia picked up the pulse-pistol, studied it for a few seconds, and then stowed it in her belt.

"Do you want to know what I think?" she asked. "I think you couldn't stand the responsibility of caring for your entire block, of losing the freedom Alora unwisely permitted her Birth-mothers compared to how I'd done it. So you fiddled with the programming of the core to free yourself, and cut off the air to every room in your block except your own."

"I would never do that!"

"Alora told us how Jacen cared for you! And now I'm hear-ing you violated the law by lying with him after having your contraceptive removed."

"What, no? We didn't do that."

"But you wanted to. Typical Blackout Generation, unable to control their perilous urges."

"I . . ." Mission swallowed her words back. Of all the un-truths spewing forth from Cassiopeia, that was one part that was true. Mission's mind took her back to the kiss in their favorite place—the way his chest pressed against hers so that she could feel his heartbeat, and how he stared at her, panting, after their lips broke apart. Now he was gone.

"I think Jacen came to murder Paul so that you wouldn't have to lie with anybody else," Cassiopeia said. "And instead, he saw what you were really planning to do to get out of a po-sition you never wanted. So you shot him to keep your little secret quiet!"

"That's not true!"

"Or maybe Alora just couldn't stand the thought of stepping down, so she got rid of everybody instead. Everybody except her favorite daughter."

"No!"

The back of Cassiopeia's hand crashed into Mission's face. "Stop lying to me! I lived through the Great Blackout and saw what it did to us. I won't stand by and watch the beginning of another one."

"I'm not . . ." Mission whimpered.

Cassiopeia stood to her full, impressive height, then exhaled. "Whatever you or Jacen or Alora were up to, we'll get to the bottom of it. Unfortunately, now we'll never know his side of things."

Mission glanced up, eyes wet. Her bloodied lips were quivering, barely able to form words. "He's dead?"

Cassiopeia's hard façade broke momentarily, and she bobbed her head. "The wound you put in him was too grave."

Mission slumped back against the wall of her cell, all the fight leaving her. She was in too much shock to weep. She didn't want to believe it. She couldn't even imagine an *Ignis* without him in it. Or walking along Block B without the chance of spotting his wry grin around any corner.

"If you take the stance that the shot was not fired in self-defense, I have no choice but to charge you in violation of our first law," Cassiopeia said. "The Collective will convene shortly to hear your testimonies and decide if your and Alora's fates will match that of so many of your undistinguished generation. If it were up to me, you'd be tried tomorrow, but thanks to whatever happened to Block B, there are more pressing matters to attend to."

Cassiopeia opened the door and went to step out. She froze in the entrance. "Enjoy your last few days, Mission," she said, her voice betraying a tremble. "It's more than you deserve for betraying us all."

* * *

I watched tears gather in the corners of Cassiopeia's eyes, but she never looked back, so Mission never saw them. Then the door shut.

"Don't lock me in!" Mission yelled, lunging at the door and

pounding. "Please don't lock me in again. Please!" Her breathing hastened until she fell back, finally giving in to the hyperventilation she appeared to be fighting for hours.

"Mission . . ." I whimpered. Her name was no sooner out of my mouth than someone suddenly grabbed me by my hair and dragged me on my back across the floor. My flailing limbs kicked and punched the canvas of bodies all around us.

"Help me!" I screamed. People groaned in pain as I accidentally struck them; nobody moved. Only those I touched even bothered to turn toward what was happening.

A door on the other end of the room swung open, and whoever dragged me stopped, but didn't let go. I clawed fruitlessly at the fingers gripping a handful of my hair. A man stood in the doorway, bearded, tired-looking and garbed in red. On his hand was the same tattoo I'd seen on the bouncers outside. The room at his back was illuminated by the glow of a vast terminal station with dozens of monitors. I guessed that he was the expert slicer the bouncers were talking about. People like him had the technical prowess to rip feeds from the High Earth Network and keep them from being shut down.

"What's the meaning of this?" the slicer barked. "This man is under the Ignis Farmers' protection!"

"He has business with Minah Dontari," my captor replied calmly.

The slicer grimaced, then nodded. "Fine, but take it outside."

"Gladly."

The grainy feeds throughout the room flickered; two went black. The slicer turned and rushed back to his terminal, slamming the door behind him. My captor immediately started dragging me again before I could get a word out.

When we emerged into the rain and the cold, he threw

me up against the wall so hard, it knocked the wind out of me. Before I could fall, his heavy fist pistoned into my gut. He caught my head and pushed it back.

"You got some nerve coming back here," my assailant growled. I was too disoriented to discern his face, but the smoldering tip of the cigarette hanging out of his mouth helped me figure it out. "Where's your visor?" He ripped off my belt and, when he saw nothing attached to it, punched me in the ribs.

"I don't have it!" I squealed. "Help!" He spun me around forcefully, searching, then back to face him. Delisted men and women roamed by. They simply didn't give a damn, too worried about where they'd scrape up their next bit of data or food. Selfish, contemptible . . . corrupt. Even the bouncers outside the bar merely watched, the smaller one wearing a smirk. And there were no public safety bots to stop it, only the blinking lights of drones far overhead, monitoring the area.

Minah's guard's hand wrapped my throat. "Resie or not, you know what happens around here to people who back out of trades with Minah? You'd better find it, or I swear I'll toss you off the outer wall."

"I can't get it," I rasped. He squeezed tighter. "I . . . I'm . . . delisted."

He released me and started to chuckle. Then, letting the cigarette fall from his lips, he blew out a puff of smoke and squished the burning tip into the flesh of my arm.

It seared, and I thought I screamed, but I'd never felt that kind of pain before in my life. If I had, my lifeband would have responded with a shot of pharma so fast I wouldn't have known. My skin bubbled.

"Just couldn't help yourself, could you?" he said, looking me straight in the eyes. "Guess I'll be seeing you around, then, friend. Minah will be thrilled."

He hoisted me up, and the blows that followed came too fast for me to count—a few to my likely already-fractured ribs. More in the stomach. The final shot to the jaw had me seeing stars, and after two floundering steps, I toppled face-first onto the street.

CHAPTER 14

Waking up dazed and unsure of where I was or how I'd gotten there was becoming a habit. Only this time, I felt like I'd been hit by a hover-car. Something tickled my cheek, and when I went to roll over, a sharp pain radiated down my side.

"You really should try to stay still," a man said.

Something frilly dangled in my face. I fought through incredible soreness to brush it aside so I could see the man who'd addressed me. He sat across the interior of a small shack, hunched over at a warped desk, hands twisting over each other like he was packing something. The walls and ceiling were made of cheap, corrugated metal that pattered with the rain outside.

"Where am I?" I groaned.

The man stood, and a segmented stick extended from his right hand. When he turned, I noticed the rag wrapping his bald head, covering his eyes and stained with dry blood. It fell loose above the bridge of his crooked nose, allowing the entirety of the Unplugged brand on his forehead to show. I knew that face.

"You?" I attempted to sit. The pain had me reeling instead.

"You remember me?" he replied. "Interesting."

"What's going on?"

"I saw what happened. Well, heard . . . Minah's man put quite a beating on you, didn't he?" He slowly approached me, waving his stick out in front presumably to make sure he didn't bump into anything. In his other hand, he held a tiny bowl.

"And you carried me all the way here?" I asked.

"Dragged. If I'm being honest."

"First, you try to kill me—now, you're my savior?" He was getting closer, so I gave moving another try. My sore ribs finally complied, but sitting up made it feel like someone had ignited a fire inside my head.

"Poetic, isn't it?" He presented the bowl. Inside was a clump of finely ground green herbs and no reprehensible meat mixed in. "Eat this."

I remained still.

"I had no real reason to choose you last time, and I have no reason to kill you now," he said. "Take it. It'll help with the pain."

He stretched his arm farther, though incidentally, in the direction of my legs rather than my head. When I still didn't take it, he sighed and dropped it on my lap. Then, using a stick, he shuffled over to a spout like the one in the show bar. A tin cup underneath it was already filled with water, and not nearly as murky as everywhere else in the Outskirts. It took a few tries for him to pick it up before returning to me.

"I'm not going to force it down for you, but I'm tired of hearing you moan." He placed the cup at the foot of the fraying couch I was on. The blind man seemed relatively comfortable walking with his stick, but squatting took a great deal of concentration. "Stuff tastes like piss, but I promise, it works. Better than any pharma you've had."

"Why should I believe anything a lunatic like you has to say?" I growled.

"You shouldn't, but one day delisted and you've already found trouble. People don't last long out here if they've got grudges and no friends."

"Do you always befriend the people you try to murder?"

He smirked in response.

"You think just because you pulled me here, I'll join your order of fanatics?" I said. "You might as well kill me now and finish the job you started. I've got nothing left to live for. Certainly not gouging out my eyes or giving raving speeches." I had to take too big a gulp of air to compensate for my rant. It made my chest burn.

"You want to let yourself die, be my guest," he said. "Seems an awful waste after coming this far."

"You call *this* far? We're in the Outskirts, where the undeserving members of the human race are exiled. Or have you forgotten? Nobody wants to be here!"

His smirk grew deeper and then, without saying anything, he turned. He dragged his stick along the grooves of the corrugated wall, using it to locate the door out of the shack.

"Where are you going now?" I asked.

"To give 'raving speeches,'" he replied. He opened the flimsy door and stepped outside. I heard the tap of his stick for a few seconds before it was drowned out by the pouring rain.

I stared at the cup he'd given me. The water rippled from the vibrations thrown down from the flimsy roof. Eventually, my willpower broke and I grabbed it, gulping down every ounce. In High Earth, thirst had been little more than a vocabulary term. VORA never gave me a chance to truly experience it. Hunger either. I was kept as nourished as my body required.

A strange new sound caused me to search the shack. When

I found nobody, I realized it was my stomach growling. That had never happened before. I felt empty, like my gut was the hollowed-out asteroid comprising the *Ignis*.

I lifted the clump of herbs the nameless Unplugged had given to me. It looked just about as appetizing as a nutriment bar . . . if it was even food. Now that he was gone, I didn't care. Maybe it wouldn't fill me up, but at least he said it would dull the pain. Best-case scenario, it would kill me. I had no reason to go on anyway. I'd allowed myself to lose *Ignis: Live*, betrayed Mr. Helix, and condemned Mission. I was as pathetic as the Unplugged madman had been when last I saw him rolling around in the grime, eyeless and cackling.

I shoved the herbs into my mouth. The texture was awful, but they didn't taste like much of anything. At first my mind continued racing, cursing myself for all the foolish things I'd done to wind up in this awful place. Then, whatever the blind lunatic fed me hit.

The pharma I'd been shot up with days prior was candy in comparison. I lay back, closed my eyes, and drifted away . . .

* * *

I had no idea how long it'd been when I woke up again. Honestly, the time had been posted so pervasively in High Earth that I barely ever had to think about it. I had very little concept of how it felt to lie still for five minutes, or even an hour, with no content to watch or VRs to engage in. All I knew was that I felt well-rested for the first time in days and that the rain pounding on the tin roof had abated.

My legs slid off the couch and pressed my feet on the floor. The cold metal against my bare soles made me remember that I'd gotten rid of my shoes just to have a few moments with

Ignis: Live. Was that how you became like the starving, delisted wretches roaming the streets? You gave away necessities one at a time for a fix until there was nothing else left.

I went to stand but fell back onto the couch. The sharp pains were gone, but I was still unbelievably achy. I tried again, and my stiff knees cracked as I straightened out. For the first time, I was able to see over the back of the couch and what inhabited the rest of the shack.

The back half was filled by rows of planters. A miniature conservatory fed by water lines running down from the ceiling so they could use the rain, and warmed by an array of low-hanging heat lamps.

There had to be at least a dozen different species of flora. Some were tall and leafy, others squat and sitting in deep beds of soil. Tomatoes, radishes, cucumbers—my brain fed me the names without me asking. A result of the brain infusers teaching me while in the synth-womb. A few plants in the back were even flowering vibrant clusters of pink and purple.

It was like my own little taste of the inside of the *Ignis*. The closest I'd been to any real plant was a hundred meters above the lawn of High Earth. I'd seen flowers and ancient forests filled with extinct animals in VRs, but somehow it wasn't the same. My finger grazed the surface of a jagged-edged leaf. A bead of water trickled down the stem, ripe tomatoes hanging from it, red as a sunset.

My grumbling stomach had me biting into one before my mind could process the action. The taste wasn't special, but the texture was delightful. Supple, succulent—the juice literally dribbled down my chin. I devoured it, then ate two more and a radish until I felt like I was ready to explode. The stuff concocted by re-assemblers had all the nutritional value without the bulk. Just a few real vegetables probably caused my stomach to expand.

I limped down the rows of greenery, smelling new scents, or

perhaps they weren't new and the VR simulations just couldn't compare. I stopped by purple flowers at the end. *Lilacs*, I unexpectedly recollected. Maybe it was the herbs the Unplugged had fed me, enhancing my senses like the scrunge many *Ignis* inhabitants snorted, but the fragrance made the tiny hairs along my arms stand on end.

I shoved my face into a clump of flowers and inhaled. For an instant, I forgot where I was, about High Earth, and Mission, and *Ignis*. That was, until I noticed a holopad sitting on a forsaken, half-deconstructed NT chair buried under drooping leaves. Not an ancient one like throughout the rest of the Outskirts either. Closer to the one built into the table of my smart-dwelling.

I brushed the flowers aside to grab the thing, ripping out a few petals by accident. A year-old model, thin like a sheet of glass and still glossy. The screen lit up, but without the fingerprint of a resident, I couldn't access an active account, and I was no slicer. I tossed it onto the couch and sighed. What a waste of tech, stranded in this lawless place with me and an owner who'd purposefully robbed his ability to see all the wonderful content it could offer.

"Are you happy now?" I said to anyone who would listen.

My legs started to get wobbly from standing. I used the wall to drag myself over to the water spout. As nice as they were to eat, the tastes of tomatoes and radish didn't mix well. When I turned to head back to my couch, I noticed that the shack's door remained cracked open. A strange noise came through. A steady lapping, like a massive brush sliding across a coarse floor.

I prodded the door a little farther so I could peek outside. The world was grayed out by a thick curtain of clouds, but I was closer to them than I'd been down in the Outskirts' entry. As if I were up on a wall.

"High Earth?"

I rushed outside, only to have my hopes crushed. I wasn't atop the wall separating High Earth from the Outskirts, but instead the outer one along the coast. Even farther away from home. To my left, beyond a high parapet, was the ocean. The sound I'd heard was its foaming waves pounding the base where the wall met a rocky shoreline far below. A sound impossible to hear from High Earth's even loftier barricade.

The stench of salt was rampant. Above me, the blades of countless wind turbines spun, their posts connected to improvised power boxes and conduits. Hundreds more poked out of the water below as well, stretching to the horizon in either direction.

To my right, the ledge of the wall was filled with more shacks like the one I'd exited. If I thought what existed down below, between the walls, was a hodgepodge, this was exponentially less organized. They were built onto the inner face of the fortification, stacked and connected by ladders, ramps and bridges all the way down to the streets of the Outskirts. And it was all handcrafted. No bots to perfectly seal edges or to polish. Not a single shack was made of materials that matched either. Like every new delisted person scavenged for parts, nailed them together, and called it a home. In fact, that was probably exactly what they'd done.

Where this area atop the outer wall most differed from the lower Outskirts, however, was in what lay between. It was more crowded, but somehow less chaotic. No VR dens or show bars were in sight. Instead, there were countless rolling stands and pedestals. People at them bartered over every type of ware I could imagine. From utensils to monitors to discarded bots like the receptionist in Minah's shop.

I skirted along the shacks at the edge of the crowd. One of

the busier bartering stands was run by a plump man in yellow, with a rectangular emblem sewn into his shirt and filled with star patterns. Dozens of racks' worth of clothing hung from it. I gravitated toward it. The coarse plasticrete walkway was rough on my soft feet after giving away my shoes. All the VR sims I'd been in, like walking barefoot along the sandy beaches of ancient Earth—they never simulated that part. I'd much rather have traded in another piece of clothing.

I never had to worry about needing new clothes in High Earth. VORA provided a fitted-everything when I'd left the synth-womb, and that was all I'd ever needed. The lack of stress in a resident's day-to-day life rarely led to wear and tear, and if by chance there was even the slightest rip in the nano-fabric everything was made from, a bot would immediately be dispatched to perform an in-home repair.

Guards in yellow watched over the stand as the shopkeep rattled on about all the goods in his possession. There were other stands like it nearby, guarded by people in corresponding clothing or with matching tattoos or hair. It was like the gangs and armies in dramas I used to watch. People under hardship, banding together under the rule of slicers to make things a little easier.

I couldn't imagine myself in a group like that. Hell, when I was in High Earth, aside from the Helix studio, I couldn't imagine myself amongst any group at all. Even there, I preferred the solitude of my virtual office.

A woman limped over to the stand run by the people in yellow. Her shoes were so worn I could see her scrawny feet covered in scrapes and bruises. An inactive lifeband wrapped around her wrist, the screen half busted. She perused the rack of footwear, then held up a pair.

"1,300 bits for these?" she asked, her voice husky.

The shopkeep scratched his fuzzy chin, then leaned in close

with one eye. It was artificial, with a spiral of light in the center. "Fourteen," he said.

"For these?"

"Cheaper than you'll get them anywhere else."

"You Nation boys run a racket." She went to turn around empty-handed, but the shopkeep stopped her.

"Thirteen fifty," he said. "And that's final."

The woman scanned the shoes, then nodded. She raised her arm and keyed a few commands on the crummy lifeband I couldn't believe was still operational. The shopkeeper lifted a holopad. I could see on the screen that they were syncing an exchange of data. The interface was too ugly to have been designed for High Earth.

I stood still, staring without realizing. It was fascinating. I never really considered what the delisted did with the data they got from residents beyond accessing content. Using the cast-off devices of High Earth, they'd turned the data we . . . they . . . took for granted into a monetary system. Siphon some out of the account of a willing resident who wanted a taste of the old world, then disperse it throughout their rotting one.

The transaction went through without a hitch. The shop-keeper thanked her for her business, then went about shouting to more people. The woman plopped on the ground right where she was, discarded her dilapidated shoes, and squeezed on the new ones. Then she got up and left.

Her old shoes were left sitting there. They were too damaged to do anything to keep out the cold, but the soles looked intact enough to help with the pain of walking barefoot. Nobody else seemed interested in them, so I grabbed them. I didn't make it two steps away before one of the stand's yellow-clad bouncers had his rusty artificial arms wrapped around my chest.

"Those don't belong to you, filth," he growled. He ripped

them out of my grasp, shoved me onto the ground, and then tossed them back to the stand. Filth. One day and I'd gone from being mistaken as a resident to the basest of their kind.

"Sorry," I said to the shopkeeper as I stood. "I didn't know."

"Newcomer over the wall, eh?" the shopkeeper said. "You want those, it'll be, uh, two hundred bits."

"I don't have any data."

"None?"

I shook my head.

The cyber-enhanced bouncer who'd grabbed me started circling me like a wolf on the hunt. One of his eyes was crooked, but the other studied me. He even gave my shirt a sniff before saying, "He smells fresh."

"Word of advice, newcomer," the shopkeeper said. "Find a visiting resie, and do whatever it takes to get some."

"I . . . I can offer clothing."

The man glanced at the bouncer with his fake eye and they exchanged a snicker. "Another word of advice, never give away what you were able to keep from the other side of the wall. But here." He tossed the wrecked shoes to me. I dropped them I was so shocked. "When your brain sorts out from the wipe, you remember the generosity shown to you by the Nation, followers of the greatest slicer in the Outskirts, Denizen Pane. We aren't High Earth, but you'll be as comfortable as anyone can get out here with us."

I lifted the shoes. They were in worse shape than I initially thought. Probably wouldn't last a day, but they were better than nothing. "Thank you," I said. "Thank you so much."

"They wouldn't have sold anyway. Now scram."

The bouncer pushed me along, growling as he did. I didn't try to fight it.

I needed to get my hands on some data somehow. It would've

helped if Mr. Helix had exiled me with my OptiVisor or life-band in hand, something that could store or receive it. Maybe I would've even been able to drain my pre-existing High Earth account. I still wasn't exactly sure how it worked. I'd never had to worry about becoming delisted before.

I spotted an obvious resident at a trading post down a short way. She stuck out like a sore thumb even though she was surrounded by delisted people. Half were on their knees kowtowing, but all were kept at a perimeter by her guardian bot.

Her neatly pressed tunic and pleated pants were programmed to whatever color she wanted—green in her case. She had perfect hair. A perfect figure. A lifeband around her perfect wrists to keep her safe. I noticed the outline of a drone flitting in the sky high above, watching over her as well.

I looked down. My clothing was already worn from rain and ripped from the beating I took. At least I was starting to fit in.

What could a resident who had everything she needed possibly want from me, or any of them? I retained all my memories, so I knew what her life was like. How did somebody who woke up in the Outskirts, with any specific memories about High Earth ripped out of their heads and replaced only with a horrible feeling that something wonderful was missing, know where to start?

I thought about what I might say to her, but then was distracted by the familiar voice of my recent savior, and formerly attempted murderer, speaking nearby.

"Then why did you come here again?" the Unplugged man said.

I edged around the corner of a shack and saw him standing in front of it, like the top of the wall was his chapel. No dais, just his feet, rags, and the bandage wrapped around his eyes. Probably better not to scare people off with two gory holes if he wanted them to listen. He spoke loud enough for anybody in the area to hear, but he addressed a single person. A child, young enough to be fresh out of the synth-womb and already delisted. He had a nervous twitch and scorch marks along his temples.

"I don't know if I can do it," the boy replied.

"You can. Trust me, you can," the Unplugged man replied. "Tell me, do you know why some of us choose to remove our eyes upon taking on the brand?"

The boy shook his head.

"Because we are so much more than the things we see." He used both hands to feel the boy's face, stopping when he located his eyes, and ran his thumbs over the lids.

"Losing these reminds us to live only with our own feelings," he went on. "I can converse, walk, eat . . . perform any task a man needs to survive. One day, the people here will realize that though they may have been cast out of paradise, they've really been set free. That they don't need to cling to the things left behind. The best programming on this world isn't seen through a screen or transmitter." He spread his arms and aimed his worthless eye sockets toward the cloudy sky. "It's here." Then he lowered his hand and patted the boy's chest a few times before stopping in the center. "And there."

The boy nodded, though his expression made it clear he wasn't convinced. "If it's so awful, why does everyone want to get back in so badly?" he asked.

"You were born out here. I know it's hard for you to understand, but for those who weren't, their minds grasp for what they can't completely remember. For shadows of a past where they were never wanting. Now, without their smart-dwellings and their VORAs, they're children. They may have been carried out of their synth-wombs, but they've never truly left them."

"But you were one of them."

My savior took a deep breath. "Once, yes. And even after I wound up here, I clung to what I'd lost. I was willing to trade anything for a VR fix. Did even worse. One time I plugged myself in at a VR den with more data accumulated than I knew what to do with and stayed there for days. I didn't stop until the Unplugged raided the place and razed it to the ground. They found me under the rubble on the precipice of death, and for what? They fed me, cared for me. When I was finally conscious enough to see myself in a mirror, I was closer to a skeleton than a living man. Right then, I vowed to change my life."

The boy's eyes widened. "Was it hard?"

"Yes. But life is meant to be hard. The Outskirts exist for that very reason. To fulfill this illusion for residents that High Earth is perfect, so they would never question their existence. We are a novelty to them, an amusement park, a place to visit and see savage things. To them, we're more content. A point of reference, just like in any program. The moment I realized that, my young friend, was when I understood that there can be another point of view. That maybe life on the other side of the wall isn't as perfect as we all think."

He unwound the bandage from his head, then wrapped it around the boy's, bloodstains and all. The boy didn't fight it. "When you have a compulsion, wear this," the Unplugged man said. "Open your eyes—truly open them—and find yourself in the reality we're all born into."

The boy nodded before running off. The Unplugged man picked up his walking stick and started off toward me, tapping the wall to keep straight.

"How long have you been there?" he asked as he passed.

"How did you—" I said before he cut me off.

"Practice. They had me wearing a blindfold long before they took my sight. I know your smell by now."

I instinctually sniffed my armpit. I wasn't sure how my own odor smelled, but whatever I got a whiff of made me grimace. It could've been me, or it could've been my soggy clothing . . . probably both. Back in my smart-dwelling, I had my resident-issue laser-detox. VORA would receive my clothing through a slot in the wall during the cleaning, and return it afterward, pressed and spotless. It barely took more than a minute.

"I . . . wait!" He didn't stop, so I used the wall to pull myself to my feet and catch up with him. "That story you told," I said. "Was it true?"

He stopped for a moment, bit his lip. "Every word."

"So you blame High Earth for what happened to you?"

"I don't blame anyone."

"Then what is it? Just because you couldn't control yourself, you'll discount all of the incredible things residents have and create?"

"To shun technology is foolish, and that is not what we seek, but to rely on nothing else? A storm can look incredible. That doesn't mean it won't whip the waves and haul us out to sea. Maybe their creations were art once, but it's all become so meaningless now."

"I'm supposed to be happy I'm stuck in this place, then? That simple? I don't care if you saved me, *I* wasn't meaningless there. I had a real purpose, helping bring millions of people joy every day. I was a damn director for *Ignis: Live!*" I was yelling by the end. I only wished that my anger was directed more toward him than it was at myself.

The Unplugged's walking stick slid along a groove in the floor, extending him too far and causing him to stumble. He caught himself against the loose-swinging door of his shack.

"Ignis what?" he asked.

"*Ignis: Live.*"

He grabbed my arm and dragged me inside. With one hand, he slammed the door shut and locked it by inputting a code of digits in the keypad despite the fact he couldn't see. Then he finally released me.

"What are you doing?" I asked.

"You remember that?" His eyebrows lifted, and if he had eyes instead of empty holes, they would have been gawking.

"I remember everything."

"But that doesn't make any sense. The new ones sent here can't recall much beyond what genre they enjoyed watching or playing. Sometimes, and I'm telling you it's rare, they can piece together the fact that they used to develop something without quite knowing what. Those ones usually become slicers. When you said you remembered me, I figured the trauma of what I'd done to you was so embedded in your psyche that those soulless bots didn't know how to erase it, but nothing so specific."

I'd completely forgotten to hide the well-known fact that I shouldn't have any of my memories before my previous answer. "I willingly betrayed the trust of a man I cared about," I said, careful to keep things vague. "Now I'm here."

"But the mind wipe?"

I thought about it for a second before answering. "I did a lot of work with brain infusers. I was able to reprogram it not to take anything, without the High Earth Network realizing it."

It wasn't exactly true. Mr. Helix had been the one to do that, but it was the only way not to put him or the show in a compromised position. Canceling the mandatory wipe of a delisted resident was not permitted, whether I deserved it or not. It would be grounds to have him exiled as well, and then *Ignis: Live* would cease to exist.

No matter what had happened, I couldn't let that come to pass.

"So you remember everything from when you were a director for *Ignis: Live?*" the Unplugged man asked.

"Now you're interested in our 'meaningless' programming?" I said. "Well, don't expect me to tell you any secrets. I'll never betray anyone I care about again. That's why I wanted to make sure I remembered how much it hurt to do that to somebody."

"How gallant of you."

"Who knows. Maybe I'll be forgiven one day, and his recommendation will get me back in when I apply for re-enlistment." It was a long shot, but I'd started thinking about it while walking the wall. My brain fed me the info. There was a policy that delisted residents could apply for re-enlistment after a certain period. From what I knew, it was rare that ever happened unless they had been a prolific developer. High Earth's space was finite. I'd try, of course, if I managed to survive long enough, but my chances were still slim without Mr. Helix's backing.

"You're delusional. Nobody who applies ever gets back in, if they even remember to. Not one." My deranged savior stalked aimlessly around the conservatory area of the shack, searching for something. He stopped by the flowers and ruffled through them.

"Looking for this?" I asked. I tapped the screen of the holopad I'd tossed onto the couch earlier so he'd hear what it was. "I found it back there. For a man who claims how much he hates everything it's used for, you seem pretty concerned."

"Would you shut up!" He scrambled back through the planters to me. "What time is it?"

I glanced down. Without access, the device wouldn't tell me. The delisted really were lost. Nothing to tell them when it was so they could know what was on or what to do. Being out here really was going to drive me mad.

He took the device from me and pressed his thumb against

the screen. Everything unlocked. Not only the interface, but complete access to the High Earth Network from a legitimate account. He was in like a resident would be. No need for a slicer or anything. He shoved it in front of my face.

"3:53 p.m.," I read, utterly dumbfounded.

"Still early for her." He exhaled. "I have to be somewhere, but you need to stay here and rest. Nobody will touch you if you stay in this shack. It's marked. And I doubt you can take another beating."

I was barely paying attention to him. "How is this working?" I asked.

"There's more data left on that account than you can use in a year. Watch whatever you'd like. Eat too. Just stay here and I'll be back soon." He started toward the exit, but I seized him.

"How did you get this to work!"

"Same way I got back into High Earth and found you, not a real thought in your useless head until I woke you."

"How?"

"I'm not delisted."

I staggered backward. I felt like I'd just been punched across the face. I'd never bothered to think about how he got in. I figured crazed people like the Unplugged had discovered ways of sneaking through the wall for short periods before bots inevitably caught them.

"I thought you said nobody's application for re-enlistment ever gets approved?" I managed to ask.

He shook his head.

"Who are you?"

He grinned and poked the device in my hands. "You've still got eyes. Read." He unlocked the door, slipped out, and sealed it shut behind him. I was too astonished to slow him down.

I stared down at the holopad. Not my preferred choice of

viewing apparatus, but there were all the icons, applications, the lists of programs, advertisements, what was popular, comment boards, discussions—all of it. The entire High Earth Network available at my fingertips. The sudden euphoria of being back in forced me to sit down. The flowers behind me could all burn. This was true beauty . . .

And then I saw the name of the resident to whom the device was registered. Virgil Rhodes. It wasn't a name most people would recognize, but I did. My favorite dating VR, the one in the golden-age western restaurant where I'd met with Dawn and countless other women who decided never to see me again for one reason or another. He'd developed it.

A resident was living in this run-down hellhole by choice.

CHAPTER 15

I stared at the name of my savior in awe until my eyes were dry. It didn't make any sense. He had the world at his fingertips. Everything he needed to survive, safety, all the tech and entertainment he could imagine. He was even one of those few residents with the capacity and creativity to create content that others cared about, however few.

I couldn't. The only worthwhile thing I'd ever done was volunteer my time to help with somebody else's vision. It was impossible to fathom Virgil's fulfillment compared to how happy I felt walking into the Helix studio every day.

Yet he'd left it all behind.

The very notion gave me a piercing headache. I searched the couch for more of the herbs he'd given me to dull it, but I'd taken them all. There was no telling where in his conservatory the concoction had come from if I wanted more. So I found solace the best way I knew how. I navigated through the Network and tuned to the many windows of *Ignis: Live*. So long as I avoided any that showed Mission, the pain of watching might be bearable.

Most feeds continued to depict the cleanup efforts after the tragedy in Block B. Every corpse had already been put through the recycler, but there was a great shift occurring. The Collective was hard at work using the core's databases to decide how many and which inhabitants should be transferred into Block B from the others, similar to the post Great Blackout period, which had allowed Mission to find her place.

They tried to keep the populations equal in each block to ensure balanced usage of equipment, but with over two hundred dead, it would take a great deal of shuffling. All that work, however, was the only thing keeping Mission from her trial. I hoped against reason it would last forever.

As I updated myself on the circumstances of the *Ignis*, I noticed one feed had a ticker at the bottom that read ANNIVERSARY FEED. It displayed old footage. I knew it right away, because I could never in a million years forget the scene being replayed. A familiar green-eyed young girl sat across from a young boy, who was scared of the dark. Mission and Jacen, long before she'd killed him.

Mr. Helix was using my idea of playing back significant events from Block B's history. I'm not sure why, but it made my blood boil.

I pressed my finger against the interface so hard I dropped the device. As I picked it up, I dragged the feed focused on Mission onto the main window. Imprisoned or not, criminal or not, she always warranted a live feed. She sat on the floor of her tiny cell next to a bowl of sloppy food that she'd barely taken a nibble of. When I last saw her, she'd been having a panic attack from being locked back away. Now, her cheeks were stained from crying. She had her eyes closed, breathing slowly and deliberately. In through her nose, out through her mouth, like she'd done all those years beneath the floor.

Then someone arrived outside her cell.

[Ignis Feed Location]
Core Cell 3
<Camera 1>

The *whoosh* of the door to her cell caused Mission's eyes to snap open. She didn't hesitate. She blew through whoever stood there and out into the corridor. An enforcer grasped at her, but he was tall and awkward. He got a finger on her collar and tore it a bit before she broke free.

"Mission, stop!" voices shouted, unclear and blurred. She was too panicked to focus. It wasn't dark, but it felt like that day the lights went off all over again. Her gaze darted side to side as she ran. She saw screens, angry faces, more screens.

She rounded another corner when a baton smashed into her stomach. She went down hard, gasping for air and clutching at her gut. Another enforcer grabbed a clump of her hair and dragged her back down the hall. She was too winded to fight.

"Get your hands off her!" Mission heard a woman yell.

The enforcer heaved Mission back into her cell. She rolled across the floor, her face stopping just over the viewport. The top of Block B was straight below her now, a view of her and Jacen's favorite spot in clear sight. There was a bit of discoloration in the center from where they'd spent so much time sitting side by side, or maybe she imagined it. The one thing she was sure about was that their spot remained empty.

"Mission!" Alora ran in and knelt at Mission's side.

"Alora?" Mission whispered.

She worried she was dreaming. The rags of any normal inhabitant hung loose from Alora's slender frame. It made her appear older than she was. Or maybe it was the new wrinkles wrapping her eye sockets, as she too hadn't slept in days.

Before any more doubt could build, Alora embraced her. Mission hugged back at first, but then her arms fell slack.

"He's dead . . ." Mission whimpered. "It's all my fault."

"No, no, stop that." Alora ran her fingers through her hair, shushing her as she often did whilst cradling a newborn. "Cassiopeia told me everything you said. I don't care what she thinks. I know it was an accident."

"I don't know what happened . . . I don't understand."

"Neither do I." She held Mission at arm's length and gazed upon her lovingly. Then she squeezed her against her chest and kissed the top of her head. Once, twice—until strands of hair were sticking to her lips. "Get up." She hoisted Mission to her feet and brushed off her shoulders.

"Where are we going?" Mission sniveled.

"To get you cleaned off." She started toward the door, but Mission didn't follow. She stood over the viewport aimed at the green surface below.

"It's okay, Mission," Alora said, extending her hand back into the cell. "I asked Cassiopeia for this one favor. For all my years of service."

"I'm exonerated?"

"Not yet. Maybe we can piece together exactly what happened down there, but not until you're finished smelling like a sewer. And no running this time." She smiled. The barest twitch of a smirk affected Mission's lips before she took a few hesitant steps forward.

The two enforcers immediately fell in around them once they were out of the cell. They had pulse-pistols holstered. Not a common sight on *Ignis*, even in the core, but it was clear they weren't taking any risks. When Mission noticed the weapons, her eyes widened. Alora grasped her hand and kept moving.

"Try that again, you'll get more than a baton," one of them growled.

"You try being locked up," Alora snapped and hurried Mission past.

They entered a brightly lit hall flush with shiny metal and mechanical equipment. The floor curved away from them as it wrapped the circumference of the core's rotating structure.

On the right, rooms slightly larger than Mission's cell branched off, most of them boasting small beds and other limited amenities. The inglorious dwellings of the Collective. A lofty, continuous space branched off on the left side, with expansive glass viewports cut around the floor. It was filled with terminals. Members of the Collective were stationed at many of them, rifling through data and charts. Others sat around tables, drawing on digital screens stretching across the walls.

Together, the thirty . . . twenty-nine now that Paul was dead . . . members monitored the core's many systems and plotted the future for those inhabitants who would be alive when *Ignis* reached a new Earth in the Tau Ceti system.

That was their most vital burden.

Nobody was sure what would happen when that day came, but they'd spent fifty years already figuring out every conceivable outcome. Even Mothers, like Mission had been for a day, weren't privy to their innumerable predictions.

Their most recent inability to keep the failures in the Block B life support in check had them all on edge and looking exhausted. The only thing able to pull them from their tireless work was glaring at Mission and Alora as they went by.

"They all think it was me," Mission muttered.

"Or me," Alora replied. She drew Mission closer and squeezed her hand tighter. "Ignore them. They're afraid, looking for answers. For somewhere to place blame. A Mother must be immune to judgment."

"Even you're lecturing me now?"

"Always."

Alora stopped and turned into a larger series of adjoined cells on the right. The enforcers escorting them positioned themselves on either side of it.

"Nobody will be permitted beyond this point until she's finished," one of them said. "Make it quick. We don't want to waste water on *her*."

"Thank you," Alora said.

"Thank Cassiopeia," the other grumbled. "It wasn't my idea to help a flame-robber."

The term caused Mission to stop in her tracks, but Alora wrapped her arm over her shoulders and steered her inside. It was a name reserved only for lawbreakers. Those who'd earned the fate of spacing and would have their flame—their energy—forever expelled. For what better punishment was there for breaking laws than knowing one made life for everyone else just a little bit harder?

"Ignore him," Alora said. "You're still a Mother. Now, let's get you cleaned up."

The cramped space was lined with half a dozen tiny showers divided by curtains. All water utilized on the *Ignis* was communal, even for the Collective. With no promise that the star system they were heading to harbored a truly habitable planet, water remained a restricted resource in case they ever had to add a new destination. Curtains, however, were a luxury afforded only to the Collective.

Alora prodded Mission into one. The curtain closed around her, and as she stood there, the words of the enforcer weighing heavily on her conscience, the water turned on. It rained on her head, straining the muck out of her hair, wringing the blood from her clothes and face.

Jacen's blood.

It swirled about the drain, squishing between her toes and running under the arcs of her pale feet.

Her fists clenched as she watched it go. The water went from reddish-brown to pink, and as it nearly turned clear, she screamed at the top of her lungs. She tore off the white uniform gifted to her when she was named Mother and threw it against the curtains. Alora waited outside, observing a viewport in the floor. The calm façade she wore up until that point cracked when she heard the scream.

* * *

I averted my gaze from Virgil's holopad as Mission removed her clothing. I'm not sure why. I'd seen countless inhabitants bathe throughout my time as director. And her plenty since she'd become a woman and the viewers clamored for it. Of course I gave in.

But it felt wrong to watch now that I was no longer in charge of overseeing the feeds. It felt dirty.

Still, I heard her bloodcurdling shriek. It sent a chill up my spine that lingered.

I longed to reach out and stroke her untidy hair, tell her that everything was going to be okay. But as I lied to her, I wondered if I would also be able to tell her that her suffering was all my fault? She could have joined the rest of those in her block who were unfortunate enough to get trapped when the air went out. Died painlessly, a superstar, and been recycled to help nourish her people in the years to come.

"I'm so sorry, Mission," I whispered.

Selfish. That was what I was. I hadn't tried to save her for her, or for the viewers, or the show, but for the sake of my own vague feelings. Me, who now couldn't even bear to look at her body, like I was some shy child.

Now we were both alone in strange places that we were never going to leave. Except only one of us had earned the ire of our entire people for what we'd done, and the other might as well have been a ghost on the streets of the Outskirts.

After Mission finished cleaning off, the enforcers shoved a protesting Alora out of the way and seized her.

"No, not back in there!" she yelled. "No, please!"

They hauled her back to her cell, naked, then threw a pair of rags at her, and locked the door. Mission slammed her fists against it too late, pounding until her arms grew too exhausted and she collapsed to her knees. She breathed, slow and steady, in through her nose, out through her mouth, eyes squeezed tight.

I could've looked away to spare myself the sight of her reversion, or put on something else, but Mission deserved better.

So I sat for hours, quietly watching her fail at sleeping and every so often peer through her cell's viewport at the rotating farms and living blocks of *Ignis*, like the drawings of the outside world she used to imagine from her hole.

My wish that Mr. Helix would've merely shown the mercy I didn't deserve, and allowed me to forget everything like he was supposed to, was outweighed by knowing that I could be there for her now. Even millions of kilometers away, at least somebody knew that she was, and always would be, innocent.

"Do you always cry when you watch those things?"

My gaze darted toward the shack's wide-open door, where Virgil stood. His ratty clothes dripped with fresh water, and only then did I notice that the rain had picked up again.

I squeezed my eyelids, forcing out what was left of my tears. "I didn't see you there," I said.

"That's all right," Virgil replied. "I didn't mean to disturb you. Sorry for rushing out. I remembered I was supposed to be meeting an acquaintance. Not as punctual as I used to be, without eyes." He tapped his way into the room.

"You're the one who chose to lose them."

"I suppose I did." He chuckled.

I looked up at him, keeping view of Mission with my peripheral vision just in case anything happened.

"Virgil Rhodes," I said. "I used to visit your restaurant VR all the time when I was a resident."

"So, you can read?" he asked, smiling wryly.

"Why the hell are you really out here?"

"I can ask you the same, Asher Reinhart. Not only a director, but chief director of Content and right hand to Craig Helix on *Ignis: Live* until the studio's volunteer credit list suddenly changed only two days ago and made it like you'd never existed."

My brow furrowed.

He grinned. "My friends can read too," he said. "What exactly did you do to fall so far?"

"Nothing."

"A man who has done nothing doesn't watch someone in silence, sobbing."

"How do you even know I was watching?"

"You don't always need eyes to see."

I thought about that for a moment, then said, "I failed my show. That's all."

"Asher." He wiped the water off his forehead, as if to accentuate the glowing mark of the Unplugged etched into his skin. "Unburden yourself."

"No. I know what this is."

"You do? Enlighten me?"

"You're angry with your life because no VR you designed ever became as popular as my show. You think that because I remember what I was, I'll tell you some secrets about *Ignis: Live*. That I'm supposed to owe you something for saving my life. Then you can leak it to discredit the show so you can end this self-imposed exile of yours and go home without feeling like a disappointment every time."

"That's really what you think?" He paused, then shouted, "I don't give a damn about your shows!" He slapped the contents off his desk. It was just a few cans with plants growing inside them, but they clattered against the wall like thunderclaps, spraying soil all over the floor. I flinched and turned my face. In the short time I'd known him, he'd barely raised his tone beyond a whisper. Even before he'd tried to kill me, though that whole event remained extraordinarily blurry.

"High Earth could burn for all I care and the Network with it," he continued. "The only disappointment I feel is that I ever cared about adding to it." His cheeks were flushed and his fists clenched.

I waited for him to stop panting before I answered.

"Then why do you care about why I'm here?"

"A few days ago, you were a VR-content-addicted sheep just like the rest of them. Now you're delisted, erased from the grandest spectacle in High Earth. I can't help but think mine was the first push that sent you spiraling down this path."

I glanced down at Mission. Footsteps passed outside her cell. She rolled over eagerly just for a chance to talk with somebody again . . . anybody. But the person went by, and she curled back into a ball.

"Well then, you'll be sorry to hear that you can't take all

the credit," I said. "My mistakes started long before running into you."

He found his way to his desk chair and sank into it. Then he drew a measured breath. "What were they?" he asked.

"You Unplugged are relentless, aren't you?"

"It's the only way to get anybody to listen these days."

I sighed and shifted on the couch so I faced away from him.

"There's more value to a real story than you people think," he said. "You eavesdropped and heard mine. I think it's only fair now that I hear yours. Consider it your first trade out here. You'll have to learn how to barter if you ever plan on surviving long enough to apply for re-enlistment. Ten years is the minimum, not that anyone ever gets approved. They just get on reality shows like *Ignis* or *Survivor 2450* and are never seen again."

I tried not to let my disappointment show. I had no idea it was that long. Honestly, I didn't even know what the process was, only that it was a possibility. Ten years seemed like an eternity—especially out here. It was roughly the amount of time it took my body to grow in the synth-womb. Almost a tenth of my potential life, though I seriously doubted life expectancy was the same in the Outskirts. Long enough to forget High Earth entirely.

"That would be a fair trade if you hadn't been lying," I deflected. "Loading into a broken-down VR chair as often as you claimed to would have left you with the same burns on your temples the kid I saw you with had."

Virgil stood, approached without a word, and fell clumsily to his knees in front of me. He took my hand, somehow in a single attempt, and quickly brushed my finger across his temple. Under the dim light it was hard to see, but the skin there was bumpier than it should've been. Like reptile scales.

"It's been some time," he said. "Scars on the body heal, even without your precious bots. On the mind, they last forever."

"That still doesn't explain why you'd ever need to go to an Outskirts VR den if you weren't delisted," I said.

I could see his frustration building. His lips were drawn tight, and if he had eyes, I could bet they'd be staring daggers my way. "I guess you never overextended your data contract, then. My VRs never built much of a following outside the lackluster dating crowd. I'm sure you know how that goes. Most residents want to upload into the spectacular, not bare their hearts. In a place where you can be anything the human mind can imagine, why be yourself?"

I nodded. I remembered my last attempt at a date at Virgil's, when I took Dawn to my own worthless creation like so many others before her. I let them inside my head, and almost every one of them stormed off. Those who hadn't left the moment they were done with me, unsatisfied, and never messaged again.

"I requested so much data to experiment and was constantly studying other people's work that I'd pushed my limits," Virgil said.

"I didn't even think that was possible."

"Neither did I until I'd managed to do it. Got a warning that I was risking probation, so I came here for inspiration on what to develop that people would really enjoy. I wound up inches from death in a VR chair I wasn't familiar with. There are no AIs watching your vitals in the Outskirts."

"Lifeband?"

"They're easy enough to hack if you know how. It's the best way to ditch the safety bots so you can use unregistered tech." He pointed with his cane toward the other side of the room. I hadn't noticed it before, but covered by vines was a High Earth

Security bot. Its chassis was coated with dust. Its eyes slowly flashed white, like my own bot's had in Minah's vault.

"Don't worry, it can't hear us," he said before I asked. "No service. That thing's been 'watching over me' for years."

I considered mentioning my similar actions and attempt to use prohibited tech, but decided against it. "Did you ever figure it out?" I asked instead.

"What?"

"What people would enjoy. You know, before you stopped."

He laughed. "No. Only that I was pathetic for caring enough to almost get myself killed over it."

"If it makes you feel any better, I loved your work and I'm not alone. It's still active. Just the other day, Joanna Porvette was there."

"Who?"

"The developer who portrays Gloria Fors in *Molecular Nation*."

"I've been out of touch. It doesn't change anything, but thank you."

"You're welcome."

"Now, if you're done with your questions, it's your turn to answer some of mine. If you still don't trust me, keep any secrets about your beloved show out. I don't care about that. I only want to hear *your* story. The life of Asher Reinhart."

My gaze darted between him and Mission on screen. He seemed earnest, though I was far more accustomed to dealing with expressionless AIs or my camera crew over comm-link. When it came to reading expressions, I was an amateur.

"I still don't understand why you care," I said.

"A deal is a deal." Virgil propped himself up onto the couch and leaned over. I was glad he couldn't see, because I had to look at the floor to avoid staring at his eyeless sockets.

"I . . . uh . . ." I wasn't sure why it was so hard to get out.

"Go on."

I swallowed against my suddenly dry throat.

"What was your great mistake, Asher?" Virgil pushed.

"I fell in love," I blurted out.

"With whom?"

"It's hard to explain. How familiar are you with *Ignis: Live*?"

"Who isn't? I wasn't always an Unplugged, remember?"

"It's . . . she . . ." I took a deep breath. "Mission."

He nodded, signaling he knew who she was. Like there was any doubt he would. If her face was as prevalent in the Outskirts as in High Earth, you couldn't miss her. Joanna Porvette's fame was a flash in the pan in comparison.

"I know what you're going to say," I said. "Everybody loves her. I'm just some foolish resident. Well, maybe that's true, but when I found out she might be in danger, I violated terms by interacting with her directly for the second time and trying to get her to safety. Mr. Helix found out and had no choice but to report me for everything. But worse than that, my actions placed Mission in a position to inadvertently break the *Ignis's* laws."

"So you're the reason she's on trial for murder?"

I glared at him quizzically, wondering how he knew about that since it happened after he was blinded.

"The streets whisper of that show lately more than most."

"Yes. It's all my fault . . ." My lips started to tremble, but I persevered. "It's what Mr. He . . . What I wanted myself to remember when I refused the mind wipe."

"You tried to help her, Asher. You can't punish yourself forever over what happened. You can only look forward now."

"That doesn't mean I'll ever forget. You see, I've been watching over Mission for nearly her entire life. In some ways we were born the very same day. I focused on her, without even realizing, to the detriment of every other character on the *Ignis*. I helped put her face on screens all over in High Earth and on adverts even out here. When I found out she might be at real risk, I came here to try to erase her from my memory, for the good of the show."

"That's why you were here, sitting beside me in the rain the other night?" he said. "Not for revenge."

I nodded. "My VORA and everyone else convinced me you weren't actually there that day. I believed it was a dream."

"The edge of reality is so very thin in our world today."

I didn't have an answer.

"So what did you do to your mind?" Virgil asked after a short silence.

"I couldn't go through with it," I said. "I decided I had to do something to help her instead. I told myself it was for the good of the show, but it was really because . . . because . . ."

"Because you felt a need to protect her," Virgil finished for me.

"Yes."

"Because you love her."

"I think so? I'm not sure how that's supposed to feel." I could hear Mr. Helix's final words echoing in my head from before he cast me out. "Or maybe something inside me is just broken and I ignored it for too long."

"You're not broken. I can hear it in your voice. You are no fool, Asher Reinhart. There is nothing more human than love for another. And love is deeper than a touch or a kiss. Whether or not you thought it was real, if my push helped even the slightest in getting you to realize that, then I can die a happy man."

Maybe I was wrong, but I thought I noticed his lips tremor similarly to how mine were. Like he was fighting back tears.

"What does it matter anyway?" I said. "I only made things worse for her. I failed her. I failed everyone."

He reached out slowly and laid a hand upon the side of my face. Nobody had ever touched me like that, not even Mr. Helix. Like they cared.

"You didn't fail her for trying, Asher," he said. "Not yet."

Again, I glanced down at her on the holopad. Additional footsteps and sounds of talking just beyond her reach seemed to be driving her mad.

"If that were true, she wouldn't be locked up in a cell," I said. "You can't see how small it is. She must feel like a child again. Like she's suffocating."

"The only person you're failing is yourself."

"Myself?" A harsh edge entered my tone that I didn't know I was capable of. I was used to being kept level by pharma and not having relative strangers question every little thing I'd ever done. I didn't need him to admonish me. I could do that all by myself.

"Yes," Virgil said. "You've given up on her."

"I'd never give up on her!"

"Then you've given up on yourself, which is equally bad. She's still out there, which means that until they kill her, she can be saved."

"Not by me," I said. "In case you've forgotten how things work on the other side of the wall, I can't access the core anymore."

"Forget the damn core! How nice is it to sit with someone and have a real conversation? To smell them, feel them, hear their breathing. So, go to her and save her yourself. Don't manipulate her life through a screen."

I dropped the holopad and stood. "You do realize that the *Ignis* is a ship, right? Circling Earth somewhere out in space."

"It's an asteroid, technically."

"Right, then you know that getting there is impossible without a spacefaring vessel, which are all stored in High Earth under Network protection. All beyond a wall and bots designed to keep filth like us out."

"Again, I know. Yet, when our ancestors looked up, they eventually found a way to get there. There is nothing stopping you but yourself."

"Everything is stopping me."

"Do you even want to save her?"

"Yes!" I screamed so loud my voice resonated off the corrugated walls.

Virgil lifted his walking stick and shuffled over to me. I was across the room by then, my hands wrapped around the lip of his worn desk, squeezing so hard my knuckles were white. Again, he placed a consoling hand on my shoulder, which somehow acted like pharma to soothe me.

"If you aren't ready to give up, I can help you reach Mission," he said.

My head whipped around too fast. The headaches from the beating I'd taken flared up again. I felt faint and had to lean on Virgil's chair just to stay upright.

"What did you say?" I asked softly.

"I can help you save her."

I stopped myself before asking how. The people of the Outskirts apparently survived on bargaining, and I was stumbling into another one. Virgil was playing me for something. I just had no idea what. This was a man who'd once tried to kill me for no reason, after all.

"What's in it for you?" I asked.

"Do you believe in fate, Asher?" he whispered.

"No. Maybe? I don't know."

"Well, I was wrong about you the other day. Maybe you are special, and I can't help but feel that in my rage I stumbled upon your home, of all residents, for a reason." I opened my mouth to respond, but he hushed me. "I understand why you'd be reluctant to trust me. Placing trust in your fellow man isn't a lesson one learns much of back in High Earth."

"Just tell me already!"

"I can't, but I can show you."

"Show me what?" I asked.

"How close to *Ignis* we really are."

CHAPTER 16

"Are you planning to tell me where we're going?" I grumbled.

"You'll see soon enough," Virgil replied.

We'd been traversing the Outskirts by foot for over an hour. All their time wasted hounding residents for data, and the delisted hadn't thought to construct anything to get around quicker. My new shoes were already falling apart. At first, it irritated me; then I began to wonder if maybe they didn't bother developing infrastructure because there was nowhere to go.

Virgil had made me leave his holopad behind, so I wasn't sure exactly how late it was. Failing streetlights made it impossible to see down alleyways. High Earth drones zipped by overhead like shooting stars, too far to help with our visibility.

Somehow, I felt safer being ignorant of what watched from the shadows, but I was far from being comfortable in my new home. And it was colder than ever. No rain, but before we left, Virgil made me change out of my resident-issue clothing and throw on a ratty shirt and cloth pants. No self-fitting waist, no thermal lining.

Every neighborhood of the endless sprawl looked the same. Signs had different names, materials changed, but the layer of filth and the dilapidation never faltered. The people were equally dirty and forlorn, even the ones who wore matching colors—as if being a part of any group could compare to being a resident.

Virgil stopped at the end of a row of rotting wooden structures, took a whiff of the air, then turned right. I followed as he tapped his walking stick along the cracked street.

"How does that feel, you piece of shit!" someone barked.

I turned quickly, fearful that the words were intended for me. Down a nearby alley, a roaring flame raged in the absence of rain. It spat glowing embers out of the windows of a decrepit structure. A group, all wearing shades of yellow like the ones who'd run the stand where I got my shoes, were outside it. They surrounded a woman in rags. She wasn't bald, but her hair was drawn back to reveal the glowing mark of an Unplugged on her forehead and a bandage wrapping her eyes.

"Next time you start a fire in one of the Nation's dens, think about this!" One of her assailants swung a length of pipe and smashed her in the side of the head. The other side cracked against the street on her way down.

"Unplugged filth!" Another kicked her in the gut even though she'd stopped moving. Virgil could obviously hear what was happening, but he didn't slow.

"Aren't you going to help her?" I asked agitatedly.

He shook his head. "There are many slicer gangs in the Outskirts who object to our methods. The Nation is the most despicable."

"They gave me shoes for free."

"Nothing out here is free, Asher. If you'd like to die, feel free to interfere. If you want to help Mission, keep following."

He turned again, and I realized that if I didn't stay close,

I'd be completely lost. And *he* was the blind one. The warren of darkness, banal buildings, and blinding adverts engulfed me. I couldn't even see either of the tremendous walls framing the Outskirts until a High Earth trash sweeper zipped by and illuminated my world for a brief second before vanishing off toward some other forsaken area of the Outskirts.

"Is that what I have to look forward to if I work with you people?" I questioned after it passed.

"She tried opening their eyes her way. That's all we can ever hope to do." He stopped. "Here."

He entered an unassuming building, abandoned by the look of it. The only light within was the little that seeped through shattered windows. The floor was covered in ash and dust, and the ceiling fractured to reveal slivers of the night sky. Viewscreens along the walls were half-melted and black.

"Virgil," said a woman with her face covered by a shawl. He greeted her. I stared. Her covering was lifted while she breastfed a baby. Just like the Birthmothers on *Ignis*. She noticed me and shifted to face away. That was when I noticed that half her covered jaw had been rebuilt with shoddy robotics.

Virgil tapped his cane. "Come now, Asher. It isn't polite to stare."

I followed him under a crooked overhang, to a room beneath a fractured steeple. Moonlight poured in through a gap in the never-ending covering of clouds that plagued the Outskirts. No sooner had I joined Virgil at the spot where its light touched than it vanished.

"How is that possible?" I asked.

"How is what possible?" he said.

"That baby. It's too young to be animated from the synth-womb. How could it be delisted already?"

"Easy. It was born out here."

"That's impossible. All residents are sterilized to control reproduction. It's safer."

"People have been out here over a hundred years, Asher. You've seen how they invent, improvise. The ability to reverse the High Earth sterilization was learned long before you or I was born."

I glanced back at the woman through the breaks in the wall. She was done breastfeeding and now hummed to the cooing baby. Yet, unlike nearly every delisted person I'd encountered so far, she wasn't focused on technology or on winning a trade.

"There are people out here who shouldn't be delisted?" I asked.

"They're all the same to High Earth," Virgil said.

I'd never heard of such a thing as delisted people ravaging their bodies to create more delisted people. I wondered if shows like *Outskirts Today* ever dug deep enough to see what awful lengths delisted people would go to in order to find some semblance of a purpose.

"Who would go through so much effort to bring a child into this world?" I asked, incredulous. "Our population is stable. Humanity endures through High Earth."

"No, we merely survive. Like we're wrapped in a cocoon."

"You can't possibly endorse illegally raising a family here. The very notion is antiquated."

Virgil ignored me. He knocked his cane along a portion of the tarnished wooden floor, only stopping when the sound transitioned from a solid thump to a softer thud.

"Virgil," I pressed.

"Nothing out here is illegal to us," he said, then, "Step back." He tapped the stick in a specific melody. When he finished, a floor hatch swung open with a cloud of dust.

I shielded my eyes and coughed. A young man popped up

through the opening, wearing the three-arced-line mark of the Unplugged, but unlike Virgil, he still retained his eyes. His gaze passed from Virgil to me, where it froze.

"Who's he?" he questioned, making no effort to mask his disdain.

"He is the friend I spoke of earlier," he replied. "May we enter?"

The man studied me a few seconds longer, then nodded and disappeared. Virgil ushered me down, but I was too focused on the word he'd used for it to register. Friend. A person who'd tried to kill me was now my *friend*?

"Virgil, nobody should want to live out here," I said. Between knowing he could leave if he wanted to, and that delisted folk were reproducing, my mind was racing. "Or want it for others."

"Want and need draw a winding line," Virgil said.

"I don't know what you're saying."

"I'm saying that you're wasting valuable time to get what you want, worrying about what others need. Now, climb down. Sight first."

I bit my lip in frustration but decided to drop it. I'd have killed for a bit of pharma to get me steady. I'd have to make do despite all of the distractions. Work through an aching head.

I stepped to the edge of the hatch. The shaft sank deep into the earth, completely black at the bottom. Virgil offered a nod of assurance and instructed me to turn around before placing my feet on the first step of the ladder. I'd never used one before.

I went slowly, both feet on each rung before moving on to the next. I couldn't tell if Virgil was frustrated by my speed or not, but by the time my foot groped through the darkness to find the ground, he was right on top of me.

We were in a downward-sloping tunnel, dated lanterns

arranged along it at wide intervals. The rock surrounding us
was roughly hewn—a far messier job than the tunnels carved
throughout *Ignis*, natural-looking even. The Unplugged who'd
permitted us entry sat by candlelight at a small empty table
with nothing to do but wait and carve a chunk of wood with a
knife. Three arcing lines.

"What is this place?" I panted, voice echoing.

"You'll see," Virgil said. "Come. It isn't far ahead."

My muscles weren't tired from descending the ladder, but
doing so was a bit nerve-racking and, along with everything
else, had me feeling light-headed. I followed the resonant tap
of Virgil's stick until we reached the first lantern and I could
actually see my own feet.

Down and down we went, with nothing to offer a sense of
time or elevation. The air was musty at first, but the farther we
delved, the crisper it grew. As fresh as High Earth even. All the
awful smells rampant in the Outskirts faded away, and the hu-
midity was far less stifling.

Virgil stopped when we reached a great circular hatch filling the entire passage, unlike any I'd ever seen. Three or four
times the size of Minah's, and there was no telling how thick
the solid metal it was made from was. Off to the side sat a small
terminal boasting a single screen. Virgil used his walking stick
to search for it, but I quickly figured out his intent and helped
move him into position. He shrugged me off without a word,
then aimed his face down at the screen.

"Forgot the secret password?" I asked after half a minute
of silence.

"This isn't like one of your High Earth dramas, Asher," he
rebuked. "This passage protects lives, real human lives."

"Sorry, I—"

I was cut off by the massive hatch stirring. It lowered backward, and then the teeth around the edges spun. The sound of scraping metal was so grating, I had to cover my ears. The *clack* as it unlocked was even louder, penetrating my hand-blockades with the sound reverberating down the rock tunnel. Then the hatch swung inward enough to reveal an opening about a meter wide before stopping.

Virgil shuffled his way through. I didn't move. I wasn't sure why I suddenly felt so petrified. In the face of an entryway seemingly built for giants, I was minuscule. There was no saying what lay beyond, and even if I believed the things Virgil had said, could I really trust him? Could I trust any of the people in the bizarre new world I'd been dumped into?

"You coming?" Virgil called back to me.

I could've turned back right then. Found a run-down shack to call my own or even built one—that would knock some days off the decade I needed to wait to apply for re-enlistment. But as I surveyed the rocky tunnel and a hatch from a bygone age, I couldn't help but be reminded of a place far away.

Virgil was right. I was here because Mission existed, and she was still alive. What else did I have to lose?

So I swallowed the lump in my throat, shook out my nervous legs, and headed through. I didn't get far before my body once again forgot how to move.

The tunnel opened into a tremendous hollow that was obviously meant to be a shrunken replica of the interior of the *Ignis*, only on a two-dimensional ground plane. As big as it was, it was probably a tenth the size of the asteroid-vessel, if that, but that didn't make it any less impressive. The entire surface was covered in a pattern of square hydroponic farm plots and, like on *Ignis*, no personal heat lamps were required. It had a smoldering fusion reactor serving as its own core, suspended in the center of the space by thick cables and releasing enough heat and light to sustain all of them.

Hundreds of Unplugged tended the plants or lurked beyond a rocky arcade wrapping the outer walls of the hollow. Their own versions of living blocks. Some were blind like Virgil, others still bore sight, but all of them wore the glowing brand of their order. And the most peculiar thing about all of it was that as we stepped in, each of them stopped what they were doing and looked up at us, paying complete attention to the new presence—me. Men, women, and even more children too young to have been delisted. There wasn't a single piece of real tech amongst them to distract. Manual tools, wrists naked of life-bands—not a screen in sight.

"This is—"

"*Ignis*," Virgil finished. "At least, our best impression of it. It isn't perfect, and we can't make it spin, but if a self-contained world with everything humanity truly needs can be created in space without the luxuries of High Earth, our leader figured, why not here?"

"Leader?"

"Yes. She would have greeted us if she were able. She's quite intrigued to meet you. I may be the only resident to ever visit this place, but you're the first one cast out from such a crucial program who remembers every detail of their past. Come. If Mission is in as much peril as you suspect, we must move fast."

He led me down a set of grated stairs leading directly into the first row of suspended crops. The verdant plants rose around me, forming an archway of green. I was transported to all those countless hours managing *Ignis: Live*'s cameras. The brightness of the core, the crags of rocks peeking through breaks in the canopy—it was like I was really there.

My unfinished recreation of the *Ignis looked* perfect. Theirs worked. I marveled at the effort of people I'd believed were savages. I breathed in the scents of countless species of flora, multitudes more than in Virgil's shack.

"Excuse me," an Unplugged woman harvesting corn said politely as I accidentally bumped into her. She smiled and made room for us to pass before getting back to her work.

"The Unplugged have spent decades studying how the *Ignis* works in order to develop this place," Virgil said. The vibrations of their core's fusion reactor were rowdier here than on the actual *Ignis,* so he had to raise his voice for me to hear him. "It's constantly being improved and expanded as we bring more into our fold, but work is tedious since it must be performed in secret. If any bots or High Earth Network surveillance systems discover that we are disrupting the bedrock of Earth's last surfaced continent, and using fusion power, they would destroy everything we've done and catapult our core into space."

"How are you managing to mask the energy output from a reactor that size, then?" I asked. "Even through all that rock, High Earth's sensors don't miss anything."

Virgil smirked. "You're more perceptive than most residents I meet."

"I spent a lot of time watching a place just like this."

"Lead. The material hasn't been used extensively in centuries, but our scavengers retrieved tons from a sunken city many kilometers out into the ocean. It blocks the bots' daily sweeps searching for elevated power activity in the Outskirts." He pointed up. "The whole ceiling is laced with it. And the main hatch. Bits of it in the core's enclosure, too."

I squinted toward the ceiling and saw what he meant. The glare of the core made it difficult to perceive, but while most of the walls were fashioned of rough rock, the ceiling undulated in a pattern too perfect to be natural. And it was completely black, like onyx.

With my initial sense of awe fading, I began to hear running water all around me. Pipes and power lines ran down from the ceiling and along the walls like stripes. Every joint and run appeared like it was made of a different variant of metal. Rusty, then shiny; copper, then steel. They fed into all the hydroponic beds and hoses being used by Unplugged farmers as well as the living areas.

"I'm guessing the water comes from the ocean, like the *Ignis*'s subsurface one?" I said. "But I don't see any re-assemblers or purifiers to make it potable."

"If we had one of those, we wouldn't need to farm, would we?"

"True . . ."

"It's rainwater, actually. The sewers and drains left beneath the Outskirts are almost a century old. Even the High Earth surveyor drones don't pay much attention to them. We rerouted a few from along the outer wall, where rainfall is heaviest, and directed them here. The natural filtration system installed directly above our core ensures it's as clean as we can get it, but it's nowhere near as efficient as the one on the actual *Ignis*. And constant stress from storms forces us to construct replacement parts yearly."

"This must have taken years," I marveled.

"Decades, actually. Excavation was the hardest part. Every inch you see was once solid rock and dug out despite our limited ability to use heavy machinery without being discovered. All human hands."

A few Unplugged men and women were up on scaffolds, installing new pipelines or repairing old ones with more corresponding pieces . . . probably foraged from trash sweepers. I could imagine my old lifeband squealing if I were ever up so high on such a shoddy structure.

"A few bots would have helped," I said.

"Our leader refused to use even reclaimed ones for fear that they were being monitored by the High Earth Network to search for prohibited operations like this, which might put Earth's health at risk. They don't really give a damn how much data or tech is stolen, you see, but mess with the careful balance of this flooded planet and being delisted will be the least of your problems."

"I never realized they cared at all about what happened out here unless a resident was in trouble."

"Of course you didn't. The Network is just doing what it was programmed to do. Looking out for humanity's future and ensuring the comfort of its present residents."

"Like the *Ignis*'s core . . ." I whispered, half to myself and half to anybody who was listening. Virgil glanced back over his shoulder, tilting his head like he hadn't heard me.

"Sorry," I said. "It's nothing."

He brushed aside the last wiry plant in our path. We turned and approached a portion of the rocky arcade wrapping the hollow. In a few, I could see the flutter of tiny insects. Not crowds like in the *Ignis*, but their stock was evidently growing. Not much else survived Earth's flooding.

One arch had two Unplugged men standing guard on either side of it. They retained their eyes and were chiseled with muscle. That was where Virgil headed.

"As you can see, our leader is a fan of your former work," he said.

"I thought you people despise all programs like it," I replied.

"The *Ignis* itself is as real as you or I."

"Why don't you live here, then?"

"One day, I hope. For now, I'm needed opening eyes."

He strode beneath the archway, and as I went to do the same, the two men standing guard grabbed me. Wordlessly, they patted down every inch of my body. They were far more thorough than the bouncers at the Ignis Farmers show bar. My shirt and pants were lifted and yanked. And they were as strong as bots, as if they alone had carved the entire hollow with their bare hands.

"You're clean," one said. "Go ahead."

They shoved me up beside Virgil. The whole process had me feeling like a plaything, but at least they didn't ask for any more of my clothing.

"Forgive them," Virgil said, his voice softening as we passed into a lower, quieter tunnel. "Our leader is in fragile health these days."

At the end of the rocky passage, a dingy curtain was pulled all the way across. A strange sound emanated from beyond, like the rasp of wind blowing through a canyon followed by a squeaky piston.

Virgil stopped and faced back in my general direction. "You must wait here until I invite you in. If it's all right with you, I must explain your situation to our leader exactly the same as you did to me."

I considered it, then shrugged. One more person knowing wasn't going to affect anything. It wasn't like he knew any actual details that might impact the perception of *Ignis: Live.*

Virgil peeled back the curtain and entered, leaving me alone. After a minute of hearing incomprehensible whispering, I thought about searching around for myself, but the warm breath of the guards who'd suddenly appeared behind me kept me still. A few more minutes passed until Virgil finally poked his head out and beckoned me inside.

"You are welcome," he said. "Whatever you do, don't draw any attention to her condition. And be respectful at all times. I know how you residents can be."

"I'm not one, remember?" I said, making no effort to hide my continued disdain for that fact.

"You aren't one of us yet, either."

I bit back a harsh response and settled on, "Who is she?" instead.

"She's the oldest of us. Of any human. Around since before the techno-revolution, High Earth, or the oceans stopping their rise. If anyone can get you to the *Ignis* quickly, it's her."

He drew the curtains all the way. The strange noise was immediately clarified. Their leader was more machine than human. She lay propped upright on a tall bed and covered in blankets. If what Virgil had said about her age was true, that would make her over two hundred years old. She looked it. She had to be the tiniest woman I'd ever seen, with wrinkles so deep, her skin looked like cloth drapery hung from her bones. Both her eyes were gray from cataracts, and a tube stretched from a hole in her throat.

It and more tubes in her wrists, one of which was cybernetic along with half her torso, were attached to a clunky piece of machinery releasing the raspy noise as mechanisms within it pumped. A neural band wrapped her head, glowing blue and pulling back the few wisps of ash-gray hair still sprouting from her liver-spotted head. She didn't wear the mark of the Unplugged, though it might have been buried under her wrinkles.

Virgil took my hand and pulled me in. The decrepit woman's head didn't turn to face me. It remained crooked to the side, as if stuck. The darker portion of her murky eyes rolled toward me, however, and her neural band started to swell and fade in color.

"This is the one, Virgil?" a young man standing behind the life-support machine said, not a hint of emotion behind any words and no facial expressions or inflection of tone. The upper half of his face was covered by a dated OptiVisor, presumably with an Unplugged brand hidden beneath it. Veins covered his bald head, with the right side above his ear completely made of tech surrounded by scarred flesh. He wore rags, but they did nothing to hide his hands, both of which were also artificial.

In them, he held an ancient-style book. A treasure of some sort, with a spine and pages and everything. He finished scrawling something on an open page with a manual writing instrument, then closed the cover. He then placed it within a safe in the wall and locked it.

Virgil approached, using the Unplugged leader's bed to guide himself. He placed a hand gently over the outline of her two withering legs beneath the blankets. They were so skinny he could wrap both ankles. One of her feet didn't show beneath the covers either. Amputated.

"Yes, Elder," he said deferentially. "This is him."

Her hand budged under the blankets only slightly. Then the young cybernetic man behind the machinery said, "Come closer, child. Let me get a look at you."

"That's her speaking?" I whispered to Virgil.

He nodded.

My legs felt like they were shaking as I took a step, but a quick check proved they weren't. The Elder's head rotated about an inch, but the effort caused spit to dribble down to her sagging chin. Virgil wasted no time using his sleeve to wipe it away.

"Excuse my need for a proxy," the young man said. "Too many years on Earth have left my body in shambles."

I struggled between looking at her and the emotionless cyborg speaking for her. I'd never experienced anything like it. It was clear how the thing worked, or at least I could guess. The neural band conveyed her thoughts directly to the chunk of tech built into his head, which showed a series of blinking lights as it received the message, then transmitted to the visor over his eyes so he could relay them. It would have been less confusing to have the machine speak for her, but I guess the Unplugged leader had to keep their standards of human-first, even though it was machinery that sustained both of them.

"Relax, I know what I look like," the proxy said emotionlessly. "Don't let Virgil scare you. If it were up to him, he'd say he'd removed his eyes just so he wouldn't have to look at me."

Virgil smiled warmly. "You know that's not true, Elder. I hope to look as good as you at your age."

"Let's hope you don't live this long. Now, come closer, Asher Reinhart. Time is one thing no technology can manipulate." Before I knew it, I was beside the bed, her life-support machines humming directly in my ear. "There you are. Healthy, handsome. They're still taking care of us well on the other side of the wall, it seems."

I managed a nod. It was even stranger conversing with her now with the proxy now behind me. I could see the slight twitch of her crinkly lips as her neural band surged with color and conveyed her thoughts. Occasionally, a quiet whistle and dribble slipped through, but nothing more.

"Virgil tells me you're interested in reaching the *Ignis*?" her proxy said.

"Yes . . ." The words escaped my lips more meekly than I'd intended. For some reason, I was more intimidated by the haggard bag of bones who couldn't move than anyone I'd met in the Outskirts so far. "Yes," I repeated louder.

"A difficult task, but not impossible. I was around when it was constructed, you know. Your ancestors transported it near the sun to melt out its innards before fitting it for space travel. It was originally intended to carry us to another star."

"I know."

"Gloria Fors invented the molecular re-assembler for it. Did you know that? It was meant to minimize resource expenditure during a centuries-long voyage, but the technology shifted the paradigm."

I shook my head. I knew about how the re-assembler fit into High Earth's history, but had no idea it was originally developed for the *Ignis*. I guess I should've paid more attention to *Molecular Nation*, though if what the Elder claimed was true history, then the infusers would have taught me that while I was developing in the synth-womb.

"Space travel, AIs, cognitive manipulation, bots," she went on. "None of it changed the fate of the human race like the re-assembler. It was built for the stars, yet it made reaching them negligible. It helped tame the oceans and make farms and animals nonessential, transforming a portion of the Earth we'd forsaken into the only place we now need. A completely autonomous Higher Earth."

"Why are you telling me all of this?"

"Because I already know your greatest desire. You at least deserve to know mine."

"Re-assemblers changed the world, but you want all people to survive without them because you're unfortunate enough to be stuck outside High Earth. Is that it?" Against my best intentions, my tone swelled with bitterness. All of the Unplugged seemed to speak in never-ending riddles. At least when Mr. Helix cast me out, he wasn't vague about it.

"I wish to return humanity to humanity. That is all. This place is a start," the proxy said. "But if we ever hope to expand any further, we need to improve efficiency without boosting power. Lead and rock can only mask our operations so long."

I started to reply, but Virgil shook his head as if he could hear words forming in my throat, and whispered, "Let her finish."

"Nobody on this side of the wall knows as much about how

the *Ignis* operates so proficiently as you," her proxy said. "From its core to how it circulates water, and everything in between."

"I wish that were true," I said, remembering my replica, which was all visuals and no beating heart. "I operated cameras to help tell our stories in the most provocative ways possible. I didn't build it. I couldn't even reconstruct it properly in a VR environment."

"But you have seen and remember more than any other person out here. Information even you don't realize you have. For years, we've conscripted any slicer who didn't want us dead to hack into Craig Helix's datahub and recover as much about the vessel as possible in an effort to perfect our life here, but his security systems are exceptional. All anyone can manage is to rip those feeds that are already live for residents."

"I'm not surprised," I said. "Everything about Mr. Helix's program is exceptional. You're looking at one fool who thought he could hide something from him."

The Elder's worthless body started moaning, and her jaw wriggled. Virgil patted his way along the bed to find her shoulders and propped her up higher, quieting her. One of her collarbones was missing.

"You are the key, Asher Reinhart," her proxy said. "Your head contains everything we need to know, and it is also the only way to get you onto the *Ignis*."

"Virgil, what is she talking about?" I asked. "If I could get us there, I wouldn't be here."

"At some point, you must have seen the *Ignis*'s orbital pattern on charts and readouts, right?" he said.

"I don't know. They were never relevant to my work. The Network handled comms details through Mr. Helix's programming."

"Even if you haven't, you've communicated with the fixer stationed there."

"Fix—how do you know about them?"

"We've discovered at least enough to know that Craig keeps a human near *Ignis* in case of emergency. We can analyze transmittal delays you've experienced with them down to the millisecond, along with directional readouts from the comm-relays and any other information you might have seen in order to establish an anticipated vector."

Excitement took hold. I clutched him by the arm. "You can figure out exactly where it is in orbit? Is that what you're telling me?"

"Theoretically, yes," the Elder's proxy said.

My enthusiasm suddenly faded. "But wouldn't you need a ship?"

"Yes, we would, and as you know, the High Earth Network monitors all of them and reserves them for approved developer purposes only. There's no other need to leave. Any sign of intrusion or altering a programmed bearing and it would be shut down instantly. Alas, the time of exploration for the sake of it ended long ago."

I pondered for a moment. "What about a ship that's already going there? I know Mr. Helix is considering bringing on a new fixer. That would mean sending someone from High Earth. Virgil can enter again, sneak on, and be there in a day. Right?" I tugged on his sleeve like a child on *Ignis* hoping for an extra portion.

"It's a plan we considered, but we don't know when he will select a replacement or send one out," the proxy said. "And there will be security bots in the city as well as on the ship. It is a difficult task to ask of one newly without sight."

"It is an impossible task to ask of anyone, Elder," Virgil remarked.

"I don't see how any of this is helping!" I groused. Watching the Elder's body remain still as a corpse while we spoke made our conversation feel like it was taking even longer.

"The one you wish to save doesn't have the time left for us to wait on a low probability," the proxy said. "There are other ships that leave the surface, destined for nowhere. Unmonitored because of it. We can get you on one of the radioactive waste vessels dispatched from High Earth's ocean plants. With careful calculations, you should be able to delay its launch until the precise moment its trajectory will collide with the *Ignis*."

I would have burst out in laughter if I wasn't so frustrated. "You want me to ride a trash can through space, with no way to stop, and slam into the *Ignis*?"

"Into the small station adjoined to it, where the fixer lives, to be more precise," Virgil clarified. "Exact timing and ejection of waste can help temper the impact. Before the techno-revolution, the Elder was involved in plans for numerous deep-space expeditions."

"That was over a century ago!" I protested.

Virgil's features darkened. "Her body may be broken, but her mind is as sharp as ever!"

The proxy leaned over and placed a comforting hand on Virgil's shoulder. His head whipped around toward the touch. It seemed to break him down a bit. His lower lip quivered noticeably for a few seconds before he regained control.

"Calm yourself, Virgil," the proxy said. "It is hard for any resident to learn to trust in others."

Virgil lowered his head and turned away from all of us. "Forgive my outburst, Elder."

"There is nothing to forgive. This is my only offer, Asher Reinhart. With the information in your head, I can help you reach the *Ignis* and spare the inhabitant called Mission the repercussions of your mistakes. In exchange, you will allow us to probe the deepest recesses of your memories and learn as much as we can about how the *Ignis* operates."

I was right back to where I'd been while strapped to Minah's chair. If I said yes, every secret about *Ignis: Live* would be laid out for a fanatical faction I still wasn't sure I could even trust to uphold their end of the bargain. They could destroy the public perception of the show by revealing studio operations, and potentially get Mr. Helix delisted when they found out that it was he, not I, who left me with my memory. On the other hand, Mission would undoubtedly die.

"Let's say I agree, and you can get me to her," I said. "How would we return?"

Assuming I could get to her in time without affecting the show, I had no clue where we would go after. The High Earth Network wouldn't remain unaware of my presence. There would be nowhere to hide.

"It is possible there are ships on standby for the acting fixer to utilize, but you would know better than I," the proxy replied. "I'm sorry, but I can only promise a way there."

"If your way even works," I remarked.

"It will." For the briefest moment, I saw the Elder's gray pupils focus on me. Then they listed back off to the side.

"You can trust her, Asher," Virgil insisted. "She saved what little was left of me when all I could see in the world was darkness. She can do the same for you. All you have to do is open your—"

"Eyes," I finished for him this time. "And in exchange, you get to learn everything about the program I dedicated my life to. No matter how much you promise you won't, I'd be handing you everything you'd need to try to destroy it."

"If we cared about the show, we have you here already and

brain infusers to spare," the proxy said. "The next waste vessel from a factory rig we can reach is scheduled to be launched at dusk tomorrow. Take the night to think over what is worth risking. Remember the stars, Asher Reinhart. They call to us."

CHAPTER 17

I reached by my side and picked up a half-eaten tomato from Virgil's garden. It was proving to be my favorite of his offerings. Tomato juice trickled down my chin as I took a bite.

The Outskirts were a rank, unpleasant place, but it wasn't so bad up on the outer wall, I supposed. I sat, tucked into a nook just outside Virgil's shack. I wanted to be alone to think about what the Unplugged leader offered, and with the rain deciding to take a break, I could find no better place. Virgil insisted I stay close if I wanted to risk using an active High Earth holopad abundant with a resident's worth of data. After what I'd seen out here, I was inclined to agree.

I hadn't slept a wink since we'd left the Unplugged's *Ignis* replica and their strange cybernetic Elder and her proxy. It was so late that the top of the wall was quiet enough to hear the show without an earpiece. All the shops and stands had long since emptied, and the High Earth factories floating out in the ocean emitted a dull glow like the moon would've if it weren't veiled by clouds. Shacks blocked the wind, so the only distraction from

Ignis: Live was the constant purr of spinning turbines and the rhythm of the waves far below.

I closed my eyes and breathed in the salty air. Then a disturbance shook the live feed of Mission, which I already had pulled up.

[Ignis Feed Location]
Core Cell 3
<Camera 1>

A second knock on Mission's cell had her up right away. She had no idea how long she'd been locked up, but this time she was composed enough not to try to run. It was always like that in the hole. After a while, she grew complacent to the darkness and the solitude. And ever since Alora's visit, even Cassiopeia stopped coming.

Many times in her life, she'd gone so long without interaction. Even growing up under the floor, Alora would pop in any chance she had. All Mission could do was close her eyes and fight the claustrophobia, occasionally peering through her eyelashes to see her and Jacen's spot through the viewport. As much as she fought it, she couldn't help but look. But hope he might appear there, smiling up at her.

The door opened.

Mission didn't jump up this time. She opened her eyes and saw Alora framed by lights, just as she used to as a child. Before she could speak, enforcers rushed in, hoisted Mission up, and dragged her out. Their strong hands crushed her wrists.

"Let her go, you brutes," Alora demanded.

"You're lucky you're not in there with her," an enforcer spat. "It was only a matter of time till one of them cursed Blackout kids nearly killed us all."

Alora glared at him. "Until she's sentenced, she is still a Mother, and you will treat her accordingly."

The enforcers grunted, then released Mission.

Alora quickly came to her aide. She took Mission's hands and gently rubbed her wrists with her thumb. "Are you okay?"

"I'm fine," Mission replied. "I didn't think you were coming back."

"Nobody deserves to be treated like this. Not until the Collective passes judgment. They're only afraid that you might know tricks to manipulate the core."

"I swear I don't."

"They haven't let me leave either, though my room is nothing like this. It's like the Great Blackout all over again. Without somebody to blame, fear and doubt will take hold of everyone."

"I can't believe this is happening . . ."

"I know, dear, I know," she shushed her tenderly. Alora embraced her and ran her fingers through her hair. Mission closed her eyes, almost pretending she was back in that hole, where at least she wasn't despised.

"I want to show you something, Mission," Alora whispered. "As long as you're up for taking another walk."

"Nope. I'd rather stay." Mission folded her arms and held them there until her lips formed the bare edges of a smile. Glazed eyes betrayed the earnestness of the expression, but it was enough to make Alora chuckle.

"There's my girl. I was worried I'd lost you. Come on."

The enforcers guarding Alora and Mission stayed even closer this time as they crossed the core. Mission noticed Cassiopeia watching them keenly from the workroom and tracking their progress, as if waiting for something. It was unnerving. Before her many interrogations, Cassiopeia was like an ephemeral figure who only appeared in public during spacing ceremonies and once a year at launch anniversary celebrations. All she brought with her was pending death and reminders that the people of *Ignis* once had a real planet to live on.

So Mission did what she couldn't do the last time on her way to the shower. She ignored all the judging glares leveled their way and stayed close to Alora. She longed to reach out and hold her hand, but wasn't sure if she'd outgrown that. By the time they reached their destination, it was too late.

"Let us in," Alora requested, her usually polite demeanor melting away.

An enforcer standing outside a pressure-sealed hatch looked them over, perplexed. He peered over their shoulders, and Mission saw Cassiopeia out of her peripherals offering a nod of approval. The enforcer positioned himself in front of a keypad and entered a preposterously long code followed by a finger-print scan before the first layer of the airlock popped open with a snap-hiss.

"Is this what I think it is?" Mission asked.

Alora didn't need to answer. They passed through the other end of the airlock and into the central chamber of the core. An accessible, enclosed walkway circled the spherical space, wrapped on the sides by data-stacks storing all the information the *Ignis* needed. About present and past inhabitants, as well as the dying world they left behind and the new one they were traveling to.

The top of the corridor was transparent, so Mission could see the core's fusion reactor suspended in the center. The smoldering orange orb was supported by thick conduits and a series of spinning metal blades and rotating inner enclosures. These obstructed any harmful radiation while also emitting enough light and warmth to feed its farms. Through large rifts and light amplifiers built into the steely enclosure, slivers of the green inner surface of *Ignis* were visible.

Sweat immediately started dripping from Mission's brow as they entered. The heat emanated by the constantly refreshing data-stacks as well as the reactor made it like being in a sauna turned all the way up. Two Collective members monitoring the fusion reactor on the other side of the glass wore bulky protective suits to keep them from boiling. With gravity so low on the inside, they were able to float from side to side.

"Incredible, isn't it?" Alora marveled, shielding her eyes with her hand as she squinted up at the core. Up close, even the tinted divider couldn't diminish the brightness enough to stare for more than a few seconds.

"I never thought I'd see it," Mission stammered. She had to raise her voice. The ceaseless *whir* of the core was so loud there it was like stepping into a tornado.

"Few of us ever do. I had the privilege of being brought here the day I was named Mother by Cassiopeia. She'd said, 'This might be the greatest feat of human engineering in history, but without the children we bear, it'd be pointless. Another lost star in the void.' We are the true heart of the *Ignis*, Mission. Never forget that."

Mission's eyes twinkled at the prospect, then dimmed. "I don't have long enough left to forget."

Alora grasped her and leaned in close. "Don't say that. I know you'd never hurt anybody, and I know how much you cared for Jacen. When the Collective stands before you, they'll see you aren't lying. We're going to find out the truth."

"Are we? I don't know how long I've been in that cell, but I've been trying to think of anybody who could have sent that message. The only other person who might have cared about me being paired with Paul is Jacen . . . was Jacen. But he would never kill all those people just to get me out of it. Never."

"Maybe he only meant to hurt Paul? If he could somehow

find a way to hack into the core's systems, he might not have known what he was doing. That could have led to the error."

"No!" Mission snapped. "It wasn't him. He embraced what I had to do. More than I did. I tried to give myself to him the day before, Alora. If he hadn't rejected me, I would've been spaced anyway."

Alora took a measured breath, probably reeling from the news. "Oh, Mission."

"He was everything to me. I don't even deserve to have been born on this ship. You know that. I just wanted something that was mine. Really mine."

Alora threw a finger over her mouth. "Never say that. The Great Blackout happened for a reason, and you're one of us no matter what you think."

"Does that mean all those people suffocated too? For more illegals born like me to sneak in."

"No, never. I'm not saying that. Just, maybe Jacen changed his mind about wanting you. Maybe he—"

"It was whoever was trying to act like him," Mission cut her off. "The one who attacked me. I just don't know why."

"There are no clones on *Ignis*, Mission."

Mission's lips twisted in frustration. "Even you don't believe me?"

"I trust you with all my heart. But if you stand by this story that there were two of him, nobody else will. Listen to me, Mission. Tell them you found Jacen at your terminal with a stolen pulse-pistol, and that you can't remember what happened, but you know someone attacked you and a shot went off. Oxygen had barely returned to the block. You could easily have been disoriented from deprivation enough to not know exactly what was going on."

Mission's jaw dropped. Exactly what had happened still

remained a mystery, but Alora was the one person she felt she could rely on. The one person who would back her no matter what because she knew her secrets. And they never openly discussed Jacen, but they never had to. She'd known since Mission was old enough to have her conception implant installed how difficult it had been for Mission to keep her distance from the first boy she ever met.

"You want me to blame him?" Mission questioned.

"I want you to live!" Alora implored. "Wouldn't he?"

"He wouldn't want me to lie! Maybe his body has already been recycled, but he'll be hated by everyone, forever." Alora's gaze drooped toward the floor just for a moment, but long enough for Mission to recognize. "It hasn't been?"

"They're waiting to resolve this situation."

"His remains would be spaced, then. His energy discarded."

"But yours wouldn't be."

"And neither would yours." Mission scowled. "Is that why you really arranged this talk? To clear your own name?"

"You know I would never! You could return to being the Mother you were always meant to be, and guide a tortured block through this terrible time. He would understand. It's for the good of the *Ignis*."

"I'd rather see the stars." Mission stormed away before Alora could respond, and approached the enforcers at the entrance. Their hands hovered nervously over the grips of their weapons until she stopped.

"This flame-robber would like to return to her cell now," Mission demanded. They were eager to oblige, but before she could follow them through the door, Alora grabbed her wrist.

"If I knew how to take the blame, I would," she whispered. "Think of everything I've done for you. All the lying and sneaking. All the sacrifices."

"I never asked you to."

"And you never had to. I don't care what the truth is, Mission. I'll always look out for you. I'm your mother."

"Except you're not."

Mission glowered at her for a few moments. Alora's lips trembled and her eyes teared, but she said no more. Mission turned and walked away with the enforcers, for the first time eager to be shut out from the world.

Now she knew why Cassiopeia had been watching them. They were hoping to pin everything on Jacen, a lowly sewer jockey, so that Mission, a Mother, wouldn't become a darker stain on her already tainted generation.

* * *

I had to lower Virgil's holopad for a moment to wipe my cheek. I couldn't estimate how many times *Ignis: Live* had lured me to tears, but it was harder to hold them back when my own influence had so directly caused such anguish. Of all the people to turn their back on Mission . . . Alora? The woman who'd hidden her, cared for her since birth, made her lawful. The woman who, for all purposes, was her mother.

I didn't know who Mission's real parents were. I never looked back at the footage to find out how she was illegally conceived. Once I was chief director, I could've scoured the logs. The thought never even crossed my mind until I watched Alora break her heart. She'd always been enough. The story behind the story.

I understood the feeling of being hurt by a mentor more than most after what had happened with Mr. Helix, but at least my actions had justified it. Mission hadn't done anything but be in the wrong place—one that I'd put her in—at the wrong time.

As she returned to the solitude of her cell, I found myself checking on the many other feeds displaying inhabitants coping with the losses in Block B. My own circumstances made it difficult to enjoy the drama. Or maybe now that I wasn't tracking them, I only cared about one storyline.

What I did know was that the *Ignis* didn't seem like it would ever recover from Mr. Helix's planned fiftieth anniversary events. It hit them harder than he'd anticipated; he'd said as much. It had claimed more lives. Inhabitants always emerged from adversity stronger. I just couldn't see it.

For the first time, the thought popped into my head that maybe this wasn't the first calamitous event Mr. Helix had been directly involved in. Had the Great Blackout truly been an accident? Was the show's directive, to which I'd dedicated my life, all a lie? Was any of it even real? Or was Virgil planning to help me reach a vessel that had secretly always been computer generated? Was Mission . . . real . . . ?

I was startled as a young boy suddenly sat by me, saving my tired mind from going further down that dark path. My brain was so used to pharma, I found it racing more easily, unable to be controlled, affecting me enough to make my heart race. I hadn't been in the Outskirts long enough to start driving myself insane with doubts.

The boy didn't say anything to me. I hadn't met enough children to have a good grasp of ages, but he was too young to have been animated in High Earth. Half his face was deformed, lumps of hard flesh covering one eye and creasing his mouth. His clothing was so tattered he might as well have not been wearing any. He clutched his knees to his chest and rocked back and forth.

I noticed him peeking over at Virgil's holopad from time to time. At first, I thought it was respect that kept him from watching someone else's device, but then I realized it was fear. His expression told the entire story. I remembered those three wretches sitting around a holopad who pretty much hissed me away when I first was exiled. I could only imagine how many times the boy had been struck or pushed away by trying to watch what wasn't his.

I placed the holopad upright on the ground in between us. Then I reached down for the sliver of tomato I had left and threw it in my mouth. He stared at the juice dribbling down my chin, and I realized that was what his eyes were focused on, not the screen.

"Oh, sorry," I said, low enough that he probably didn't hear me.

He edged toward me so he could see the holopad better. I struggled not to move. He had a monstrous look to him with his deformed face, small as he was. He slid a little closer still until only an arm's length separated us.

And then, over his shoulder, I noticed the strangest thing. A resident stood across the way, under the shadow of a shop's awning. I didn't spot a bot guardian with her, and her clothes were set to dark gray, like she wanted to hide. The fact that no delisted folk seemed to be flocking to her meant it was working. But she looked straight at me.

Her clothing might have been colored to help her stay inconspicuous, but not her hair. It was dyed bright purple, shaved on half her head and flopped over the other. There was pain in her features, and I thought I recognized something in her eyes.

I stood, and she looked from side to side like she was ready to bolt.

"Do I know you?" I asked.

I took another step closer, then almost got whacked in the face by the door of Virgil's shack. The boy quickly scurried a few steps away. In one hand, Virgil had his cane, in the other, a cracked box filled with produce. He tossed a ripe tomato to the child with unexpected accuracy—as if he expected him to be there—and said, "That you, Colin? Enjoy." The boy caught it and darted away.

I moved around the door to see if the resident was still there, but she was gone. I then realized that a small group of dirt-covered children had accumulated around the corner of the shack, many with physical deformities, though none as bad as the first. They waited patiently to step up one by one as Virgil distributed food. He might as well have been wearing a re-assembler on him, chiming for every serving. A few older folks watched as they began setting up their merchant stands, some unsavory looking, others desperate. Virgil didn't have a guard of any sort in sight, but they kept their distance.

I stood to approach him myself and promptly had to shield my eyes. Beyond the wall, the sun was rising, a fiery globe sitting on the horizon, light splintering like shattered topaz across the crests of waves and the corners of a faraway factory. So much like the *Ignis's* core. It instantly warmed my cheeks and sodden clothing. Made me feel more awake than I had in days.

"You could never feel the sun on your face like this with all those towers around, could you?" Virgil said as the last of the children claimed their food. "The Outskirts. You stay here long enough, and it grows on you. There's beauty in chaos."

"I suppose I understand that . . . a little," I replied.

"We'll make a delisted man out of you yet."

"Do you feed everyone born naturally out here?"

"If there was enough food. Perhaps when we finish our *Ignis*."

"What's wrong with all of them?" I asked.

"Nothing is wrong with them, Asher. They are as they were born. Imperfectly perfect."

"You can't believe that. It's dangerous."

"Life is dangerous. It's why people love your old show. It's why we're kept around. *Ignis: Live* may be your top-rated reality program, but out here? This is the longest running." He spread his arms wide toward the ocean. "Us. Here. Addicted to what was your birthright, begging like fools to get a taste. A carnival of thrills, open any time."

"You're sick."

"Isn't it wonderful?"

Virgil laughed and nudged me in the leg with his cane. Then he slid down beside me and his features darkened.

"We can't wait much longer, Asher," he said. "She needs to know."

"I know." I gazed up, where the few visible stars struggled to remain visible through the cloudy sky. "She's up there, somewhere, isn't she? I'd never really thought about it while sitting in my director's chair, but one of those stars might really be *Ignis*."

"We'll find it soon enough."

"All you need is to look inside my mind."

"All *we* need is to look inside your mind."

I sighed. "I promised not to betray Mr. Helix's trust ever again."

"The Elder is only interested in how the *Ignis* works. Whatever secrets you know will stay hidden, and we can go about saving Mission once we arrive however you think is best for your show. Viewers, Mr. Helix, nobody ever needs to know anything. Hurting one show won't change your world. I'm not sure it even can be changed."

"Even still."

"I give you my word. You help us. I help you. It's a simple trade."

"And I'm supposed to trust it? Mr. Helix provided me everything I could have ever wanted, Virgil. Gave me a purpose."

"A friend doesn't allow another to be exiled for following the affairs of the heart."

A seaward breeze kissed the sweat drawn onto my brow by the warmth of the rising sun. It was a remarkable new perspective on the sun, glistening unevenly off the unpredictable ocean rather than refracting through a uniform grid of glass towers. Maybe Virgil was right. Maybe Mr. Helix could have done something else besides give up on me. Considering the fiftieth anniversary event and state he left my mind in, he was very clearly capable of bending rules, both his own and High Earth's.

It was too late to worry about what he'd think. There was one point that Virgil was undeniably right about. I couldn't give up on Mission. Not yet. I'd watched over her for our entire lives, cared about her, made her famous, protected her . . . loved her.

Now it was time I actually went to her and made things right. No matter the cost.

"I'll do it," I said. "But only for her. Not for you and your gang."

"I wouldn't have it any other way." He patted my leg, then used his cane to stand, groaning all the way to his feet. "You're finally starting to understand what a trade means."

CHAPTER 18

The moment Virgil and I arrived at the entrance of the Unplugged's *Ignis* replica with news that I would help, everyone flooded out. Only then did I get a true understanding of how many dwelled within. One by one, members bearing the three-arced brand climbed up the ladder like programmed bots. When they were all through, a makeshift pulley system raised the Elder along with all her life-support equipment. The last one up was the half-metal proxy who spoke for her.

"I am pleased by your decision." The proxy spoke the Elder's thoughts to me. "We must hurry. There is no time to waste."

I regarded the motionless husk of the woman whose words he dictated, and then the proxy pushed her past me until her people surrounded her. The throng of Unplugged then horded onto the winding, rainy streets of the Outskirts. A weaponless army in rags, making the Elder untouchable. Too many to count were blind. Others were too old to hold their backs straight. Yet they all somehow maintained the same steady pace.

Virgil took my arm as we fell in behind them. His walking

stick stopped tapping. It was easier to keep up while using me as a crutch considering he was one of the newest to lose his sight, though I doubt he'd ever admit that.

"Rarely does the Elder move," he whispered in my ear. "She must be protected."

"Why now?" I asked.

"Why ever?"

Delisted folk cowered wordlessly into back alleys and buildings as our Unplugged mob barreled down the cramped street. Eyes actually glanced up from weathered holopads and cracked OptiVisors. A visiting resident threw open the doors of a balcony, a woman surrounded by naked men and her guardian bot. She watched in awe.

Members of all the different slicer gangs I'd encountered and more glowered from their VR dens and show bars. People deep inside virtual worlds were yanked away from their neural transmitters, I supposed out of fear of the mob's intent. I remembered the Unplugged woman who'd burned a Nation venue down the night before, and in the story of his past Virgil had said he too got caught in a VR den razed by the Unplugged.

We headed in the direction of the High Earth wall, then turned. More and more Unplugged seemed to appear from the shadows, swelling our numbers. The bearded preacher by the lifts was the only one who didn't join in. He continued to expound, though with everyone having fled, there was nobody to listen except for those who'd already agreed with his ideology.

"We're here," Virgil said.

The mob stopped, filling an entire alleyway and overflowing into the adjacent intersection. They parted so that the Elder could be rolled by, and suddenly, I was no longer aiding Virgil. He returned to tapping his stick and led me down the alley, which I now recognized. Minah's Brain Miner was at the end. One of the *I*'s had completely fallen off since my last visit, but there it was.

I freed myself from Virgil and halted.

"What is it?" he asked.

"You're not expecting me to see her, are you?" I answered.

"She is the best wiper outside of a High Earth med-bot."

"And the reason you found me half-dead on the street."

"Minah is the one you saw to erase Mission?"

I nodded. "She thinks I stole from her, but what I took still belonged to me. I didn't go through with the exchange."

"Relax, Asher. With the Elder here, she'll do exactly as she's told."

"She works for the Unplugged?"

Virgil snickered and tapped on along toward her doors. "She *works* for nobody. And you're lucky you didn't go through with it."

I froze for a few seconds, mind racing, and then caught up with him. "What are you talking about?"

"She helps those of us she respects who have difficulty breaking habits. And she's seen enough of the Elder's mind to respect her. Almost everyone else, she steals their tech and strips their minds. For residents . . . well, if you'd stayed, we'd already have access to everything we need to know. And you'd have walked out without any recollection of where home really was. A clean slate. Lucky Mission."

Again, I stopped, now right outside the door. "Your leader allows that? That's awful."

"Any worse than watching the inhabitants suffocate?" he said. "Look around you, Asher. You think honorable people erected this place? We're rats to High Earth. Pests. And if you thought I was the only one with access to the lifts to steal tech and spread our word, then you haven't learned a thing out here. I'm just one of the few who remembers why I do it, and who hasn't been caught yet."

"Yet I'm supposed to trust you?"

"It doesn't seem you really have a choice, does it?" He smirked, then struck me in the shoulder with his cane with exceptional aim. "Now, would you come on already? The waste vessels are always launched promptly, and we have one chance if we want to make it today."

He opened the heavy wooden doors with his stick. I could smell the awful musk of Minah's lobby, now accompanied by the newly learned fact that the moment I stepped into her shop the first time, I was damned to wind up stuck in the Outskirts, whether I stayed or ran.

I swallowed the lump in my throat and in my mind, repeating the very thing that had gotten me out of her chair to begin with. *For Mission.*

"Gree-eetings," the unsettling bot receptionist stuttered the moment I got inside. It was overloaded by the number of Unplugged in the lobby, repeating the phrase time and time again as its eerily human head turned to face each of us.

"My, my, look who decided to come back!" Minah exclaimed. Her faulty artificial leg was twisted even worse than last time from when I made her fall, but she limped over to greet me. She ran one of her long fingernails across my cheek, her rancid breath filling my nostrils as she leaned in.

"Handsome as ever," she said. "So sorry if Patrese hurt you. I had no idea you were so special. You don't have to worry about him anymore." She gestured toward the staircase leading down into her flooded basement. The man who'd guarded her shop and beaten me lay facedown, body half-floating in the water, which now bore a rusty tinge. I shuddered. I'd never seen a dead body in person before. In the VRs they didn't smell anywhere near as foul or, rather, like anything at all.

"Let's go, Minah," the Elder's proxy commanded. "There is no time for your games. You'll see what you've been craving."

"You can't rush a reunion with old friends." She wrapped her chubby arm around my back to lead me in farther, and her hands slithered so low on my back I cringed. "You couldn't stay away from old Minah, could you?"

"Apparently not," I muttered.

"Minah, we really need to hurry," Virgil said.

She maintained a big toothy grin while grasping my hand. "I just want to hear how much he missed me. Don't they teach you manners on the fancy side of the wall?"

"It's . . . It's nice to see you, too," I forced out.

"I knew he missed Minah!" She chortled and pulled me into a hug. Her nose pressed against my chest as she breathed in my aroma. I was glad she was so short or she might've kissed me. "Come, dear. Let Minah help you."

She guided me past her bot receptionist still continuously greeting everybody around its desk. It was only a matter of time before its voice box exploded. Virgil remained still.

"You aren't coming?" I asked him.

"You'll be fine, Asher," he replied without looking. He remained facing one of the room's cloudy windows.

I tore free from Minah. "No. I need you in there. She can take everything from me, and I won't know the difference."

"The Elder made a deal with you. She won't go back on it."

"Well, I don't trust her—either of them. I . . . I trust you." It wasn't easy to get the words out, but I think I meant them. A few days ago, Virgil had tried to kill me, but since then, we'd shared more words about things other than *Ignis: Live* than I ever had with anybody else. I turned to the crippled

Elder and said, "I'm sorry, but unless he's in there, my mind will remain sealed."

"Isn't this romantic," Minah groused. "Minah grows bored."

The Elder's neural band glowed, and for once, I recognized hints of frustration on the usually staid face of her proxy. "He may enter," he uttered. The proxy then turned toward the dozen or so other Unplugged who were inside the shop. "Nobody else gets in. The Nation is livid about one of their dens being razed yesterday. Watch the rooftops."

"Yes, Elder," one of her burly guards replied.

"Placing your trust in a blind man to watch a screen." Virgil snickered as he tapped his way past me. "You're still just as foolish, I see." My lip twisted. I hadn't even thought of that. "You'll be fine," he promised again before I could think of anything to say.

The Elder's proxy rolled her into Minah's operating room. The hatch into it locked shut once Minah, Virgil and I entered, causing dust to swirl down from the ceiling. It made me cough.

"You ran out like a scared cat last time," Minah said, patting me on the back. "But now, Minah finally gets a look into that pretty brain of yours. What secrets will Minah find?"

"*Ignis: Live* doesn't get touched, right?" I addressed Virgil.

"For the last time, I promise, we don't care about what happens with your show."

I pictured the dead piled high around air recyclers . . . twice. Once during the Great Blackout, shortly after I was animated, and again, for the fiftieth anniversary. At least one of those catastrophes was far from the accident the viewers were meant to think it was.

Minah was about to see that too. Maybe it was wrong, intervening like that. But that one moment would undermine years of inhabitant lives experienced by viewers—decades of genuine moments that deserved to be remembered fondly.

"After this you might," I said softly.

"Why are you still protecting it, anyway?" Virgil said. "Your old friend Craig Helix cast you out. You're as good as dead to them. Erased from the credits."

"The original applicants to the *Ignis* came from this place. They gave everything to be a part of something. Their children struggle every day to keep it going. Without the show, they have nothing. No purpose." I didn't think before answering. On the cusp of having my mind pried open once again, I was trying to be honest this time. With myself, and with them.

"Without the show, they'd be exactly where they are," Virgil countered. "Working to survive. Life goes on; only the setting changes. They don't know they're being watched, and they sure as hell don't care. They're people, Asher. Same as you or me. The sooner you accept that, the easier this will all be."

Virgil's words reverberated in my head as I was strapped into the rickety brain infuser chair I'd once been so eager to get out of. The Elder's bed was arranged just beside me, and her proxy worked with Minah to connect her neural band to mine with cables.

"It will be quicker to calculate trajectories if your memories are synced directly with mine," the proxy explained. "Anything of value I discover will be kept in my mind. No records, as per your agreement with Virgil. Minah has already acquiesced to these terms."

"Minah still gets to see." Minah chuckled. She rearranged my head in the bowl of neural nodes and transmitters. The blue light lit her chin as she leaned over me, making her portly face appear like something out of a nightmare. When she was done, she regarded me with a broad grin. That was even worse. She was like a jack-o'-lantern I'd once seen in a period drama.

She ran her fingernail along my neck and leaned so close I

could feel the moisture in her breath. Then she pulled my restraints as tight as she could. That gained my attention. With my head strapped, I couldn't do anything about it, even if I wanted to.

"Don't want you running away again," she said. "Just relax, my dear. It will all be over soon." She creaked away on her metal legs, still cackling.

The neural nodes behind my head amplified, and a tingling sensation built up around my ears. That was when my heart started racing. Again at Minah's mercy, but with newfound information about what she really did to her everyday clients. I glanced over at the immobilized body of the Elder beside me. "Remember your promise, Elder."

Her eyes twitched, as if to view me in her peripherals. Her life-support machine whirred as it pumped air into her; then her lips quivered. They formed words in the faintest way, but the only slightly audible one to slip through was "eyes."

Minah cracked her artificially enhanced fingers alongside her real ones. "Here we go!" They clacked across her keyboard, and the neural transmitters amplified. No warm-up period to get a read of my brain this time and provide an opportunity for me to change my mind. She was diving straight in. The last thing I saw clearly was Virgil standing amongst the shadows in the corner of the room. His arms were crossed and his eyeless face rested securely on me.

My mind retreated.

It was like uploading into a VR, only without any clarity. Images and pictures flashed across my consciousness. I saw the synth-womb I'd been developed in—a memory I didn't even know I'd retained. My first day alive, when VORA first showed me *Ignis: Live* and, more importantly, Mission. I saw my smart-dwelling and the gleaming towers of High Earth. All my tech and gadgets and favorite programs. The Helix digital studio and the crew. Mr. Helix regarded me pridefully on my first day as Chief Director, and then heartbroken on my last.

It was like someone made a visual scrapbook of my life.

The director's screen array in my old office, which I'd spent countless hours in front of, surrounded me with visions of the *Ignis*—of Mission and all the others. My conversations with fixers past and present. Yet, at the same time, I was privy to footage from another show.

It must have played in the background of my vision so often I never noticed, but as much as I saw Mission, I saw the events of *Molecular Nation*—the brilliant Gloria Fors as she invented the molecular re-assembler, signaled the techno-revolution, and ended war, famine, and the need for colonization from a failing Earth. I had no idea the show started as early as her birth, but I could see through her eyes as they opened for the very first time. An ancient city surrounded her, rife with hovering cars, strangely dressed people, and buildings made of brick and stone. Explosions from bombs being dropped during a war followed. Screams and blood and death . . .

My body lurched. Something pressed down on my chest to keep me down.

"There you are, Asher Reinhart," a voice said. "Welcome back."

"VORA?" I asked, breathless. I couldn't see straight. They couldn't get the restraints off me fast enough. I rolled off the chair and made a mess of Minah's floor with the contents of my stomach.

"Let it out," Virgil whispered as he patted me on the back, his voice growing clearer. I spit up some shreds of tomato and then fell back onto my rear. It felt like someone had taken a vacuum to my mouth.

"The Elder's brain function has ceased," her proxy said, voice marginally elevated for the first time.

Virgil dropped me and rushed over. His knees bumped hard against the base of the chair I'd been in, but it barely slowed him. I turned over. The proxy repeatedly slapped the OptiVisor used to convey the Elder's thoughts. He seemed wrecked without her guiding him, leaving Virgil to take charge.

"Minah, what's happening!" Virgil questioned. "The deal was you got her through this alive. Only you had the skill."

"There was too much stress on her psyche! Minah is trying." Her artificial fingers flew across the controls. I couldn't fathom how she was able to operate them so fast. That was when I realized that if the Elder died, so would Mission. Everything I'd just risked would've been for naught.

I scrambled to my feet, still woozy, and staggered over to the Elder. Her eyelids were fully closed, and both of her hands quivered. I grabbed one of them and squeezed. It was so frail it felt like it might crumble into dust.

"Wake up," I begged. "You have to wake up."

Virgil pushed the proxy away and knelt by her life-support machine, which continued to pump oxygen into her even though her body was rejecting it. A series of compartments were built into the base, and he rifled blindly through them all.

"Got it!" he cried, then hurried back to us.

He patted her chest a few times, then raised a needle and plunged it into the center of her rib cage. "Minah, provide a surge with everything you've got!" The neural transmitters around the Elder's head amplified, painting the entire vault-like room blue. Virgil threw the needle aside and clutched the Elder's face.

"Your work isn't finished," he whispered.

The Elder's proxy suddenly placed a hand on Virgil's

shoulder. Tears stained his soft cheeks, but his voice and expression were as relaxed as ever. "Worry not, Virgil. It is not
my time yet."

"Thank goodness." Virgil exhaled. I too released a mouthful of air.

"Nothing to worry about," Minah boasted. "Minah is the
best there is!" She waddled over, leaned on the Elder's chair,
and bent to kiss her on the cheek. For once, she showed a bit
of deference.

"Now I see," she whispered to her. "It's all I've ever wanted
to see."

"Then you'll stop asking?" Virgil said.

"See what?" I asked.

"A memory of the Elders," Virgil clarified. "Nothing that
concerns you.

Minah turned to me and grinned her rancid grin. "Don't
worry, that brain of yours is fascinating too. All the horrid people
Minah has seen out here, and your Mr. Helix is worse than all
of them."

I glared at her, and she playfully raised her hand over her
mouth.

"Of course," she said. "Secrets, secrets. Minah does hope
you'll visit again, though you probably won't be able to stop
yourself, considering what Minah put in." I grimaced. She
chuckled. "Oh, stop worrying. One day, you'll get used to my
jokes. Minah will make sure of—"

A tremor shook the entire room, nearly hurling me off my
feet. Knocks at the entry hatch were followed by muffled yelling.

"The Nation has come for revenge!" someone shouted.

"We have to get the Elder out of here immediately," said
another.

"We're coming," the proxy said. He quickly unfastened the

Elder's chair from Minah's machinery. Virgil took my arm and we hurried toward the door. I remained disoriented, so he was helping me as much as I was him.

"Minah, are you coming?" Virgil asked when we reached the opening.

She stood by her infuser chair, affectionately running her hands over the seat. All her bravado melted away. Revolting as she was, I imagined that the expression she wore currently was like how I felt all those times strolling into my office at Helix studios, like there was nowhere else I belonged. There, in her "operating room," she was home.

"You go on without old Minah," she said calmly.

"Every slicer in the Outskirts will know you're with us now," Virgil replied.

She cradled the bowl of neural nodes with both of her hands. "I'll say you all forced me to help. If they don't believe me, I'll make them." She chuckled and then turned her gaze upon me. "You sacrificed so much for her. I hope she's worth it, Asher Reinhart. She may have the looks, but I'll always be here waiting if you're ever looking for something . . . more."

Virgil yanked me out of the vault, leaving Minah behind, crowing to herself. We rushed back to the lobby, where we were greeted by the vacillating glow of real fire from outside and the deafening crack of gunfire.

"This is over what we saw the other night?" I asked Virgil. I recalled the burning structure and that Unplugged woman being beaten to death by Nation people in yellow.

He nodded. "That and more like it."

A window shattered and the head of an Unplugged standing only a few feet from me exploded with red. The body toppled over, a gaping hole at the base of the brand on his forehead dripping bits of brain onto the moldy floor. I gagged.

"Don't they realize we're helping them?" someone shouted. "Protect the Elder!" screamed another.

Unplugged surrounded us before I could question anything else. I was caught in the current, dragged into the alley where the bedlam was strongest. Silhouettes in yellow lined the rooftops all around us, firing down with guns dating back to every age of humanity I could think of. They couldn't penetrate the shield of bodies surrounding the Elder, her proxy, Virgil and me.

A stray explosive fell near us, and one of the Elder's followers picked it up and tossed it away without aiming. It bounced through the open door of Minah's shop and blew its street-front open. The blast momentarily threw us to the ground as debris from the devastated building flittered overhead.

Intense heat from crackling flames licked my feet as I stood with Virgil's help, burning my already worn shoes to the point where I was better off without them. There was no lifeband in the world that could level me during such wanton violence.

On the street, Unplugged armed with makeshift weaponry engaged the Nation assailants. They picked up fallen guns and fired at the rooftops. Some of the blind ones were even more proficient fighters than their seeing counterparts. They helped us push through a mob of yellow with the Elder surrounded.

We rounded a corner. The bearded preacher at the plaza outside the High Earth lifts took a shot to the leg. Then three more to the chest. Blood splattered all over the plasticrete. I saw the bright clothing of residents fleeing up the lifts, swarmed by drones. The Elder's proxy broke rank and scaled half a building in a single leap. His artificial hands dug into the wall and pulled him the rest of the way. He snapped the neck of the shooter on the roof like it was a twig, stole his weapon, and shot at the others.

I stayed as low as I could as I ran with Virgil on my arm,

until I spotted someone through the legs of the mob. Amongst all the delisted people running for cover, one resident stood in the plaza and didn't run. A poncho was pulled tight over the man's head to combat the rain, and his eyes were glued open. I remembered him from my first visit. The drone hovering over his shoulder recorded the chaos for *Outskirts Today*. The best footage he'd likely ever seen.

Bullets zipped by, snapping against the street and kicking up dirt in the direction of his feet. The crowd surged, and an Unplugged bumped into him. That same mother I'd seen the other night. Without thinking, I released Virgil and shoved through the crowd to reach the woman. I just grazed her fingers when I heard it.

"You have been asked to step away from the visiting resident," a security bot said. "Lethal force will now be required."

The bot behind the director resident raised its hand, and a surge of pure energy shot out. The mother's body lurched, and an instant later, she was vaporized into a cloud of red mist. My eyes stung as it engulfed me. I swatted at my tongue. I could taste her, like metal.

Virgil tackled me, and another burst of energy crackled over our backs. The preacher was its next unlucky target. At the same time, another explosion blew out the wall of a nearby building. The ground quaked, and the director finally gave in to the bot and retreated. I knew what it meant to get the perfect shot, but I couldn't believe anyone would go to such lengths.

A row of public safety bots had formed by the lifts. Enough to end the fighting with nonlethal weaponry with ease, yet they remained still.

"We have to go!" Virgil yelled into my ear.

I was too petrified to move. Buzzing sounded overhead, and the lights of security drones grew bright. "You are utilizing unlawful weaponry and must be disarmed." Robotic voices filled the air. Then they started to zap the combatants on the roof without offering a chance for compliance.

Blue bolts of electricity coruscated around bodies, making them convulse. Some fell from their perches; others collapsed and vomited. One struck the proxy in the arm. The electricity surged around his limb, but he seemed to be able to absorb it with his tech long enough to break free and leap down off the building.

"Get him!" Virgil yelled.

The proxy's impossibly strong hand grasped the back of my shirt and heaved me to my feet. The touch of his electrified hand sent a jolt up my spine that made me feel like I'd plugged into a VR. He dragged me back into the protective shell of bodies so we could keep moving.

Screams rang as the fighting died, thanks to the intervention of drones. Stray bullets still stung the street and the ranks of the Unplugged, but the Elder made it safely until all the shooting ceased.

"We're okay," Virgil said, his arm wrapping my waist. "They made their hit, but we're crossing Ignis Riders' turf now. They won't start a war."

I thought my wobbly legs would've given out without his aide. I'd dealt with more trauma in the last week than ever in my life, but a firefight was something I'd never expected. Something I didn't think anyone could get used to.

Apparently, out here, it was just another day . . .

CHAPTER 19

We sealed back behind the main hatch of the *Ignis*'s replica. The Unplugged ranks broke apart along the walk, scattering through back alleys and buildings in an effort to maintain the secret nature of their manufactured paradise. Most of those who'd returned were bloodied. I could only hope that, for their sake, their farms grew more medicinal herbs like those Virgil had given me to mitigate my pain.

As it was, I fell against a wall to catch my breath, scratching at my arms, which itched incessantly. I could feel the remnants of that woman coating them. Feel her underneath my fingernails, at the back of my throat.

There was no telling how many had died, or if Minah had managed to avoid being crushed by her own beloved shop. Maybe I'd be better off if she didn't make it, considering the things she knew. I hoped against reason that wasn't the case. I could relate to someone who loved their work as much as her, wicked as it might have been.

Many of the Elder's personal guards didn't survive either.

Her proxy and Virgil did, however, with barely more than a few scratches. Whatever I thought about the Unplugged before, one thing was clear to me now: they were devoted. The way they shielded their leader was unlike anything I'd ever seen, even in a period drama. It made me feel better about imperiling *Ignis: Live*'s future with them.

Virgil backed against the wall beside me. I was too busy with my hands over my ears and squeezing my eyelids to regard him. The ringing from all the chaos didn't end. The screams . . .

"Are you all right?" he asked.

"All right?" I said, seething. "All right? Is that normal to you, seeing a woman turned to mist like that?"

"It's what happens when our problems bring us too close to visitors."

"That was more than a problem, Virgil."

"It means they're scared. Of us. Of what this place could be."

"People died!" I screamed. I looked at him, eyes filled with tears from both shock and dust. That was when I saw him cradling that same newborn the dead mother had been, stroking its hair.

"People die on *Ignis* all the time."

"That's different, and you know it."

"Do I?"

I swallowed back a response because I didn't really have one. An older Unplugged woman approached from Virgil's side, tapped his shoulder, and he handed over the infant. She started humming a tune to the baby to keep it from crying. I only noticed it because it was one Alora always used with newborn inhabitants.

"Take the time you need, Asher," Virgil said. "We're not in a smart-dwelling anymore."

"No." I used the wall to rise to my feet. My legs remained

weak, but I forced myself to think of happy thoughts to calm down. Of Mission, free of her cell. Shown to be innocent. I didn't have healthy pharma at my fingertips to steady myself anymore. I had to learn. "She can't wait."

Virgil gave my shoulder an affirming shake. "Now you're getting it. Come with me."

We returned to the Elder's chamber. Her life support and brain seemed to have returned to proper functioning, but the attack sucked the life from their entire underground world. Nobody spoke; we merely panted, waiting for her proxy to break the silence. I stood opposite her, watching her cloudy, stagnant eyes. She knew everything about me. Like one of Mr. Helix's datahubs in fleshy form. I couldn't wait any longer.

"Did you find everything you need?" I asked with enough urgency to draw a glower from one her guards, who remained by her side rather than outside the room. With the knowledge she'd gained from me at Minah's disposal, apparently, the Elder had become even more valuable.

"She damn well better have," one of her protectors growled. "We lost too many to get inside your head."

"Leave us," the Elder's proxy requested.

"What?"

"Everyone, leave us. You too, Virgil."

The guard grumbled something and stormed out. Virgil offered me a nod of encouragement before leaving as well. Only when the curtain closed behind me and the echo of footsteps drowned out did a single finger of the Elder beckon me forward with the feeblest twitch.

"I have seen your mind," her proxy said. His head rotated to face me, but through the OptiVisor conveying the Elder's consciousness, it was impossible to know exactly where he was looking from so far. I shuddered. Being alone with them made me nervous.

"That's what you wanted, isn't it?" I said.

"Yes. I have what I need now. Do you?"

"That's up to you."

"I know the secrets you really wish to keep buried, Asher Reinhart, even if you do not. The truth about Craig Helix's involvement in what happens on the *Ignis*, and how willing he was to bend the rules during your expulsion." I started to sweat, but she quickly reassured me. "They are safe with me, as promised. The claims of delisted 'lunatics' would count for nothing on High Earth Network message boards. Words lost to the ethers."

I edged a little closer. "Thank you."

"I only have one question," the proxy said. "Are you keeping his secrets to protect the integrity of the show, or is it to protect yourself?"

"From what? There's nowhere worse I can be sent . . . No offense."

"Remember that I have seen within you. You must know that the blood of the *Ignis*'s inhabitants is on your hands as well as his. Saving Mission won't change that."

"I . . ." My lip twisted. I had no idea how to respond, and thankfully she didn't give me a chance to.

"You don't need to answer. Just know that Craig Helix is wrong. The inhabitants' reaction to adversity is not what makes the show real. Even the simplest AI can be programmed to react randomly. What makes it real is that they believe. They believe so fervently they are carrying the torch of humanity that they would sacrifice anything to preserve what little they have."

"You want me to tell them the truth when I go?" I asked. "Is that it?"

"No. They have their truth as their core's deceptions have helped them define it. Their mission is as real to them as the air you're breathing now. Every one of their deaths in service to it is final. Every conversation, as genuine as what we share now."

"I know. It's why people love the show so much."

The edges of the Elder's wrinkled lips creased into a meager smile. Her proxy walked over to a wall safe and entered a code into a small keypad. Inside, I noticed the ancient book he'd written in the other day. He grabbed something else and returned to me with what appeared to be a folded space suit. It was shiny, with armored joints and a carbon-fiber underlay. An angular oxygen tank with carbon filters was affixed to the back, attached through tubes to a sleek helmet. It bore a logo on the side. An *F* with a curved tail that circled the globe. Beneath it the words FORS TECH were printed—the company under which Gloria Fors had invented the molecular re-assembler a century ago.

The proxy placed it in my arms. The oxygen tank gave it some heft, but the remarkably light weight overall informed me that the suit was likely designed in the late twenty-second century, right before the techno-revolution.

"A relic from a golden age of war and poverty," the Elder explained. "You will need it to reach Mission."

I raised the helmet and blew on the visor. Dust scattered, revealing my own filthy face staring back. I hadn't even realized how much blood spatter was on me from the ambush. The crinkles around my eyes were deeper than ever, and the amount of gray in my hair seemed to have doubled since my exile. It was so bad that back on High Earth I might have considered requesting a med-bot to come and smooth it all out.

"What do I do with this?" I asked.

"My voice will guide you." Her proxy returned to the safe and emerged holding two more FORS TECH space suits.

Just then, the curtain at my back slid open. In strode Virgil. He used his walking stick to navigate to the side of the Elder's bed then whispered in her ear. She mouthed something imperceptible in response. He turned and extended his arms for a space suit.

"High Earth Network programming expertise may also be necessary when you reach the waste vessel," the proxy stated as he removed some more gear from the safe and stowed it in the packs on either side of his suit's oxygen tank. "Virgil spent his prior life as an expert at such. He will accompany you as well, with your sight to guide him through the process."

"I told you to open your eyes, didn't I?" Virgil said to me, smirking.

My attempt at returning the expression was thwarted by the unexpected arrival of tears at the corners of my eyes. I regarded Virgil, the Elder and her proxy. "I can't ever thank you all enough."

"You already have," the proxy said, finally finished gathering gear and again facing me. "Soon, our world will thrive as the *Ignis* does, thanks to you. A trade made in good faith must always be upheld. The good parts of humanity believed in that once. Now go. Your ride leaves shortly."

"I know the way, Elder," Virgil said.

"You always have, my friend."

The Elder's hand suddenly shot forward and wrapped my wrist. It was as pale and scrawny as a skeleton's, with withering flesh as cold as the rock all around us. The bony tips dug into my arm like the tips of daggers, and the grip was so unexpectedly tight that I couldn't pull free out of fear of ripping her arm off.

"Never forget what I told you," she whispered. She wheezed through every word, her voice as small and brittle as she was. "Go to *Ignis*, Asher Reinhart. Only there may you find your freedom."

CHAPTER 20

[Ignis Feed Location]
Core Cell 3
<Camera 2>

Mission glanced up from the viewport in the floor as the door of her cell opened. Cassiopeia stood outside. Her usually pristine white outfit had lost its crisp hems and was dappled with grime. She no longer regarded Mission with an accusatory glower. Exhaustion had stolen her edge.

"The Collective will convene shortly to hear your and Alora's cases," she said. "Do you still maintain that the death of Jacen-14133 was due to self-defense, and that you had no part in the theft of a Collective emergency pulse pistol?"

Mission gazed back down through her cell's tiny viewport at her and Jacen's spot. If Cassiopeia appeared exhausted, then there was no word accurate enough to describe how she felt. She was growing used to her cell. Safely locked in again. At least there, everybody, even her own mother, couldn't look down at her.

"I do," she muttered softly.

"And do you deny any role in the manipulation of core programming that resulted in the suffocation of two hundred and thirteen inhabitants?"

Hearing the number again made her wince. She nodded.

Cassiopeia exhaled slowly, then stepped into the room, knelt, and stared quietly until Mission had no choice but to meet her gaze. "Think long and hard. I hope you have a better story than what you've told me. I've seen enough people die this past week for a lifetime. I . . ." Her voice cracked. "I'd rather not have to space another."

Again, all Mission could manage was a nod.

* * *

Virgil stopped walking. He'd led me and the Elder's proxy through the warren of dilapidated structures and filth I was growing all too used to. I lowered his holopad playing the live feed focused on Mission. I had to keep track of her situation to be sure we'd reach her in time.

We stood at the base of the Outskirts' outer floodwall, blanketed by a shadow so oppressive I could've mistaken it for nighttime, even though sunset was only just underway. The proxy had placed our space suits in a cart covered in rags. Both he and Virgil had hoods up, and other Unplugged watched over us from the shadows. After the Nation ambush we'd survived earlier, I didn't blame them for wanting to remain inconspicuous.

Virgil's head tilted toward the sky and he inhaled deep through his nostrils. "This is the place," he said.

"What's here?" I asked. Besides being in close proximity to the outer floodwall, it looked the same as anywhere else. Data beggars and whores were crammed around holopads; VR addicts waited in line to get a fix. A visiting resident and his bot stood amidst a crowd, testing them with ridiculous questions to see who would earn his data donation that day.

The only perceivable difference was that the area was slightly more crowded with people standing around, doing the same as the rest of the Outskirts. It made me anxious.

"Just wait." Virgil reached into a satchel, withdrew three apples from the Unplugged lair, and handed one each to the proxy and me. "Eat now. It's the last you'll have until we reach *Ignis*."

I didn't hesitate in taking him up on his offer. Hunger was new to me, and I wasn't too fond of the feeling. I was almost done wolfing mine down when I heard a distant hum. It grew increasingly louder until my insides were vibrating. I could only get half a word out before I figured out what it was. Hovering toward us, with all its suction tubes retracted, was a High Earth trash sweeper. A portion of the seemingly impassable wall peeled apart for it to pass through.

The crowd around us started clamoring and sprinting through the opening. The Elder's proxy pulled a circular magnetic device out of our cart and looped it to his artificial arm. Then he grasped Virgil's hand and rushed into the breach. I quickly stowed the holopad and followed right before the gate closed again.

The salty aroma of the ocean grew pungent as we traversed the solid guts of the wall. On the other side, the coast trailed off on a steep slope littered with sharp rocks as far as one hundred meters from the shore. Rusty fishing boats filled their crevices, and many of those who'd fled the Outskirts alongside us headed to them. Others scoured the rocks for shreds of seaweed to fill baskets, which could be hooked onto ropes dangling from the top of the towering wall. Some people even hung onto them as they rose, and risked falling.

It wasn't safe, pleasant harvesting like on the *Ignis* at all. It was a race. I saw a woman slip and crack her head open on a rock before being towed out into the water by a strong current. Nobody stopped to help her.

Suddenly, Virgil clutched my forearm, and my body was lifted into the air. His strong grip held me steady. The magnetic device in the proxy's hand had latched onto the side of the sweeper as it floated out.

My feet dangled above the ocean, paralyzing me with fear. All the water I'd ever drunk had been clear, yet this was a wall of dark liquid. Gray waves swelled all around me, transforming the horizon into a vacillating line with the tops of twirling wind turbines poking out like spiky traps. Even the factory rig we were heading toward disappeared behind whitecaps.

It was hypnotizing. I lost myself in the terrifying, undulating depths.

Rising and falling . . . rising and falling . . .

"Asher!" Virgil yelled.

I snapped back to reality and realized Virgil was losing his grip on me. Ocean spray slicked my forearm, so he had me by the wrist now. I swung my other arm to take his and tucked in my legs. The Elder's proxy did the rest. I watched the gears and circuits in his artificial arm tighten as we were hauled up onto a narrow ledge protruding from the side of the sweeper. When my feet finally touched, my legs felt as nebulous as the ocean. The proxy directed me to sit.

"We'll be there shortly," he stated. "Put this on." He had our cart of supplies pinned to the side of the sweeper with the magnet and distributed our FORS TECH space suits one at a time. After we all had one, he allowed the rusty metal cart to fall and sink into a watery abyss. In seconds, I couldn't even distinguish its silhouette.

"You expect me to get changed here?" I questioned.

"It is not a request." Something shifted in the proxy's tone. It was more direct and forceful, as if I'd heard his true voice, for once not being dictated by the Elder.

I mustered the courage to glance down at what we were sitting on. The tiny outcrop—or rather, indent in the hull of the sweeper—was slender enough for me to sit on and no more. Purely for aesthetics. A few meters below, the sweeper kept altitude just above the crests of the waves by sucking in water and shooting it back out from its many vacuum tubes.

"The High Earth Network monitors its production facilities closely," Virgil said. "We keep our distance to avoid automated security. You won't see any scavengers getting close."

"Won't we be spotted, then?" I asked.

He patted the suit slung over my outstretched arms. "These are relics of the old world. In the Outskirts, we would have surely been robbed had we worn them. To High Earth, they're trash. The Elder has had them specially lined with rare materials that minimize our life signatures."

"If we are not fast, they'll get a read of us anyway," the proxy added. "Put it on now and check the seals. If bots do not kill you, radiation aboard the waste vessel will."

That got my attention. It wasn't the easiest way to get dressed, but every little action proved more trying outside High Earth. Thankfully, the suit came in one piece, minus the helmet mag-latched onto the back. I checked Virgil's holopad to ensure Mission's trial hadn't started yet, then stowed the device and got to work.

My legs went in first before pulling the suit up my body, twisting carefully from side to side to avoid falling. Watching Virgil put his on with such ease encouraged me. He couldn't even see, although that might have been an advantage. As I threaded my arm through the second sleeve, I incidentally looked down, saw something secreted amongst the waves, and almost tipped.

"Careful," Virgil said as he braced me.

A square of rusted metal punctured the water, with a tall,

slender pylon poking up from its center. A handful of rafts floated around it, delisted men and women on them gripping fishing lines. One wore a bulky suit with a bulbous helmet connected to a long air hose. He flipped over the side of a raft and sank into the ocean.

"What is that one doing?" I asked

"There are many relics worth trading left to find in the old, sunken world," Virgil replied.

I released a breath and sealed the suit up to my collar. "Mr. Helix's office," I ruminated.

"What?"

"Mr. Helix displayed useless treasures from the old world in his smart-dwelling. I've seen it in interviews. He'd portray the same things in our studio VR. I wonder if the people he traded with found them here."

"It's possible. Countless ancient cities remain hidden beneath the waves."

"I always wondered why he cared about things like that when he had so much. I think I get it now. There's so much lost beauty on Earth, isn't there?"

Virgil turned to face me. I knew he didn't have eyes, but it felt like nobody had ever seen me as he did then. No OptiVisor in the way. No subliminal adverts all around.

"You have no idea, Asher," he said. He smiled and turned back to the ocean. "Now, helmet on."

I took one last moment to take in Earth. The longer we spent over the ocean, the less terrifying I found it. It was the randomness at first, I thought, but that no longer seemed like such a bad thing. No bots were needed to tend the waves. It simply was. In all its power and majesty. It couldn't be tamed, only respected.

The outer floodwall, which separated it from the Outskirts,

stretched across my view behind us. We were so far now that when I lifted my hand and squinted, I could fit it between my thumb and index finger. An aura of light from High Earth bloomed above it. Opposite it, darkness fell upon where we were headed. I could no longer tell where the ocean ended and the sky began. All I could hear was the hissing of waves and the gentle hum of our ride.

Never in a million years would I have thought that in a place where the menace of death and darkness literally surrounded me, I'd feel more at peace than ever before.

I lifted the helmet and placed it over my head. It fit snugly and locked into my collar with a gentle hiss. The world then muted. With the elegant visor curving over the contours of my nose, I had no idea how the Elder's proxy fit his outdated OptiVisor inside.

"The suits are all set to the same frequency," the proxy said. "Listen to my directions." His impassive voice surrounded me via an in-helmet comms system. It was like I was back in my director's office issuing orders, only now *I* was on the receiving end.

"I can't use my walking stick well in this," Virgil said. "Asher, you'll have to help guide me."

"All right," I said. "What next?" Darkness answered me. The sweeper we rode moved beneath a suspended slab, enhancing the blackness in ways I thought impossible. After a few seconds, it stopped and began to rise.

"We aren't dead yet, so that's a start!" Virgil had to shout to be heard.

As we ascended, the sound of running water became thunderous, even through my helmet. An incessant stream of droplets sprayed my visor as well, combining with the night to render me as blind as Virgil. He grabbed my arm as if to reassure me. Then my internal organs shrank as the sweeper returned to traveling horizontally, now safely atop the platform.

"We're on," the proxy said.

I tried to determine where we were, even though the helmet didn't allow for much movement. Bots had no need for light, so it was murky, but I could tell we were aboard the factory rig's main landing platform. A structure, fabricated from metal, towered adjacent to us. A rift in the side allowed a peek within, where it seemed like a lightning storm raged. Conveyer belts and machinery were everywhere. Mechanical arms pieced together the components of new VR chambers. Thousands of them. Maybe millions. The entirety of the next line of the device, which would be provided to every resident upon the new issuing. I remembered looking forward to those releases, to virtual experiences getting even more seamless and engrossing.

The factory's interior rose dozens of stories, with production lines at each level. At the bottom, it dipped into the ocean, where water was churned into a vortex, then sucked up to both provide power and have its molecules rearranged by a re-assembler into required materials. A seemingly endless supply thanks to the invention that also ensured the planet-wide water level never rose again. It would take a billion years for it and every other factory to expend all the water on the flooded planet, if that was even possible.

In High Earth, new devices appeared for me whenever VORA said they would. I never cared to see where they were made, but now, I was drawn toward the sparks of production. My foot stretched out from my seated position to tap the landing, but Virgil barred me with his arm.

"You'll be detected," he warned.

I nodded and turned my attention to the landing platform. Even with the minimal lighting, I could tell it was tremendous. At the very center loomed the outline of a tall cylindrical vessel with no visible cockpit or viewports. Humankind rarely had need to visit outer space any longer, unless it was for a show. Drones swarmed about the solid, conical top, providing almost all the light available to us. The trash sweeper stopped beside it, set to transfer its contents through an access hatch on the vessel's side that promptly folded open.

"Let's go," the proxy said.

We went to step down, but Virgil continued to hold out his arm. A drone zipped by within a few meters of us, darting from side to side like a hummingbird. My heart thumped against my rib cage; I was so nervous. Antiquated materials really must've done a number on its sensors, because after a few seconds, it continued on.

"Okay, now," Virgil said. He took my arm and pretty much pulled me down from the ledge. We were higher than expected and had to support each other to keep from falling. The youthful cybernetic proxy didn't have any trouble.

"The time is 6:53 and forty-seven seconds," he said. "Launch is scheduled for 7:00. We need to delay precisely two minutes and eleven seconds. It won't take off so long as the loading hatch remains unsealed. Virgil, we need to angle seventeen-point-four degrees north by four-point-seven degrees west to intercept the *Ignis*. Radiation will mask our signature a little longer, but I will prepare our defenses."

The proxy positioned himself by the loading hatch and placed the magnetic device he'd used to grapple onto the sweeper in the opening. Then he started piecing something together from parts in the pack built into his suit.

"Asher, look for a manual override control panel in the lower hull," Virgil requested.

I skirted the circumference of the massive ship with Virgil in tow. The ship's exterior shell was like a single piece of composite something. No joints, no breaks, except for the hatch currently receiving more radioactive waste.

"I can't find it," I said.

"It will be covered by a removable plate, most likely. High Earth may be run by computers, but it was designed by people. Think like one. You'll be able to reach it."

I placed my hand on the hull and dragged it along. Turn on a light to see any clearer, and we might as well invite a swarm of bots set on protecting High Earth products from the delisted. We'd get ourselves vaporized like that woman, a thought that made me shudder.

I circled the ship all the way once, then released Virgil so I could use two hands sliding up and down. Halfway around again, I located a tiny groove.

"I think I found something!" I called.

"Come get me," Virgil said.

With his helmet on, he had no way to navigate except with touch. I traced my steps back to him and somehow led him back to the right spot.

"All right," he said. "Elder, are you ready?"

"Weapon armed," the proxy answered. "Open it."

Virgil undid the seal of one of his gloves and exposed his hand. Instantly, the dots of drone lights filling the black sky got a reading of a human presence and aimed at us. Virgil placed his palm in the groove I found, and it signaled a small portion of the hull to pop open. Within was a screen that read: RESI-DENT OVERRIDE.

"I'll be delisted after this," Virgil said. "Asher, get on the terminal, and I'll block you."

I struggled not to keep peeking up at the gathering security drones. "I . . . I don't know how to use it," I said.

"I'll guide you. Just tell me what you see."

A *slam* rang out. The sweeper had emptied and was backing away, but the proxy had jammed the waste ship's hatch open.

Light now flooded us from the spotlights of innumerable security drones, drifting closer and aimed directly at both me and Virgil as well as the proxy.

"Resident Virgil Rhodes, you are in danger," a mechanized voice announced loud enough for me to hear clearly through my helmet. "Please step away from the intruders and you will be returned safely to your smart-dwelling on the thirty-third floor of Residential Tower 4, Block 3C."

My hand slipped. All my years of living in High Earth, what were the chances? Virgil's smart-dwelling would have been straight across from mine on the adjacent tower, facing each other. I'd never even noticed him. Why would I have, when I had the show?

"Asher, focus," Virgil whispered.

"I wasn't random. That's why you picked me? Familiarity."

"Now isn't the time. Focus."

I shook my head and forced my attention to the screen. "There's a detailed 3D schematic of the ship," I said. "The thing looks solid, yet there are so many parts."

"The vessel is catapulted into orbit by a launchpad built into the platform." Virgil spoke hastily, though, somehow, maintained a calm demeanor. "According to the Elder, it is then accelerated with molecular re-assembler–generated chemical reactions with water stores in its stern engine. The bots build each new vessel around the launchpad, so I need you to select the detachable couplings."

"I can't. I can't select anything. I'm locked out!"

A line of blue slashed across the sky. One of the drones spun aimlessly before bursting into pieces. The proxy had constructed some sort of electricity blaster like the ones the drones themselves used, and affixed it to his artificial arm. He fired again, a surge of pure energy zipping past another drone.

"Another relic from old wars," Virgil said. "Security is onto us. Relax, Asher. I've never been as good at anything as I was at programming. Just follow my instructions exactly. Key in command . . ."

He rattled off jargon so fast I didn't have time to process it, only listen and key. I became his eyes and hands. It was incredible. As a man who developed VRs, I knew he had to be proficient with programming, but this was slicer level. In no time, even security couldn't keep me out, and we were admitted into the launchpad controls.

The pad sat on an axle, able to be tilted to a limited extent in every direction to avoid impact with any satellites or debris in space, and of course the moon. This way, irradiated waste from data chips, processors, and other unwanted devices which were hazardous for molecular re-assembling couldn't accidentally come crashing down to High Earth or pollute the ocean.

It was then, as I keyed the commands to angle the ship in ways that were imperceptible to my naked vision, that I realized just what Virgil had sacrificed when he chose to lose his eyes. He could've been a slicer in the Outskirts, with access to his own legitimate data as well. He could've presided over an entire gang of his own like the Nation. He could have had everything. Access to High Earth tech, followers—he could have been more than even the Elder seemed to be. A king, in the modern sense of the word. Instead, he chose to tap blindly through the streets where he never had to live, handing out wisdom and food to bastard children.

"Seven o'clock, Virgil," the proxy said. "Are you finished?" The ground started to rumble as the ship's launchpad gathered power. The proxy's jam on the hatch kept it grounded.

"Almost there," he replied, then returned to directing me.

"Resident, you have been deemed a threat to society," the

mechanized voice of the High Earth Network pronounced through the only drone to survive the proxy's onslaught. "Stand down, or lethal force will be req—" A burst of electricity had shards of it peppering the hull a few feet above me.

An ear-piercing *boom* filled the sky. A hover-transport arrived over the platform, and a unit of public security bots dropped out. The same model that guarded High Earth's wall. The platform cracked beneath their heavy chassis. They could turn us all to red mist.

"Focus, Asher!" Virgil yelled.

I tore my gaze away from them and continued heeding his guidance. The proxy drew their fire with the electricity blaster, but his cover behind the waste vessel's half-closed hatch would be compromised after the bots had fanned out. He was fortunate that the plating of the vessel was designed densely enough to resist radioactive waste and could resist their energy weapons.

"7:01 and eleven," the proxy said. "You have one minute."

"Almost there," Virgil said.

"Tilt is set!" I shrieked, unable to contain myself. I was never a fan of action-simulator VRs, or even violent dramas, let alone my second shoot-out in as many days. My heart was ready to pound through my chest. Sweat greased my every pore.

"Good," Virgil said. "Now, they'll try to ground us. Authorize launch and we're done."

"How?" I asked.

"Just enter the—" He paused, then grabbed my back and shoved me toward the loading hatch. "No time to teach you. I don't need eyes for this." I glanced back as I stumbled. His bare hand flicked along the screen with the same grace that Mr. Helix's did when he was coding. Electricity crackled over my shoulder, and one of the bots bearing down on us toppled in a heap of sparks and smoke.

The proxy grabbed the back of my suit and hoisted me up through the narrow opening and into the vessel. I didn't go far. My back butted against a pile of hazardous refuse stacked in compressed blocks up to the height of the lofty vessel.

"Got it!" Virgil shouted.

"Trace the circumference back," the proxy said. "I'll retrieve you."

I scrambled to regain my bearings in the stifling darkness of the vessel's interior. Blue sparkled out through the open hatch as the proxy poked outside and fired his weapon. Shrapnel from a broken drone stung the outer hull like hail. Bot energy weapons wailed and distorted sounds.

Before I could make myself useful, Virgil arrived and the proxy grabbed hold of him. I took another of Virgil's arms to help heave him all the way in, but I knew the proxy's artificial limb did all the work. He fired off one last shot with his other hand, said, "Switch on oxygen," and then released the hatch to seal us in.

The rumbling beneath us augmented. My shaking fingers searched desperately for the button that would switch on the oxygen tank connected to my suit. The ship clattered, stray scraps falling all around me in the cramped air pocket the three of us were crammed into.

"7:02 and eleven seconds," the proxy said softly.

There was no space for me to be thrown downward, but the pressure exerted on my body as we launched was beyond compare. G-forces pressed on my ribs and made my eyes feel ready to pop out. I guess the suit was supposed to help a little, but not enough to quell the roar of pain festering in my throat. The others screamed with me. The pressure built until my skeleton felt like it was going to be ground into dust.

Then it was gone.

Weightlessness took hold. The sudden shift to a completely opposing sensation was jarring. The ship stopped shaking, and scraps began to float all around me.

"Are we clear?" I asked, panting. The pressure had my throat hoarse. Before anyone could answer, a red droplet splashed against my visor.

I twisted my confined body so I could look down. Virgil was positioned with his back against the sealed hatch, with more red globs floating over a gash in his stomach.

CHAPTER 21

"Virgil!" I yelled into my comm-link.

It took some effort, but I coiled my body so I faced him and drew myself down. I wished I'd spent time testing weightlessness in a VR. The chamber allowed for a perfectly calibrated experience.

My hand pressed against a wound in the upper portion of Virgil's abdomen, and he grimaced. A large chunk of shrapnel had hit him, and the g-force of launch had caused it to bury deep into his body.

"Pressure helps, I think. Right?" I was no medical expert, but Mission was, and she'd done something similar while trying to help Jacen.

"The synth-womb taught you well." Virgil chuckled, then groaned.

I searched for anything loose in the vessel that might help. I found nothing except blocks of waste. Maybe there was something on my suit. I started to pat around in the darkness, but Virgil grabbed my wrist. "

"Forget it, Asher," he said. "I'm already exposed. I won't survive the trip."

"Don't say that." I turned to the proxy, who floated in a corner. Through his OptiVisor, I couldn't tell what he was thinking, but his lips drew a straight line, as usual.

"You have something that can help him, right?" I asked. "Anti-radiation medication or something!"

"That is reserved only for those who operate directly on our replica core," the proxy replied.

"That can't be true! You knew we were getting on this thing."

"Asher," Virgil whispered, "even if he did, there's nothing that could help me now."

"I don't believe that."

"We are eight hours and fifty-three seconds away from impact," the proxy said. "It is possible the medical supplies aboard the fixer station may be able to help."

"I won't make it," Virgil said.

I hushed him and pressed harder on the wound. I only had to keep him from bleeding to death until we made it. Hopefully, that was before his insides cooked . . . or whatever might happen. The synth-womb didn't leave me with extensive knowledge of radiation poisoning. Any hazardous material around High Earth residents was promptly sealed away inside one of the great big tubes we now inhabited, and shot into space.

Virgil moaned as I stuffed his arm back into the suit and clamped down on it with my other hand to stop exposure.

"There you go," I said. "The Elder's right. Fixers risk exposure in the secret routes through the *Ignis*. I'm sure Lance keeps something that can help."

He coughed and tilted his head to the side. "Thank you, Asher."

I finally leaned back as well and tried to relax. The proxy

watched us in silence, or I thought watched. Struggling to distract myself, my mind wandered to how hypocritical it was that
he wore an OptiVisor at all times, even if it only displayed words
scrolling across. Would the young man the Elder used as her
body ever get to "open his eyes" like the rest of the Unplugged
did? Or was he nothing more than a tool to them?

"I lied, Asher," Virgil grumbled.

I'd save that thought about the proxy for another time.

"I know," I said, turning back to Virgil. "Your picking me
wasn't random."

"You're right. I spent years looking out my window, and I
never saw you come outside. Not once. When I had to pick a
resident, I guess I had to know who was inside."

"It's okay, I—"

"But I don't mean that," he cut me off. "I suppose I lied
twice."

"What are you talking about?" I asked.

"I try to honor the deals I make, but we don't live in an
honest world."

My heart skipped a beat. "We're going to the *Ignis*, right?"

"Not that . . . You told me your story, but I didn't tell you
the truth about mine."

"What?"

"The Unplugged didn't save me from a VR den. I never . . ."
He coughed and slumped backward. A bit of red sprayed against
the inside of his helmet. "You ever wake up one day when you
were a resident and realize you were bored with life? That no
program scratched that itch? That no VR gave you a thrill?"

I shook my head slowly. It was the truth. I'd go to sleep
thinking about *Ignis: Live*, Mission and the other inhabitants,
and wake up doing the same. If my sleep-pod allowed for
dreams, I'd probably have dreamed about them, too.

"That restaurant I designed, you remember it?" Virgil asked.

"Yes." I leaned down closer.

"I made it to stand out to other people. There was something romantic about the place that real ones loved. I didn't want the simulations anymore. So I spent every night there, and every night I found a resident to take up to the rooms who was looking for a good time. And we had one, but afterward, it was *Ignis: Live* this or *Molecular Nation* that. They wanted to talk about every bit of content that, for some reason, I couldn't stomach any longer. I had no idea what was wrong with me. I met with more people than I could count; asked them to program their avatars to older women, younger women, even men. Eventually, I started convincing some to leave VRs and visit my smart-dwelling personally. I thought that would cure my boredom, but it felt the same. The sex. The senseless talking after.

"So, one morning, I trekked to the Outskirts. I figured there must be a reason why some residents do it when we have everything we could ever need already, and can see the place any time on *Outskirts Today*. Boy, was I right. I found a delisted woman named Clara and, because I was a resident, she didn't even bat an eyelash before sleeping with me. People who fight to survive know something about enjoying the good times, I'll tell you.

"I never wanted our night to end. But it did, like always, and then it was exactly the same. She asked for some data if I wanted to go again, because she didn't want to miss the next episode of some show I didn't even bother to remember the name of. I ran away so fast my bot thought I was having a panic attack. Afterward, I tried to return to all the things I used to enjoy. Stories. Programming. None of it helped."

"Did you ever try having your memory wiped?" I asked. "Disassociation can be a side effect."

"I couldn't tell you, though I suppose that's the point." He tried to laugh, but all his body could muster was wheezing.

"All I know is that I wanted to be free of living," he went on. "I went back to the Outskirts with plans to travel to the far wall and leap into the ocean. I only made one stop before, and that was where I found out that poor Clara was pregnant." He sniffed, and I noticed his lips beginning to tremble even more than they had been just from enduring the pain of his wound.

"She was born in the Outskirts, you see, so she wasn't sterilized like resident women. The kid wasn't mine, couldn't possibly be since I was a resident, but she died pushing him out. She died alone, except for me. And that boy, that child, he saved me."

"But he wasn't yours."

"So? He would've starved in her room, and nobody would've noticed. I stayed in the Outskirts for good that time and spent every day with him. Used my data to keep him healthy. I couldn't tell you how much tech was stolen from me over the years out there, but I didn't care. Oran was my son. I was going to wait at his side until he was fully grown and I could petition for him to become a resident."

"Is that even possible?"

"I didn't care. I just knew I had to try. Oran's excitement over everything in life inspired me to enjoy all the things I used to. That shack you stayed in? I built it for him and traded data for pieces to put together our very own VR station so he could use it. The thing's collecting dust now. By the time he could talk, we were developing programs together using my data. He loved it all. For once, I didn't care if anyone else did. He loved to pretend he was an ancient warrior, so we made a VR. It looked like an ancient Japanese dojo . . . so ridiculous." The rate of his breathing started picking up with every subsequent word. I was too enthralled to interrupt.

"Oran would battle whatever demented monsters I could conceive," he said. "Then he always wanted me to think of something even crazier. Like a fool, I listened. I just wanted to make him happy. By the time he was fourteen, we didn't spend much time together outside of VRs, and it went like that until I actually did exceed my data contract and was issued a delistment warning. That's one of the few things I told you that was the truth. He threw a tantrum when I told him we needed to slow down, disappeared into the streets, and by the time I found him, he was in the shittiest Nation VR den in the Outskirts. No monitors to assure nobody stayed plugged in too long. Data brought in by whores instead of slicers.

"The smell when I walked in . . . I'd have a memory wipe take that away if I could choose one thing. The stink of burnt flesh from overpowered neural emitters was so thick on the air, it was like paste. I can still smell it. Worse than the shit-and-urine-stained VR stations without feeding tubes or waste receptacles. Oran had strapped himself into one and never got off. He . . . he starved to death."

I considered putting a hand somewhere, anywhere, to comfort him, but my body was frozen.

"His body, Asher . . ." he continued. "It was like tissue paper wrapped around hollow tubes. I could lift him with one arm. Not a single person noticed him lying there. Not one. I snapped. I burned the whole place down around me and let my guardian bot vaporize anybody who got too close until every delisted bastard was dust.

"The Unplugged found me in the rubble, next to the damaged bot, and took me in. They nursed me back to sanity, but I couldn't hide from the truth . . . I killed him . . . I got my baby boy addicted and killed him." He lurched in pain and clutched the chest piece of my suit. A stream of blood trickled around my makeshift bandage and crossed the air in a steady stream. I choked back tears and squeezed his hand.

"It wasn't your fault," I said.

"You have opened many eyes since, Virgil," the proxy said. "Most would have given up."

"Stop, both of you," Virgil moaned. "I've carried the anger of denial with me for too long. Carried it when I entered High Earth for the first time in a decade that day to complete my initiation." His heavy breaths sounded like air being squeezed through a faulty air recycler on *Ignis*. "I saw myself in every carefree resident there and wanted to shake the life out of all of them just to see if it would fill the hole inside me. But I chose your home, Asher. It's true, you didn't seem special, you were just a neighbor, but I'm so glad I did."

"So am I," I whispered. "Even if I was too much of a fool to know you were real."

He steadied his breathing for a moment and smiled. "No, you aren't. But after you get to her, you will be." He repositioned his body, groaning as he reached around me and removed his holopad from my pack. He placed it in my lap, a smudge of blood rubbing off on the corner from his finger. "This was his. They . . .. they'll deactivate my account soon. Make sure you're ready. I couldn't s-s-save him." His arm was starting to go slack, so I squeezed as hard as I could and held it straight.

"Virgil, stay with us," I said. I tapped his helmet. His scarred eyelids froze in an open position; his lips cracked just enough for air to whistle through. "Virgil!"

His finger tapped the holopad's screen directly on top of Mission's face. "Look . . ." he rasped. I ignored him and placed the holopad to the side, forgetting it'd just float. I clutched him by his shoulders and shook.

"He is truly Unplugged now," the Elder's proxy said without a shred of an emotion.

"Are you just going to sit there?" I growled. "He gave his life for you! Help him!"

"He did not give anything for me. He made his choice, as we all must. Make yours."

"Is anything about you still human? Using this thing to talk for you."

"This proxy's mind was destroyed by VR addiction, similar to Virgil's adopted son. For us, tech does as it was meant to—allows us to live our best possible lives. To make a difference."

"Make one for him."

"I already have. Now, if you continue to exert yourself, you will deplete your oxygen stores before we ever reach *Ignis*."

I ignored him and shook Virgil until my fingers gave out. My heart didn't race, it simply felt like there was a vacuum where it had been. I couldn't even cry properly. Tears rolled out, but they did so as my mouth hung open silently. Was this what it was like to lose a friend?

Virgil's weightless body rose slowly, and as if in a final message, the top of his helmet tapped his holopad. I grabbed it before inertia caused it to rise the length of the vessel. The screen appeared blurry from tears, but I blinked hard a few times to dry them out. Then I saw her.

[Ignis Feed Location]
Core Entrance
<Camera 7>

Only a single path existed to reach the Core from the inner surface of *Ignis*. Its major structural axis ran from one vertex of the oblong asteroid to the other, at the points where the centripetally generated pseudo-gravity was too weak to allow access by foot. On one side, the rock wall was littered with an unnavigable maze of machinery and metal nodes—all a part of its tremendous engines. On the other, a lift descended from the vertex, able to carry people to the green-covered surface, where the vessel's spin could take hold.

In the area between the steep arc of the asteroid's inner wall and the start of its hydroponic farms, the Collective convened. A series of broad, sweeping terraces extended down from the lift, as if ancients built the site to worship the stars. The Collective sat along the uppermost step, with Cassiopeia in their center. The five Mothers, absent Alora, sat on the level below them, accompanied by their Birthmothers. Infants, too young to be left alone, were cradled in their arms, some nursing, others sleeping or crying.

Mission stood across from them with Alora beside her. A line of enforcers waited at their backs in case they were stupid enough to run, not that there was anywhere they could go. Mission was too big to hide beneath the floor now.

The rest of the inhabitants watched from the edge of the farms, the crowd filling the entire circumference of the *Ignis*'s tapering end. Those from Block B who had survived the recent catastrophe were positioned at the front.

"I'm sorry," Alora whispered to Mission as they awaited trial. "I should never have asked that of you."

Mission glanced up. She'd been staring at the floor, deep in thought. "No, you shouldn't have," she replied, unable to mask her contempt.

"You have to understand, I don't care what our titles are. It's my duty to protect you."

"You're not Mother anymore."

"No, but I'm *your* mother."

Mission lost her train of thought as Alora took her hand and pulled her close.

"Back away," an enforcer promptly ordered.

They listened but continued staring into each other's eyes.

"It's always been me, Mission," she said.

"But the accident—"

Alora shook her head. "Me. When I was named a Birth-mother, a man attacked me. I didn't know who he was, and the DNA never matched any male inhabitant. Cassiopeia helped hide the pregnancy, and when you were born, I was supposed to recycle you to keep the whole thing hidden, because we weren't sure the Collective would believe me. Only when I looked into your eyes, I couldn't . . ."

"So you hid me," Mission said. She wasn't surprised. A part of her had always known, somehow. She wasn't one yet, but only a mother would risk so much to protect her child. Only *her* mother.

"From everyone, until the Blackout changed everything. I didn't tell you because . . ."

Mission ignored what the enforcers might do and took Alora's hand. "To protect me. Like always." She brought the hand to her cheek and nuzzled in its warmth. All her anger melted away. Alora—her mother—was simply trying to spare her a fate worse than death by blaming Jacen. It was what any parent would do for their child.

"I shouldn't have reacted that way," Mission said.

"No, you were right. Mission, I may not have done what we're accused of, but I deserve to be on trial. For so much."

"Don't say that."

"We aren't supposed to have favorites, but biological daughter or not, I've loved you most from the moment I held you in my arms for the very first time. I would've picked you to succeed me even if the core didn't."

"I don't—" Mission was interrupted when Cassiopeia stood and raised her arms to hush the crowd.

"Whatever happens next," Alora whispered, "know that I do believe you, and that I'm so sorry I wasn't there to keep you safe. I failed you."

"No, never." Mission squeezed her hand as tightly as she could.

"When our ancestors built the *Ignis,* it was not lightly that they placed the flame of humanity in our hands," Cassiopeia began. She didn't have to shout, as being at the narrowest point within the *Ignis* projected her voice across the gaping hollow. The steady hum of the core, distant and glowing both above and below fields of green, was all that competed with her. "Earth has fallen. We remain."

"We remain." The thousands of inhabitants echoed her words.

Mission and Alora were too focused on each other to join them. Their fingers locked, and if they remained there, Mission felt that nothing could hurt her. She wasn't alone.

"Purity of population, moderation and preservation," Cassiopeia said. "These three notions must always be upheld if we are to survive our voyage to a new Earth. The two inhabitants before you today stand accused of violating the very laws that hold the *Ignis* together. Their defense shall now be heard, without interruption, for all of your Collective to judge."

"Flame-robbers!" someone called out from the crowd. Another hollered something similarly disparaging.

"Silence!" Cassiopeia bellowed, her voice carrying like a thunderclap. "It is with a heavy heart that I condemn any man or woman to death without recycling. So, I ask all of you to open your minds to their stories. Mission-14130, step forward."

"I believe you," Alora whispered in Mission's ear. They

exchanged a heartfelt nod, and then enforcers spurred Mission to shuffle forward until the glowing core was positioned directly behind her, and her elongated shadow ended at Cassiopeia's feet.

"Mission," Cassiopeia said, "you are the 14,130th of us to share the light of the core. In the name of both it and the everlasting energy you employ, do you swear to speak the truth?"

"I do," Mission replied meekly. Seeing so many people arrayed before her, specifically staring at her, was unlike anything she'd ever experienced. She'd prefer solitude to how this made her feel. Clearing her throat, she spoke louder. "I do."

"Then we shall judge you without bias," Cassiopeia said. "All witnesses perished in the calamity of the fiftieth anniversary, so you must speak only for yourself." The entire Collective rose to their feet, an imposing line of lanky men and women garbed in white. The Mothers below them remained seated with their children, but their heated glares bored into Mission. She'd been one of them, after all, and even though it was only for a day, it was like Alora had said, no other position was held in such esteem.

"Bring him," Cassiopeia said. The Collective parted, and two enforcers carried a body in a vacuum-sealed pod down from the core's lift. They placed it carefully on the ground in front of her.

Mission tried to rush to it as soon as she realized that Jacen lay within it. Enforcers grabbed her arms and held her still.

"You are charged first with the murder of a fellow inhabitant using this firearm," Cassiopeia said. The member of the Collective beside her raised the ill-fated pulse pistol for all to see. "You have claimed to me that it was in self-defense. We will now hear your full testimony and decide. The punishment for both murder and attempted murder is the eradication of your energy through spacing, so as never to taint us. If you are found innocent, it will be assumed that Jacen somehow stole the weapon from the core, and his body's energy will cease to be."

Mission stared at Jacen's body. Everything that had happened seemed like a bad dream until that moment. She felt like she was going to be crushed beneath the weight of the truth. She'd replayed the moment when she'd shot him countless times since that day, and she would never understand what had really happened, but the one thing she couldn't deny was that she'd shot him. She could've shown restraint, but she'd lived up to her generation's bad name and pulled the trigger without thinking.

It was an accident, but that didn't make her innocent.

"May I?" Mission asked softly.

Cassiopeia regarded the rest of the Collective. More than half of them nodded.

"You may come closer," Cassiopeia said.

The enforcers helped her approach, but she was stopped just before she was near enough to touch him. Her legs gave out, and she fell to her knees. They immediately lifted her back up. Jacen's skin was usually coated in grime from his work, but now, it was almost gray so much color had left it. His eyes, which had gaped in horror when Mission pulled the trigger, were shut, and his face appeared tranquil. Clothing covered the hole she'd put in him.

"Jacen . . ." she whispered. "I'm so sorry." Again, she attempted to reach out, but Cassiopeia stopped her.

"Enough. This has been delayed too long."

The enforcers dragged Mission back to her position and stood her upright.

"If you are innocent, defend yourself," Cassiopeia demanded.

Mission turned slowly from Jacen to look back at Alora. Somehow, she managed to retain the same proud, loving smile she wore on every big day in Mission's life. A mother's smile. Mission did her best to return it and then took a deep breath.

Saying goodbye to Alora was going to be the hardest thing she ever had to do.

Two decades had passed, and the Great Blackout remained a haunting memory in the waking minds of her people because it was so senseless. Like a hurricane wiping out a coastal village in ancient Earth. Her generation was its deadly wake. The young lashed out against the core's necessary rules because fear born from that disaster drove them toward a dangerous tendency to live for the moment rather than the future.

Mission couldn't bring Jacen back and couldn't prove that what had happened on the fiftieth anniversary wasn't her fault, but she could shoulder the blame for it. She could shoulder the blame for her entire eschewed Blackout Generation so that her people could stop being angry about all the awful things that had happened and look forward instead. She, the girl who was never meant to be born, could make her life worth something.

"I'm not innocent," she stated. The Collective gasped, but she hadn't spoken loud enough for Alora or any of the thousands behind her to hear. "It was me!" she yelled. The sound of shock that followed was as if the *Ignis* itself had drawn a colossal breath.

"What are you doing!" Alora shouted. Enforcers had to restrain her to keep her from charging to Mission's side.

"Alora and Jacen had nothing to do with it," Mission went on. "It's like you said, Cassiopeia. She named me Mother and I couldn't handle the responsibility. I loved Jacen . . ." She paused, having to battle her trembling mouth to speak. That was the only truth in anything she was saying. "So much. I couldn't bear the thought of being with someone else, so I tried to reprogram the core to suffocate Paul in my quarters and make it look like an accident."

"Mission, don't do this!" Alora yelled. "She's lying, don't listen to—" An enforcer covered her mouth.

"She's only trying to protect me! I stole the weapon so I could keep Paul in my room when the air recyclers malfunctioned, but I accidentally caused a malfunction in the entire block. After the emergency, Jacen came to check if I was safe, and I professed my love to him. I told him what I'd done so that we could be together, and he rejected me. He tried to take the gun, but it went off and . . . and it killed him."

The *Ignis* grew quiet, like it had been turned inside out and exposed to the void. Even the core seemed to hush. The jaw of every single member of the Collective hung agape.

Then came an eruption. The edge of the hydrofarms rustled as thousands of livid inhabitants swelled through the boughs. The enforcers tightened their stances, but they were vastly outnumbered.

"Silence!" Cassiopeia boomed. "Silence!" Even her resounding voice was lost in the commotion. "In light of this confession, Mission is sentenced to death by spacing! She will enjoy one last meal, as is custom, and then her flame will be extinguished forever!" She gestured to enforcers to seize Mission before the mob reached her. Alora had also broken free and grabbed her as well.

"Mission, don't do this!" she said as the strength of a dozen enforcers drew all of them toward the core's lift.

"Block B will need a new Mother," Mission replied, calm despite the wave of animosity closing in around them. "Help her, like you always did me."

Alora lost her grip and fell backward in the mob. "Mission!"

The door of the lift shut behind Mission, and it shot up toward the core. Half of the Collective made it in. The rest were trapped within the horde of inhabitants.

"I've never seen anything like this," Cassiopeia panted, staring down through the glass floor. Enforcers had to pull a few people off the structure of the lift to keep them from trying to climb. She turned to Mission, only she didn't appear angry at all.

"That was a brave thing you did," she said. "I'm so sorry, Mission."

Mission's brow furrowed. "For what?"

"I was named to the Collective for a reason. I'm not stupid. However much of that story was a lie, the *Ignis* needs someone to blame for what happened or it would've been the Great Blackout all over again." The lift stopped and everyone piled out. Cassiopeia stayed put and held Mission with her.

"If you have any last requests, I promise to do my best to fulfill them," Cassiopeia said.

Mission opened her mouth to reply; then her lip twisted. "Now Jacen will be recycled?"

"He will."

"Let me say a proper goodbye?"

* * *

The image froze, and I was returned to the home interface of Virgil's holopad. The message invalid account awaited me. He'd been trying his damnedest for so long, and now Virgil was finally delisted.

Any other time, I would've shaken and slammed it out of frustration, desperate to see only another minute of the show. Anything. But I didn't need to see any more this time. Not after learning everything Virgil had done for a child, and now all that Alora had sacrificed for Mission. Like her, I wasn't surprised at Alora's truth. It was almost relieving to know.

Someone horrible had attacked Alora. An inhabitant somehow hiding who he was, a tech error caused by Mr. Helix, maybe even a depraved fixer back then with a thing for her—none of it mattered. The only truth was that against all odds, that darkness had created Mission, just as it had set Virgil on his path. A part of me only wished that Alora and Mission could've met Virgil and known they weren't alone in letting love change everything. Now I knew why he wanted to help me—he understood.

"I won't let you down," I said, glancing between the holopad's frozen screen and Virgil's petrified features. "Either of you."

"What was that?" the Elder's proxy asked.

I looked up at him, still wondering if there was anything left of whoever he used to be before the Elder made his body useful. It certainly didn't show.

"Nothing," I said.

"Try to sleep, Asher," he said. "The more oxygen we can conserve, the safer we will be if our landing attempt does not go smoothly."

"I thought you said this would work?"

"There are no absolutes in space travel."

"Now you tell me." Against my expectations, it didn't make me feel any more anxious. I merely leaned my head against the back of my helmet and closed my watery eyes.

Despite everything I'd done to put Mission in her impossible position, the sacrifice she made all on her own had transformed her from a villain to a hero. And she hadn't done it because she knew she was being watched by millions of viewers on High Earth. She did it to offer catharsis to the people she cared about, just as Virgil would have happily done for his son with a redo on life. People were more than they appeared on the outside. More than their avatars.

It didn't matter that one of their worlds was based on a lie— perhaps even both. I now understood what the Elder had tried to tell me. *Ignis: Live* wasn't reality because it was unscripted and unpredictable. It was reality because it was filled with people. Real people—delisted volunteers or not.

My eyelids might have been closed, but my eyes were open now. I'd been planning to save Mission ever since Virgil made me believe it was possible, but I didn't think I was truly prepared to until that moment.

CHAPTER 22

Pressure on my shoulder startled me awake. The proxy's foot had pushed off it, propelling him quickly toward the top of the vessel some twenty meters or so above.

"What's going on?" I groaned. I went to wipe my groggy eyes, forgetting they were behind a helmet visor.

"We are approaching the *Ignis*," the proxy replied.

"Already?"

"Your body needed rest. Our expected impact is within a few seconds of my initial calculations."

"Is that bad?" I asked.

"We are as blind in here as you, but we are about to find out."

"What's the plan?"

"I'm planting a contained explosive charge at the bow, which will slow our approach as the pressure shift sucks out the waste."

That got my attention. I pulled myself upright, only to find I was face-to-face with Virgil's corpse. I averted my gaze straight up toward the proxy.

"That's what Virgil meant by ejection of waste?" I asked.

"Yes," he answered. "These vessels are not constructed for evacuation. If we remain fastened toward the base, however, we should remain unharmed."

"Should . . ."

"At our current velocity, the chances of either us or the fixer station surviving the collision are marginal. Explosive decompression is our only option."

"No absolutes in space, right?" I sighed. "I hope you were as good at space flights in the old world as Virgil said."

"My specialty was outfitting them for long expeditions, not piloting."

I nervously groped at the stark bottom of the vessel. The surface was entirely smooth, but the magnetic device that the proxy had used to latch to the side of the trash sweeper stuck to it. I grabbed hold of it and realized it wasn't magnetic at all. I'd seen too many old-world dramas. It utilized pressurized suction for its grip. Magnets were mostly useless with most modern tech comprised of synthesized materials, so essentially, we were gambling Mission's life on a glorified suction cup.

"Are you sure this will hold?" I asked.

"Yes. It was designed in AD 2233 to help with space station construction and allow for mobile tether anchors. This is the last one we have left." The proxy pushed off the top of the vessel and floated back down to me. He grabbed the belt of my suit, which I figured was just for show, and extended it. There was only about a foot of slack, but a link at the end could be tethered directly to the suction device. The proxy attached mine and then his own.

"Our window is closing," he said. "Are you ready?"

I glanced up at the tower of waste pinning us against the vessel's hull. The explosive charge blinked red at the top, set to space all of it like a criminal on *Ignis*. I stopped myself before answering upon remembering Virgil. I unfastened and pushed up to grab him.

"We are safer without him."

"He's coming with us." I didn't wait for a response. I carried his weightless body down and latched myself back onto the anchor. We were too confined for his belt tether to reach as well, so I stuffed his arm back into his suit and resealed it. Then I fixed his buckle to my suit and wrapped my arms tight around him.

"I'm ready," I said.

The proxy opened his artificial palm, revealing a single-switch detonator. No turning back. "What are your oxygen readings?" He tapped a switch on my collar. Data projected onto the lower corner of my visor.

"It's . . . um . . . twelve percent."

"That's enough. Just try to stay conscious."

"Why wouldn't I—"

Before I could get the words out, the proxy pressed the detonator. The flash was blinding. My ears rang. Indescribable forces tugged on my body in every direction as the change in pressure tore open the ship's bow and violently yanked out the waste, Virgil's holopad along with it. Rapid deceleration had the anchor pulling on us in the other direction.

Our launch from Earth had been agonizing, but this made me feel like my skin was being peeled off my bones. I squeezed my eyes shut and clenched my jaw as hard as I could, both to battle the pain and keep my insides where they belonged.

A block of radioactive waste near the bottom of the vessel was jarred loose, and without anything to jam my legs against, the three of us were wrenched upward, or sideways . . . there was no up or down in space. The force of my tether being drawn taut was enough to misalign my hips. My head felt like it was stuck in a vise constantly squeezing harder and harder. White spots danced around the inside of my eyelids.

Just as I started to grow faint, my fingers, which had been locked on the other side of Virgil's body, were slowly pried apart, and he started slipping away. I squeezed with all my strength and clasped my wrists to keep him tight.

My helmet slid over his shoulder, and I peeked through eyelashes to see the silvered remnants of the vessel's bow fraying into the blackness. Space squelched any flames from the explosion like a thumb and forefinger squeezing a lit candle. Through that ruptured maw, the *Ignis* was visible barreling through space and growing fast. The gray, wrinkled exterior of the almond-shaped asteroid rotated faster than I'd ever imagined. On one end, its tremendous inactive nuclear propulsion system spread like petals of a rose. On the other, a station clung to the rock like a tiny metallic spider.

"Asher, can you hear me?" the proxy strained to ask.

"Still conscious!" I shouted.

"I'm going to grab you to brace for impact. Keep your body relaxed."

I couldn't gather a response. Like he'd instructed, my breathing was rapid to counteract the discomfort, which was almost so pervasive that my whole body grew numb. I was a mass of aches and tension, muscles assaulted by the unseen forces of the universe.

I stole glances of the rapidly approaching *Ignis* as often as I could manage without my eyeballs feeling like they were about to pop out. After a few times, the asteroid expanded beyond the opening. The details of every crag were emerging by the second, as if at that very moment, they were being sketched upon the rocky canvas by a god.

Hovering over a large crater near the vertex, the fixer station appeared a speck no more. It was a ring, with the top face almost entirely transparent, except for a series of three massive comm relays jutting out. Sweeping beams on the bottom connected to tracks wrapping the circumference of the crater, allowing the station to rotate constantly while also remaining attached so that the fixer could enjoy centripetally generated gravity within. Through the ring's hollow center sat the small outer seal of the *Ignis* airlock I'd seen so many condemned inhabitants go through, like the pupil of a giant eye. Emitters around the rim projected an adjusted view of the stars on the side facing them, per their imaginary location.

We were headed straight for the fixer station . . . well, at least close to it. I don't know where the Elder planned on hitting, but the waste vessel was going to collide on an angle with the lip of the crater.

"Elder!" I grated through the pain. "We're going to miss!" Maybe that was a stretch. For essentially being inside a bullet shot thousands of kilometers through space, hitting the right crater seemed like a miracle in itself. But miracles couldn't save Mission.

"Even a millisecond delay at launch could have altered our impact zone," the proxy replied. "Stay calm. We remain on target."

Pain couldn't stop my eyelids from widening in terror as the asteroid drew ever closer. I might as well have let myself fall off my balcony all those days ago if splattering against the ground was going to be my fate anyway. The proxy wrapped his strong arms around my back, and I squeezed Virgil's body as tightly as I could.

We struck in total silence, at a speed I couldn't fathom. There was no explosion. The vessel's shell rippled and cracked, and before I knew it, we were dangling loosely in the empty tube.

The angle we came in at caused it to ricochet and topple end over end until the stern slammed into the fixer station. The sudden change in momentum should've caused us to be thrown back against the inside of the vessel so hard all my bones would've shattered, but the proxy released our tethers just in time. The momentum of the spin caught us, and we were thrust through the wrecked top of the vessel.

I broke free of the proxy's grasp and tumbled out into the starry abyss with Virgil in my arms, disorientation and awe paralyzing me. The stars shone everywhere, spinning with me.

"Asher." Unusual urgency in the proxy's voice drew my focus. "You are moving away from the station."

I couldn't stop my weightless body from rolling, but I twisted my head in my helmet to gather my bearings. The top of the fixer station was below me, slowly distancing. The waste vessel had gashed open its side on it before bouncing off. It came within feet of smashing into me and carrying me off into space.

"What do I do?" I asked. Opening my mouth after all the spinning made me want to vomit, but I swallowed it down.

"You need to use Virgil to redirect yourself. Cut the tether and push off when I say."

"He'll be lost!"

"He promised to get you here. Do not let it be for nothing."

I relinquished my embrace on Virgil so that his short tether held us far enough apart that I could see his face. Lawbreaking inhabitants of the *Ignis* were cast into space so their energy would never be recycled into the vessel again. It was the worst fate imaginable for them. I'd spent so much of my life with the show that I never cared to consider what happened to High Earth residents after they died. Were they recycled? Were people from the Outskirts dumped into the ocean or devoured by the starving?

Even in death, Virgil had one last trick up his sleeve to help me. An eternity in the void wasn't an insult to him like it would be an inhabitant. Maybe, one day, his body would reach another star and open the eyes of whoever else is out there, like he had for me.

I had to let go.

"Now," the proxy said.

"Thank you," I whispered. For all the reasons he'd decided to try to kill me on that fateful day on my balcony, or chose afterward that I was worth helping, this much was true—he, not Craig Helix, was the only true friend I'd ever known.

I took one last glimpse of his face; then I unlatched his tether from my belt and pushed off. The momentum from cutting off our revolution at the right time redirected me. I still wasn't floating straight, but I arced back toward the ravaged side of the fixer station where the waste vessel had hit.

I approached too fast, fruitlessly flailing my arms to slow me as if I was in water.

"I need to slow down!" I yelled. "How do I slow down?"

No answer.

Before I knew it, I smashed into the station. I flailed to grasp the edge and missed completely. Before the spinning ring threw me off, the proxy grabbed hold of me with his powerful artificial grip. A human hand would never have been capable of such a feat of strength.

He clung to the breach as he swung me inside. Before I knew it, I was facedown on the inner surface, the familiar sense of gravity again holding me down. I gasped desperately for air until a beeping sound and a message on my visor warned me that my oxygen levels were at one percent. It was like I was back to wearing a lifeband.

CHAPTER 23

"This sector is compromised," the Elder's proxy said. "We need to reach life support."

He heaved me to my feet. A sharp pain in my injured hip struck, and my legs gave out. All the adrenaline from flying through space had dwindled, and soreness radiated throughout my body from everything it'd endured. The only thing that made all of it somewhat tolerable was that my hip hurt exponentially worse.

"I can't move," I groaned.

The proxy lifted me by the helmet with his metal hand, then placed his arm under my shoulder to help me walk. I could barely even move my legs. Instead, they dragged across the ground like limp sacks of meat. It didn't seem to slow him.

"In my time, we used to be trained to tolerate the high stress of space travel," the proxy said. "My proxy was addicted to a piloting VR. He has been preparing for this his entire life."

As I was dragged along, I studied my new surroundings. The entire inhabitable portion of the station was a wide cylindrical space, with a transparent wall on one side aimed at space. Emergency shutters divided the area we were in from the rest, and all that remained of whatever equipment had been inside were sparking outlets. Explosive decompression from when the waste vessel collided had sucked it all out.

The edges of the gash were bent back so far, it was as if it the station were made of tinfoil. Through the hole, the blue orb of Earth receded behind the horizon of the ever-spinning *Ignis*. A single brown splotch of paradise coated a small portion of it. High Earth.

"It looks so small," I marveled through clenched teeth.

"The sky, space, other worlds in this system—Earth was the one place we never learned to tame," the proxy replied.

"High Earth was larger when you were born?"

"There was no High Earth when I was born."

We stopped in front of an emergency shutter, which must have lowered automatically to prevent damage to the rest of the station.

"Can you stand?" the proxy asked.

"I think so."

He placed me near the bulkhead, and I quickly learned that I was half-right. I could stand if I leaned the majority of my weight against it. He kneeled in front of the door's control panel.

"Locked," he said. "The other side remains inhabitable. We need key codes to override."

Again, my suit beeped. "My oxygen tank is almost empty," I said, growing anxious. All that heavy breathing during our "landing" really did me in.

"There is still oxygen remaining in your helmet and suit. Just breathe slowly—it should be enough while I override the lock. High Earth programming was Virgil's specialty, but I should be able to get us through."

The proxy held his artificial hand over the control panel. The screen flickered as he was able to communicate with it without contact. The lights in the tech latched onto his head sped up in their blinking pattern.

As I watched, I wondered if it was the Elder or her tool doing the work. Could she see through his eyes and tell him what to do, or was he mostly alone with nothing but her blind advice? It helped me to focus my thoughts on something. Distracted me from how tiny my breaths were, and how strained my chest felt from doing so.

Suddenly, the controls chimed and the door shot up into the ceiling. We should've been blasted backward by the sudden change in pressure, but we weren't. A man in a space suit, uncannily similar to ours, appeared in the opening. His visor was fogged, and he held a pulse-pistol. With no air or comm-link to carry a voice, whoever it was waved us in with the weapon, never breaking aim.

The proxy was hesitant to enter, but I didn't have time to think. I ignored the pain racking my body and lunged in, forcing him to follow. My head was getting light, and without air, I had no idea how much longer I had left. Another resource I never had to worry about in High Earth.

The emergency shutter resealed behind us, and then the familiar, soothing robotic voice of a VORA announced: "Repressurizing station." Lights along the tall ceilings blinked red, and the loose vent cover of an air recycler started shaking.

I fell to a knee, tore off my helmet, and breathed in so deep it hurt my organs. Hearing VORA's voice sent a calming sensation rippling across my body, like I was entering my home.

Only I wasn't.

The person holding us at gunpoint removed his helmet as well. He had a wrinkled face with a messy beard and hair that looked like it hadn't been brushed in ages. He looked like someone straight out of the heart of the Outskirts. I didn't recognize him.

"Who are you, and what are you doing here?" he asked.

I *did*, however, recognize his voice, as abrasive as the surface of *Ignis*. It belonged to Lance Alsmore, the *Ignis: Live* fixer I'd worked with for years. The very same who'd worked in secret to rectify our mistake after helping Mission. I'd never actually seen him when he wasn't wearing the holographic face of an inhabitant. Apparently, Mr. Helix hadn't replaced him yet.

"Helix Productions has been notified of the intrusion," VORA said. My gaze was drawn to the security feeds tucked into the ceiling. They would have already transmitted my image back to Earth for Mr. Helix to see if he wanted to.

"Thank you, VORA," Lance said. "Now, I'll ask again, who the hell are you?"

The proxy faced Lance and stood still, without even bothering to remove his helmet. My attempt to stand failed, so I remained kneeling.

"It's nice to finally meet you, Lance," I said.

The sights of his pulse-pistol bounced between the proxy and me. His left eye twitched. "How do you know my name? Are you here to replace me? Mr. Helix said there'd be a bot."

"No, it's me . . . Asher. Chief director of Content."

"Asher Reinhart?" His face lit up. "By Earth, I knew you sounded familiar! They told me you retired after the fiftieth."

"Not exactly."

"So, you are here to have me replaced?" He turned to the proxy and raised his pulse-pistol again. "Is this him? Is this the one?"

"No, Lance. Nobody is here to replace you."

"Then why are you here?" He squeezed his gun tighter and

took a hard step forward. He looked like he was ready to snap. One eye twitched every so often, and the other lagged behind, unable to focus on anything. "They said I failed and didn't fulfill my probation. Might not get re-enlisted. What in High Earth's name are you doing here!"

I didn't have a chance to respond. Blue streaks raced across the room and struck Lance in the chest. His body convulsed and flashed from the inside out. I could see the silhouette of his skeleton through his skin. A stray shot from his pistol gashed the floor a few feet from me before he crumpled into a smoking heap.

"No!" I shouted. I crawled to him and flipped his body over, only to find that his mad eyes had rolled back into his head and the center of his suit was charred. I turned, aghast, to see the Elder's proxy with his electricity blaster armed.

"Lance, I am no longer receiving readings from your lifeband," VORA indicated. "A med-bot has been dispatched."

"Why did you do that?" I yelled at the proxy.

A slot in the wall opened and a many-limbed med-bot floated out. Another blast from the proxy's weapon promptly overloaded it, causing half of its arms to pop out as it sparked and toppled over. A few more shots cooked the surveillance feeds tucked in along the ceilings.

"Lance, I am no longer receiving readings from your lifeband," VORA repeated, and then twice more as if she was malfunctioning before silencing.

"He was a threat," the proxy said. He finally removed his helmet and proceeded into the room.

"That doesn't mean he had to die!" Adrenaline fueled me and I rushed him. I took him by the collar and drew his OptiVisor-covered face toward my own, so close that I could see the pale outline of eyes beyond the screen. Both were cybernetic.

"No more risks can be taken. Helix knows we're here now." He pushed me off. His charged weapon crackled beside me, making my entire body tingle and the hairs on my neck stand.

"So you'll kill anyone else who gets in our way? You don't even care about being here!"

"Nobody else is in our way, Asher. We have made it."

He turned to face a vast viewport comprising an entire wall. Earth was no longer visible, and the *Ignis* asteroid had revolved far enough that the sun glared in the lower corner. Radiation shielding ensured the brightness wasn't hazardous, but I still had to use my hand to shade my eyes. This was the view Lance had to live with every single day, rotating between Earth and the sun. Constantly being reminded how minuscule he really was. It was no wonder he looked like he was on the verge of cracking.

"I suppose you have another plan for how to get inside?" I asked.

"No," the proxy said. "We are here to fulfill a promise to you. How to proceed is your choice. You are the expert on *Ignis*'s people."

The proxy turned, strolled across the room, and stopped in front of a cluster of powered-down holoscreens. We must have been in Lance's living quarters. A lonely chair was positioned in front of it with an OptiVisor hanging off the arm, but it wasn't a VR station. In fact, there was nowhere for him to enter a VR at all and interact with anybody.

Adjacent to the chair was a small kitchen much like the one in my smart-dwelling, complete with water dispenser and a re-assembler. A half-eaten nutrient bar sat on a round table nearby with two table settings. The food lay in front of one, where I presumed Lance ate, and a neckband projecting the photo-realistic face of Jacen in 3D was at the other. As if they'd been "sharing" a meal together.

Then I noticed a succession of purposeful scratches on the floor. Some were complete nonsense, others more deliberate etchings. From meaningless spirals and symbols, to the hand-scrawled ravings of a lunatic in script I could hardly decipher.

The wall beside the holoscreens had the most. Thousands of tally marks were lined up along it, top to bottom. The last one was fresh, inscribed with a handmade chisel made from one of the med-bot's arms that was missing even before the proxy got to it. Lance had been counting down the days until his probation ended and he could be a proper resident again. I always knew Mr. Helix chose people who were on the brink of delistment to volunteer for this as their penitence. The intense nature of the work meant a shortened period.

"Who would choose this?" I said.

"To live alone with an AI?" the Elder's proxy replied. "Every resident does."

"Not like this . . . and it's not like we have a choice."

"Of course you do, and you made yours. Now you are here."

I glanced back at Lance's body. His usually crass attitude and impatience when it came to repair operations finally made sense to me. The way he stayed behind until the very last second to install a new camera and the smirk his false facade wore as he'd fired at Mission during the fiftieth anniversary events. Without any ability to load into VRs, it was the only interaction he ever got.

"At least he died before he had a chance to be let down again by paradise," the proxy said.

"Shut up," I snapped. "Was he not good enough to have his eyes opened before you killed him? Being older than everyone doesn't mean you get to choose who stays blind. Virgil wouldn't have—"

"Virgil is dead because of his decision to aid you. Unless you want Mission to join him, I suggest you stop trying to understand things beyond your control and focus. I made a deal to help you save her, and I intend to honor it."

I squeezed my fists as tight as I could, then exhaled. The Elder was right. There was time before her spacing, but that didn't mean there was enough to waste arguing.

"Fine," I conceded. "VORA, please turn on any live feeds of *Ignis: Live* currently tracking Mission-14130." It felt so natural to ask it of her. Like old times. Only I'd never speak with the one designated to me again.

"I am sorry," she replied. "I am programmed only to accept commands from Lance Alsmore or Craig Helix. I am no longer receiving readings from the former's lifeband, and there are no med-bots available. Can you verify his status?"

"He's . . . dead. Now, please activate the screens." She didn't answer. Her processing matrix, which threaded the controls and tech throughout the station, suddenly powered down. We were lucky a VORA couldn't harm a human being and the life-support systems remained active.

The proxy waved his artificial hand across the display and switched on the holoscreens manually. An episode of *Molecular Nation* was the first thing to pop up. The actress portraying Gloria Fors was in a lab, tinkering with a strange gizmo. A suit hanging in the background bore the same FORS TECH logo that the one I currently wore did. For some reason I felt like I'd viewed the scene before, even though a watermark indicated this was a new episode. The proxy quickly changed channels to *Ignis: Live*, where Mission was, as usual, front and center on a live feed.

I released a sigh of relief. She was still alive.

[Ignis Feed Location]
Recycler Hollow
<Camera 14>

Cassiopeia stood beside Mission in the *Ignis* recycler hollow, as well as numerous enforcers who didn't appear overly pleased with her being permitted there. The chunky machine comprised an entire wall. Tubes extended from it in either direction, like arteries branching from a heart. In the center was a rectangular mouth of metal large enough to fit a human. Once bodies went in, they never came out, but their energy lived on. Jacen's corpse lay naked inside, his body painted like sunlight by the hellish glow. It made the roughly sewn wound in his gut harder to notice.

Mission glanced at Cassiopeia, who returned a stern nod. She placed down a bowl of her last meal, which she'd hardly touched. Then she approached the body cautiously, as if afraid it was going to spring back to life.

"He'll be with us forever now," Cassiopeia said. "Helping us carry the flame of humanity."

"Good. You'll need him." Mission fought her trembling lips to form a smile. "All he ever wanted to do was help our world."

"It's all any of us can hope to do."

"I used to hope there was more."

"There was," Cassiopeia said, "but our impulsive ancestors destroyed all of it. Our burden is crushing, Mission, I know. I only wish I'd spent more time with your generation, helping them see why all of this is worth it, instead of teaching them only to fear losing it."

"Why is it?"

"Excuse me?"

"Why is it worth it?"

She sighed. "There was a time back on Earth when a girl could meet a boy and they could love each other without restrictions. One day, our children's children will step off *Ignis*, purified by the rigors of our journey, and into a new world where that may be possible again. Where they'll be free. Until then, we remain. Against all the forces of the universe, we must remain."

"I never got the chance to tell him how I felt."

"I'm sure he knew."

Mission placed her quaking hands on the edge of the slot where Jacen lay. She closed her eyes and let her head sink. She wondered then how Alora, her real mother, felt, holding her as an infant here when she couldn't go through with it. If it had been this difficult.

When her eyes opened again, she saw that Cassiopeia had placed the star-speckled pendant Jacen made in front of her.

"Alora told me this belongs to you," she said.

Mission quickly grabbed it and squeezed it as hard as she could while holding it against her chest. In all the chaos, she'd forgotten about it.

"How is Alora?" Mission asked.

"She continues to insist that you're lying and that she's going to find out what really happened."

Mission put on a brave face. "Good. She needs something to keep her busy."

"Whatever the truth is, I hope you understand why I have to accept your confession as the truth and punish you according to our laws."

Mission nodded. It was what she'd anticipated when she decided to tell the Collective and everyone else in *Ignis* what they secretly wanted to hear. To give them a villain to direct their anger toward: a girl who never really fit in. They were angry and scared, even if they didn't realize it. The core was the face of their laws. It couldn't be rebelled against or overthrown, it was simple data.

"Earth has fallen . . . We remain," Mission recited. For once, she said it like she actually meant it.

Cassiopeia put on a solemn grin and backed away. Mission reached out to graze Jacen's chin. The coolness of his flesh caused her to recoil at first, but then she cupped her entire hand around the back of his head. She lifted it and placed the necklace he'd made for her around his neck.

"You keep this," she whispered, pressing the pendant against his bare chest. "I'll finally see the stars for myself soon."

She leaned over him and ran her fingers through his hair. At first, the body appeared to her like a bad wax replica of her oldest friend, but as she got closer, she no longer doubted it was him. She could still picture him on that first day she sat beside him to look out upon their world, smothered in darkness. Unlike then, now he appeared to be at peace.

"They say our energy lives on forever, Jacen," she said. "Now you'll be a part of the plants you loved so much."

Cassiopeia laid a hand on Mission's shoulder. "It's time."

Mission got even closer, until her and Jacen's faces were mere centimeters apart. "I don't know if you can hear me," she said, "but I know now that I would have let the whole of *Ignis* die for you. So I can't stay, you see? Even if I wanted to. Even if I belonged. I love you, Jacen."

She pressed her lips against his and kissed him like she'd always wanted to, unimpeded by her responsibilities or the core's laws. She held there until tears rolled directly from her eyelids onto his stony cheeks.

She had to draw on her entire reservoir of willpower to pull her lips away. A part of her wanted to crawl in there with him so they could be reduced to pure energy together, but it was too late to be selfish.

She backed away slowly, holding back her tears, and said: "I'm ready."

Before she could change her mind, Cassiopeia activated the recycler. The doors of its maw shut, and the machine roared to life. Through all its vibrating tubes, his energy would be transferred into fertilizer for the farms, feed for the insects, fuel for the lights. He would live on forever as a part of the *Ignis*.

* * *

"How will you reach her?" the proxy asked.

I wiped my cheeks. Jacen's death had never really impacted me beyond how it'd wounded Mission so deeply. I thought a part of me had always been jealous of the time they got to spend together, but now Virgil taught me what it was like to lose a friend. Nobody had been closer to Mission than him. Not Alora. Not even me.

"How will you reach her?" the proxy repeated.

"Sorry . . . I'm thinking," I answered.

He pulled up a station schematic on another holoscreen. "Fixers are able to traverse the station's structural beams directly into the asteroid's pipes and ductwork. We can reach her through them."

"She'll be watched constantly until she's spaced. We'll be seen."

"Does that matter? Remember, I saw your mind. We know the *Ignis* well enough to escape with her before anyone can do anything about it."

"It won't work," I argued.

"Are you really still worried about disrupting the show after all of this? You are no longer its director. Think of your arriving to grab her as one of the natural phenomena Craig Helix used to rationalize his actions."

"I know what I am now, but you heard Lance's VORA. Mr. Helix will know about our intrusion by now. They'll send bots here. But if they think Mission is dead, they might overlook her. She can sneak back to Earth on their ship. It isn't perfect, but perhaps your replica *Ignis* will suffice as her new home."

"What about us?"

I shrugged. "You couldn't promise a way back. Besides, all they can do is toss us back into the Outskirts with our memories wiped, where we already belong."

"Belong is a peculiar word choice for you."

"At least it's somewhere," I said.

"As glad as I am to hear that, that is still not a plan to retrieve her."

I scratched my chin and tried to pace. After a few limping steps, a bright line of pain up my side reminded me how injured it was. I slumped backward into Lance's lonely chair. His OptiVisor slipped off the armrest it was balanced on. Out of reflex for protecting the tech I used to worship, I scrambled and caught it just before it crashed into the ground.

That was it!

"I'm going to catch her," I said.

"What?"

I pointed at the solid inner face of the station. "The *Ignis*'s airlock is directly below us, right? When they eject her, we can quickly catch her in space."

The proxy studied the schematics of the station in relation to the airlock. We were at least fifty meters away from the surface, in a ring with about ten times the diameter of the airlock itself.

"The only way out there is by tether," he said. "Bots preserve the station, so there are no thruster-suits available for exterior maintenance. And they won't operate now. With VORA offline, all bots are on standby."

"I don't have time to learn how to use anything new anyway. Can it work?"

"Pressure will draw her out fast. You'll have to be extended far to grab her, with the strength of my proxy to reel you back in. And if you miss—"

"I won't," I said.

"Arriving ships dock at an airlock on the inside of the ring to shield them from any stray debris caught in orbit. It's the closest way in or out of the center, but it would still be a long period for her to be exposed to vacuum."

"How long?"

"If we pull you in as soon as you grab her . . ." He, or rather the Elder, paused to think for a bit. "Roughly ten seconds."

"Could she survive?" I asked.

"That depends on whether or not she tries to inhale. The extreme change in pressure might prevent her from doing so at first, but once you have her . . . I can't predict that."

"Could she survive, Elder?" I asked sternly.

"I still suggest we infiltrate and remove her from the inside."

I pictured Mission crying over Jacen's bloody body from when Mr. Helix set it to replay repeatedly. Thanks to Virgil, I was starting to get a clearer picture of the type of man he really was.

"I can't say what Mr. Helix might do to her right in front of me out of anger," I said. "Catching her is the only way to keep her survival secret. Can you retool Lance's uniform into a mask? I'll cover her mouth and nose as soon as I grab her, and you get us back in."

"If you are absolutely sure about taking this risk, then yes, it can be done."

"There are no absolutes."

Flickers of a grin touched the proxy's lips for a moment, then faded. He keyed a few commands on Lance's terminal.

"I'll start working, then," he said. "I have now deactivated all surveillance throughout the station. You head to the dock. There should be an emergency tether there. Based on the schematic, you will need exactly twenty-four-point-four meters to reach the midpoint vector of the *Ignis*'s airlock. Make sure it's long enough."

"Got it."

I groaned as I rose to my feet, but I'd worry about my battered body later. I analyzed the schematics for one last moment, then started off deeper into the station. The proxy stopped me.

"Here," he said.

He opened a med-kit he'd found in the kitchen and revealed a few stims. Calming pharma, painkilling—everything that came with a standard-issue lifeband. I quickly reached for them, then stopped, hand hovering over them. Sweat dripped down the back of my neck. My very skin seemed to want to extend from my bones for the shots of sweet relief.

"No," I decided. "I need to be clear."

"Good for you." He closed the kit and tossed it aside. I regretted it as soon as I heard the snap of the top sealing, but I couldn't back down now. "As soon as she is safe, we have upheld our end of the bargain, correct?" the proxy asked.

"Yes," I replied before continuing along the curving passage. If I waited any longer, I'd shoot up every ounce of medication the station had.

One more trade nearly completed. I was becoming a true delisted man after all.

* * *

The docking airlock was on the other side of the station. Because of our breach, I had to take the long way through a lengthy space filled with exercise equipment. A bot reminiscent of my guardian in the Outskirts stood silently by a rectangular table with a low net strung across the middle and paddles lying on either side of it that looked like they hadn't been touched in ages.

Its eye lenses were pale, but for some reason I felt like it was watching me. I limped by and into the next space. This one was empty, meant for loading supplies, and a ladder across the way led up into the docking airlock. It took some time for me to climb with the shape I was in.

The airlock poked out toward the center of the ring-station, with the outer seal positioned straight above me. The tiny chamber stored a tether just like the proxy anticipated. I worked as fast as I could to extend it all the way back down the ladder and across the floor. Its interface provided a measurement. About a meter short, but after some quick thinking, I removed my own suit's belt. With that added on, I was left with a bit of slack that the proxy could use to his benefit while dragging Mission and me in.

When I was finished, I made my way back and found the proxy in the exercise room. I sat across from him, eager to rest my throbbing hip. He'd ripped off the faceplate of the bot by the netted table and was busy using Lance's homemade chisel to shape it. He then pried off the bot's arm and used its sparking end to fuse a tube to the portion over the mouth and nose, which connected on the other end to Lance's now unneeded oxygen tank.

"As soon as it's on her face, hit this switch on the tank, and the pressure will be enough to make sure that when she does take a breath out there, her lungs don't collapse," he explained.

He showed me the contraption. The mask looked like something out of a horror drama.

"That switch," I said. "All right, easy."

"And wrap this around her body immediately to limit radiation exposure." He slid a wrinkly silver blanket over to me. Lance's suit lay off to the side with the lining cut out of it. The Elder-proxy team worked exceptionally fast.

I raised the shimmering blanket. It'd been stitched together from at least a dozen pieces. "This is all incredible," I said.

"If you must know, my exact specialty in old Earth was research and development for aiding safe interplanetary travel. I miss using my own hands more than anything. Not that he has his." The proxy finished a last bit of fusing and twisted things into place. "I am compelled to warn you again that this is extremely dangerous. More so than any operation I supervised in my youth."

I was too busy staring at the proxy to answer. As the young man sat there tinkering, a thought popped into my head about the Elder. Her age, her technical prowess, the logo on her proxy's chest, but the real clue had been seeing *Molecular Nation* earlier, right after learning about Alora's true nature. I realized what was so peculiar about the brief scene that had come on Lance's screen. I'd seen something similar when the Elder was looking into my mind, only there was something off about it.

"You're Gloria Fors, aren't you?" I said quietly, hardly able to formulate the words. It was rarely in my nature to be awestruck by a High Earth star, but if I was right, the woman who'd invented the molecular re-assembler and sparked the techno-revolution was sitting directly in front of me . . . sort of. Without her, High Earth as I knew it would never have been possible.

The way the proxy's gaze snapped up toward me, even with an OptiVisor on, answered the question before he could. A thousand different responses flashed across his usually demure

features before the woman dictating his words settled on the
truth. "In another lifetime, perhaps. Yes," he said. "I was wondering how long it would take you to realize yours wasn't the
only mind opened that day."

"That's . . . Does anybody else know? Did . . . did Virgil
know?"

"If he did, he never cared to say."

"Why aren't you in High Earth? The med-bots could help
you, couldn't they? Fix your body. I don't know. You deserve—"

"What? A throne? That new show about me the residents
adore so much takes many liberties with my life. As did all that
came before it. The molecular re-assembler was meant to help
us settle the universe in response to our dying planet, not to
stay behind on it. But the technology was bought out by the developers of what became the Higher Earth Network, and I . . .
Let's just say you aren't the only one with mistakes to rectify."

I crawled forward. "It's many things, but High Earth isn't
a mistake," I said. "It just needs the same help you and Virgil
have given me. They need to be reminded to stop from time to
time and look at each other."

"No," Gloria said, shaking her proxy's head. "High Earth is
perfect. It's what humanity has striven for since the first time a
Neanderthal picked up a rock and sparked a flame."

"What about all that stuff about opening eyes to the reality we're born into?"

"The reality we live in is broken. I can change thousands in
the Outskirts, but they will always be the people stuck on the
other side of paradise's wall. If ever that wall disappears, not one
of them would turn down the chance to cross over."

"Virgil would have. He did."

"Pushing you that day released the anger he clung to, but
he was still a man. And the human struggle to survive ended

the moment I made a machine that could turn dirt into wine. Food, water, shelter, and mental stimulation—in those regards of necessity, High Earth *is* perfect. You can't fight perfection, Asher. However, humankind is anything but."

"So then why are you even here?" A mixture of pain and anger had me raising my voice. "There's more to it than a trade with me, isn't there?"

The proxy calmly stood, reached behind his belt and removed the OptiVisor that had belonged to Lance. "For now, to save a girl." He handed the device to me. "We can't waste any more time with talk. Put this on and refill your oxygen tank. You can keep track of Mission until the spacing, and the moment you have her, I'll be listening on our comm-link frequency to know when to pull you in."

Just holding a legitimate High Earth bit of tech in my hands again felt like seeing an old friend after years apart. At least, what I could imagine that felt like, as I was new to friendship. I'd be a liar if I said I didn't miss it. Would I too return to paradise like Gloria thought?

I looked back up at the Elder's proxy, into the reflection of the OptiVisor that essentially stole his sight and being.

"And I thought I was the one who was lost," I said under my breath.

I lowered the OptiVisor over my face and turned away. The last time I wore one, I thought Mission was going to die before I was exiled to the Outskirts. Now, as her face came on screen, I was so close I could almost feel her amber-colored hair between my fingers.

"I'm coming, Mission," I said.

CHAPTER 24

[Ignis Feed Location]
Recycler Hollow Exit
<Camera 2>

Mission left her unfinished final meal behind in the recycler hollow and began the long trek across *Ignis* to the airlock hollow. The path took her directly through the heart of her world, past the entrance to the living blocks, and all the surrounding farmland. Inhabitants usually convened around the airlock for a spacing ceremony, but this one was different. They lined the path, the older ones hollering and cursing, the younger watching in disbelief. The entire Collective and their enforcers surrounded Mission to keep her from being torn to pieces before the ceremony.

Rocks thrown by inhabitants penetrated the enforcers' ranks and pelted her. Spit slicked the rock in front of her every step, as inhabitants issued the revolting insult of willingly discharging water. Mission focused on the glowing core above as she walked, trying her best to ignore them. They were nearly to the airlock hollow when a sizable rock cracked her in the head. She fell over, tearing the side of her clothes as she slid on the ground.

"Back away!" Cassiopeia roared.

Mission scrambled to her knees, blood trickling down the messy strands of her hair. She couldn't get up further. More food and refuse struck her from every side. She'd expected outrage, but this was on another level. Twenty years of pent-up ire fueled every throw. She had welts all over her body the size of cherry tomatoes.

Alora broke through the line and covered Mission, taking on the brunt of the assault. One of the enforcers then fired a pulse pistol round into the ground. The crack reverberated across *Ignis* and momentarily silenced everyone. Few but Mission had heard a gunshot out in the open since the time of the Great Blackout when keeping order had become paramount.

"I've got you," Alora said. She lifted Mission and covered her head as they walked. "Just keep moving."

Side by side they strode into the yawning hollow of the *Ignis*'s only airlock. Spacings were usually solemn occasions, but the more inhabitants who filed in, the more raucous it became. The armed enforcers had to flaunt their weapons just to keep the mob from wiping them away.

They stopped by the edge of the airlock's circular inner seal, surrounded by inhabitants on every side. Alora held Mission in her arms as they waited, silent.

"Our laws are simple!" Cassiopeia yelled, straining her voice to be heard. "The delicate balance of resources provided by *Ignis* must never be tested. We are the last! We carry the lasting flame of humanity!"

"Just space the flame-robber!" someone shouted. The sound of more than one hundred people spitting in Mission's direction was as loud as the core's hum. It rained down upon the Collective, Mission, and Alora.

"Leave her alone!" Alora screamed. Mission held her back from doing something foolish with her welt-covered arms.

"It's okay, Mother," she whispered. The word drew Alora to embrace her again. All the Birthmothers and Mothers cared for the inhabitants of their block equally. Family was the community, was *Ignis*. Another reason Mission knew she didn't belong. Now, especially, she only saw one Mother amongst the thousands around her.

"Stop this madness!" Cassiopeia yelled. "We are better than the ancestors we left behind."

"She deserves worse! She gives even her generation a bad name!" That cry from the crowd was followed by Cassiopeia being hit hard in the side by a whole vegetable.

"Seize him!"

An enforcer swung his way through the crowd with a baton. A brawl erupted in the area.

Cassiopeia looked exasperated as she struggled to move the ceremony along. "For the crimes of—" Her words trailed off when Mission limped out toward the center of the airlock's seal on her own, Alora helping her every step of the way. Most offenders had to be forced out, but not her.

"I'm going to find out the truth, Mission," Alora said. "All these people are going to think back to this day and know how wrong they are about you, I swear it."

"I've always wanted to see space," Mission replied.

"You're the bravest person I've ever known." Alora embraced her daughter, squeezing as tight as she could. Mission's countless welts ached unimaginably from the pressure, but she didn't mind. It was worth being held in the arms of her mother one last time.

"Don't . . ." Mission's knees buckled, but Alora kept her upright. Then she stood tall and gazed into her mother's eyes. "Don't forget to relax."

Alora laughed through her tears. She kissed her daughter

on the forehead and backed toward Cassiopeia, one slow step at a time. Mission stared at the incensed crowd. By now their insults were like white noise. She was only grateful they'd run out of things to throw.

She removed her clothes, as was customary. The energy of a criminal was cast away, but their belongings remained in the *Ignis* for the rest of its time. When she was completely divested, she nodded in Cassiopeia's direction.

Cassiopeia swallowed hard. "For the crimes of murdering your fellow inhabitants and tampering with the core, your . . ." Her voice was uncommonly hoarse. She had to pause to gather herself. "Your energy will be expelled from the *Ignis*. Never to taint us again. Never to be recycled."

She started off toward the airlock's controls, but Alora placed a hand on her shoulder to stop her and went in her stead. A member of the Collective had to unlock the console since she was no longer a Mother.

The spectacle of Mission stripped bare over the airlock calmed the crowd enough for Cassiopeia to be heard. "May you find peace in the void." She regarded her people, her face darkened by disappointment. "Earth has fallen! We remain!"

That was usually the point when Mission turned away from spacings, unable to stomach watching another young soul be evacuated into the void. This time, she stood still and maintained eye contact with Alora.

"We remain," Mission mouthed.

Her mother's hand hovered over the command to open the inner seal like she was supposed to, shaking uncontrollably. The echo of the inhabitants repeating after Cassiopeia hung in the air, eerie silence prevailing once it was gone. They all waited anxiously for Mission, the Mother who'd betrayed so many of their fallen brothers and sisters, to get what they thought she deserved.

Mission shuffled across the seal to the control console. She reached over the screen and placed her hand over Alora's.

"Maybe I can tell them the truth about us," Alora whimpered. "Maybe I can change their mind."

Mission smiled. Then, without a word, she helped Alora press the command.

"No!" Alora gasped. "No! I can't!"

It was too late. The inner seal peeled open, and Mission fell through the opening onto her back. Members of the Collective had to grab Alora to keep her from jumping in too. Then they, Cassiopeia, and anyone else who could fit circled the edge of the hole and stared down. The ceiling started to seal over Mission, locking her back in a hole like she'd been so many times before.

When she was very young, Alora used to have to calm her to get her to go to sleep down in the darkness. She'd stroke her hair and hum a song and wear a brave face. Now, it was Mission's turn. She held Alora's tear-filled gaze the entire time.

"I'm coming, Jacen," she said. Her lips curled into a frail, relieved grin as the inner seal closed with barely a sound. She wasn't sure how long she lay there, waiting for the outer seal to release. It seemed like eternity. Her entire life passed before her eyes. She'd achieved much in her short time on *Ignis* after Alora had helped her become an inhabitant, but the only thing that stood out to her was that moment only a few short days ago when she kissed Jacen for the first time, in their favorite spot. It felt like the only time outside the hole that she'd ever been honest with herself.

She didn't allow her mind to linger on the horrors that followed and stole him from her. She stayed in that fleeting juncture of true happiness. His warm breath on her neck, his scent, his strong fingers digging into her back. As Cassiopeia said, humans were beings of passion. Mission was only happy she got to feel that once in her time, no matter how briefly.

The floor suddenly dropped out from beneath her. She drew one final gulp of fresh air, and then she was pulled out into the sublime, star-filled blackness.

* * *

"Now!" I shouted into my comm-link. I used my eyes to deactivate the OptiVisor over my face, which had allowed me to keep track of Mission on *Ignis: Live*.

I watched from my end as the outer seal of the *Ignis* airlock opened and Mission's pale, naked figure shot out, slightly off center, and passed through the projection of stars keeping the inhabitants ignorant. There was no time to ask the proxy to provide a few more meters of slack. I stretched out as far as my aching body could and kept my eyes on her as she fell upward like a leaf caught upon the wind.

Only seconds passed as she flew toward me, unaware, but each one felt like a lifetime. No lifeband. No pharma. It was me and her against the void, attempting something that even the most brilliant inventor of a bygone age thought was insane.

I believed. I had to.

With one hand, I gripped with all my might the respirator mask Gloria Fors's proxy had fashioned. My other arm cradled the fully unfurled space blanket cut out of Lance Alsmore's suit. The silvery strands of Mission's hair fluttered like she was submerged in the Earth's vast ocean. Her eyes were peeled wide open, like the stars were even more beautiful than she'd ever imagined. And it was that sense of awe that kept her alive.

The sight left her breathless so that she didn't open her mouth and let the vacuum of space in. She was too smart for that. I knew she would hold in her last gulp of air so that she could marvel at the world beyond her own until her vision went black.

She didn't, however, notice me. My space blanket enveloped her wildly gyrating body as we made impact. It happened so fast and so hard that my shoulder was yanked out of its socket. My arm wrapped her waist and I refused to let go, even as we started to tumble violently. Somehow, I managed to slap the mask over her face and switch on the oxygen with my thumb.

"Pull!" I howled into my comm-link.

The proxy tugged with all his enhanced strength and sent us hurtling toward the ring-shaped station. The only thing that kept me from being too dizzy to keep my hand over Mission's mask was her. There had always been a lingering fear buried deep in my skull that everything on the *Ignis* was nothing more than a computer simulation, like countless other shows. She was no special effect. Her eyes were rolling back into her head and growing more and more bloodshot with every agonizing second.

My back slammed against the inside of the fixer station's airlock. My suit was the only thing that kept my back from breaking. I served as her buffer. My hand flew off her mask so wildly that it struck the ceiling, likely fracturing a few knuckles.

The outer seal of the airlock closed, and oxygen flooded the chamber. She didn't move. I wrenched my arm out from under her and crawled on top of her. I ignored the pain and threw off my helmet.

"Mission!" I rasped. "Mission, wake up!" I shook her body. I didn't care how much it hurt. As I lowered my head to listen for a heartbeat, her eyelids sprang open, her back lurched, and she gasped.

CHAPTER 25

"W . . . Where am I?" Mission asked me after she had her fill of air.

She scrambled backward, panting and unable to focus on any one thing. The wrinkling sound of the space blanket underneath her made her flinch. Then she slapped her hands against the ceiling and the walls, searching for a way out.

Seeing her face so nearby trapped a response on the tip of my tongue. The *Ignis*'s cameras were supposedly life-quality, but her eyes were somehow greener than I even imagined. Her skin more flawless.

I reached out to stroke her impossibly soft cheek, but she slapped me away. She flipped over, threw off the blanket, and scurried down the ladder into the station. I tried to follow but couldn't grip the rungs properly with my injured hand and arm. Instead, I slid all the way down.

"Gloria, stop her!" I yelled.

Despite reeling us back in, her proxy was nowhere to be found. Mission darted back and forth through the hall in a panic, her welt-covered body bare. The space blanket fluttered down over my head. I grabbed it and hurried after her.

"Mission, calm down!" I coughed and slipped back to my knees. An entire half of my body felt like it was on fire. I had to crawl.

Mission reached the station's exercise space and shrieked the moment she saw the stripped-down humanoid bot positioned inside. She ran from it as if she'd seen a monster, toward Lance's former living area. I drew myself to my feet and staggered toward her along the wall, falling a few times. By the time I reached her, she'd already stopped. She was on her knees facing the holographic mask replicating Jacen's face.

"Wh-what is this?" she stammered.

I finally caught her and wrapped the blanket around her back. After being in space, she must have been freezing. She completely ignored me.

She steadied one hand with the other and reached out to touch Jacen's face. Light diffracted around her skinny fingers. Her eyes bulged. She grabbed the band it projected up from and spun in, swiping her hands through over and over. "What is this!" she yelled. She flung it and scrambled away.

"It's not real." I took her by the shoulders. "Mission, you're safe now."

She smacked my hand away. "How do you know my name? Where the hell am I?" She stared right through me, unable to tear her terrified gaze away from the device as Jacen's expressionless face rolled across the floor. "Where . . ."

"I'll explain everything. I promise."

She squeezed around me, drawn suddenly to the holoscreens. Gloria's proxy had left them on, and *Ignis: Live* played. Enforcers were cleaning up the airlock hollow after the ceremony.

"That's . . . *Ignis*. How?" She whirled around and froze again from what she saw through the viewport. As the asteroid the station clung to rotated, blue Earth became visible amongst the sea of blackness and stars. A crescent of sunlight bloomed along its rounded edge.

"What is . . . ?" She fell, clutching her chest as it heaved.

"Mission, just breathe," I begged.

I'd played how our first interaction might go countless times in my head since I'd decided to save her, and it was never like this. I cursed my tendency to fantasize. I thought back to being released from my synth-womb for the first time back in High Earth. I understood there was a world and everything about it, but it was all disconnected. Like pieces of a puzzle spread haphazardly across a table, which my VORA helped me piece together. The difference was, I had been where I supposed to be. To her knowledge, she was light-years away from any star. Yet there, right before her, was a planet and a sun.

I didn't know how to begin to explain.

Mission bent over and threw up bile. I took a cue from Virgil, kneeling behind her and rubbing her back. "It's okay," I whispered. "It's all going to be okay. Let it out . . ."

I lost my train of thought as I saw a ship flit across the viewport. It moved too rapidly for me to see any markings, but there was no question in my mind whom it belonged to.

"No," I said to myself. "No, no, no, they can't be here that fast. That's impossible." We hadn't been on the station for more than an hour after the Network had been warned about an intrusion.

I wrapped my arm around Mission and tried to lift her, but my body was too battered to support her full weight.

"Mission, you need to hide," I groaned. "Mission." She was in no condition to understand what I was saying. She continued to stare blankly at Earth as if her brain had been switched off like a circuit board. I scurried about the room, half on one knee.

"Gloria, where are you!" I yelled. "Come help me."

An alarm wailed. VORA's systems buzzed to life. "All station occupants, prepare for imminent arrival of *Ignis: Live* developer Craig Helix," she announced. "Please clear the docking area."

"Gloria!" My foot kicked Lance's handmade chisel. It slid across the floor and banged into the wall filled with the tally marks he'd carved over the years. A new inscription ran across them. Words that could only have been carved by her proxy. REMEMBER THE STARS.

My breath fled my body. Gloria was gone. She'd lied and was here on *Ignis* for something else, while I was about to be caught with Mission because of it. After everything we'd gone through.

"No!" I told myself. I wasn't going to be hindered by doubt and self-loathing again. I'd endured enough of that when I was cast out into the Outskirts, and now I was far across space with an inhabitant of *Ignis*—a star of the show to which I'd dedicated my life—beside me. A young woman whom I cared for deeply, who needed me now more than ever.

I limped over to Mission and grabbed her. My side burned with bright lines of pain as I lifted and hauled her across the room. The cabinet the station's med-bot had hovered out of before the proxy zapped it remained open. It was big enough to fit her. We tilted from side to side as I walked, and every time I had to plant my left foot to gain balance, it felt like I'd been shot.

I shoved her inside the tube just before crumpling. The pain was unbearable, but I rolled over and couldn't help but marvel at her. Even in her state of shock, she was more beautiful than anything I'd ever seen.

"You have to stay in here, Mission," I said. "I'll figure out a way to sneak you onto that ship. You're going to be fine."

All I wanted was for her to make eye contact with me, to trust that I could help, but it didn't happen. So I draped the space blanket over her head, hoping it would disrupt scanners as well as it did radiation. Then I grabbed the cabinet's cover and pulled. It was jammed. Positioning my feet against the wall, I pushed as hard as possible, screaming until it slammed shut. Losing my grip threw me backward, and I slid across the polished floor. By the time I came to a stop, a unit of High Earth public safety bots flooded the kitchen.

"Intruder, do not move," they ordered. "You have been deemed a threat."

I couldn't convince my body to move any more even if I wanted to. They surrounded me on every side, their weaponized arms aimed. Then I heard someone clapping.

Two of the bots parted, and in strode Craig Helix himself. His resident-issue tunic was programmed to purple, every bit of it pressed and clean. Only there was no OptiVisor covering his face this time. He regarded me with blithe fascination.

"Well done, Asher," he said. He clapped a few more times as he joined the circle. "I couldn't have scripted this better myself."

"Mr. Helix," I groaned, "what are you doing here?"

"There I was, on my way to introduce a new fixer to this station, when surveillance informs me that Asher Reinhart crashed a waste vessel right into it." Another clap. "Brilliant. Absolutely brilliant."

"I had to get out of the Outskirts," I lied, improvising. "You don't know what it's like."

He ignored me, smirking as if he was in on a joke while he walked over to Lance's charred body and tapped it with his foot. That was when I noticed the fixer's pulse-pistol and cursed myself for not taking it.

"A shame," he said. "I guess I have to thank you for solving that particular problem. It would have been impossible to support ending his probation after his failure."

"You're welcome, sir." I was trying to stall, to think of how I was going to get Mission out of the cabinet and into Mr. Helix's ship without anyone noticing. "You can't even imagine how good it is to see you again."

He strolled all the way back to me before responding. "Where is he, Asher?"

"Who?"

"I saw the footage of two people entering here. Feeds showed that one bore the brand of an Unplugged behind his visor. Now tell me where he is. There's no need to lie anymore."

"I don't know."

He kneeled so we were on the same level. "Asher, you don't have to be scared," he said. "I'm not upset with you this time. In fact, I wish I had been smart enough to record you after your exile. I could've never even imagined you'd go this far when I left your memory intact. Throwing in with the Unplugged just so you could be close to the *Ignis* again. What you did has haunted me for many nights as I took back control of my show. I even considered having the memory wiped so I wouldn't have to keep asking myself how you could be capable of such deceit. But perhaps I underestimated your dedication."

"That's all I wanted you to see."

"Then you must know that dangerous men like an Unplugged can't be allowed near the show. They live to see the pleasures of High Earth shut down so we can all wallow in despair with them. So please, Asher, tell me the truth. Seeing you go through all of this for the show has made me think I might have acted rashly in reporting you without really hearing your side."

I took a deep breath. Was he offering me a chance to get back to High Earth? I wasn't the expert trader Virgil had become, but an answer in exchange for returning home seemed fair.

Unfortunately, whether I wanted to go back or not, Gloria's proxy had disappeared without a trace.

"I swear, I don't know where he went," I said.

His calm façade vanished. "Take him."

Two security bots seized me by the arms and started to drag me.

"I don't know, Mr. Helix! Let me go!" I kicked and screamed, but it was no use. I thought I could appeal to his better nature, but maybe Virgil and Gloria Fors were right about him and it didn't exist. We crossed the exercise room. Adjacent to the entrance to the airlock was a sealed door I hadn't noticed earlier.

"VORA, please open the infuser entrance," Mr. Helix commanded.

"Right away, Mr. Helix," she replied, powered back up again. The door opened to reveal a small circular room. The only thing in it was a top-of-the-line brain infuser and its control terminal. The bots shoved me into the chair and locked me into the restraints.

"Leave us," Mr. Helix ordered. They marched out and the door shut behind them, leaving us alone again. He had more privileges with the Network, thanks to his standing, than I'd ever even imagined.

"If you're going to once again withhold the truth, then I'm going to find it myself," Mr. Helix said. "It seems the Outskirts hasn't taught you anything, Asher. And this, here, this is my world, where the Network bends to me. My program." He took his position at the infuser's control terminal.

"I swear I don't know where the Unplugged went!" I protested. "He won't hurt the show, Craig. He was honoring a trade, getting me here. Just let me stay. I'll be the new fixer, do whatever you need."

"I'm sorry, Asher," Mr. Helix said. "It is as I feared. You are beyond repair, and I can't take any more risks. It's time to see everything you're hiding."

The neural nodes surrounding my head sparked to life. A glowing blue transmitter band descended over my temples. Mr. Helix wasn't anywhere near as gentle as Minah had been. In an instant, my ability to do anything but scream was rendered useless. My head felt like it was being split open, brain leafed through like the pages of an ancient book. Everything that had happened since Mr. Helix cast me out flooded my consciousness . . .

* * *

When the infuser finally powered down and my head slumped forward, it felt like it'd only been seconds. Of course, it hadn't. Mr. Helix stood in front of me, newly shaved and manicured. He had his arm around Mission's shoulder. She was cleaned up as well, wearing a resident's tunic that fit snugly to her lithe body. Her naturally messy hair was straightened and shiny, the red in it highlighted, and her pale skin washed of *Ignis*'s grime.

The only thing the same as when I'd last seen her was that she wouldn't focus her eyes on me. Thanks to a heavy dose of pharma clearly administered by the lifeband now around her wrist, her eyelids could barely open. She looked detached. *Is that how I used to look?*

"Mission . . ." I moaned. I couldn't stand to see her gifted mind neutered like that.

"You have quite a collection of new friends, Asher," Mr. Helix remarked. "You may have been telling the truth about that Unplugged, but the location of their nest, as well as Gloria Fors being alive? Befriend a man who actually did try to murder you in your own smart-dwelling? It's hard to believe you wouldn't report all of it. I know, after all of this, to still be surprised by your recklessness. You truly are broken. The High Earth Network will put an end to Gloria's dangerous, unsanctioned operation straight away."

"Please . . . don't hurt her . . ." I reached for Mission, but a bot impeded me.

"Why would I do that? Misguided as your intentions were, your knack for capturing raw human emotion is undeniable. Our fans will be thrilled to see her. Not on a screen. Not in a VR. I'll walk her along the skywalks themselves, and people will leave their homes and raise their visors just to look upon her face. To touch her. Then they'll know how real the *Ignis* is." He regarded me warmly. "I don't know why I didn't think of this sooner, Asher. Engaging viewers directly in person. Answering their questions and visiting with them. Mission is going to be a star for the rest of her now-lengthy life, and it's all thanks to you."

I rocked my body forward so hard the bots had to restrain me. Pain swelled everywhere. "Mission, don't listen to him!" I yelled. "I know none of this makes any sense to you, but when you get the chance, you have to run as fast as you can!"

Mr. Helix rolled his eyes. "You're unbelievable, Asher. I find out that you came all this way to save her, and now I promise you she'll live comfortably forever, and still you're not pleased. I'm sorry it has to be this way, I truly am, but you're too unpredictable now to leave with your memory."

I ignored him and focused on her. "You taught me what it means to live, Mission," I said. "Don't let him take that from you."

"It was wrong of me to erase you from the show's credits like you had no impact," Mr. Helix said. "I let disappointment cloud my judgment. You're only human, after all. I'll tell High

Earth that you retired, like the chief director before you, but that you had one last flicker of brilliance to leave behind for the viewers." Mr. Helix sighed, as if he actually felt remorseful. He patted me on the chest. "Don't worry, Asher. I'm going to send you someplace you loved more than anywhere else in the universe. You won't have to worry about her anymore."

The infuser hummed back to life and threw my mind into a frenzy. The world grew blurry, but I fixated on Mission. "You've been my life from the moment I was born," I said. "You opened my eyes, Mission."

My consciousness started receding the moment I got her name out. For a heartbeat, she was there, looking directly at me. And beneath all her drug-addled confusion, I could tell she was listening. Finally, after so long, she heard me.

That was my last memory . . .

Uploading . . .

New High Earth Resident: [Mission-14130]

CHAPTER 26

"Good morning, Mission," a strange, feminine voice said, echoing all around me.

My eyelids jolted open as I woke from the strangest nightmare I'd ever experienced. After being spaced for my crimes, I had been rescued from the void by a man who somehow knew my name. Who could see inside *Ignis* as well as Earth. But there were others. Walking humans made of metal, an older man in violet . . . it was all so hazy.

"Welcome to the thirty-third floor of Residential Tower 3, located on Block 3C of High Earth."

Hearing the voice again startled me. My hands struck a plane of glass stretching over my head, but before I could pound on what seemed like a transparent tomb, it slid open. I threw myself over the rim of the container and spun. I was in a colorless room. White walls, white floor, white everything, but nobody else in sight.

As I turned, more memories from my nightmare swamped my foggy brain. The confusion sent me to my knees, where I clutched my head like it was about to explode.

"Your world is part of a High Earth reality program," the man in violet had told me as he showed me a screen where Alora cried for me over the sealed *Ignis* airlock. "A documentary about real inhabitants on a generational ship sent across the stars."

He showed me recordings of volunteers stepping onto the *Ignis* fifty years ago, with their memories reprogrammed. Memories that became the story of my world. My own birth, Jacen's death—everything in between. And then there was shouting. He and the man who'd saved me from space disagreed on something. *On me?*

"You opened my eyes, Mission." So much was a blur, but those words rang clearer than any. They'd come from the mouth of the one who'd saved me. He was in terrible pain.

My mind spiraled around that moment, and I couldn't make sense of any of it. Yet the clarity was unlike any dream. It made me feel nauseous. I squeezed my eyes until a dull red light blinked bright enough to perceive through my eyelids. A chirping noise synchronized with it.

"You are experiencing an episode of heightened anxiety," the same feminine voice said, emotionless. "This can be harmful to the healthy functioning of the human mind and body. I have signaled your lifeband to administer the proper medication."

One by one, my heavy breaths slowed. The onslaught of bizarre memories faded into the recesses of my psyche, and I was left sitting on the floor, eyes still shut out of fear of seeing something else, but calm.

"Am I dead?" I wheezed.

"No," the voice replied instantly. "You are in your peak years of physiological well-being, though currently considerably malnourished and under immense psychological strain."

"This is real?"

"Objectively, yes."

I opened my eyes and stood. The container I'd rolled out of was more like a bed stuck within a raised pod. The inside was cushioned throughout, the imprint of my body still showing. The blinking red light came from an unassuming band wrapping my wrist. I tapped it and a round screen lashed out. I wasn't fast enough to dodge it, but quickly realized it was only light. In my nightmare, Jacen's fake head had been comprised of something similar.

I ran my fingers through it and watched the pixels bend around them. A body was projected on the screen, with myriad fields of data and readouts. It looked eerily similar to the imagery that would pop up when I searched a specific inhabitant through the *Ignis's* core. Whoever it displayed was a woman, with a slight build . . . *Me?*

I glanced down to see if the bodies matched and realized I was wearing a new outfit. The elegant cut was reminiscent of the suits the Collective wore, only there wasn't a speck of dust anywhere to be found, and it was a verdant green.

"Who am I?" I asked. The question seemed even more ridiculous once it escaped my mouth.

"You are Mission, surname unverified. A resident of High Earth."

"High Earth?"

"A fully autonomous city designed to provide humanity with a safe, carefree environment. It was founded in AD 2267 by various interplanetary conglomerates, including Fors Tech, Sol-wide, InhabiCo and App—"

"Stop," I interrupted at the risk of my headache worsening. "So, you're the core or . . ."

"I am your personal Virtual Occupant Residency Aide, or VORA. I have been programmed to tend to your needs and well-being, both physiologically and psychologically. Your vitals tell me that your most recent dose of pharma did not ease your discomfort fully. Would you like me to place you in a more familiar setting and see if that soothes you?"

"This isn't the *Ignis*?"

"*Ignis*: Formerly an interstellar vessel constructed using a hollowed main belt asteroid before the start of the techno-revolution. Currently, the setting of the popular reality show developed by resident Craig Helix, *Ignis: Live.*"

The room transformed. White was replaced by rock, metal, rusty pipes—sights I'd known my whole life. Even my feet stood atop it. Yet, through the soles of shoes I couldn't recall putting on, I could tell the surface was smooth and flat. Falsified by more light manipulation. I backed away slowly, and a door disappeared into the ceiling before I hit the wall, and I stumbled into a larger room.

Now hydroponic farms surrounded me, wrapping all the way around me, near and far. I could even smell the familiar scents of all the different crops merging throughout the tremendous hollow. I could see the flurry of insect wings in the containers behind their rows. High above me, the *Ignis*'s core shone in all its warming, homey glory, only it wasn't far at all.

As I scurried along the wall, patting my hands along the smooth surface, I realized the room was just like the last. A rectangular box, like a cell.

"After your journey, you must be starved," said the voice that referred to itself as VORA. "I must encourage you to increase your portions in order to attain optimal weight." Something else chimed loudly. I spun nervously, then saw a machine on a counter spit out three granular bars. "I do not know your flavor preference yet, so I have assembled a variety based on the habits of other residents."

I crept toward the machine, constantly checking over my

shoulder for the core-knows-what. I poked one of the bars. Each was identical, void of color and ground into perfect rectangles. The machine they popped out of didn't appear dangerous.

"This is food?" I questioned. No line to wait in for a feeding period. No server rationing portions.

"Yes. Every resident-issue re-assembler is able to produce all required daily nutrients," VORA said. "This information should have been uploaded during your synth-womb or re-enlistment process. Shall I report an issue with the infusers?"

"The what?" I said while chewing on a mouthful of food. Sometime while she was talking, I couldn't help but grab one. I hadn't enjoyed a proper meal since being detained, and my grumbling stomach forced action before my mind could say no. The taste was smoky and delicious, and far from any vegetable I'd ever tried. A tall cup of water appeared beside the machine as I swallowed my last bite.

My fingers wrapped the cold glass, but I froze before lifting it to my mouth. I looked up at the ceiling disguised as my home, where water was so precious, and asked, "May I?"

"Of course you can," a new, gruffer voice replied behind me.

The cup slipped from my grasp and spilled all over the floor. The older man in purple from my dream strode into the room. The same grin he'd worn in it was plastered on his clean-cut face, but that was the only visible part of it. The rest was covered by a strange device bulging over his ears with a semi-translucent visor stretching over his eyes. The inside face of it flickered with motion and color.

I dropped to the floor and unsuccessfully tried to wipe up the water with my sleeve. It beaded along the waterproof tile. The man placed his hand upon my shoulder.

"My dear, please don't worry about that," he said. "VORA, clean this mess and provide Mission here with another water."

A second full cup of water emerged from the counter. The man took it and held it out for me just as a tiny metallic box zipped along the floor. I leaped out of the way as it dried and scrubbed the area with many limber arms under its chassis, again clarifying that the rock below my feet was false. Before I knew it, the thing returned through a hidden hatch in the wall.

"I'm still dreaming, aren't I?" I said.

The man attempted to place the water cup in my hands. I was too distracted to take it, so he put it down and replied, "Far from it. In fact, try to imagine that you're finally waking from one."

I extended my hand slowly and poked him in the arm. "So . . . you're real?"

"Of course I am." He lifted the visor from over his eyes. They were strikingly blue, warm and inviting. "Where are my manners? I know so much about you, yet you know nothing about me. You were still in shock from space exposure and required a heavy dose of pharma when we first met, but I am Craig Helix. I am the developer who filled your world and programmed everything within it." He took my hand and shook. "You can't begin to imagine what a pleasure it is to meet you."

I pulled back and took a healthy stride away from him. "And the *Ignis*?"

"It's as I tried explaining to you before we departed its station. Physically, the *Ignis* is as real as you or I. We watch your lives on a reality program called *Ignis: Live*, but we have no interference in them. Everything that has happened in your life is completely unscripted."

"A program . . ." I muttered.

My legs felt wobbly. My head faint. I started to lose balance, but Craig caught me.

"Precisely." He frowned. "I really do apologize, Mission. I

would have had infusers acquaint you with our world as it is, but my viewers value authenticity, and it was hard enough programming your residential status to be approved. When people hear from you, I don't want it to seem as though you're already one of us. You are so much more."

"I still don't understand why I'm here," I said. "Is this a test? Am I still in the aptitude exam?"

"This isn't a test." He chuckled. "I think everything will be much clearer if I show you. You have no idea how special you are. Everyone is dying to meet the first inhabitant of the *Ignis* ever to leave."

"Everyone?"

"Come." He smiled, extended his arm around my shoulder, and started to walk me toward the entrance he'd appeared through. I planted my feet. It was mostly out of reflex, but the last time I was with him, I woke up alone in a pod. The words "you opened my eyes" again echoed throughout my consciousness.

Craig turned and took me by the arms. "You have nothing to fear," he insisted. "Never again. Now, I know you've always wanted to see the outside with your own eyes. Let me show you."

My brow furrowed. I'd told Jacen that the last time we ever talked. Real or fake or whatever, I could never forget that. Hearing Craig say the same drew me forward in my haze of confusion, and before I knew it, I'd followed him onto a lift similar to the one that descended from the core.

I understood how gravity worked, how it held everything on Earth to the surface. It was part of our education on the *Ignis* to understand rudimentary physics since it was those principles that kept the ship operational. Members of the Collective studied it extensively. But as I stepped outside and saw the sky of what Craig Helix promised was Earth, I finally comprehended why Jacen found it too overwhelming to even contemplate.

A field of blue nothingness stretched far overhead—no rocks or plants littering its surface. Even though my feet were stuck on a walkway, I felt as if at any moment I could be sucked up into it. I couldn't stop staring until Craig halted me and gently tilted my head down.

A series of glistening towers soared high into the vacant, blue canvas. The Core had provided many historical images of how human civilization built on Earth, but they couldn't begin to capture the enormity. Each structure would have scraped the opposite surface of the *Ignis*'s main hollow had they grown within its center.

Layers of walkways were strung between them, seemingly floating. Hundreds of real humans lined the walkways in front of us. Most wore visors like Craig's while others stared down at handheld viewing devices. Shiny vessels darted overhead, some large enough to fit a person, others the size of my head.

I staggered forward until more towers were visible. One after another, in every direction, arcing away from me instead of wrapping up overhead like I was used to. Moving images shone through the windows covering them, visible on the nearest tower. So many images made no sense to me, projecting strange pictures alongside titles, but ones of what Craig called *Ignis: Live* were more prevalent than any. They all depicted either me or the massive interior of my world from vantages that I knew weren't possible to achieve.

"You aren't merely another inhabitant down here," Craig said. He stepped in front of me and gestured to the swelling crowd. A bot stood before them on the skywalk to keep them at bay. My mind flashed back to my spacing ceremony, surrounded by my own people wanting to see me dead. These people, on the other hand, looked thrilled to see me.

"Every one of them has been watching you for your entire

life," Craig said. "They worship you, and rightly so." He guided me toward a raised platform positioned directly in the center of the entrance to the tower behind us. Lofty holographic screens suddenly rose on either side, displaying live images of me so that people could see from far away.

"You're really here," a woman said. "Wow." Her bright blue hair was swirled atop her head. The bone structure of her face was perfect in every way. I knew, because as a Birthmother we measured such things. She took my hand in one of hers and helped me up. In her other, she held a viewing device with a rectangular holographic screen projected above it.

"Vivienne Poole will be your human assistant during the daily greetings and competition entries," Craig said. The woman flashed him a smile, but as soon as he wasn't looking, Mission noticed her expression sour.

"I still don't get what the big fuss is," said a grumpy man beside her. His arms crossed as he studied the crowd. "I have a show to help run."

"Laura can handle it," Craig said.

"I've been around longer. I can't believe you still have me on the nigh—"

"I'd rather our quality not fall any further than it has since our last Chief Director of Content."

Frederick flushed a shade as red as his tunic, then stepped back to watch from the shadow.

Vivienne spun me toward her and patted down my outfit before using her finger to undo a knot in my hair. "You really are beautiful," she said. "Different. A part of me understands him now."

"Understand wha—" She spun me back around to face the crowd before I could finish.

"I am astounded that so many of you showed up here

today!" Craig announced. His voice was being artificially amplified so loudly it filled the yawning valleys between each tower. The countless onlookers slowly lifted their visors and glanced up from any other devices they were holding.

"To bring entertainment to so many," he went on. "I don't think there is any greater calling for a man. Today, I reward your viewership! Despite all the recent calamity that befell the *Ignis*, there is a light. Pulled from space only seconds before her death by my former Chief Director of Content in his last gift to you, she will now have the chance to see how *we* live. My fellow residents of High Earth, I did not invite you to gather here, outside your homes, for no reason. I am proud to present to you the girl who stole your hearts. Innocent or guilty of the crimes her people tried her for, she is the inhabitant who dared to love. Mission-14130!"

His smile spread wider than ever as he gestured to me. At the same time, the tiny flying ships projected holographic screens into the air all around, each of them showing me. My gaze moved between each of them, which was then displayed live for everyone too far to see in perfect clarity.

"Every week, one of you can apply to win an evening in her company," Craig continued. "Real volunteers from my staff will help sort you. Mission's life on *Ignis* is yours to discover."

There was no outcry of cheers like there'd been when I was sentenced to death back home. In fact, none of the thousands of people said much of anything. They didn't even converse amongst each other. But the robotic men allowed the first person in line to pass, and he sprinted over to me. His visor sat atop his head, revealing a perfect, almost plastic face. His skin was as smooth as an infant's. His thick, blue-dyed hair was perfectly groomed and his bone structure flawless. The core would've approved him for reproduction in a heartbeat.

He didn't say a word. He simply strolled in a circle around me, as if I were a trophy encased in glass, scrutinizing me from head to toe. The way his eyes seemed to be undressing me made my stomach curdle. Nobody would ever regard a Birthmother like that on *Ignis,* even if they resented me. Despite everything Craig had tried to explain, that feeling was the first time my new surroundings didn't seem like just a bad dream.

The band on my wrist started to blink red.

"Just try to relax," Vivienne whispered in my ear. "Nobody will hurt you here." She then used her viewing device to scan the man's retina. Afterward, he scurried away.

"They've never seen anything like you," Craig admired. "Enjoy yourself, Mission. You've earned this. Take care of her, Vivienne. You gained my trust in telling me the truth. I look forward to the day when you and Laura can take over all the day-to-day." He shot a look at the one called Frederick, who slunk back farther into the shadow.

Helix walked away, and before I could watch where he went, somebody else arrived to gawk at me.

"I can't believe it's really you," a woman said. She could hardly contain her excitement. Like the man before her, she was aesthetically flawless in every way. "I have so many questions." She tapped my arm and squealed when her hand didn't pass through. The band on her wrist started blinking red even more rapidly than mine.

"Did you know?" she asked.

"Know what?" I answered, rotating to try to keep track of her so she couldn't get behind me. "What the hell was going on?"

"All questions are reserved for private engagements," Vivienne told the woman.

"Yeah, move along," Frederick added.

Vivienne pulled her aside to scan her retina, incidentally

providing me with an open view of the screen of her viewing device. I couldn't hear anything, but I saw the familiar rock and metal walls of my home.

Instinct kicked in. I leaped off the platform, grabbed Vivienne's device and ran as fast as I could.

I had no idea where I was going, and I bumped into countless people wearing visors. Eventually, my legs were too exhausted to continue. I collapsed on the walkway and stared blankly out upon the glistening towers of my new surroundings. I felt like I wanted to cry, but tears wouldn't come. Instead, I raised Vivienne's screen and watched . . .

A feeding was taking place inside the familiar galley of *Ignis* Block B. Usually they were a time of leisure, when inhabitants could unwind, escape their daily regimens, and carouse with friends. Only, many of the people present were strangers to each other. New faces filled the galley, brought over from every block during the redistribution of the population. They waited in somber reflection, as if in line to view a corpse at a wake.

Much of the damage from the tragedy of the fiftieth anniversary had been repaired, but some remained to serve as a constant reminder of those who'd died. A portion of the wall near the main conduit remained charred, and the air recycler vents so many had tried to escape through were permanently dented.

A new feedmaster mixed insects and flora in giant vats behind his counter to continue serving. He didn't utter a word to anyone. His thousand-meter gaze held firm as he slapped the same amount of mixture into bowls one at a time, without looking. He was almost done when a man staggered into the galley.

He was completely naked, covered in filth and bruises from head to toe. His eyes darted around the room as if piecing together the world for the very first time.

He stumbled into a table, chasing everyone at it away. He

only made it a few steps more before his wobbly legs gave out and he fell to his knees at the serving counter. His lips mouthed something incomprehensible, then his wet, shriveled hand slipped, and he collapsed onto his side, unconscious.

"Mission, are you all right?" Vivienne asked.

She startled me so much I dropped the device.

"Why is he there?" I asked. The inhabitants didn't recognize him, but I did. That stranger in the Block B galley was the one who'd pulled me out of space. All I could picture was him covering my shoulders with a silver blanket. Then he was strapped down. Screaming.

"Why is who?" As Vivienne glanced down at her device, the air seemed to be sucked from her lungs too. "I . . . he looks just like his avatar."

"Why is he there?" I jumped to my feet and pulled myself along the walkway's railing. "Mr. Helix!" I rasped. "Mr. Helix!" Vivienne squeezed my wrist before I could shout any louder.

"Don't," she whispered sharply. "He's part of the show now."

"He's the one who saved me. Who is he?"

"A dangerous man." Vivienne retrieved her viewing device and stowed it in her belt. "Please, forget about all of that and try to seem comfortable. The fans have high expectations."

She escorted me back to the platform in front of the eager yet distracted crowd. I was too tired and perplexed to do anything about it.

Another observer arrived to scrutinize me. And the next after that. One by one, people in a line so massive that it made the ones for feedings on *Ignis* seem minuscule waited only to spend a few seconds beholding me up close.

After about an hour and a few hundred visitors, the sick feeling in my gut gave way to emptiness. Someone would step up, then return to the walkways while calmly staring at whatever devices were near their faces. It was like they had nowhere to be, nothing to clean or farm. Countless perfect-looking people wandering aimlessly around a perfect city in a perfect world. I'd rather have been under the floor.

CHAPTER 27

"Are you ready, Mission?" Craig asked, standing beside a peculiar glass chamber covered in nodes. He told me that through it, I was going to be spending time in digital space with one of the people who'd come out to see me earlier, which made absolutely no sense.

Clusters of wires and a tube draped off the back of the thing, with a band hanging from its ceiling that glowed blue. Craig positioned me in front of it. Vivienne stood quietly beside him, focused on her handheld device.

"You opened my eyes." Again, the words of my rescuer came to me. Hearing them made me wince, and I suddenly remembered something else from when he'd said them.

"That's like the chair you put him in," I said.

"Excuse me, dear?" Craig replied.

"Why doesn't anybody know who I'm talking about!" I tore myself free from his grasp. "The man who rescued me!"

"Vivienne, please go get Mission some water."

"I don't need water!"

"You're agitated."

"No, *you* aren't telling me everything. You put him in something with a band just like that and he screamed. Just tell me what's happening!"

"Mission . . ." Vivienne said softly. She took my hand to try to calm me, but I pushed her away.

"Why can't I go home?" I demanded.

Craig sighed. "Leave us."

Vivienne regarded me with genuine concern for a few seconds, then obeyed.

"The man who saved you is very ill," Craig said. "His obsessions placed the *Ignis* in grave danger, and I needed to look into his mind to keep it safe. The device you saw was a brain infuser, which allowed me to do so. This here is very different. It is merely a conduit to allow your mind to enter programmed virtual realities, where you will convene with our first winning resident."

"If he's so dangerous, then why did I see him there . . . on *Ignis* . . ." It seemed too ridiculous to think that he was now in my world, yet I wasn't.

"He is being used to help draw out an unknown criminal we believe is hiding somewhere on the ship."

My eyes went wide. "Is it the one who looked like Jacen?"

Craig's brow furrowed like he was deep in thought. "It is . . . a possibility. We're still trying to piece together exactly what happened that day."

"Then you have to let me help him!"

Back on *Ignis*, I'd completely given up on discovering the truth. Oxygen deprivation, mysterious clones, it was all too mystifying to make sense of. But I was sure about two things: I hadn't stolen that pulse-pistol from the core, and I didn't want to use it to shoot Jacen. Now, I felt a flicker of hope that justice might be served, until Craig promptly shut me down.

"If only I could," he said. "But to your people, you are dead, and that cannot change. You must trust me, Mission, when I say I'll do whatever it takes to protect *Ignis*. The man who saved you would never purposefully put the show or your world in jeopardy. He's sick."

"I . . ." I choked back tears. "I just want to go home."

"It's time you started thinking of this as your new home. I promise, you won't miss it at all. Now, my dear, we have a schedule to keep."

"I know, but I need . . . I need some time alone to think. Would you mind if I went for a walk outside first? I won't be long." I wasn't sure if that last part was a lie or not. A piece of me thought that I might take off and not look back, like when the Great Blackout happened.

"Unfortunately, that won't be possible," he said.

"So I'm your prisoner?"

"No!" He looked appalled. "Never. It would merely be dangerous to allow you on the skywalks unsupervised until you're more acclimated to your new surroundings. We don't want anything happening to you." He took my hand and led me to the strange chamber. "Once you're in there, your mind will be uploaded into a virtual world, where you'll be able to walk as far as you want."

"But not alone. I don't want to meet anybody right now."

"You must. The promise of meeting you will generate a lifetime of fans. *Ignis: Live* is the largest production in High Earth. The second our viewership falls too far, we risk losing the tech needed to keep it going. We're in this together now, Mission. Without us doing all we can to maintain resident interest, the *Ignis* will stop running, and then our people there will never be able to uncover the truth of the fiftieth anniversary."

I wiped my eyes. *It really grows on you though, being a part of the ship.* Jacen had said that to me once about working on the *Ignis*, and now, like him, it was all I could hope for.

"All right," I conceded. "And you'll tell me if you discover anything?"

Craig nodded, and I reluctantly stepped into the chair. Craig placed the band over my head. It was cold.

"I'm so proud of you, Mission. VORA, please begin the uploading process. Sync Mission with our winner, Dawn Trevell. Wherever she would like to be."

"Mission, do you wish to upload?" the robotic voice of my smart-dwelling asked me, as if I had a say.

"Yes," I said softly.

"Right away, Mission."

The band on my head, stretching from temple to temple, began to glow blue. With that came a tingling sensation behind my ears. The nodes around the chamber started to hum, and my feet lifted off the floor. I struggled to pull away, terrified, but I couldn't move.

My vision folded . . . or at least, that was the best way I could describe it. Everything in front of me retreated, then warped in on itself, and in a few seconds, I stood somewhere new.

A flaming shard of metal flew at me. I wanted to dive out of the way, but my mind was petrified. Instead, I closed my eyes. The projectile passed right through me, and I spun to see it disintegrate as it struck the ground.

I was in the concourse of a stadium of some sort. cygnus creations bot fighting league was written in large letters all around the outside walls. Extending below me was a massive crowd, eyes glued to the central arena. Two metal behemoths battled in the sand, swinging their tremendous limbs at each other. One evaded the other using jets, then fired off a volley of missiles. A few struck home, while the others raced into the crowd.

I squealed and went to look away, but the missiles exploded harmlessly, to the delight of the crowd. The bot that absorbed the fire collapsed to one knee, the other blown off. But the fight went on.

"Mission, is that you?" shouted someone behind me.

I turned to see one of the women who had come to observe me earlier that day. The only reason I remembered her out of the thousands was because she was the woman who'd tapped me just to make sure I wasn't a mirage. Before, she was flawless, now she was such that my definition of flawless changed. Her breasts were larger and her hips more slender. Her skin was so smooth I wasn't even sure she had pores, and her hair was now jet-black and fell to her hips with impossibly tight waves. She pranced over, giddy like a child at her first public feeding.

My brow furrowed, and on one side of my vision, information flickered. Her name, something called account standing, age. I closed my eyes and shook my head, and the data vanished.

"I can't believe this," she said. "I can't believe I won. You have no idea how long I've dreamed of meeting you."

"Where are we?" I asked.

"Bot fighting. Programmers create war machines based on real-world physics and . . . Don't worry, they can't actually hurt you in here. It's all virtual." She grabbed my arm and led me around the concourse and into a private, glassy booth. It popped out over the rest of the stadium in a way that didn't seem structurally sound. Two seats were arranged with a clear vantage of the arena. Floating screens along our flanks provided up-close views of the battling giants in seamless detail.

"I hope this is sufficient?" she said, indicating my seat. "I don't usually upload into VRs like this, but, I didn't want to bore you. I thought about maybe a medieval festival where we could get all dressed up—listen to me, rambling."

"It's . . ." I wasn't sure what to say. The damaged bot was now using a sword as a crutch and slashed upward, slicing off a piece of the other's shoulder. It flew over the crowd and smashed to pieces against the glass right in front of me. I flinched. The crowd roared.

"It's fine," I exhaled.

"Good, I'm so glad." She sat and pulled up a holographic screen on the edge of her chair. "Are you hungry?"

"I'm fine." I joined her in sitting, if only because any more surprises might have given me a heart attack. "So this isn't real?"

She pondered it for a moment, then laughed. "I suppose not."

"But High Earth is?"

Dawn giggled. "Here, why don't you try some of this? Our ancestors called it corn. It really is good, even if it isn't *real*." She keyed a command and a colorful bin materialized on her lap. It was filled with small amorphous white puffs—nothing like the corn we had back on *Ignis*. She grabbed a handful and shoved it into her mouth. Crumbs dropped all over the floor but quickly vanished before they settled.

After a few seconds went by with me not trying any, she swallowed what she had. Her lips twisted. "Sorry. I'm not usually nervous like this. I've just been watching you for so long and you're *so* much more beautiful in person."

More beautiful? I stared at her, dumbfounded. In here or on the skywalks, I couldn't find a single thing wrong with her. Perfect bone structure, fat index, skin, and voluminous hair. She had the structural genes to be named a Mother back on *Ignis*, presuming her intelligence quota was up to par. At the very least, a Birthmother.

I must have stared too long because she blushed and averted her gaze. She reached into her bucket of strange corn and held some out for me. Finally, I gave in, grabbing a single kernel and biting off the smallest lump on it I could find. Like the bar VORA generated for me, it was delicious. A flavor I couldn't even imagine tumbled down my throat as I scarfed down the rest of it and a few more. It definitely didn't taste like any corn I'd had back on *Ignis*. No matter how much I ate, I never felt any fuller either.

"I'm glad you like it," she said. I was about to shove another piece into my mouth when her hand fell upon my upper thigh. The gesture wasn't aggressive, but it caught me by surprise, and I coughed. She didn't remove it.

"You know, I never agreed with any of the message board fiends who pronounced you guilty," she said.

"Message board?" I asked.

She chuckled. "It's a place on the Network where every resident can post their opinions and reviews on programs. I read the ones about you every day, and I never stopped believing you were innocent."

My eyes widened. "Does anybody know what happened? You can see everything, can't you?"

"Not everything all the time . . . I met a director once though." I must have looked perplexed, because she paused to clarify. "They're in charge of which of the camera feeds go live. Maybe he knew? All I saw is you running back to your room. Then Jacen appeared and you shot him, but you didn't look the same as when you got there. It looked like you had been attacked, just like you said you were!"

I turned my entire body to face her, not caring as her hand slid higher on my thigh. "You're saying a director would know the truth—" I couldn't finish the last word because her lips pressed against mine. The shock immobilized me. She pushed hard, running her one hand as far up my leg as it could go and pulling my head closer with the other.

For a moment, my eyes closed and I recalled the only kiss
I'd ever shared with Jacen. It seemed like a lifetime ago. Then
I snapped to and pushed her away, mouth ajar. She appeared
equally aghast.

"I'm so sorry," she stammered. "I . . . I couldn't help myself."

I stared blankly.

"Mission, please," she said. "I don't know what came over
me. I'll keep my hands to myself this time."

"What did you just say?" I whispered. I'd said something
like that to Jacen after our first kiss. Maybe that exact phrase.

Is she copying me too?

"I'll control myself this time," Dawn said. "I promise."

She was. I didn't think twice. I sprinted out of the booth
and pounded on the first wall I could find. Out in the concourse, my voice was drowned out by the raucous crowd, but
I shouted anyway.

"How do I get out of here? Let me out!"

Just as Dawn appeared beside me, pleading, my world
again folded in on itself. It didn't hurt, though it seemed like it
should've. Momentarily, I was nowhere; then the faux-*Ignis* walls
of my domicile reappeared. My whole body was numb, and a
tube slid out of the back of my throat as restraints fell off me.

My sensations returned, and with them came a crushing
dizziness and nausea that sent me stumbling into the wall of
the VR chamber.

"Welcome back, Mission," VORA said. "Your engagement
ended earlier than expected. I sense that you are feeling ill. The
first use of a neurotransmitter chair can have that effect. Let
me help you."

I felt a pinch under the blinking band wrapping my wrist.
Afterward, my vision and heartbeat started to level out. I no
longer wanted to puke, but my stomach still felt like it was

twisted into a knot. I held my mouth as I turned and studied my room.

"Where did they go?" I groaned.

"Mr. Helix and Ms. Poole had other business to attend to and left you in my care. Are you hungry? Thirsty? I would be happy to—"

"Message boards! I want to see the message boards."

"You will have to be more specific."

"Um . . . Message boards referencing me. Mission-14130."

A portion of the wall across from my couch suddenly transformed from rock to a window displaying the city, and then a giant holographic screen. It was filled with text, top to bottom. I crept over and poked at it. Even though it was made of light, my hand was still able to manipulate where the contents went. There were so many messages—thousands, maybe millions—each marked with a signature and with replies of their own. I read a few out loud.

i can't wait to see mission tomorrow.

mission looked amazing in person. even if she is a killer.

if i win a one-on-one with her, i'm going to—

I couldn't stomach finishing that one. It was so lewd it reinvigorated my nausea. Yet, for whatever reason, I kept scrolling. I couldn't stop myself. Message after message discussed me, some even with snapshots posted next to them of me from when I was on the *Ignis*. In many, I was completely naked in the communal showers.

"*Ignis: Live* . . ." I whispered. The screen suddenly broke into a cluster of windows, each apparently displaying a live broadcast feed of my home. They showed my people doing everything from farming, to sleeping, to their most private activities.

In some, Mothers and Birthmothers lay with male counterparts as the Collective strove to rebuild the population. In a smaller window still displaying message boards, a constant stream of comments appeared to discuss it. One even referenced me under the floor, meaning that was common knowledge here too.

It finally hit me what Mr. Helix meant every time he uttered the word "show." I must have spent an hour gawking from one feed to the next, then reading the comments affiliated with each. Finally, one feed caught my attention enough to break me out of my confounded trance. Alora and Cassiopeia stood in a cell in the core across from the man who'd saved me.

He was cuffed, on his knees and a complete mess. They'd provided some rags to keep him warm, but that was all.

[Ignis Feed Location]
Core Cell 3
<Camera 2>

"Who are you?" Cassiopeia asked, her tone betraying her calm demeanor. Alora didn't try nearly as hard to mask her disdain.

"Answer her!" she growled.

"I . . . I . . . I don't know," the stranger muttered. It was obvious by the way he studied the farms beyond the viewport in the floor that the inside of the *Ignis* was strange to him. Nobody could be that good an actor.

"There are no records of you in the core's database," Cassiopeia continued. "No DNA matches to *any* other inhabitant past or present. Where are you from?"

"I don't know." His lips creased as he strained his mind to think harder.

"Do you have a name?"

"I don't know!" His frustration finally reached a breaking

point and he banged on the glass. He then keeled over, gripping his head as if by squeezing hard enough he could draw out the memories he was somehow missing.

Cassiopeia pulled Alora outside the cell and whispered, "He's not lying."

"Or he's lost his mind," she retorted. "Doesn't this remind you of when I was . . . There was no data then either. Nothing."

"I try not to think about that day."

"I never stop. Do you think he could've been born in secret down in the pipes like Samson? Maybe his parents erased anything that might lead to him from the core's database."

"They'd have to be members of the Collective to pull that off. The core is studying his samples to determine his exact age, but look at him. He's in his mid-twenties. That long down there would drive anyone mad."

Alora clutched Cassiopeia by the shoulders and shook her. "Cassiopeia, Mission said somebody attacked her that day! Now this?"

"She said it was Jacen."

"There was barely enough oxygen in there to breathe, you know that. Don't you find it a little odd that a day after she's spaced, a stranger shows up in Block B? It has to be connected."

"Or he's a terrible accident, and you're seeing through the lens of your own personal trauma. Our system allows us to live, but it isn't perfect. Mistakes happen. You know that better than most."

"Cassiopeia, he's lying!"

"It doesn't matter. We need to give the core time to process his genetic information so we can proceed with *all* the details. You're angry, I get it."

"I'm more than angry."

Cassiopeia exhaled. "I've allowed you up to help because I

too believe there's something bizarre going on, and Mission deserves something for her sacrifice. Don't make me regret that, Alora. I need you to be patient. We have to get this right."

"Be patient?" Alora bit her lip in irritation. She glanced into the cell, where the stranger traced his finger on the floor in an effort to spell something, whispering to himself like a lunatic. "Patience won't bring Mission back," she huffed, then stormed away.

* * *

I stood, stroking the pixels of light comprising the face of my mother.

"I'm going to find out the truth," I said. It was her final promise to me after I'd already given up on such things. But no matter how far away I was now, I decided I was going to help her do it.

I had no idea how any of the High Earth tech worked, but I'd always been a quick study. I manipulated the screen without needing VORA's guidance and made it so that a dozen feeds at a time were visible as well as relevant message boards. Then I sat back to watch and read everything I could, searching for clues until my eyes were dry, and my racing mind finally surrendered to sleep.

CHAPTER 28

"Mission, wake up." Vivienne shook me. "Mission!"

I peered up at her, eyes groggy. I'd fallen asleep on the floor by the couch, half my body tucked under it. I guess I was used to sleeping in a rocky nook.

"You need to get ready," she said. "Residents are already arriving outside to see you. More this time. Two days in a row, I've never seen a gathering like this in High Earth. Ratings for every other program are down."

She and VORA instructed me toward gadgets that helped me clean up, and I was too tired to fight it. My own personal shower surrounded me with static-filled air and decontaminating beams that made my entire body tingle. I didn't even have to scrub. It did all that while VORA simultaneously received my clothes and cleaned them. Back on *Ignis,* water was only expended to wash clothes every few weeks.

I discreetly glanced around, wondering if cameras watched me here, too. Seeing none, I stepped out, and a mechanical arm by the sink whitened my teeth and another straightened my hair. Before I knew it, I looked as well-maintained as Vivienne had, without having to lift a finger.

"I heard that your meeting with the winner didn't go too well last night," she said as she grabbed my shoulders and rushed me toward the tower's lift.

Her touch finally stirred me from the fog of exhaustion. I shook my head. "Do you know?"

"Know what?" she asked.

"What really happened that day when I shot Jacen?"

Vivienne paused. "Nothing more than you do. I'm an assistant. I only help where Mr. Helix needs me."

I stopped her. "You must know something. I can see it on your face."

She thought hard for a second, nose twitching, then pulled me into the lift with her.

"Mission, if you don't let all of this go, you're going to drive yourself crazy. I'm just looking out for you." Her features darkened. "Asher deserves at least that for me getting him exiled."

Asher. My rescuer finally had a name.

"You knew him?" I asked.

"Not well. Like I said, he's dangerous. Please try to focus on presenting yourself as naturally as possible. I promise, you'll get used to it. This is your home now. Better than under a floor, right?" She forced a nervous laugh.

The lift opened as we reached the lowest floor. Brightness from the sun blinded me, but as my eyes adjusted, I saw a crowd stretching across the platform surrounding this residential tower, all around the skywalks, and to more towers. The giant holo-screens projected above the skywalk, each recording me from different angles.

Vivienne was right; there were more people this time—many more—with additional robot men to organize the crowd.

The man named Frederick stood beside my dais, wearing a visor and manipulating whatever he saw through it with his hands.

All the thousands of comments I'd read about me raced through my thoughts. Any one of the people could've written any of the vulgar things about me or what they wanted to do to me and with me.

I leaned against the wall to keep upright as the sight overwhelmed my senses, desperate to ignore images of my people from the hundreds of feeds I'd watched through the night before. All the people arrayed before me had been living vicariously through us for their entire lives. Watching during every fight. Every incident. Every tender moment.

Everything.

"*You opened my eyes.*" The words of my savior, Asher, rattled around my brain again, only this time, the trauma of viewing my lustful crowd sparked me to remember more of what came before them.

"*Mission, don't listen to him!*" he'd screamed, strapped down on that strange chair and referring to Craig Helix. "*I know none of this makes any sense to you, but when you get the chance, run as fast as you can!*" Craig then said something to him softly, but Asher's gaze had remained fixed on me as he uttered these final words. "*You've been my life from the moment I was born. You opened my eyes, Mission.*"

"Are you coming, Mission?" Vivienne asked, waiting for me at the lift's doors.

The memory was finally starting to settle. How could this Asher person love me? I'd never even met the man. If he'd watched from the moment he was born, that meant he was like all the other residents gathered to observe me like I was some rare animal in some ancient zoo. But there was something more between him and Craig. It was personal, and Craig had referred to him by a specific title when he addressed him. What was it again . . .

"Director?" I muttered under my breath.

They were the people whom Dawn had said might know more about what really happened on the *Ignis*. Everyone had been telling me how dangerous Asher was, but he seemed so genuine. I didn't know how he could possibly claim to love me, but I was sure that he meant it. His expression had looked exactly like Alora's had before I was lowered into the airlock.

He'd urged me to run from Craig Helix for some reason, but now running was the last thing on my mind. Between my new home and my final days on *Ignis*, I was tired of being talked at. Of being told how to feel, what to do, and what I'd done. I decided, instead, that I wanted to know what Asher meant when he'd said I'd opened his eyes. Why he'd traveled across the stars to save me from my fate. Somehow, he was connected to what had happened to Jacen, and if Craig and Vivienne weren't going to tell me exactly why, then I'd make them.

I snatched Vivienne's handheld viewing device and slammed it against the wall. It fractured, the slim surface breaking into two shards with sharp edges. The band on my arm seemed to calm me whenever I was riled, so I pried it off, slicing the top of my wrist longways. Then, raising the shard to Vivienne's neck, I edged out of the lift, careful to keep a wall at my back.

Vivienne was too scared to form words. Everyone in the crowd gasped. Some even cheered. Like it was all a game. Only the robot men turned from the crowd to face me, pale eyes shifting as they slowly marched forward while saying in unison, "Please release your weapon and step away from your fellow resident."

"You don't want to do this," Vivienne sputtered.

I didn't want to hurt her. She'd been kind. But all the rage that had been building in me since the day I was named Mother bubbled to the surface. Probably from even further back. I held the shard closer and shouted, "You!" at Frederick.

His head aimed down, then up. "Me?"

I forced Vivienne closer, again using the wall and the tower's overhang to protect me. Hoping, against all odds, that the robot men wouldn't risk hurting Vivienne. Or the tiny ships that now swarmed overhead. I pressed the shard tighter until it drew a thin line of red. More gasps from the crowd. "Oohs" and "aahs" like I'd heard in that fake bot fighting arena.

Frederick lifted his visor off his eyes, his face contorting to wear a baffled expression.

"What's the meaning of this?" he asked. I could see dozens of tiny windows displaying scenes from the *Ignis* on his up-turned visor.

"You're a director."

"*Night* director," he grumbled.

"You're going to tell me everything or I'll slit her throat!" That last threat got Vivienne to start crying.

"I don't know what you're talking about."

"Tell me about Asher!" I shifted the shard so it was pointed directly at Vivienne's jugular. The bots once again requested I disarm. If they hadn't fired yet, I hoped it meant they wouldn't.

"Listen to her!" Vivienne shrieked. "Please!"

The sheer terror in her voice changed the way the crowd watched. Many now appeared afraid, or perplexed, like they'd never seen violence before. Murmurs about me being a true murderer carried on the air. Still, none of them tried anything to help. They just watched.

"All right." Frederick held up his hands and approached us. I tilted the shard, and he stopped before getting too close. "That sick bastard Asher's mistake followed us all the way back here," he grumbled. "Mr. Helix should have dropped him when he had the chance."

"What mistake?" I asked.

"The fool contacted you directly through your terminal, so we sent in a fixer." He kept his voice low, so only he, Vivienne, and I could hear over the gentle hum of wind and the robots' demands.

"What's a fixer?"

Frederick hesitated.

I lifted Vivienne's head so her throat was completely exposed. The sound of her crying made me wince, but I didn't back down.

Frederick cracked a smirk. "I know you're not really a killer, Mission. I know everything about you. Stop this before you accidentally hurt her."

"You don't know anything about me!" I shouted and, just as he'd predicted, accidentally cut Vivienne deeper. She screeched in pain, but I knew it was more from shock. I'd been trained in medicine for much of my life and knew she'd still be fine as long as I controlled myself. I knew where to slice if I didn't want to do any real damage.

"They work on *Ignis*," Frederick said, his grin vanishing. He stared at Vivienne's stream of blood, now looking like he was going to faint. "The problems your people can't fix or don't know about, they sneak on to handle. We sent one in to subdue you and erase Asher's message from your memory so that you didn't look into it."

"Jacen," I said. More memories from the dreamlike fog of events that had proceeded Asher pulling me out of space came to me. I saw Jacen's holographic face rolling across the floor like . . . like an empty mask. "That's who attacked me?"

"And he screwed up too, dammit," Frederick cursed. "I

swear, Lance and Asher were born to work together. Both useless. If you want to blame anyone for what happened to Jacen,
blame them. I had nothing to do with it. I'm just stuck cleaning up their messes, and getting no respect!"

I threw Vivienne to the side and dashed at Frederick. One
of the robot men fired something, a stream of energy. It crackled over my right shoulder. Frederick cowered, toppling over
with ease as I crashed into him. His visor cracked when we hit
the floor. I quickly rolled and faced his back to the robot men
and placed the shard to his neck.

By then, a sense of trepidation had really stolen across the
crowd. They were stunned to silence. Even Vivienne didn't run,
just gawked at us from the floor of the platform.

"Why did Asher want to contact me?" I asked.

"I don't know!" he yelped.

I stabbed the shard against the floor inches from his head,
then raised it directly over one of his gaping eyes. "Stop lying!"

"H-h-he claimed he wanted to save you."

"From what?"

"Mission, stop this!" Craig Helix shouted from the open
door of a flying vehicle. It landed on a nearby platform, and he
stepped out, his thick gray hair swaying in the wind.

"They think you're a threat, but I know you aren't," he said.
The crowd parted and permitted him to pass, until he reached
one of the robot men, who informed him not to proceed.

"I know you're still just adjusting," he continued. "Let him
go and we can talk alone. I'll tell you whatever you want to
know."

I ignored him. "From what?" I repeated to Frederick. It
was only after asking again that I realized I was panting like an
animal. I lowered the blade toward his eye. Frederick squeezed
it shut and turned away.

"From suffocating with everyone else!" he sniveled. "You were supposed to die with the rest when Mr. Helix programmed the fire-suppression system to malfunction!"

All the air was sucked from my lungs. The crowd gasped in shock. The shard slipped out of my hand, scratching his face before clanking against the floor. Frederick rolled over and started crying hysterically.

I fell backward.

"No!" Craig shouted, stepping before the bots and spreading his arms before they could shoot me.

"She has been deemed a danger to society," they said. "Resident Craig Helix, we request you step aside."

"No. She's having a panic attack. I can help her." He backed up slowly, ensuring they had no shot. They never averted their aim.

"He knew what was going to happen to us?" I whispered. I turned to Vivienne, surprised to find that she was no longer terrified. Instead, like me, she looked completely dumbfounded. "You all knew?"

She shook her head profusely. "I swear I didn't."

"He said our lives were real . . ."

Craig turned to face me. The bots remained behind him, their soulless eyes tracking my every movement. "Just relax, Mission," he said. "Nobody needs to get hurt. I know it's been a difficult adjustment, but it's only going to get easier."

He smiled. Like everything was okay. Two hundred and thirteen people died that day, and according to Frederick, it was all his fault. And everyone who watched knew it too. Their whispers grew in volume, sounding surprised and revulsed.

"Mission, please calm down," Craig implored. "We have so much work left to do. Frederick is making things up because he's scared. I can explain everything."

I grabbed the shard and squeezed it so hard it sliced into my palm. I wanted to ram it through Helix's heart just so that he could feel what I had, and I was seconds away from lunging for him when every screen around us suddenly transitioned to the same feed. On the giant holodisplays, on Frederick's damaged visor, and all those in the crowd angled so I could see. On every viewing device held by viewers, and through every single open window on the High Earth towers.

Asher was on his knees in his cell, quaking in terror with blood dripping from his mouth. Alora stood in front of him with a pulse-pistol aimed at his head, the same one that I'd used to shoot Jacen. I'd never seen her look so incensed.

The volume on every device in High Earth rose to max so we could hear her.

"I'm not going to ask you again. Who are you!" Alora barked. When Asher didn't answer, she cracked him across the face with the barrel of the gun. "Tell me!"

"What is this?" Craig questioned. "Frederick, stop blubbering and fix this!"

Frederick wiped his face and drew a viewing device from his belt. He swiped through controls. "I-I-I'm locked out."

Suddenly, I wasn't important at all. Craig ran out in the open to get a look at their surroundings. I flinched, expecting the robot men to shoot, but their eyes flickered and their heads twitched. Then they didn't move at all.

I still kept behind Craig for safety, the blade in my grip. He spun a holographic screen over his lifeband, his fingers flurrying across controls and bringing up rows of data I didn't understand.

"What is this?" he said. "The *Ignis* comm-relay isn't broadcasting anything but this feed! Is this live?"

"I-I . . ." Frederick sputtered.

On the feed playing everywhere, Alora wound up to strike

Asher again, but this time, something grabbed and disarmed her. She went to pull free but was promptly put in a headlock. A strong arm squeezed her throat until her eyes started to close.

"Alora!" I screamed. "What's happening to her?" I made a movement toward Craig and poked the shard against his back. The robot men shifted their aim with me. Craig didn't budge at all, just stared at the screen hovering over his hand.

Alora was lowered to the ground, and despite the proficiency of her attacker, it was slow and gentle. She was still breathing. Behind her stood a broad-shouldered young man with forearms and hands covered by metal—no, *made* of metal. A visor covered his eyes, like so many other residents I'd seen, only peeking out from the top of it was a brand on his forehead, which glowed blue. Three arcing lines growing from bottom to top.

"No!" Craig barked. "Frederick, get our new fixer in there right now. Take the Unplugged down!"

Frederick pawed for his cracked visor and threw it on. He tapped the wildly blinking band around his wrist, then started conferring orders to somebody through some sort of comms. "Laura, Laura, can you read me?"

"Shut all feeds down, dammit!" Craig said. "All cameras!"

"A terrible thing to lose control, isn't it?" All eyes snapped toward the sky as the man Craig referred to as Unplugged spoke into the feed broadcasting around High Earth. His cold, impassive voice echoed in every direction. It sent a shiver up my spine. "That's what it is to live."

"This is impossible!" Craig said, spinning, searching for answers in the faces of the awestruck crowd or the faulty robot men. "We shut down her operation. I shut her down!"

"I speak the mind of Gloria Fors," the one Craig referred to as an Unplugged said, all around us. "Craig Helix may have filled the *Ignis* with life, but I was there at its conception. He may have reprogrammed the core in his image, but I helped script its very first code."

The Unplugged knelt in front of Asher, who appeared as baffled as we were. "Thank you for opening my eyes, Asher."

"Y-y-you know who I am?" he whispered.

"You are the reason I'm here. Come with me and I will remind you." The Unplugged stuck out a hand. Asher wavered for a moment then took it and followed him out.

The feed didn't transition to track them, and wherever they disappeared to was unclear, but what I could see were a few unconscious members of the Collective lying in the hallway outside the cell.

CHAPTER 29

"She can't lock me out," Craig raved. "The *Ignis* is mine! Frederick, have Laura get the fixer there now, and make sure Mission doesn't go anywhere before we can get her on an infuser. I'm going to my terminal downstairs. I'll shut the damn core down if I have to!"

He went to walk by me toward the skywalks. A drop of blood reminded me of the shard in my hand. If he could shut down the core, then that meant scripting the Great Blackout was also possible—anything. This was my chance to stop him and his show, to avenge all those people whose deaths I took the blame for.

I charged at him. Craig must have seen my reflection in his visor before I got there, and stumbled to the floor. I stood over him. The robot men might not malfunction forever. I wouldn't be able to escape them when they came back online. This was my only chance. My blade would fall and sink into the monster who tortured my world.

"Don't!" Vivienne jumped in front of me. "Don't be the

killer they made you. Open your eyes, Mission. This is your chance to run. There's a place where you can hide."

"Now isn't the time for this!" Craig hollered as he clambered away along the floor. "Subdue her immediately," he ordered the bots.

This time, their eyes slowly flickered back to a cool, steady red. Their heads snapped upright and their weaponized arms rose toward me. I was about to rush Craig again to try to beat them, until Vivienne took my hand and placed the blade at her own throat.

"They are programmed not to allow residents to be harmed," she said. "Hold it and me close, and they won't risk touching you."

Craig's jaw dropped. "Vivienne, what the hell are you doing?"

"Sir, I . . . I only volunteered here because I had to. I felt a void growing inside me that no VR could fill. I thought being a part of something real would help me—a part of the vision of the great Craig Helix. I'd thought what you did to Asher was the right thing, but nothing seems right anymore. All of *Ignis* seems false."

"Asher Reinhart wanted nothing to do with you! You were worthless to him. A talentless, thoughtless consumer just like all the others."

She didn't react to his insults. She turned to face me, no longer afraid of the sharp edge shaving her neck. "He gave up everything to save you," she said. "All of this. That has to mean something, doesn't it?"

I glanced between her and Craig, and then the Unplugged man was back, filling every screen and device in High Earth, once again stealing everyone's attention. He and Asher were entering the very inner sanctum of the *Ignis*'s core, where the brilliant fusion reactor churned beyond a tinted veil.

[Ignis Feed Location]
Core Reactor
<Camera 1>

A member of the Collective turned just in time to be punched across the face by the Unplugged. He then led Asher to the reactor's control console positioned below a thick conduit.

"What's going on?" Asher asked nervously.

"The ship we're on was always intended to remedy the mistake I created. No more cheating through life. Fors Tech's last project—one final hope for a new world."

"What mistake? I don't know what you're talking about, and I don't know you!"

"You did." The Unplugged ran his artificial fingers over the controls. The interface should've been locked to anybody who wasn't a member of the Collective, but he somehow entered with ease. "Two centuries ago the High Earth Network took the *Ignis* project from me, only for it to be transformed into a glorified stage. I thought trying to construct a replica would be enough, but thanks to you, I have hope again that at least a shred of humanity in High Earth remains unplugged."

"What are you talking about?" Asher asked, unable to tear his petrified gaze away from the smoldering fusion reactor. It swirled within blades of revolving metal, like a miniature star, yearning to scorch everything around it.

"I'm going to finish what I started a long time ago."

An earsplitting bang rang out. A bullet shredded the Unplugged's shoulder and knocked him back. He whipped around while falling, and a weapon extended from one of his artificial wrists to fire. A stream of electricity lashed across the corridor and struck a stranger standing in the entrance with a pulse-pistol drawn. His face flickered as he convulsed; then a band around his neck burst. The face he wore vanished and a new one was revealed, eyes frozen open.

"A new fixer," the Unplugged groaned. "Someone will have heard that. Asher, help me." Asher was busy staring at the smoking corpse. "Asher!"

Asher snapped out of it and wrapped his arm around the Unplugged's back. Blood oozed from the gaping wound in his shoulder, from which his cybernetic arm now hung slack.

"You need help," Asher said.

"I'll be fine." The Unplugged propped himself back up in front of the console and went back to work with one hand.

"Who was that?"

"Nobody anymore."

"Step away from there!" Cassiopeia commanded, bursting into the room with a cohort of enforcers and other members of the Collective, armed with guns. Unlike the attacker before them, they didn't risk shooting and puncturing the core's enclosure.

"I told you he was trouble," Alora said. She leaned on the wall behind them, rubbing her aching head.

"It's too late." The Unplugged entered one last command and stepped back. "The coordinates for your new world are set. They've always been set."

"Step back or we will fire!"

Asher looked back and forth frantically. The Unplugged took his hand. His thin lips curled into an almost robotic smile, the rest of his facial muscles barely flinching. "Remember the stars, Asher Reinhart," he whispered. "They call to us." Then he struck an execute key with both of their fingers.

A shudder knocked everyone in the walkway sideways. The floor and data-server-covered walls began to rattle, and the glow of the core's reactor augmented until all that was visible were their silhouettes cast against orange light as brilliant as fire.

* * *

"What is he doing!" Craig screamed as High Earth was flooded with orange light. He darted past me as if he'd forgotten I was there. He shoved cowering Frederick out of the way and then looked straight up.

The light didn't wane. It bounced off every shimmering tower outside, above and below the skywalks, as if a new sun were rising. All the screens in the city, which had once depicted me or views of the *Ignis*, were still set to the same feed depicting the blinding interior of the core.

Vivienne approached the edge of the platform window slowly, and I had no choice but to follow, keep the blade at her throat, and rotate away from the robot men.

"This is impossible!" Craig shouted. "Frederick, do something!"

The director remained on the floor, whimpering and totally stunned.

"Laura, somebody, do something!"

"*Ignis*," Vivienne whispered. She pointed toward a bright spot streaking across the blue canvas of Earth's sky.

"What's going on?" I asked.

The images of the core on everyone's feed started to flicker so rapidly it was like we were caught in the heart of a violent, rainless electrical storm. Then, suddenly, the feed cut out, and every viewing device in High Earth went dark.

"No!" Craig and I shrieked at the same time.

"It's okay! Look, it's still there." Vivienne ran her finger along the glass where the white mark she claimed to be the *Ignis* jetted across the horizon. And she wasn't alone. All of the crowd did the same. And up the towers surrounding us, residents here and there who hadn't come down to see me stepped out onto their balconies to look up.

"This is impossible!" Craig cried. The band on his wrist flashed so fast it might as well have been solid red. He pulled out a device like Vivienne's, and his quaking fingers darted across the keys. "She can't take *Ignis* from me. Nobody can!" He slammed the screen on the floor and ran to one of the bots. He grabbed it by the shoulders and shook it, earning their attention. "Fix this!"

"They're actually sending it," Vivienne said.

"Where?" I asked, unable to take my eyes off the tiny white blemish in the sky. *Ignis* had been so close to Earth that the people there could see my world if only they'd removed their visors and looked up.

"Where you always thought you were going."

Another piece of my memories after Asher had saved me jumped into my head. I recalled seeing Earth while running from him. It was blue and brilliant, and while I wasn't an expert on astrology like a member of the Collective might be, I knew the *Ignis* shouldn't have been close enough to see it at all.

It really was all a lie . . .

"You did this," Craig turned and said to me, his face flushed. "You planned it with Asher, didn't you? He wanted to get back at me, so he helped Gloria take my show from me."

I didn't answer. Instead, I stared at him. His entire body was trembling. Tears stained his cheeks as he sat amongst the wreckage of the console. He looked like a child in one of the *Ignis*'s nurseries, throwing a tantrum.

"You took my show from me!" He sprang at me, but I stepped back with Vivienne. He tripped again and cut his hands on the countless shards of the screen. He gaped down at them as blood started to bubble out of him.

"Why would you do this?" he whimpered. "I made you a star. All of you ungrateful . . . Kill her!" he yelled at the robot men, but with Vivienne there, they couldn't. Craig lunged again and grabbed my calf. He was so physically weak that I was able to shake free with ease, but as I went to retaliate with a kick, my foot stopped just in front of his face.

Vivienne was right. If I killed him now, I'd become the very thing he'd allowed his show to make me. I'd learned back home that there was a fate worse than death. Our criminals, people like me, were cast into space so that their energy would be lost forever. I never imagined I could pity the man who had caused my world so much pain and suffering, but I'd never seen someone look so pathetic. Asher and the Unplugged had taken from him the one thing in the world he valued, just as he had taken my Jacen from me.

"You said there was a place the bots can't reach?" I asked Vivienne.

She nodded.

"Show me."

I turned without even bothering to say the innumerable insults to our monstrous benefactor that I wanted to. Craig Helix didn't deserve my attention.

"You can't run from this!" Craig bellowed. "The Network sees everything!"

With the makeshift blade at her throat, Vivienne led me toward the skywalks. The bots parted to allow us to pass, reiterating how I was a threat to society and requesting that I release my weapon. I wondered if maybe they too had no idea how to handle a situation like this. Real violence in their perfect little world.

"She's an inhabitant, for Earth's sake!" Helix yelled to the crowd who'd come to meet with me. "Someone grab them and I'll make you director!"

None of the residents did anything to block us. They were completely confused, some terrified and fleeing me like I was a monster. Others were too busy staring at Craig while he unraveled. More watched the bright mark in the sky that was apparently *Ignis* setting off on the long-awaited journey across the stars I always thought I was on.

"You're all useless!" Craig screamed. "After all I've given you people. You don't deserve it. You'll be delisted for this, Vivienne! You'll never see High Earth again, you hear me! Neither of you!" His maddened howls now filled the studio.

Vivienne glanced back as we entered the lift. For a second, I noticed hints of regret affect her features; then the doors closed behind us.

CHAPTER 30

Security bots followed as the moving walkways carried us by all the flabbergasted residents. Vivienne braced me and ensured my weapon didn't budge.

I watched *Ignis* in the sky all the way across High Earth and its innumerable rows of identical towers. More and more residents exited onto their balconies to look up with me. When we arrived at the end of High Earth, the now barely perceptible dot of *Ignis* was obscured by clouds.

Water splashed on top of my head, an endless supply. *Rain.* I stuck my tongue out and tried to catch the droplets as Vivienne directed me onto another lift, which descended a towering wall.

Robot men manned it, but due to my threat to Vivienne, they let us pass. We sank into a dark, wet world.

"This is the place?" I asked as the lift stopped and the doors reopened.

"You'll be safe in there," Vivienne said. "At least from us."

"You're not coming?"

"I'm still a resident. A bot will guard me at all times, even out there."

"I'm one too."

She shook her head. "Mr. Helix is the best programmer I've ever seen. He falsified everything for you, like so much else. I overheard him say it to Frederick in the studio. You were never fully uploaded into the Network, only the lifeband you broke. Disappear, Mission."

"Why are you helping me?"

"I reported the things I saw Asher do for you, and he was delisted. Nothing felt right after. I watched *Outskirts Today* constantly until I saw him caught up in some battle. I even came out here and found him one night. I knew he wouldn't remember me, but I wanted to apologize . . . I just couldn't. If I hadn't distracted him with my questions that day, he wouldn't have—"

"You do know that I have no idea what any of that means?" I interrupted.

"Right . . . Sorry."

"Just—do you know why he saved me?"

"I used to think he was just crazy, but . . . I think maybe he realized that it was wrong for Mr. Helix to hurt so many of you simply for ratings. That *Ignis: Live* was more than just *his* show."

"It was my home."

"All I know for sure was that he really must have cared about you, Mission. To do all this."

"I'll never get a chance to thank him, will I?"

"No."

I craned my neck to look back while I still held the shard in place. Vivienne's eyes welled with tears.

"I came out here once and couldn't keep out of trouble," she said. "I guess I was meant to choose your show to volunteer for. Don't look back, Mission. And if you ever see me out here, remind me who I was."

Before I could do anything, Vivienne pushed off of me, then shoved me out onto the streets. The robot men didn't fire, but they quickly positioned themselves in front of her and signaled the doors to shut. She smiled at me before the lift carried her up, back to her home.

I turned and faced a city filled with dilapidated structures and grimy-looking, diseased people with their attention glued to devices. Colorful ads blinked on every building, some showing my face. I didn't know what to do, so I just walked, past beggars, whores, and brawls—the very things that we'd learned on *Ignis* had led to Earth's ruin.

I reached an intersection and spotted someone staring at me. Every other person in the disgusting nightmare of a city was busy paying attention to something else, but not him. As I got closer, I realized he couldn't see me. His eyes were covered by a bloody bandage, and he leaned on a cane because he was blind. But under the shadow of his hood glowed that same Unplugged mark as that cybernetic man on *Ignis*.

"Hello?" I said to him.

He didn't answer. He turned and strode down the street, past all the people too busy to give a damn, and ads showing me and other insane things. He clacked with his cane to find his way. I followed him until we reached a half-collapsed building that appeared like it'd endured a fair share of fires.

He ducked under a low passage, and for whatever reason, I didn't stop following. Dozens of men and women with the same glowing brands waited inside, watching us from every angle if they had eyes, or listening to our footsteps across a rickety wooden floor if they didn't. At the back of the building, a trapdoor was stuck open.

"What is this place?" I asked when he stopped before the door.

"Home," he said.

"What does that mean?"

He didn't answer, only climbed down. Curiosity had always been a trait of mine. I knew, because it frustrated Alora to no end.

I descended next, and he was already on his way down an unlit path until a huge open hatch led into a tremendous hollow. My gasp resonated across it as I entered. A fusion core was suspended in the very center, deactivated but still glowing enough to illuminate the whole space. Farmland filled the floor, but every crop was slashed. Pipes leaked and conduits sparked along the craggy walls. Branded people were everywhere with flashlights, cleaning up scraps. Even the blind helped.

Someone, or something, had swept through, devastated the place, then left it to crumble.

I looked down and the man guiding me was nowhere to be found, so I wordlessly crossed the wrecked interior that was so reminiscent of *Ignis* that, for a second, I felt like I'd never left. A cluster of more marked people waited under an arch at the other end of it. They gestured for me to enter.

Inside, an old woman lay on a bed.

As I got closer, I realized that she wasn't like any elderly woman I'd ever seen before. Her flesh was so shriveled it hung loose from her bones. Her hair had long since withered away. Half her chest was made of machinery.

My first instinct was to check for a pulse. None. Her skin was as cold as the rock surrounding us. She was dead, yet on her face existed a most peculiar expression for a corpse. Her lips were almost too desiccated to see, but they were curled upward at the edges. It was a smile as meager as the one the Unplugged on the *Ignis* had worn before finally launching my people toward the stars, but there was no question it was there.

On her chest lay a handmade book, the kind history lessons aboard *Ignis* said were ancient. The real paper pages were creased and tarnished by age. I lifted it carefully and blew off a thin film of dust. The first page came loose and flittered down onto her bed.

I could just make out the faded title scrawled on the top. HIGH EARTH AND THE END OF THE WORLD by Gloria Fors.

EPILOGUE

Alora strode by the busy workstations of the Collective. Something had happened when those strangers manipulated the core, and all of *Ignis*'s brightest minds were busy trying to find out what. Even inhabitants from the blocks were brought up to help.

It was like the *Ignis* changed course, throwing everyone to the side. Then it straightened, but there was something else—a force, pulling at Alora's body as if caused by a shift in the *Ignis*'s acceleration. Coordinate readouts all went wonky, some placing the *Ignis* far from where it had been only days ago.

A team led by Cassiopeia prepared to run an EVA, purposefully moving beyond the airlock for the first time to try to evaluate exactly where the *Ignis* was in the vast expanse of space.

Alora didn't understand, but it wasn't her job to figure out. Her world had changed the moment Mission was spaced, and somehow, she knew the strangers who'd altered the *Ignis*'s direction had something to do with what had happened to her.

So much so, Cassiopeia had broken protocol to put her in charge of the continuing investigation of where they'd come from and who they were. An investigation that, unfortunately, was going nowhere.

The tattooed one had gone silent the moment after the *Ignis*'s core went hot. He now lay unconscious on a Collective medical bed, hooked up to oxygen. Every Mother had evaluated his condition, and each came to the same conclusion—he was in a coma and would probably never wake up. It was up to them when to pull the plug.

The other stranger? He was alive, locked in the very cell Mission had been in before her judgment. Presently, Alora stood outside it, wishing with all her heart that she could open it and find Mission running out to embrace her.

But she didn't, and wouldn't, and never could again.

The door *whooshed* open, revealing the stranger on his hands and knees, palms pressed against the glass, staring down at *Ignis*'s hydrofarms.

"If you've come to ask me again what happened, you'll get the same answer," he bristled without bothering to look up. At first, Alora had mistaken his frustration for anger. But she'd pressed him for days now, and his amnesia didn't seem to be an act.

She didn't understand how, but someone had buried all his memories, down to his very name. He was like a child in a man's body.

"I haven't," Alora said.

"Then why are you here?"

"Honestly, I don't know." She stepped in, moved to the back wall without his invitation, and sat cross-legged on the floor. He glanced up, his brow in a deep furrow.

"I'm just so tired," Alora said.

"I wish I could help. Honestly, I do," he said. "Maybe if you let me out, show me this world, something will come to me. I . . ."

"That isn't up to me."

He frowned and dragged his hand along the glass. "I don't know what you want me to do."

"Bring her back?" Alora scoffed. That was all she wanted— one more day with Mission where she forgot about protocol and rules and treated her how a beloved daughter deserved to be treated.

The stranger bit on his lip, then sighed. "I don't know who you're talking about." He slid to sit across the cell from Alora.

"I know." Alora closed her eyes and drew a deep breath. She could still smell Mission in the cramped room. It was nothing anyone else would ever notice. Only a mother. When she opened them, she found the stranger sitting upright, staring at her. A look of concern washed across his face, quite different from the usual combo of anger and confusion he wore. He didn't look like a killer or a manipulator. He looked . . . normal. Decent.

"Are you okay?" he asked.

The question caught her off guard. Locked up, accused, probed, and questioned constantly, and he was concerned about her?

"You really don't remember anything, do you?" Alora asked. He shook his head.

"Then we both lost something impossible to replicate," she said.

"What did you lose?"

"A daughter."

"I'm . . ." He paused, as if to consider his next words carefully. In the end, he settled on, "I'm sorry."

"The worst part is that I'm envious of you. I wish with all of my heart that I could forget her. That it wouldn't hurt so much."

"I don't think that'd be any better," he said. "Trust me."

Alora chuckled meekly. "Yes. Perhaps not."

Silence passed between them. An enforcer marched by the open cell, checking in to make sure nothing was amiss. Finally, the stranger straightened his back and slid a bit closer.

"Tell me about her?" he said.

"Why?" Alora replied.

"Because all I can do is stare through that glass at a world you people won't let me into. Because I don't know anything else. Because . . ." He caught his breath. "Because I don't know what to do."

Alora watched the frustration beginning to bloom in him again. His hands had balled into fists. She couldn't imagine what he was going through, racking his brain constantly for even the slightest clue about anything. His head must have been pounding.

Yet, here was a man who didn't believe that Mission was a murderer and a traitor like most of *Ignis* did. Here was a man who might believe the truth. He wanted anything to think about besides the countless memories he couldn't access, but maybe he could help her too.

It wouldn't bring Mission back. It wouldn't absolve her. But someone else would know that she'd given her life to help her world.

"Her name was Mission," Alora said.

The stranger's eyes went wide, glinting.

"Mission," he said slowly, like he was testing the name. "Mission." He slid a bit closer. "Tell me about her."

ABOUT THE AUTHOR

Rhett C. Bruno is the *USA Today* bestselling and Nebula Award nominated author of *The Circuit Saga* (Diversion Books, Podium Publishing), *Contact Day* (Aethon Books, Audible Originals), *Children of Titan Series* (Aethon Books, Audible Studios), and the *Buried Goddess Saga* (Aethon Books, Audible Studios); among other works.

He has been writing since before he can remember, scribbling down what he thought were epic stories when he was young to show to his friends and family. He is currently a full time author living in Delaware with his wife and dog Raven.

Find out more here: RhettBruno.com

Also, please consider subscribing to his newsletter for exclusive access to updates about his work and the opportunity to receive limited content and ARCs. For a limited time, you'll also receive his Free Starter Library!

Subscribe Here: RhettBruno.com/newsletter/